ROOT WEAVER

ROOT WEAVER

FIVE FORCES BOOK ONE

MICHAEL HARDCASTLE

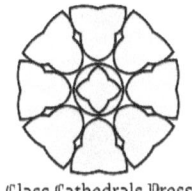

Glass Cathedrals Press

ROOT WEAVER

ISBN 979-8-9942517-0-6 (paperback)
ISBN 979-8-9942517-1-3 (ebook)

Published by Glass Cathedrals Press.

www.hardcastlewrites.com

For Zarena.

CONTENTS

Chapter 1: Anya the Pig...1

Chapter 2: The Redsmith's Apprentice 18

Chapter 3: The Stranger and the Crow...34

Chapter 4: A Change of Luck...50

Chapter 5: Aen's Spring..65

Chapter 6: A Broken Mast 79

Chapter 7: The Testing 93

Chapter 8: Dowsing and Healing..107

Chapter 9: Choices for a Future...129

Chapter 10: Negotiations..140

Chapter 11: Fivewells 156

Chapter 12: Through the Forest 169

Chapter 13: The Training Pentad 184

Chapter 14: The First Day...201

Chapter 15: The Gauntlet..220

Chapter 16: The Second Day..239

Chapter 17: The Wheel...256

Chapter 18: The Sea Docks 273

Chapter 19: The Fish Docks...291

Chapter 20: The Missing Mirror 306

Chapter 21: Incursion...326

Chapter 22: Captain Lahmeer...344

Chapter 23: The Portal Opens 358

Chapter 24: The Long Night 376

Chapter 25: A Blending 395

Epilogue: An Answered Question..413

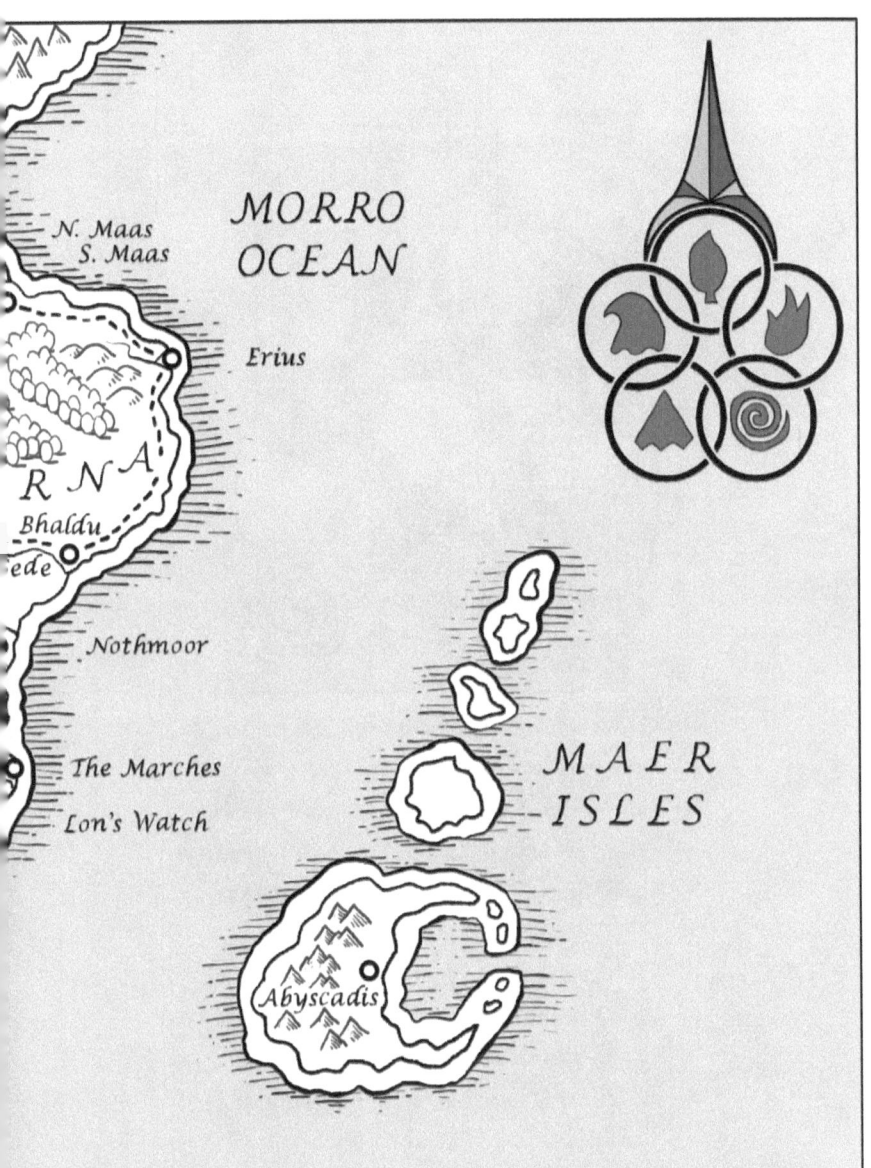

MORRO
OCEAN

N. Maas
S. Maas

Erius

R N A

Bhaldu
ede

Nothmoor

The Marches

Lon's Watch

MAER
ISLES

Abyscadis

ALDRIA AND ITS ENVIRONS

Root enhances Flame, as wood feeds the fire.
Flame enhances Aether, as heat warms the air.
Aether enhances Stone, as wind shapes the rock.
Stone enhances Wave, as banks guide the river.
Wave enhances Root, as rain fuels growth.

Root consumes Aether, as trees break the wind.
Aether consumes Wave, as the sky drinks the sea.
Wave consumes Flame, as water quenches fire.
Flame consumes Stone, as fire melts iron.
Stone consumes Root, as the axe hews wood.

Chapter 1
Anya the Pig

RYN WAS ON THE HUNT. He stood at the edge of the yard, scanning the trees. The woods had grown unusually quiet in the last few days. Normally, the forest surrounding his aunt's cottage was alive with constant sound and movement. Songbirds, crows, and the occasional hawk would fill the trees, flitting from branch to branch, calling to one another, or hunting for insects. Red squirrels and tiny chipmunks were always stirring up the leaf litter.

That morning he saw and heard nothing. Not even a breeze ruffled the leaves, and the trees stood unnaturally still. There weren't even any deer, which always gathered in the morning, because Ryn's aunt would sometimes feed them dried apple slices. Silence like this often meant there was a predator in the woods, but that didn't worry Ryn much. The woodcutters had hunted all the wolves out of the Sylphren Wood a century ago, and the black bears didn't bother you if you kept your distance. A jackhound might frighten the birds away, but they were scavengers who wouldn't go after anything Ryn's size, though he was scrawny and not especially tall for his age.

Ryn ran a hand through his mop of blond hair and shrugged his shoulders, adjusting his rough linen shirt. His aunt sewed all his clothes, and they were always too big, as if she still anticipated a late-stage growth spurt from the boy. His belt was the only thing keeping his trousers up, and he stuffed the excess into his sturdy leather boots.

He pursed his lips and whistled, imitating the call of a sandlark. Growing up in these woods, he'd mastered the sounds of every songbird. Nothing responded, and his whistle echoed through the still woods and died. That made him shiver. It was spring, a full week past the Equinox, but he hadn't heard a bird in three days. Still, he needed to hunt. The silverbells he sought would sustain him and his aunt far better than the modest income she earned as an herbalist.

He heard footsteps and turned to see his aunt coming around the side of their simple wooden cottage, leading Anya on a rope. Aunt Marla was taller than him and lean. She wore a green linen dress and boots, with a leather satchel slung across her chest. She kept her long auburn hair perpetually trained into a single braid down her back. Gray flecked her temples and strands ran through her hair like veins of silver. Deep creases lined her face. She had not earned them from smiling overmuch.

Anya was a pig, a gift Marla had been given years ago for helping one of the farmwives down in Aen's Hollow with a difficult pregnancy. Marla had been intending to fatten the piglet up just enough to sell it to the village butcher, but Ryn, whom Marla was always scolding for being an overly sensitive boy, had convinced her to spare the pig and let him keep her as a pet. Marla hated dogs and cats and had never let the boy have a pet before. Despite that, even Marla had grown slightly affectionate toward the pig, though the relationship was at times uneasy. They kept Anya in a shed behind the cottage, and Marla lived in constant fear that the pig would somehow break loose and find a way into the well-fenced herb garden or, worse yet, down into the root cellar beneath the house.

Anya was small for a pig. She was a Stoudfield grunter, a breed that did not grow very large but was said to have sweet and succulent meat. Course white hairs covered her round body, with patches of black down her back and on the tips of her ears. They kept her fed on table scraps, gristle, and the parts of plants that Marla couldn't use. The pig was an exceptionally smart creature, and Ryn had trained her to follow simple commands. The villagers of Aen's Hollow also believed he had trained her to sniff out silverbells, but that was a lie, and not even Marla knew the truth of it.

His aunt handed him the pig's lead. "We'll need foxfeathers, of course."

"Yes, Marla," Ryn said. His aunt had taken him in when Ryn was barely old enough to remember, but she never let him call her Auntie or anything more endearing than her name. She wasn't exactly cruel. The way Ryn saw it, Marla was simply set in her ways and had been unwilling to bend more than she had to when a small child was thrust into her life. That old wooden cottage had held little warmth for a frightened child, but they got along after a fashion.

Marla continued rattling off her list of plants and mushrooms to be on the lookout for: cat's clove, spinetails, winter daisies, sorrel weed, whitecaps, and king's lances. The lances would be hardest to find this time of year, but they were indispensable for women suffering from what his aunt called "weak blood" during pregnancy. "Oh, and some kettle leaf if you see any," she added, finishing off the list. Kettle leaf was only good for making tea, but it was delicious.

"Yes, Marla," Ryn said again.

She unslung her satchel and handed it off to him. He put it on. The satchel was her own design, something the village tanner had made custom for her. It consisted of a large pouch and a thick strap that now ran across Ryn's chest. The strap was studded with small ceramic canisters, each with its own tight-fitting copper lid. Any silverbells Ryn found would go in the large pouch, and the individual containers were for sorting and storing whatever items from her shopping list he could find and harvest.

Marla turned to go but hesitated, frowning down at him. "And you be careful out there."

He frowned in turn. That was not something she typically said.

"Look for signs of bears and steer clear," she continued, apparently not done giving advice. "Stay out of the bogs. They're still too wet with snowmelt. You'll lose a boot if you go in there after any gallroot or mercybalm. We've plenty of that in the cellar still. If you see any village boys out with their pigs, you go rooting somewhere else. It's not worth starting a fight over."

"Marla," Ryn said, "what is this? You're acting like I've never left the house before."

She looked away, out into the trees, and shook her head slightly. "Something just isn't right with the woods today."

Ryn turned and studied the silent forest again with his aunt. Anya sniffed idly at the ground, rifling through the leaf litter with her short snout. It was the only sound they heard. "They are over quiet," Ryn said.

Marla turned back to him. "Don't go out too far. Get what you need and come back. We're not trying to get rich, just get by."

He furrowed his brow and studied the lines on her face. "You really are worried about me, aren't you?"

She scoffed and couldn't meet his gaze as she said, "I've never been the maternal type, the Maker knows, but I hope you don't think that means I don't care about you."

He nodded slowly. "I know."

"Like it or not, we're the only family each other has." She reached out and ruffled his hair. "You look more like him every day, you know."

"My father?" Ryn had only the vaguest memories of his parents.

"You have his eyes." She shook her head. "My brother's eyes…" That last part was said more to herself than to him. Ryn's eyes were green, like hers. He got his light-colored hair from his mother, or so he had been told.

"You're starting to make me feel worried," he said.

"Oh, it's nothing," she said after a long pause. "I'm just getting over fearful in my old age."

He laughed. She was certainly older than the mothers of the boys his age he knew in the village, but she was decades short of being elderly, not like the old-timers who spent their waning days gossiping together in rocking chairs on their covered porches or bowling on the village green when the weather was nice. "Well," he said, "I'd better be off."

She only nodded.

He tugged on Anya's lead. "Let's go, girl," he said. The pig snorted and began trotting along beside him into the woods. He'd been facing east all the while, and that was the way he went. Every time he went in search of silverbells, he set off in a different direction, but he always found at least one. A few paces into the underbrush, he paused to look back. Marla was still standing there, staring, though her gaze seemed unfocused, like she wasn't quite looking at him.

He shook his head and kept going. She was strange, but she had always been strange. It had taken him several years to learn her moods and her ways. He'd cried often at first, missing his parents, though he had only the faintest recollections of them now, but his tears had no effect on her. She gave him space but provided nothing in the way of comfort. Still, he could never bring himself to hate her exactly.

Ryn lived a lonely life. Their cottage was over a mile outside the village of Aen's Hollow. As soon as he was old enough, Ryn had taken over for his aunt making the weekly trips down to the village to buy or trade for whatever they needed. He knew most of the villagers, but none he called friend. Though she lived apart, Marla played a vital role in the community of farmers and woodcutters, as the village herbalist. She was respected but not well liked, especially by the children of Aen's Hollow. An older woman who lived alone in the woods and only visited them when they were sick and made them drink foul-tasting concoctions? Naturally, she had to be a witch. So the rumor ran among the kids. When Ryn arrived, about twelve years ago, he fit right into their superstitions. They whispered to one another that this pale, sickly boy had to be some kind of changeling and refused to play with him. It had been nearly a decade since he had bothered trying to join in their games.

The woods were his playground and he knew them well. Marla had been indifferent to his general education, securing him a book of grammar and another of basic mathematics and leaving him mainly to puzzle it out for himself. She had schooled him well in one area alone: botany. The villagers called her an herbalist, but Marla knew far more about plants than how to make salves and tinctures to treat ailments. She'd filled his head with knowledge of every seed, berry, fruit, root, herb, weed, bush, vine, and tree that could be found in Sylphren Wood, and he'd pored over her one illustrated book of plants dozens of times.

Marla said Ryn had a natural aptitude for the subject, and compliments were rare from her. Marla was considered the best herbalist in all of Sylphren Wood, and herbalists and doctors up in Ashborne or down in Thorpe would sometimes send to her for advice or mixtures. Villagers who were too old to consider Marla a witch still whispered that she must surely be a Root Weaver. When Ryn had asked her about that, she denied it, and she did so in a tone that meant he was not to ask any more questions on the topic. He had learned to get along with her by stepping gingerly and avoiding any topics that might upset her.

As such, Ryn knew very little about Weaving in general. A few of the villagers were said to have the gift, but none had any great capacity for it and seemed to prefer living their lives without ever using it. Boris Achon the village blacksmith and Miles Mithers the tanner were both said to be Stone Weavers, which supposedly enhanced the quality of their wares in a way Ryn had never understood. He felt too embarrassed to ask anyone to explain it to him. It seemed like something he should already know.

The boys of the village were especially obsessed with Flame Weavers. When he was younger, he would spy on them from the woods as they played, longing to join in. Flame Weavers made the best soldiers, it was said, because Weaving enhanced their ability to fight somehow. The village boys seemed to think a Flame Weaver could throw balls of fire or call down lightning, so that's what they pretended to do as they ran and played together. Ryn was doubtful. That wasn't the sort of thing a human could do, he reasoned. What he knew for certain was that Flame Weavers needed fuel, and a lot of it. A good part of what the village woodcutters hewed and what the coalmen up in Ashborne mined from the Levent Hills was shipped south by the wagonload to supply Aldria's Standing Army. How exactly the Flame Weavers used it, he didn't know. The village boys seemed to think they ate the wood and coal, but he doubted that too.

As Ryn wended his way through the woods, Anya plodding along beside him, he continued to scan the forest. Each tree or shrub his eyes focused on stood out to him in sharp contrast to the surrounding vegetation, almost as if lit by a faint halo. In his mind's eye, a cloud of words floated around each plant, giving its name and any known uses for each part of it.

Here was heartsvine, named for the shape of its leaves. Those leaves gave some people a mild rash, easily treated with foxfeather and cat's clove. The flowers could greatly enhance the flavor of any tea, though it was poison to those same people who got a rash from the leaves. The roots, when added to a salve, were great for sealing wounds, and it did no harm to those allergic to the rest of the plant.

There was a white cherry tree, uncommon for these woods. The bark, when dried, was a good source of tinder, burning well and long. The leaves, when chewed, helped blood to clot, though they shouldn't be swallowed. The berries were too bitter to eat from the tree, but when mixed into preserves, with plenty of sugar, they weren't bad.

On the lists ran. Rindwort, good for breaking fevers. Boxsorrel, which when mixed with spinetail leaves, could dry out a runny nose. Kindmarrow. Queen's barrels. Geldknot. The trees here were mostly crown oaks and gray maples, which weren't good for much beyond firewood.

Within twenty minutes of leaving the cottage, he had found his first destination: a foxfeather bush. The leaves were small and round, clustered alternatingly along the stems. It looked a lot like foolsgift, a shrub that was useless, as far as Ryn knew, except that foxfeather leaves had silvery undersides. Ryn had memorized the location of twenty different foxfeather bushes spread out around his aunt's cottage. It was the ingredient she used more than any other in her tinctures. It was unparalleled for treating headaches and sore muscles, the most common complaints among farmers and woodcutters, her primary clientele. He filled three canisters with leaves. The tender new shoots worked best. He was always careful not to overharvest any of the bushes. If he found nothing else of use, he could stop here again on his way back home.

He knew of a few other spots where he could find the other items on Marla's list, excepting the king's lances, but the silverbells could be anywhere within the woods. They were little mushrooms that grew beneath the soil, considered a delicacy in Aldrian cuisine—shaped like bells and worth their weight in silver, hence the name. By the time their fruiting bodies breached the surface, they were past the point of edibility, so you had to unearth them before that. Silverbells were Aen's Hollow's second chief export, after the wood. It was said they made it all the way to the tables of the Pentarchs in Appencourt, though Ryn knew little about that. Half the families in the village kept mushroom pigs, all Mayline sows, especially bred and trained for the job. Even as far from the village as he was, he was still liable to run into one of the local youths, trotting along beside a hulking pig on the hunt. This time of year was the peak season for silverbells.

Anya didn't have a nose for them, but she did seem to enjoy her walks in the woods with Ryn. That was his secret. He started walking further east, guided by a feeling he could not quite explain. He had never tried explaining it to anyone. It was too foreign a subject to broach with Marla, and he didn't have anyone else to talk to about it, besides Anya. He certainly couldn't smell the mushrooms, often buried two feet or more under the soil and spread out across miles and miles of woodlands, but he had a knack for finding them. That's what he called it, his "knack."

He'd found the first one by accident last year. He'd been walking through the woods on an errand for Marla, looking for herbs, when a barren spot of soil caught his eye. It wasn't a sound or anything he could see, but some force drew him to it. Unsure what he would find, he started digging. When he unearthed the mushroom, the size of a baby's fist, he'd been astonished. When he rushed home and showed it to Marla, she broke into a rare smile, talking of how much it could fetch them on Market Day and what they could do with the money. Then she frowned and asked him how he had possibly found it. He couldn't tell her the truth—he didn't understand the truth—and so he lied and said Anya found it.

The extra income didn't quite transform their lives, but it certainly improved them. They had all new clothes, a new set of cookware for the kitchen, and new pestles, mortars, mixing bowls, and vials for Marla's work. Ryn purchased over a dozen new books to read, and Marla was also able to commission her herb-gathering satchel and have a thatcher and a carpenter out to make some much-needed improvements to the house. If he brought in a good harvest this season, she was talking of adding another room to the cottage. As it was, there were only two rooms: Marla's bedroom and a larger room that served as the kitchen, the living area, and Marla's workshop. Ryn slept on a pallet in the corner. The added room would be his own private bedroom. He smiled at the idea.

He walked on, compelled by that unseen, barely felt force that drew him to where he knew a silverbell would be. The force never strengthened or weakened, and he had no way of knowing how far it would take him. From experimenting, he knew it wasn't necessarily taking him to the nearest silverbell. Still, he knew he would find one, if only he kept going.

Somewhere off to the right, a twig snapped in the brush. Ryn froze. Normally, he would not even have heard the sound, but the woods were so eerily quiet that the small noise seemed to echo through the trees. He turned and scanned the undergrowth. The canopy here was thick, blocking out much of the midmorning sun. It came through in splotches, painting everything with a dappled pattern of light. Ryn couldn't see far in any direction with all the green spring foliage. The path he followed through the woods was a meandering game trail. He saw no signs of movement.

He looked down at Anya, who kept her head down, sniffing in the dirt, unbothered. It was probably just a jackhound. He rarely saw them, and when he did, they would always run. Many of the villagers feared the jackhound, though they had never been known to attack humans. The skittish canines were somewhere between a wolf and a fox, in both size and appearance, with large ears and brown or gray coats. A lot of village superstitions surrounded the jackhound, associating them with untimely death or disease. They were omnivorous scavengers and none too picky. They'd even been known to raid the village cemetery, digging up freshly buried corpses. Marla was not one for superstition. She scoffed anytime she heard mention of such things, and so Ryn wasn't superstitious either.

Still, he wondered what kind of rational explanation could account for his knack for finding silverbells. Sometimes he wondered if he himself were a Weaver, a Root Weaver even—they seemed to have something to do with plants after all. Weavers were supposed to be able to do amazing, unnatural things, but he doubted that extended to finding mushrooms, no matter how profitable it was. He couldn't talk to Marla about it, and so he could only wonder.

He continued in a straight line until he came to the edge of a bog. The ground turned muddy, spotted with brown pools of standing water. The oaks and maples gave way to moss-covered pinefirs and reeds. He remembered his aunt's warning to avoid the bogs. He also knew that silverbells never grew in soil that wet, so his quarry had to be somewhere on the other side of the bog. He broke away from the force drawing him and picked his way along the edge of the mire. The woods here were just as quiet, though this time of year the croaking of swamp frogs should have been deafening.

It took Ryn nearly an hour to make his way around the bog, but he was able to quickly pick up the unseen trail again once he was past it. Along the way he found a couple of whitecaps growing in the shade of a fallen tree. The tiny mushrooms had over a dozen medicinal uses, though they weren't nearly as tasty as the prize he sought. The force led him southeast. If he kept going, he would eventually reach Aen's River, a misleading name for a little stream that was narrow enough in most places for Ryn to leap across without getting his boots wet.

He found the silverbell well before he reached the river. The patch of earth in a small clearing gave no sign of the buried treasure, but he knew it was there. He looked up at the sky through the hole in the canopy. The few wispy clouds gave no hint of impending rain, and the sun lay an hour shy of its zenith. He was off to a good start.

He dropped Anya's lead and removed his satchel. The pig was trained enough not to wander off on her own. His belt had two leather sheaths. One held a small knife; the other, a trowel. He removed the wood-handled trowel and knelt down in the dirt, brushing away leaves and twigs. The soil here was rich and brown, and he made a pile of it, taking small careful scoops. Though his knack had never failed him, he still smiled with delight when he unearthed the silverbell. He set the trowel aside and used his hands to dig it the rest of the way out, careful not to nick or damage the mushroom. The dirty mass looked something like a lump of coal.

Reaching back, he pulled the satchel closer. He loosened the drawstrings on the bag and deposited the mushroom within. He would clean it when he got back to the cottage, rinsing it with water from the pump and leaving it out only long enough to dry, before storing it in the dark, dry root cellar until the next Market Day, when the traveling merchants came through town. He used his fingers to wipe dirt from his trowel, before placing it back in its sheath. He rubbed his hands on his pant legs to get off some of the dirt.

He prepared to stand up but froze. Suddenly, he felt a new sensation tugging at his mind. It was a force, something like the one that led him to silverbells, but this one felt distinctly different. Whatever this was, it was coming from directly behind him.

A series of strange sensations washed over him. He wanted very much to turn around and see what was there, but every instinct told him not to look, not even to move. He felt the hairs on his neck and arms begin to rise. He remained frozen for mere moments, but it felt much longer. Then, like a held breath suddenly released, time seemed to speed up, and a lot happened at once.

Anya squealed as she never had before and bolted, running away from Ryn and whatever force loomed behind him. Her long rope lead trailed through the leaves behind her like a snake. He made no effort to grab it. Nevertheless, her sudden flight seemed to break the spell over him and allowed him to move. He jumped to his feet, spinning around at the same time. His hand went to the knife at his belt, a tiny thing only good for whittling and cutting samples from plants, but he never drew it.

His mind reeled and his eyes unfocused, as if his body refused to perceive what stood before him. It was like something leapt straight from a nightmare into the waking world. He blinked, forcing himself to focus on the creature. That was the only word for it. It stood barely five feet tall but was twice as wide as a man. The whites of its black eyes were jaundiced and bloodshot. It was vaguely human in appearance, but with leathery gray skin, no hair, and large pointed ears. It wore tight brown breeches and a vest and carried a curved shortsword. Its hands and bare feet looked too big for its body and were tipped in thick black nails that came to claw-like points.

Ryn knew he should run, but he stood rooted to the ground, not even breathing. He became dimly aware of two other creatures like the first, emerging from the tree line into the clearing, but his mind was focused on the one standing directly in front of him. Its broad lipless mouth parted in something like a smile, revealing sinister pointed teeth, and its small, hooked nose wrinkled.

Ryn's mouth felt dry and his legs began to shake, but still, he couldn't move. The two new creatures came to stand on either side of Ryn, boxing him in. One held a small hand axe; the other, a club studded with spikes.

The first creature spoke. "Gris ick dewon?" Its voice was hoarse and gravelly, as if it wasn't accustomed to speaking. Ryn didn't understand the question, but the creature didn't seem to be speaking to him.

He became aware of the two others standing very close to him. He felt their breath upon his neck, but still he could not move, his eyes fixed on the one standing before him.

"Grood bee," the creature to his right said after a moment.

The creature to his left, a foot shorter than the other two, made a raspy, barking sound that could have been a laugh. "Gree no tink so," it said.

The first creature looked Ryn up and down, as if considering. "Gree no tink so," it said. He felt he could almost understand what it was saying, but his mind still reeled, clouding his ability to think clearly. The creature lashed out suddenly, raking its clawed fingers across Ryn's face. Ryn flinched and stumbled back, feeling the gouges across his cheek burn. His hand shot up to his face and came away wet with blood. One of the slices had come dangerously close to his right eye.

The sudden flash of pain freed him from whatever force kept him fixed to the ground. He turned away from the creatures and ran. He made it halfway across the clearing before he fell to the ground. He landed hard in the dirt and lay stunned for a moment. Fiery waves of pain radiated from the small of his back, his heart beat rapidly in his chest, but his mind still screamed to keep running.

He dug his hands into the dirt and tried to pick himself up, but his arms gave out after another spasm of pain. The creatures behind him were braying those inhuman laughs. He lifted his head and looked toward the woods. There at the edge of the clearing was a cluster of king's lances, like delicate white spires. They were good for… He couldn't remember what they were good for… He felt a fog settle over his mind, and the light seemed to dim at the edges of his vision.

Still, that voice in his head screamed at him to run. He crawled, digging his fingers into the dirt and pulling himself forward, inch by inch. His legs didn't seem to work anymore; he could feel nothing below his waist. He couldn't understand why, and so he pushed the question away and focused what remained of his awareness on crawling, dragging himself along on his belly.

The creature took its time catching up to Ryn, but it did soon enough. "Ick has corrage," it said. Ryn understood that. He realized they had been speaking the King's Tongue the whole time, just with garbled accents. The creature planted a foot on Ryn's back, pinning him to the ground. He felt a strange pressure on the part of his back from which pain continued to radiate, and then the shooting anguish bloomed anew as the creature seemed to straighten up. Ryn screwed his eyes shut, taking long ragged breaths.

The foot came off his back, and a hand seized his shoulder. The creature lifted him and flipped him over. Ryn cried out in agony, realizing it was not the first time he had screamed. He struggled to open his eyes. The gray-fleshed monster stood over him, holding that curved sword, now drenched in blood. Ryn's blood. When he had turned to run, the creature must have hurled the sword after him. That was what struck him in the back, severing his spine. Then the creature had pulled the blade out before turning Ryn over. It took every fiber of Ryn's remaining wits to piece that all together, and even still he understood it only dimly, like trying to remember the details of a dream upon waking. His gaze was drawn once again to those bloodshot yellowed eyes.

The creature slowly raised its sword, turning the point downward. Ryn no longer had the strength to move. His entire back felt wet, as if he were lying in a puddle. In one swift motion, the blade came down, plunging into Ryn's stomach. He spasmed again, choking and trying to scream at the same time. He couldn't move his arms or lift his head. He stared up at the blank blue sky.

He felt the sword twist in his belly, but he barely twitched that time. The pain was sharp and threatened to overwhelm his mind, but his strength was spent and his body felt leaden and immovable.

The sky went black, but no, he had just shut his eyes again. The blade pulled free, and another shockwave of pain rocked his mind. Something rigid and cold dragged across his chest—the beast cleaning its blade on his shirt. He heard footsteps crunch through the leaf litter, away from him. Garbled voices whispered together, diminishing into silence.

Ryn felt his mind fading, slipping away into unconsciousness. He struggled to stay awake, to force his eyes back open. He saw the empty sky and spreading tree branches. The nightmare creatures had left him alone. He knew he was losing a lot of blood from the jagged wound in his gut, but he had no strength left to move. All he could do was breathe, and those breaths came fast and shallow. He shut everything else out of his mind and focused on his breathing, on slowing it down. He breathed in, trying to hold it, but released it in a sputtering cough. He tried again, taking a deep breath in, holding it, and then slowly releasing it. He breathed again. In and out, slowly. In and out. In and out.

Chapter 2
The Redsmith's Apprentice

THALIA MOLDO SWEPT the stone floor of the redsmith's shop, but her mind was not on the work. The open storefront looked out onto Rigel Square, named for the ancient fountain at its center, which was also the namesake of her hometown. A woman in a green riding dress and a brown cloak had been standing for some time at the base of the fountain, looking up at the stone face on top. Thalia knew the woman was going to ask the fountain a question, and she was curious to hear the answer.

The woman turned, glancing over her shoulder, and Thalia dropped her gaze, knowing it was rude to stare. She continued sweeping the shop, though in truth, she had finished that just before the stranger arrived at the fountain. The shop was spotless. Thalia took great pride in her place of employment. She had been apprenticed to Master Foster for two years now, but she was still overjoyed that he had taken a chance with her, and she worked tirelessly every day to prove herself. At sixteen, she had been the oldest person in Rigel to be apprenticed to a master craftsman in recent memory—and the only girl, possibly ever.

Thalia's dream was to be a bladesmith, like her father had been, but Rigel's master bladesmith had flatly refused to take her on. As had the blacksmith, the whitesmith, the silversmith, and even the farrier. Master Foster, who had known her father, had reluctantly agreed to give her a shot. In the past two years, she felt she had proven herself worthy, and Master Foster doted on her like she was his own daughter.

Thalia turned her back to the open storefront and swept her eyes over the shop. Squeezed in between a jeweler and an embroiderer, the workspace was a narrow, rectangular room. Behind her, a door and a huge open window faced the square. A countertop ran along the base of the window for dealing with customers. A wooden awning, now propped up by two poles, could be lowered and bolted in place to cover the opening and secure the shop at night. Sturdy workbenches ran the length of both walls to either side of her, cluttered with works in progress and all the tools necessary for smithing copper: vises, shears, saws, ball hammers and raising hammers, wooden mallets, scribers, compasses, and various other tools for specialized work. Above them, samples of her master's work hung on pegs—largely pots, pans, pails, and kettles, the mainstays of a redsmith's wares. On the far wall sat a small furnace with a flume leading up through the ceiling, a water barrel for quenching, three different-sized anvils and sandbags for shaping the metal, a buffing wheel that could be worked with a foot pedal, rolled sheets of copper, and another barrel full of scrap pieces.

Her first few months as an apprentice, she had only been allowed to sweep up the shop and hand tools to Master Foster, but this was typical for an apprentice. She did the work without complaint, but she watched everything Master Foster and his other apprentice, a boy four years younger than her named Raef, did. Eventually, she moved up to buffing finished pieces and crafting copper rivets from scrap metal. In her spare time, she also practiced various techniques on the scrap pieces, using hammers and mallets to shape the ragged metal. She wasn't making anything wonderful or even practical, but that first step into smithing had begun to satisfy a yearning she had felt all her life: to create.

Her father's income as a bladesmith—mostly making knives—had afforded Thalia, her mother, and her two older sisters a comfortable life in Rigel. Her mother had instructed her in the finer arts practiced by second-echelon Aldrian ladies, including needlepoint and watercolor painting. While Thalia displayed some talent in these areas, quickly surpassing her older sisters' expertise, they never truly appealed to her. She would much rather spend her time down in her father's smithy, watching him work with his apprentices and journeymen. The whole process fascinated her: the sweltering heat of the forge, the glowing metal, the violent clang of the hammer. That was the kind of creation she desired, to make something both beautiful and practical, something like her father's knives, which could serve a cook, a tradesman, a hunter, or even a soldier reliably and efficiently for years. Two years ago, with her father dead and her sisters married off, she begged her mother to let her become an apprentice, and Mrs. Moldo had reluctantly agreed.

They weren't knives, but Master Foster's copper cookware and utensils had a beauty and simplicity of their own. After her first year working with him, he started letting her do the kind of work that Raef did—she'd caught up to the boy's skill level quickly and had since surpassed him. Fortunately, Raef did not resent her; they worked together to improve each other's skills. He was like the brother she never had. Thalia had mastered the basic methods of working copper, and Master Foster was instructing her on the more advanced techniques, like how to crimp pieces and edges together into a smooth seam.

The other smiths who'd turned her away had said a girl could never develop the strength needed to work with metal, and truthfully, copper was easier to work than most metals. It was soft and pliable and didn't need to be heated up before shaping it. Steady, rhythmic hammering over the anvil or a sandbag could mold the metal any way you wished. Only for the more complex jobs, like the decorative sconces or candelabras sometimes commissioned by the second-echelon citizens of Rigel, did Master Foster fire the furnace. Heating the copper and then rapidly quenching it in water somehow made it even easier to manipulate. Master Foster handled those elaborate jobs himself, though Thalia had managed to hammer out some serviceable copper earrings and bracelets from scrap pieces, which she had gifted to her mother and sisters at the Winter Feast.

Still, redsmithing could be exhausting work, and two years at it had wrought its own changes on Thalia's body. She had always been tall for a girl, topping out at six feet by the time she was fourteen, with naturally broad shoulders. Working in the shop had toned and enlarged her arms and back muscles. She didn't come close in size to the hulking town blacksmith and his teenage apprentices, but she still turned heads sometimes as she made her way through town. She had mixed feelings about that. She was taller and stronger than any other girl in town, and that made her different. She had never given much thought to the prospect of finding a husband. Only a brawny smith could make her look dainty and feminine by comparison, and none of the tradesmen in Rigel had caught her eye. The masters were all too old and the apprentices too young.

On weekends and feast days, she would spend time with the other apprentices, mainly to question them about what they were learning in their trades—she aspired to work with more than just copper someday—and all those boys viewed her as a protective older sister. Still, when she stood before the mirror each morning, studying her well-defined arms, her taut brown skin, and her wavy black hair wrangled into two braids, she considered herself beautiful, like a sturdy tool crafted for practical use. Most mornings, anyway.

Thalia leaned the broom against the wall in its usual corner. Lost in her thoughts, she had forgotten about the woman at the fountain, but when she turned back around, there was the woman, standing at the counter and looking at her. Thalia flinched.

The woman smiled. "Good evening," she said. The square behind her was mostly empty. All the other shops facing it had shuttered for the day, and only a couple hours remained till sunset. The woman looked to be about forty, with an angular face and straight black hair that hung to her shoulders. She had smooth white skin that didn't look like it had seen much sunlight.

Thalia nodded in greeting. "I'm afraid we're closed up for the day," she said. "Master Foster has already gone home." The shop held a few pieces that were waiting for customers to pick up, but Thalia knew all of Master Foster's clientele, and she had never seen this woman before.

The woman's smile faltered. She slowly shook her head. "No, I'm not a customer," she said. She glanced to the left and right at the shop's interior as if only just now noticing it. "A redsmith…" she said, almost to herself. Her eyes locked on Thalia again. "And you're…?"

"Master Foster's apprentice. Thalia Moldo."

The woman looked her up and down with those quick dark eyes. Thalia resisted the urge to squirm, wondering what this woman would think of her. She wore a sleeveless dress under her leather apron that showcased her muscular arms and shoulders well, and this late in the day, she knew dozens of curly strands of hair had no doubt broken free from her braids to hover about her head like flies. Whatever the woman thought, her smile only broadened. "Well, Thalia," she said, "my name is Mina Bellain. I've no need for copper pots or kettles at the moment, but I was hoping I could ask you a few questions about that." Without turning around, Mina pointed backwards toward the fountain.

Thalia looked out at the square again. Only a few people still moved through the broad cobblestone area, stepping quickly toward one of the cross streets. None of them even glanced at the fountain. They were all locals, accustomed to its oddity. Thalia nodded. The fountain was a major attraction to travelers passing through Rigel. It fascinated her too. It stood about twelve feet tall, built in three tiers. Water spilled out from the second level into the third. A stone obelisk rose from the top tier. Each side held a carving of a human face. Three faces—resembling an old woman, a girl, and a boy—had their lips puckered and spewed a constant stream of water into the tier below. The fourth visage, an old man, faced toward the redsmith's shop and emitted no water. His lips curved into a knowing smile, with wrinkles at the corners of his eyes.

"Well," Thalia said, "I can't tell you much, only what everyone else knows. It's a Runeform, and it's older than Rigel, older than Aldria itself."

As Thalia spoke, Mina turned around and leaned her back against the counter, joining the apprentice in staring at the fountain. "Yes, a Runeform," she said. She paused for a long moment before continuing. "No matter what you might have heard, they were built by men, humans just like you and me. We've only just forgotten how it's done."

Thalia nodded. She wished she knew how one could build a Runeform. With that knowledge, the potential for creation was seemingly limitless.

Mina glanced over her shoulder at Thalia. "No, I don't expect you to know where it came from, Thalia Moldo, but can you show me how to use it?"

Thalia looked around the shop. The only thing left to do was lock up for the night, but that could wait. "Of course," she said, taking off her apron and hanging it from a peg, before stepping out the door to where Mina waited.

The two women walked side-by-side toward the fountain, stopping at its edge. Thalia gestured toward the stone face. "You speak its name to activate it, and then you can try asking it a question."

"Yes, 'try.' That's the part that interests me. I've heard its answers don't always make sense."

"You're a Scholar." Thalia didn't mean to say that; she just blurted it out. The realization had come to her suddenly as she studied the woman, wondering who she was. Up close, Thalia could see Mina's riding dress was well-cut silk with vines embroidered along the hem. Yet she didn't have the bearing of a first-echelon lady and didn't seem to mind chatting with a teenage redsmith's apprentice. If she was a Scholar, then that meant she was also a Weaver, a Root Weaver if the vines on her dress were any indication.

Mina smiled and nodded. "Yes, I suppose I fit the stereotype, don't I?"

Thalia blushed. "It was only a guess. I've seen plenty of Scholars passing through town." Rigel sat on the west bank of the

River Aldria. A short walk or ride across the Rigel Bridge led to the neighboring city of Falport and the Golden Lands beyond that, considered the heart and soul of Aldria. Hundreds, if not thousands, of people passed through the town each day.

"I'm sure you have," Mina said. "Your shop is perfectly situated for studying this particular Runeform. Tell me, how many people ask it a question each day?"

Thalia laughed. "Oh, at least a dozen."

"I hear that it's more likely to give a straightforward answer to foreigners or people who live far away, but to the locals it only speaks nonsense."

"That seems to be the case. From the shop, we usually can't hear the question being asked, but we can hear the answers, and you can tell by how the questioners react if they understand it."

"And have you ever asked the Runeform a question?"

"Only once. I asked it…" Thalia blushed and went on quickly. "Well, it doesn't matter what I asked it. It should have been a simple yes-or-no question, but what it said was something along the lines of, 'What you seek lies in the third well.'"

"The third well? And you don't know what that means?"

Thalia shook her head. "There are dozens of wells in Rigel, so I don't know which could be the 'third' one. And I wasn't seeking anything that could be found inside a well."

"Hmm, curious. Perhaps it is defective. Are there any questions it won't answer?"

"It won't answer a hypothetical question, or if you ask something like, 'What should I do?' Oh, and you can't ask a bunch of questions in a row. After one question, it will still respond to others but not to you. Then you have to wait a day or so before it will answer you again."

Mina studied the stone face overhead for another long moment. Thalia glanced back at the shop. She needed to close up and get home soon, but she was genuinely curious to see what sort of question this Scholar would ask the Runeform and what its answer might be. As if reading her mind, Mina flashed her a smile and said, "Well, let me give it a go."

Mina stared up at the face a while longer before asking her question though. Perhaps she was deciding what question to ask or how best to phrase it. Scholars had a reputation for always having their heads in the clouds, but they were also known for their keen intellects. Unlike the Watchkeepers and the Flame Weavers in the Standing Army, who were only focused on using the Five Forces as weapons, Scholars studied every aspect and application of Weaving and had made countless advances in science, medicine, and metallurgy over the centuries.

Finally, Mina cleared her throat and said in a clear voice, "Rigel!"

In response to hearing its name, the carved face came to life. The eyes lit up, illumined from within by a white light. The face shifted as if looking down and focusing on the one who had spoken. Its stony features were surprisingly animated, conveying a distinct sense of personality. There seemed to be laughter in those glowing eyes and in its voice whenever it spoke. Mina studied it, clearly fascinated.

Thalia leaned forward. "It won't speak until you ask your question," she said in a whisper, though she knew the statue would only respond to Mina now.

The Scholar nodded. She flashed another smile at Thalia and asked the fountain, "What will I have for dinner tonight?"

The Runeform began speaking as soon as the question was out of her mouth. Its voice sounded almost human, though it was much louder than a normal speaking voice and seemed to echo across the courtyard far more than another voice would. It said, "ONLY THOSE WHO HAVE TASTED DEADLY POISON AND LIVED CAN STOP THE RIVENING."

Thalia stared up at the Runeform in stunned silence. What could that possibly mean?

Mina slowly shook her head. "Well, that was unexpected," she said. "Hopefully that doesn't mean I'll have poison for dinner," she added with a laugh.

Thalia laughed too. "But it seems you'll survive it if you do."

Mina shrugged. "Perhaps, and then I can stop the… Rivening? No, but I suspect this particular prophecy isn't about me." She paused, seeming to stare off at nothing. Thalia wondered what thoughts were racing through her mind. "Well," she said, shrugging. "Thank you immensely for your assistance. I must be off now. My fateful dinner awaits."

Mina extended her hand, and Thalia reached out and shook it. The Scholar's grip was surprisingly firm. Thalia watched her as she turned and walked away, disappearing down a cross street. She looked up at the Runeform, shook her head, and walked back to the shop to close it up for the night.

But her day wasn't finished yet, and somehow, it only got stranger. Before she had finished lowering the awning, she was interrupted by a pair of wooden shoes clacking toward her from across the square. Thalia looked up to see Mrs. Finston bearing down on her. Mrs. Finston's husband made clogs, normally not a popular footwear option in Rigel, though for some reason they had recently become quite fashionable with the more respectable second- and third-echelon citizens. Thalia had been hearing wooden shoes clacking up and down the cobblestones all week. Mrs. Finston was a portly woman, well past her middle years, who usually wore a charming smile. She didn't look happy today. In one arm she cradled a copper tea kettle; in the other hand, she held its handle.

Thalia's eyes widened. She recognized the piece. She herself had riveted the handle on just days ago.

"Thalia," Mrs. Finston said. "Thalia Moldo!" She brandished the broken tea kettle by way of elaboration.

"My goodness," Thalia said, doing her best to remain calm and pleasant. "What happened?"

Mrs. Finston scoffed and plopped the two pieces of the kettle onto the shop's counter. "That's exactly what I want to know. The cursed handle just came right off in my hand. I nearly poured scalding water all over myself! As it was, I singed the cat's tail, and now she's up a tree somewhere. Master Foster has always done good work, but I've had this kettle less than a week! That's unheard of."

"I'm so sorry," Thalia said, picking up the broken handle. It was a simple curved piece of metal attached to the kettle by two rivets. She remembered driving those rivets in herself. It took steady confident swings to drive a rivet in cleanly without crinkling the metal and making it look ugly. She'd driven them in perfectly. One of the rivets was missing, and the other had split evenly down the middle. That was something she had never seen before. If any part of the kettle was going to fail, that shouldn't have been it. "We'll get this fixed for you right away. No extra charge, of course."

Mrs. Finston sighed and waved a hand. "Oh, I know you will, sweetheart. I don't mean to be snippy. It's just been a long day. Oh, and things were going so well!"

"Oh no, did something else happen?"

"Mr. Finston took a nasty spill down the front steps this morning. Apparently, a roofing tile had come loose and fallen on the top step. He didn't see it and slipped right down the stairs. We think he broke his ankle. It turned purple and swelled up like a melon!"

"My goodness, is he all right?"

"Now he is, of course. We sent the shop boy to run and fetch a healer from the Guild, but either the boy or the Guild got the address mixed up and the healer never found us! We waited for hours, and Mr. Finston was in so much pain. We sent the boy back twice, and finally he had to take the Weaver by the hand and walk him straight to our house."

"Wow, that's so strange."

"They still charged us full price for the healing, of course. Not that it was a problem the way business has been going." She gestured toward her wooden shoes.

"I bet. I've been seeing your husband's clogs everywhere I look lately."

"Yes, Mr. Finston always swore they were the height of fashion in Iscerna, but you know how fickle the high-society types can be. Well, they finally caught on three days ago. I remember, I was coming back from your shop, with that very kettle, and who should I find in my husband's shop, but Gloria Bastion herself!"

Thalia shook her head. She had no idea who Gloria Bastion was.

Mrs. Finston scoffed. "Really, Thalia," she said. "Gloria Bastion is the queen of fashion in Rigel. She sets the taste standard, and everyone else follows. Well, there she was, sitting in a chair, while my husband fit her for a pair of clogs. He had no idea who she was either! Gloria said she had been walking by the shop window, and my husband's work just happened to catch her eye. Well, she wore those clogs out the door, and by the end of the day, we had a line around the corner! We sold our entire stock, and Mr.

Finston and the boy have been working like madmen to fill orders. The other cobblers in town have started making their own clogs, but nothing beats a Finston original." Mrs. Finston stuck out her foot and twisted her ankle this way and that to model the shoe. "I can get you a pair at a discount, my dear."

Thalia smiled. "Well, I'm glad to hear business is going well," she said, setting the handle back down. "I'll get this kettle sorted first thing in the morning, so don't you worry. I would focus on all your good fortune and not let one bad day spoil your mood."

Mrs. Finston smiled. "Quite right, my dear." She patted Thalia on the arm. "Oh," she said and gave the arm a tighter squeeze, no doubt surprised at how firm it felt. "My, you are getting to be a strapping young thing, aren't you?"

Thalia blushed. She felt awkward anytime someone commented on her size. She certainly wasn't ashamed but maybe a little embarrassed.

The two women said good night, and Mrs. Finston turned to leave but stopped when she noticed someone else approaching the shop. Mrs. Finston arched an eyebrow. "Another one?" she said.

Doug Ponter stopped at the counter, holding a copper frying pan in one hand and its handle in another. He shrugged, eyeing the broken kettle already on the counter. "Sorry to bother you so late, Thalia," he said. "It only just broke and I live right around the corner, so I hoped I might catch you before you closed."

Doug Ponter was a talented Wave Weaver. He sold his services through the Rigel Guild, and he had set wards on half the businesses in town, including the redsmith's shop. The ward was invisible to non-Weavers, but supposedly it stopped robbers from being able to break in.

Thalia took the broken pan from him. She had worked on this piece too, crafting the handle and driving in the rivets on the same day she finished Mrs. Finston's tea kettle. The rivets had also split here, and a huge crack ran down the length of the handle. What had he been doing with it? That kind of damage couldn't occur from normal usage in less than a week. Still, she couldn't accuse Doug Ponter of abusing the cookware.

"I sincerely apologize, Mr. Ponter," Thalia said. "We'll get this repaired and back to you tomorrow. I'll see to it myself."

"Thanks, Thalia," Doug said with a half-smile. He was a lean, handsome man, around thirty years old, though with gray hairs already flecking his temples. "I don't hold it against you or Master Foster. I know how these kinds of things can happen. Luck is... a fickle thing."

Mrs. Finston laughed. "Yes, Mr. Ponter, I hear you've had quite the run of good fortune lately."

Doug's smile turned sheepish. "Oh, you've heard about that, have you?"

Mrs. Finston patted his arm. "Don't worry, Mr. Ponter. I mean no slight. I know some people consider it a vice, but I would be lying if I said I've never placed a bet or two on the Sunday races."

"You don't say."

"Come, Mr. Ponter, you can tell us. Thalia and I are no gossips."

Thalia didn't gossip, but she knew that Mrs. Finston surely did.

Doug shrugged. "Yeah, I suppose I had a good run." He stared out across the square and smiled. "Truth be told, I had a streak of uncommon good luck."

Mrs. Finston gave him an encouraging smile.

Finally, Doug sighed and told the whole story, with Mrs. Finston coaxing him along with grins and friendly comments. "It started two nights ago. Some of the fellows from the Guild have a weekly game of cards, just small stakes, you understand, copper pennies mostly. Well, I won every hand. We had to call it a night early because I'd cleaned everyone out. The next day I was feeling pretty good and had this extra pocket money, so yeah, I went down to the tracks. I've always been interested in the sport more than the betting, you understand. I fancy I have a good eye for horseflesh. I only placed a few bets, but each one came up a winner. After that I guess you could say I got a little carried away. I just kept winning, you know. Horses, cards, dice, it didn't matter. I was raking it in, hand over fist." He sighed. "Until today anyway."

Mrs. Finston gasped. "Bless the stars! Don't tell me you lost?"

He nodded. "Big time. I lost almost the whole pot. I'm a little ahead of where I started, but not by much."

"You have to tell me what happened."

Doug laughed, though there was no humor in it. "It was the most peculiar thing. I went to the track this morning, and there was this nag. A little scrawny, with long odds, but I liked the look of her flanks. Truth be told, I had convinced myself I could not lose. So I emptied my pockets and put everything on the nag."

"And she lost."

"Oh, spectacularly. At first, it seemed great. She pulled ahead of the pack and was barreling down the line. She must have hit a divot or something, because all of a sudden she was sprawled out on the ground, her leg shattered. She threw her rider, and the lad almost got trampled by the other horses. They had to put the cursed nag down."

While Mrs. Finston expressed her disbelief, Thalia looked back and forth between the broken pan in her hand and the broken kettle on the counter. There was an obvious similarity between the two defective pieces and the weeks their recipients had experienced, but it made no logical sense. It had to be some kind of coincidence.

Hearing more footsteps, she looked up to see two more customers approaching the redsmith's shop, clutching broken pieces of copper in their hands. One walked with a limp, and the other had a black eye. That was only the beginning of it.

Chapter 3
The Stranger and the Crow

RYN AWOKE WITH A GASP, his body convulsing. He lay on his back in the dirt, staring up at the trees and the darkening sky overhead and panting to catch his breath. He didn't know where he was at first. The woods, of course, but how had he gotten there? Had he passed out? After what seemed like minutes, he started to remember.

He had been attacked. Stabbed. Twice. By human-like creatures he had never seen before. He tensed his muscles, moving his fingers and wiggling his toes. He didn't feel injured. In fact, he felt great, like waking up from a restful night of sleep. So it was all just a dream then? A nightmare? That didn't explain what he was doing lying on his back in the woods.

Slowly, Ryn sat up. His eyes widened as he looked down and saw that his clothes were covered in blood, now dried and flaking. His hands shot to his torso and he found the ragged tear in his shirt, but when he lifted up the sticky fabric, peeling it from his stomach, he could not see or feel any kind of wound, not even a scratch. He still remembered how it felt as the sword went in, slicing deep into his guts. He touched his cheek. No claw marks. He touched his back. There was the slit in his shirt where the thrown blade had gone in, but no wound.

Ryn looked around. His wounds had vanished—if he had been wounded—but something else had happened to the forest. Everything looked... dead. The low ground cover that blanketed the clearing had shriveled up, turning brown or black. It looked like a drought had cursed the land, or else a forest fire. Even the surrounding trees had been stricken. At first he thought they had dropped their leaves all at once like a sudden return of winter, but no, each leaf had withered on its stem, turning brown and curling up.

"What?" Ryn said aloud, and the word encompassed so many questions. He couldn't even begin to make sense of what had miraculously healed his wounds and blighted the forest. The two things had to be connected, but how? Weaving had to be involved; that was the only explanation he could think of. But if so, who had done it? Where was the Weaver now?

Ryn climbed to his feet. Despite his reeling mind, he felt steady. He felt he could walk twenty miles and not get tired, actually. That part, feeling so great, somehow made the situation more unnerving. He should be dead.

He shook his head and walked across the clearing, the lifeless vegetation cracking and crumbling under his feet. He reached the nearest blighted tree and touched it. The bark flaked off beneath his fingertips. These trees would not recover; something had struck them dead faster and worse than any plant disease he had ever seen or heard of. It was like every ounce of moisture and life had been sucked out of them.

More details of the attack came back to him. He remembered Anya running off into the woods. He opened his mouth to call her name but stopped. The creatures. Were they still in the area? Could they come back to finish the job? He shut his mouth. Anya was a smart pig; hopefully, she could find her own way home.

The sun was behind the trees now. He doubted he had more than an hour or two of daylight left, and he had no desire to be caught in the woods after dark. He glanced back over the clearing, spotting the satchel. He picked it up and swung it over his shoulder. It felt lighter than it had been, but he didn't stop to check the contents.

He moved quickly through the forest, heading straight for the cottage and only deviating to skirt around the edge of the bog. The strange desolation had only struck the trees immediately around the clearing where he'd been attacked, and the rest of the woods looked as verdant and healthy as ever. The forest, still devoid of animal sound or wind, somehow felt even quieter than before. He replayed the attack and its aftermath in his mind, trying to make sense of it all. He shook his head to clear his thoughts, reminding himself that he should be watching the trees, alert for any sign of the creatures. But the questions just kept coming back, and he retraced his steps to the cottage more by memory than by active navigation.

Suddenly, the woods opened up, and there was Marla's cottage, just as it had looked in the morning. He froze, seeing movement in the yard. An animal loped out from behind the wooden house, heading toward the woods. It was a lanky, medium-sized canine with big ears—only a jackhound, but what was it doing so close to the house? The jackhound froze when it saw Ryn. It met his gaze, its eyes small and black. Ryn took a step forward, and the animal bolted, trotting off into the trees.

Ryn quickly closed the distance to the front door. He stepped inside and took in the large main room with a single glance. It was cluttered but well-organized. A long table that might have served other families as a dinner table stood directly before the door, covered with Marla's herbalist equipment and lots of glass bottles with paper tags, all labeled in Marla's small, tidy handwriting. A wood stove stood off to the right, beside a large wooden bureau and a little rectangular table shoved up against the wall, where they did take their meals. It had only two chairs. None of their visitors ever stayed for tea. At the back, beneath the window, lay his pallet. A large iron-bound chest at its foot held all his possessions.

"Marla?" he said. "I'm back."

No one responded. The house sat as quiet as the woods. He maneuvered around the table to the door set in the left wall. He knocked, pushing it open when he heard no answer. Marla's room, dominated by her bed and dresser and not much else, stood empty. Where was his aunt?

He exited the cottage and moved quickly around the side of the house. The backyard held the outhouse, Anya's shed, and Marla's herb garden, fenced in with chicken wire to keep animals out. Marla was not in her garden, and she certainly wouldn't be in the pig shed. At the back of the house, a set of doors built into the ground provided access to the root cellar. The doors were thrown open, exposing the steep stairs leading down into the earth. Marla had to be in there.

Ryn walked quickly down the steps, eager to find his aunt. In the cellar, he found another bewildering scene. In the narrow rectangle of light at the base of the stairs, he could see the scuffed bottoms of his aunt's shoes. She lay on her back on the packed dirt floor, between two rows of wooden shelves. In the hazy twilight beyond the pool of light, Ryn could see a shadowy figure crouching over Marla. Something else moved in the darkness, something small like a bird flitting from one shelf to another, but Ryn had no time to notice that. He stumbled backward, falling against the steps as the dark figure straightened up and turned toward him.

The stranger stood taller than the creatures from before. It raised a hand toward Ryn, fingers spread wide. "Whoa, kid, this isn't what it looks like." A man's voice. He was only a man, not one of those gray-skinned monsters.

Ryn stood and staggered forward, intent on getting a closer look at his aunt. Marla had not moved. He dropped to his knees at her feet.

"I swear I didn't do this, kid," the stranger said, backing away, both hands up now to show he was unarmed. "She was like this when I found her."

Ryn nodded slowly. "I know what did this," he said, speaking more to himself than the stranger.

Blood stained the front of Marla's dress, a rip in the fabric exposing a puckering black wound. Claw marks marred her face, and her glazed eyes stared up at the ceiling. He touched her leg. She was already cold.

Ryn stumbled to his feet, turned, and scrambled up the steps back into the yard and the fading daylight. He hunched over and retched. The remains of his breakfast splattered the dirt and his boots. The creatures had been here too, and whatever miracle had saved him had not spared Marla.

He heard the man coming up the stairs behind him. The stranger cleared his throat. "Listen, kid, I'm sorry you had to see that. Do you live here? Was that your…?"

Ryn turned around. "Marla," he said. "My aunt."

"Curse me, kid," the man said, staring at Ryn's torn and bloody shirt. "Were you attacked too? Was it the Kobolds?"

Ryn brushed at his shirt. The material had grown stiff and scratchy from the dried blood. "This is… I'm fine. I'm not hurt," he mumbled. "Kobolds?"

Ryn looked at the man closely for the first time. He appeared to be about ten years older than Ryn, with tan skin and a lean build. Stubble covered his jutting chin, and feathery black hair framed his face. He wore a black wool shirt with the sleeves turned up and the collar spread wide, over gray trousers and tall black boots. He had his own satchel of sorts, slung over one shoulder and hanging at his side. The hilts of two weapons, probably swords, peaked out from over his shoulders.

The man shook his head. "Kobolds," he repeated. "They're these nasty little humanoids, come down from the Coldreaches. You'd know one if you saw it."

Ryn frowned. The Coldreach Mountains lay leagues to the north. They marked the border between Aldria and Silgaria. Silgaria was a place of legends to the people of Aen's Hollow, a frozen and rocky land supposedly inhabited by warlike tribes of humans and any number of fantastical creatures, like Drakes and Sprites. Ryn, following Marla's lead, had never believed any of the stories. Still, a Kobold would fit right into the Silgaria of folklore.

Something fluttered out of the cellar behind the stranger. There had been a bird down there. It circled once around the yard before alighting on the edge of the thatch roof. It looked like a crow but with weird blue eyes. Ryn couldn't pay it much attention, his mind still overwhelmed with processing the day's events.

Ryn kept his eyes on the stranger. "Who are you?" he said. "What are you doing here?"

The man bowed with a strange flourish of his arm. "My name is Max. I'm just a traveler, passing through the woods from Ashborne. I stumbled across this cottage and had approached only to ask directions. That's when I found…" He trailed off, rubbing the back of his head and glancing at the still-open root cellar.

The bird on the roof cawed. "His name is Max!"

Ryn's eyes shot up to the eaves. The bird cocked its head, seeming to study Ryn. "Did…" Ryn sputtered. "Did that bird just…?"

Max sighed and let out an awkward laugh. "Yeah, that's… Corvus. He's not exactly a bird."

Ryn stared at the talking creature. He stepped closer without realizing. It was about the size and shape of a crow, but everything else was wrong. Its individual feathers looked too rigid and had a strange sheen in the slanting evening light, almost like metal. Those feathers were a dark shade of blue rather than black. Its gray legs and beak also seemed too smooth and shiny. The joints of its toes were hinged like the articulated limbs of the marionettes vendors sometimes sold on Market Day. And those blue eyes, they seemed to glow like two points of cerulean light.

"What is it?" Ryn blurted.

"Corvus is a Runeform."

"A Runeform?" Ryn turned back to the man. "Those are real too?"

Max barked a short laugh. "Curse me, kid, your whole worldview is shattering today, isn't it?"

Runeforms. Legendary objects that could do marvelous things, created by ancient people long ago before the Burning. Was it all true? He thought about what the villagers said, about how the jackhound could foretell death. He could only gape and shake his head. He wasn't sure how much more bewildered he could get.

Max stepped closer and patted Ryn on the shoulder. "I guess you've been pretty sheltered, huh, kid? Living all the way out here in the middle of nowhere."

Corvus squawked again. "No one lives here," it said, its voice raspy.

"What does it do?" Ryn asked. If the legends were true, then each Runeform had been created for a specific purpose, to fulfill a specific task.

Max laughed again. "Oh, Corvus, he mostly just keeps me company."

Ryn finally broke his gaze off from the strange bird that wasn't a bird and regarded Max again. Max scanned the yard, idly rubbing his left forearm with his other hand. Ryn recognized the tense look on the man's face, the wrinkling at the corners of his eyes. The man was in pain. "You're injured, aren't you?" Ryn said.

"What, this?" Max said, regarding his arm. Whatever injury he had was under the sleeve. "This is just a scratch, but blight, kid, look at you. Whose blood is that if it's not yours?"

Ryn dropped his gaze. "It's my blood, but…" Who was this stranger, really? Should Ryn even be talking to him? Max was right, Ryn had lived a sheltered life. He'd never had a real friend and no one to talk to besides his aunt and Anya. His aunt was touchy about too many topics, and Anya never answered back, not like Max's bird-thing. Now Anya had run off and Marla was… He had to talk to someone, so why not Max?

Still, he fumbled over his words for a moment, trying to figure out how to explain it. Finally, he just started talking. "Something strange happened in the woods. I was out hunting for mushrooms with Anya. She's my… my pig. I was attacked by three creatures, those… Kobolds? One of them slashed my face with its claws. It had a sword and it stabbed me in the back and then in the stomach." He pointed to where the wounds had been. Max nodded along to the story, his eyes wide. "Then they just laughed and walked away. I was lying there, bleeding out in the dirt. I thought I was going to die. I should have died, the way they sliced me up… Anyway, next thing I remember, I'm waking up. Hours had passed, but my wounds were gone, and the trees and plants around me had all withered up and died somehow. I know it sounds insane."

Max shook his head. "No, kid, it sounds like a Root Weaver, a powerful one too. But you were alone when you woke up?"

Ryn nodded.

"Are you a Root Weaver?"

Ryn shook his head. "I don't think so, but I don't really know, to be honest. People say my aunt is a Root Weaver, but she denies it."

Max made a dismissive gesture with his hand. "But that wouldn't explain it anyway. That's the whole rub of Root Weaving. You can't use it to heal yourself. Maybe if you could lace it with Aether… but no, that's impossible too."

Ryn frowned, not understanding Max's words.

Max shook his head. "Anyway, maybe you *can* help me." He rolled his shirt sleeve up further to reveal a red inch-long scar on his arm.

Ryn let out a breath. "That's infected."

"So you are a Root Weaver?"

"No, my aunt… was an herbalist. She taught me everything she knew. If I had to guess, you got cut by a sourthorn bush? Red splotchy leaves and thorns about this long?" He held two fingers apart to show the size.

"Yeah, I suppose I might have… stumbled through some brambles a few days back."

"The pain will only get worse if you don't treat it. I can make you a salve that will draw out the toxins." Ryn ran through the necessary ingredients in his mind. Marla had only needed to teach him a recipe once, and he could remember it. "I'll start with some foxfeathers," he said, more to himself, and popped open one of the canisters on his satchel strap. He expected to find crisp round leaves inside, but it felt like dirt. Confused, he dug some out and held it in his fingers. The foxfeathers had disintegrated. Of course. The satchel had been within the ring of desolation.

Max saw the powder in his hand and the surprised look on his face. "I'm guessing those herbs were fresh this morning? Listen, kid, it was definitely Root Weaving that healed you, and I can't imagine why someone would go through the bother of mending your wounds, just to leave you unconscious and defenseless in the woods with Kobolds about. The only explanation that comes close to making sense is that you are a Root Weaver, and you just manifested a truly one-of-a-kind Etching."

"What's an—" He stopped himself from asking the question. He had barely processed every other revelation Max had dumped on him, and he didn't think he could handle a single thread of additional information at that precise moment. He needed to focus on something simple, something he could manage, like making a salve for sourthorn itch. He met Max's gaze. "Listen, the sun's going down. Let's go inside and I'll make you that salve. In exchange, I want you to promise to answer any questions I have about Weaving and… Etching?"

Max extended his non-wounded arm. "You got a deal, kid. I'll tell you what I can."

Ryn shook the proffered hand. "You can call me Ryn."

Ryn stood over Marla's worktable, trying to ignore his two strange house guests, as he ground up the ingredients for the salve in a large mortar. He had used up the last of the foxfeather supply. He would need to gather some more… The mindless work of grinding freed his mind to dwell on other things. He wondered why he wasn't crying. Marla had been his only family for most of his eighteen years. His parents had died when he was about six, taken by the ash fever. Ryn himself had nearly died of the same disease, but somehow he'd recovered. Ryn didn't hate his aunt—it took him years to realize it, but she did the best she could—but maybe he didn't exactly love her either? What would he do now? Could he just take over his aunt's business, becoming the village herbalist? Were the woods even safe anymore? Hopefully, those creatures had kept moving and weren't lurking around somewhere nearby.

He glanced up from his work. Max stood in the kitchen. No walls or divisions separated it from the rest of the room, but Ryn still considered that spot of floor the kitchen. Corvus perched atop the bureau where they stored cookware and food. For the most part, the Runeform creature convincingly aped the mannerisms of a real bird. Max turned in a slow circle, taking in the whole house. Ryn had noticed that of the two weapons strapped to the stranger's back, only one looked like a sword. Its scabbard was long and tapered to a point. The other scabbard held a broader but much shorter blade, like a large knife. He'd seen merchants' guards carrying similar-sized weapons. They would wield the sword in their dominant hand, carrying a dagger in their other hand for parrying attacks. Max must be left-handed then, judging by the position of the sheaths, strapped to his back on some sort of harness that looped over his shoulders.

Max glanced at Ryn and offered a weak smile. "Sorry again about your aunt. Do you… Do you have any other family?"

Ryn shook his head. "No, my parents died when I was little. Ash fever."

Corvus squawked. "You're an orphan!" it said.

Max narrowed his eyes and shot a glare at the Runeform. "Corvus! That's not… polite." He turned back to Ryn. "Sorry, that was… He doesn't normally say things like that."

Ryn shrugged, looking away from the man and the crow. He concentrated on finishing the poultice, using a little wooden spoon to scrape the sticky green paste from the mortar and into a glass vial. He screwed a copper lid onto it and walked it over to Max. "Apply a dab of this twice a day for a week. Finish out the week, even when it starts to look better. I added foxfeather and cat's clove, which will help with the itching too."

"Thanks, Ryn," Max said, taking the vial and tucking it in the front pocket of his shirt. "I know your aunt trained you as an herbalist, but making potions like this is exactly the sort of thing a Root Weaver does."

Ryn laughed and shook his head. "It's not a potion. It's just a salve. Anyone who knows the recipe could make it."

"Still, I bet your salves are twice as effective as a normal herbalist's."

"Maybe… Listen, could a Root Weaver use his abilities to find mushrooms?"

"Mushrooms?"

"Silverbells, specifically. I told my aunt that I'd trained Anya to sniff them out, but it isn't Anya who finds them. I can just sense where they are somehow."

"Yeah, that's exactly the sort of thing a Root Weaver could do. It's called an affinity. You have an affinity for plants, just like a Stone Weaver has an affinity for metals."

"How do you know so much? Are you a Weaver?"

Max opened his mouth but hesitated. He looked up at Corvus. "What do you think, pal? Can we trust this kid?"

The bird cocked its head to the left and then to the right but didn't answer.

Max shrugged, turning back to Ryn. "Yeah, I'm a Weaver, an Aether Weaver specifically."

Aether. Root. Stone. These were all things he had heard bits and pieces about growing up but had never really understood.

"Yeah, I can tell by the look on your face that this is all a little much. Let me give you a super simple rundown of the Five Forces. You got Aether, Stone, Wave, Root, and Flame." He used the fingers on one hand to count them off. "The interactions between the five are all very complicated, but you should just focus on Root. Clearly that is where your natural talents lie, though theoretically you could learn to wield any of the Five Forces. Each force has two complementary forces and two opposing forces—forces you can use with Root and forces you can't. For you that would be..." He paused, looking up and tracing a shape with his hand, as if envisioning some kind of diagram. "Yeah, Wave and Flame. If you knew the proper techniques, you could Blend Root with either of those. Your opposing forces would be Aether and Stone. If you ever find an injury that you can't easily heal, chances are it was made with a Stone-laced weapon. On the other hand, you could easily undo any of my Aether lacings."

Ryn screwed his eyes shut and shook his head. "I'm not following any of this."

Max shrugged and gave him an apologetic look. "I'm sorry, kid. A Scholar could explain it better, or one of the Watchkeepers. Truth be told, I've only ever focused on wielding Aether and tried to avoid any other Weavers."

"All right, but what can I actually *do* as a Root Weaver? Do I control plants or something?"

Max laughed. "No. While there are some similarities and they use the same names, the Five Forces are not the same as the five elements. You only have an affinity for Root and can use it to enhance your Weaving—like how you sucked the life force out of all those plants to heal yourself, if that is what happened—but you can't control the elements like some kind of Sprite. Before you ask, Sprites aren't real... At least, I don't think so. Anyway, you can't control plants any more than a Flame Weaver could throw fireballs."

The village boys had been wrong about that part at least.

Max continued. "Root Weaving is more about... restoration and growth, if that makes sense. Its primary and most practical use is in healing. You can use it to cure wounds, diseases, even fatigue, if you know how."

"Can you show me how?"

Max shook his head. "Sorry, you would need another Root Weaver to teach you that. Like I said, Root and Aether don't play well together."

"Well, what can you do, as an Aether Weaver?"

"This and that. Aether means wind, but it also means breath, and by extension life. In practice, it's almost the opposite of Root. Root can only be used on others, while I can only use Aether on myself. With the right lacings, I can run faster and jump higher than anyone. Aether is the power of enhancement."

"How could I have healed myself then, if Root can only be used on others?"

"I can't tell you definitively what happened out there. I didn't see it. I'm just saying you might have been able to do it through an Etching."

"And that is?"

"That's kind of hard to explain too. Look at it this way: Your inherent talent is as a Root Weaver. There is a certain pool of techniques, different kinds of lacings, that you and any Root Weaver could perform with enough training and practice, though of course your overall strength as a Weaver is a factor too. However, Weavers can sometimes manifest unique talents, lacings that only they know how to use. Those are called Etchings. Healing yourself is a unique variation on the Root Weaver skillset, so that must be your Etching."

Ryn nodded slowly. So, he was a Root Weaver... He wanted to learn more, to figure out what he was actually capable of. Max said he needed to find another Root Weaver for that. Did anyone in Aen's Hollow have that talent? He knew that a certain small percentage of people were born with the ability to Weave. In Aen's Hollow, anyone who manifested a strong gifting never stuck around for long, or so he'd heard. Most left to join a Guild in one of the larger towns to the south, if they didn't go farther. Some traveled to Lon's Watch to become Scholars, while others enlisted with the Watchkeepers in Falport. Gifted Flame Weavers often went to join the country's Standing Army. Those with weaker abilities, as far as Ryn could tell, simply ignored their talents and continued in the same trades as their parents, just like all the people who couldn't Weave.

Ryn looked up. Max studied him with narrowed eyes. Ryn never could conceal his feelings well, and he wondered what sorts of emotions had passed over his face as he had stared at nothing and pondered about his future.

"Listen, kid," Max said. "I know we just met, and maybe you have too much going on right now. However, I'm also thinking maybe you could use a distraction, something to take your mind off things. I actually came to Sylphren Wood because I'm looking for something. If you know the area, maybe you can help me find it? I can pay you for the assistance."

"What are you looking for?"

Max shook his head. "It's late. You need sleep. I need sleep. Corvus... Well, he doesn't sleep. Don't decide anything tonight. I'll explain everything in the morning, and you can decide then. How does that sound?"

Ryn nodded, realizing suddenly how tired he was. He had too many unanswered questions, but they could wait till daylight.

Chapter 4
A Change of Luck

THALIA STOOD OFF to the side, out of the flow of pedestrians, watching the two streams of traffic make their way across the Rigel Bridge. The bridge itself was a single arch of white granite, crafted from rough-hewn Stone-laced blocks, which fitted together so seamlessly that the whole expanse looked to be one single piece, like a natural rock formation spanning the nearly-mile-wide River Aldria. The river broadened and slowed as it flowed south toward the Morro Ocean, before splitting into dozens of smaller streams that snaked through the muddy and shallow river delta just south of the bridge. The delta was hard to navigate, so for convenience, the bustling city of Falport had two separate docks: one in the northwest corner along the river and one to the southeast along the coast. Most of the riverboats anchored at the northern Fish Docks were small Aldrian shipping vessels, while the southern Sea Docks entertained large trading ships from as far away as Iscerna and the Maer Isles.

While Rigel bordered the river and the sea as well, its two sets of docks were tiny affairs, only used by local fishermen. This was always the case between the town of Rigel and the grand city of Falport. Whatever Rigel had to offer was but a shadow of its sister city across the river. Anywhere else outside of the Golden Lands, Rigel would have been considered a city in its own right, but the citizens of Falport saw it as little more than a bridge town. This disparity was also the reason why Thalia's journey today would take her east across the Rigel Bridge. She just needed a moment to stop and think first.

The last day and a half had been bewildering. The four customers returning broken copper pieces that night after Thalia met the Scholar had been followed by seven more the next day. It took only a few questions to determine that all eleven people had had the same experience, more or less: two days of uncommonly good luck beginning with receipt of a copper piece Thalia had been working on, followed by a day of catastrophically bad luck that coincided with the cracking or shattering of the copper Thalia had touched.

The individual experiences had been widely different. Some found business or financial success like the Finstons. A fisherman whose family owned a few boats had closed a deal to acquire five new vessels from a rival who had previously had no plans of selling. Two separate customers had received large inheritances from distant relatives they never knew they had. For many it was personal success. A shy bookseller who had been secretly pining after a young Root Weaver from the Rigel Guild for years had come to the redsmith's shop joyfully announcing their engagement. Apparently, *she* had approached *him*, admitting that the affection had been mutual. It turned out the woman's parents had disapproved of the idea—they were a second-echelon family—but they'd recently had a change of heart. A farrier's son had fallen from a third-story window only to land unharmed in the bed of a wagon laden with hay that happened to be passing in the street below. Another customer's aged father, who seemed days away from passing from a wasting disease, had suddenly recovered his strength and stood on his own two feet for the first time in over a year.

The mishaps that struck when the luck ran out were varied as well. Freak accidents had wounded or maimed many customers or those closest to them. Wagons had broken axles. Family heirlooms had been lost or stolen. Two of the fisherman's newly acquired vessels had capsized in a rogue wave that had arisen on a seemingly calm day. Thankfully, no one had died. And the bad luck never fully canceled out or undid the good luck. When events were taken as a whole, the customers had all come out at least a little bit better off than they were before.

As Doug Ponter had said, luck was a fickle thing. Good fortune and bad fortune could strike anyone at any given time. One run of good luck followed by a day of bad luck was unremarkable, but for the same pattern to repeat itself eleven times...

"There's only one explanation," Master Foster had said, after apologizing to customer number eleven for a broken piece of copper. He wiped his hands on his leather apron and placed one of them on Thalia's shoulder. "You've got the gift, my girl. You're a Stone Weaver." He offered her a smile from beneath his bushy red mustache.

Thalia only frowned. "But how?" she said. "Of course, I always dreamed of having such a gift, but I thought it ran in families. Neither of my parents, or even my grandparents, could Weave."

Master Foster shrugged. "It certainly can run in families, but it doesn't always. It's not unusual for someone like you to be born with the gift. Likewise, someone who comes from a long line of Weavers is not always guaranteed to have it."

Thalia still wasn't convinced. "I know Stone Weavers can alter the attributes of metal and even enchant it... But luck? I've never heard of an enchantment that could make someone lucky. I wasn't even trying to enchant the copper. I wouldn't know how!"

"It's more fantastic than that, my girl. Such an enchantment, if it could be done at all, would normally require a Blending of Stone and Aether. If you did it without even realizing, then it must be an Etching."

"An Etching... I suppose that could make sense. Well, what should I do now?"

"There's a way to test for it, to see if you truly have the gifting. I've no doubt you do, but this way you can be certain too."

"Do I go to the Guild?"

Master Foster shook his head. He walked over to watch Raef work. The other apprentice had started in on repairing the broken pieces of copperware. Master Foster kept his eyes on the boy but spoke to Thalia. "Not the one in Rigel. No Stone Weavers there. You could go to the Falport Guild, but I have a friend with the Watchkeepers. He's a good man, and if you like, I can send a runner with a note to let him know the situation, and you can go see him tomorrow."

A network of runners, composed of fourth- and fifth-echelon boys and girls too young for more skilled work, was the backbone of communication between Rigel and Falport. One could send letters through the post, but they could take days to be delivered. It was always faster to send a runner, and the youths were so ubiquitous that one usually only needed to whistle and jingle a few copper coins, and a grimy-faced child would appear, promising a speedy delivery.

Thalia nodded. "I suppose it would be good to find out for certain."

Master Foster turned back toward her. He nodded and seemed to hesitate before continuing. "Until we do get this sorted, I'm afraid I can't give you any more work."

Thalia's jaw dropped. She started to protest but stopped herself when she eyed the pile of broken metal Raef had only just started to restore. Of course. No one wanted copper work that would shatter within days, and the wild swings in fortune that came with it were downright dangerous.

Master Foster must have understood the crestfallen look that passed over her face. "Have heart, my girl," he said. "This is a truly magnificent thing. Tell me. Why are there no Stone Weavers with the Rigel Guild?"

She didn't have to think about that one. "Because anyone with a lick of Weaving moves across the river."

Thalia couldn't blame them. Wages and opportunities were so much better in Falport. Master Foster was a truly talented craftsman, but because he couldn't Weave, his wares would always be second-rate. The city siphoned away the brightest and most gifted citizen of Rigel. Their relationship was why Rigel could never escape Falport's shadow. Her hometown's sole claim to fame, the only thing it was known for, was that Runeform fountain, and even that was more of a curiosity, an imperfect oracle that only gave an intelligible answer a fraction of the time. Raef, who was just as fascinated by the fountain as Thalia, had a working theory that the fountain would often give you answers to other people's questions. He reasoned that if they could record every single question and every single answer, they could sort out and match the proper answers to the proper questions, like solving a massive puzzle. But who had time for that?

"This gift will open doors for you," Master Foster said. "Just you wait and see. I know you have bigger ambitions than being just a redsmith. Only the most talented of Weavers manifest Etchings. If you can learn to harness your gift... Well, you'll never have to worry about anyone turning you away for being a girl."

Standing beside the bridge, watching the flow of traffic, Thalia smiled to herself. Master Foster was a good man, and regardless of what happened, she would always be grateful for his kindness and for teaching her to create. She still didn't know what to think and struggled not to dwell too much on the future before she knew for certain she had the gift.

Her mother agreed that she should go see Master Foster's friend, a Stone Weaver named Rohan Caston. Master Foster had arranged an appointment for her. Looking up at the sun, she realized she needed to get going, lest she be late. Glancing back toward Rigel, she joined the stream of traffic filing across the bridge.

A cool breeze blew north off the sea, bringing the smell of salt and brine. Gulls soared overhead, their caws drowned out by the din of commerce on the bridge. The river delta just visible to the south was a warren of seabird nests. A blue ribbon of sea stretched to the horizon beyond. Rigel's walls were ten-foot brick structures, while a massive gray Stone-wrought escarpment surrounded the great city of Falport. Apparently, if Thalia had the gift and could master it, she would soon be able to detect the lacings of Stone that held the walls together and strengthened them. She looked forward to such a day. A Stone Weaver could build almost anything. Most female Stone Weavers crafted things that required more finesse than muscle, such as jewelry, but it wasn't inconceivable that one might be a smith, even a bladesmith.

Traffic moved in four distinct lanes, though there were no demarcations. Carts, wagons, carriages, and riders kept to the center of the bridge, one stream moving west and the other east. Foot traffic moved on the outside lanes. A series of black bollards connected by iron chains kept pedestrians from spilling over the edge into the river. Those features had been added sometime in the last two centuries by safety-minded Aldrian officials; the bridge itself had been built without any railing back before the Burning, making it at least a thousand years old. The narrow spaces between the bollards and the edges of the bridge served as unofficial extra lanes, used only by the runners. The youths, contrarian by nature, moved in the opposite direction of the pedestrians on the other side of the barrier. Thalia looked away every time a runner came along, dashing full speed down that precarious path, only about a foot wide. She had never heard of anyone actually slipping off and falling into the river, but it still made her stomach churn to watch.

The press of traffic made her progress slow, and it took her half an hour to cross the river. The bridge led directly into an opening in the city wall, called the Rigel Gate. A massive iron portcullis hung over the bridge, with only the spiky black tips sticking out through a slot in the ceiling, but the gate had never been lowered in her lifetime. The walls were twenty feet thick, with crenellations and walks for archers on top. Five large towers anchored the corners where the walls met. Seen from above, the city would almost resemble a rectangle with the southwest corner sliced off. There the wall banked southeast away from the wide mouth of the river. The northeast corner was also set too far out, so that the north and east walls were not perfectly perpendicular to their neighboring walls. Four proper gates with gatehouses and guard stations also interrupted the smooth, seamless expanse: one on the northwest corner opening onto the river docks, one on the north wall leading to the Appencourt Road, one on the east for the Farhaven Road, and a massive set of gates built into the south wall for the Sea Docks.

Across the bridge and onto the cobblestone streets of Falport, she began winding her way toward the Watchkeepers' Citadel. She had never been to their compound, which dominated that misplaced northeast corner of the city, but she knew more or less how to get there. One could not walk very far in a straight line in Falport. The buildings here were grouped into square city blocks crisscrossed by narrow back alleys, but the blocks were all offset, so that there were hardly any four-way intersections in Falport. Thalia had visited Rigel's neighbor only a few times in her life, and each time she looked for ways in which it was inferior to her hometown. She knew of course there were not many.

These zigzagging streets were one flaw, in Thalia's mind, though the avenues were quite broad. Rigel was built along a perfect grid, its blocks interspersed with dozens of open squares and parks. Supposedly, Falport's streets had been laid out to confuse and delay any invading armies that managed to breach the walls, a feat that had not been accomplished in nearly two centuries. That was back before Aldria existed as its own nation. When Aldria split away from Tamor, the civil war had been bloody. Though the war eventually ended, tensions remained high, and conflicts had been common over the ensuing years, especially since Tamor had christened itself an empire some fifty years ago. The threat of Tamor to the west and the occasional raids from Silgaria to the north were the main reasons Aldria maintained its Standing Army.

The faces and fashions Thalia saw among the throngs of Falport were far more diverse than the Rigel crowd. Southern Aldrians like Thalia and her neighbors tended to have brown or beige skin with darker hair and eyes, but here the pale-faced and fair-haired northerners were just as common. Most of the foreigners she spotted in the streets were Iscernaens. Some had the distinctive tawny skin or hooded eyes associated with Iscerna, but many were only distinguishable by their brightly colored clothing, often considered garish by Aldrians. She spotted a handful of grim-faced traders from Mirkwald. Their men, as well as their women, mainly wore leather sandals and long tunics that draped past their knees, usually without trousers. At one point, Thalia had to press herself against a wall to make way for two towering Silgarian men. They wore leather jerkins with steel plates sewn on and apparently never trimmed their beards. Mercenaries, probably.

She lost track of how many corners she turned, wending her way north and east. She knew to avoid the center of the city, which held the Magistrate's Palace, a massive castle encircled by its own five-sided wall, like a miniature version of the surrounding city. The palace had four slender towers that rose much higher than any other structure in the city. She caught the occasional glimpse of those gray monoliths and used them to help navigate. She also checked the position of the sun periodically as she went. She was supposed to present herself at the compound's entrance at noon. She needed to hustle.

Falport was a beacon for Weavers and foreign merchants and mercenaries, but it also drew the impoverished. Every street corner seemed to have a designated beggar, calling softly for alms, and looking down any back alley offered glimpses of men and women with gaunt faces and sunken eyes. Seeing the poor and the homeless always unnerved Thalia. There were hardly any beggars in Rigel. Why would they stay in the bridge town when a trip across the river gave them access to far more people with far deeper pockets? Larger purses did not always translate into more generous hearts, however. Thalia felt bad for not wanting to make eye contact with the alms seekers. She wished she had the pocket change to spare. Her family had been comfortably third echelon, but now Thalia and her mother lived mainly off the savings her father had amassed from his smithing business, along with his soldier's pension. Ten years ago, his bladesmithing skills had earned him a short-lived commission smithing for the Standing Army, until he had been killed in a skirmish along Aldria's unstable western border with Tamor.

Eventually, with the sun standing directly overhead, she found herself at the entrance to the Citadel. Two smaller walls broke off from the main city walls to enclose the compound in a crooked rectangle. A simple wooden door set into the wall near the southwest corner signified the entrance. Though it looked unassuming, Thalia knew the Citadel had to be warded by so many lacings of Stone and Wave as to be far more impenetrable than the Magistrate's imposing palace.

Two guards in the gray tabards of the Watchkeepers leaned on either side of the door, chatting idly as Thalia approached. Pins at their breasts indicated where their giftings lay. One, a thin man with wideset eyes, wore a pin shaped like a curving blue wave. The other, a stout woman with round cheeks, had one shaped like a red flame.

The guards ceased their conversation when Thalia stopped before them. The woman arched an eyebrow, and the man eyed Thalia up and down. Thalia was nearly as tall as he was, wearing a finer cotton dress than any she would wear to the redsmith's shop, but it still had no sleeves. She found she had little tolerance for any length of sleeve; it restricted her movement far too much. Neither guard offered her a greeting or actually spoke a question. Still, Thalia kept her back straight and met the man's gaze. "I'm here to see Master Rohan Caston," she said, as confidently as she could. "I have an appointment."

The guards exchanged a glance. The man nodded and hooked a thumb at the woman. "She'll take you inside," he said.

Thalia followed the woman through the wooden door and into the Watchkeeper compound. She expected cobblestone streets like the rest of the city, but the ground here was carpeted with dense grass. She saw dozens of Watchkeepers moving about the grounds and even some mounted riders, yet no dirt paths had been worn into that blanket of grass. Perhaps the Root Weavers here had some way of keeping it alive.

At the center of the compound stood an enormous building that looked more like an ancient cathedral than a keep, with slender spires and spindly buttresses. The entire structure was composed of some black stone she did not recognize. The field around the main structure was crowded with dozens of outbuildings, each a different size. Some were made of stone, some wood, and some brick. Some roofs were flat, while others were peaked with wooden or clay shingles.

The female guard led Thalia in a wide arc around that central building to a long, covered structure built against the north wall. The familiar clang of metal on metal alerted Thalia to the building's purpose long before it came into view. Of course, a compound full of Stone Weavers would have a smithy, but this slanted-roofed pavilion was unlike anything Thalia had ever seen.

It had space for dozens of smiths to work at once. A bank of furnaces, forges, and smelters lined the wall, and Thalia could feel the heat from several paces away. Sweaty-faced men and women worked those forges or hammered out metal over anvils of every size and shape imaginable. Others worked on various projects, standing or sitting at benches spaced throughout the area. They all wore gray tabards, but only a few wore yellow triangular pins. Perhaps that mark had to be earned somehow. They worked with a huge array of metals—she saw steel, iron, copper, bronze, silver, and even gold in her first glance. She didn't recognize half the tools they were using. Some seemed designed for jewelers. They weren't all working with metal. Off to the right, she heard the rhythmic sawing of carpenters cutting and planing wood. To the left were a handful of tanners working with animal skins stretched taut over wooden frames. No, these people weren't just tanners or carpenters. A talented Stone Weaver could practice multiple trades, and a truly gifted one could master them all. In short, this was the kind of place Thalia had only ever dreamed could be real.

The guard led Thalia to a tall man, working alone at a bench. Sitting on a stool, he had a golden necklace spread out before him. He held an oval-shaped ruby using a curved tool that looked like a large pair of tweezers. He carefully inserted the gem into a slot on the necklace. Thalia saw no means of securing the ruby to the gold, so he had to be merely checking the fit. Apparently, it was good, as he nodded to himself before carefully returning the ruby to a suede jeweler's bag. Only then did he look up. With a nod to the man, the guard departed back to her post.

Master Rohan Caston was well into his fifties, but his muscular arms, toned but not bulky, showed he was still a match for men half his age. He wore the yellow pin of a Stone Weaver, a triangle with a ragged bottom edge like a stylized mountain. His brown hair laced with gray hung well past his shoulders. He kept it restrained with a leather cord tied at the nape of his neck. His face looked carved from stone, with a pointed and angular nose and chin. Those harsh features softened when he saw Thalia.

"Ah, you must be Thalia Moldo, Master Foster's unusual apprentice," he said. He flashed a brief grin and extended his hand.

For some reason, Thalia offered as firm of a handshake as she could. Normally, she would not squeeze at all when shaking hands, lest someone feel the need to comment on the surprising strength of her grip. Master Caston made no comment, but a sudden wrinkling around his eyes seemed to indicate he knew what Thalia was doing.

"Master Foster gave me some brief details," Master Caston said, "but I would like to hear the full story from you. Tell me about your customers and their... changes in luck."

Thalia tried to keep her story brief, but Master Caston kept interrupting her with questions, pressing for more details. He seemed to want to know everything. By the end, she had given him detailed descriptions of each customer, along with any facts she knew about their backgrounds and personal lives. She discussed each piece of copperware that had broken, detailing every step of its creation, including which parts had been handled by which worker, whether it was Master Foster, Raef, or her. She'd had a hand in each piece, even if it was just the rivets. She even described how she made the rivets and hammered them in, though a master craftsman like Rohan Caston would know such basic processes by heart. All the while, the din and heat of the smithy swirled around them, but Master Caston seemed to tune it all out, focusing solely on Thalia, nodding solemnly along as she spoke. This went on for nearly an hour before she had given him enough details to satisfy him.

"I'll be happy to test you," Master Caston said, "but I've no doubt you have the gift. True, I've never heard of an Etching being able to alter a man's luck, but that is often the way of Etchings. I've known Weavers who could do some fairly miraculous things."

"I still can't believe it," Thalia said. "And I'm not sure I understand it. If I am lacing the copper, why does it break after two days, and why does the luck swing the other way?"

Master Caston turned and looked over the smithy. He walked over to another workbench that no one was using at the moment. On the bench was a stand for weapons. Carefully, he picked up a sword that had not yet been completed. The blade looked well-forged, but no handle had yet been fitted to the narrow steel tang at its base. He looked back at her.

"Stone Weaving," he said, "is unique among the Five Forces, though of course each force is unique in its own way. Unlike the others, which require a fuel source to strengthen them, we draw our strength from the materials we lace. A Stone-laced sword like this one may be stronger than a normal sword, but it is also lighter. Something is lost in the process. There are always trade-offs when working with the forces. Other Weavers use other names for it, but we call it the recoil. Stone, especially when Blended with Aether, can create some powerful enchantments, but the stronger the enchantment, the stronger the recoil, and you won't always be able to tell what that is. I could lace this blade so powerfully that it would be almost impossible to break, even by a Flame Weaver, but there would be a cost to whoever used it. Perhaps it would sap their strength, shortening how long they could last in a fight. Or perhaps the lacings would only last for a year, before the blade fell apart on its own. That could be disastrous to a soldier."

"So, the copper breaking and the bad luck... That's the recoil?"

"Correct. Altering a person's luck is a powerful tampering with the universe. However, because we now know the limitations, we can still find a utility for your Etching. The time limit seems to be about two days, though we'll need to experiment to find the exact window. If we equipped a Pentad with your laced copper and sent them on a mission, their success would practically be guaranteed, so long as it was completed quickly. Then we could lock them away in some remote cabin for a day—probably separate cabins—while they weather the recoil. That would take some trial and error as well, of course."

Thalia's eyes widened as Master Caston rambled on, the excitement building in his voice. She had not yet considered the practical applications of her Etching. Perhaps seeing some concern in her expression, Master Caston stopped and held up his hands.

"I'm sorry," he said. "I have a tendency to get ahead of myself. I'm really not trying to force you into enlisting in the Watchkeepers, but I would be honored to train you."

Thalia looked around at the smithy. It was a marvelous place, and if joining the Watchkeepers would give her access to it… She shrugged. "I would need time to think about that and talk it over with my mother." And Master Foster. Joining the Watchkeepers had never crossed her mind before, though of course she hadn't known she could Weave. She knew little about the organization, other than that they helped to keep the peace in Aldria and were not as militant as the Standing Army. The army protected Aldria's borders from foreign threats, while the Watchkeepers were more internally focused.

Master Caston nodded. "Of course. You don't need to decide anything today, but I will make you this promise: I will help you learn to control your Etching so that you're not manipulating the luck of unsuspecting customers. After that, you can do what you want. The Watchkeepers pay decent wages, but with a talent like yours, you could make a fortune with the Falport Guild—or any guild for that matter. There are many who would pay well for your services. If you decide to go that route, I will understand. In fact, I'll be your first customer."

Thalia smiled. It seemed her Etching had altered her luck as well.

Chapter 5
Aen's Spring

RYN SCOOPED ONE FINAL CLOD of dirt onto the grave and patted it down with the shovel. Max leaned against the side of the cottage. To the stranger's credit, he had helped Ryn dig the grave for Marla without being asked. Ryn had only the one shovel, but they'd taken turns. They'd neither heard nor seen any signs of the Kobolds during the night, though the forest lay as quiet as ever. Ryn let Max spend the night in Marla's room, not having the heart to sleep there himself. Corvus, the metallic Runeform, silently watched the men from the edge of the roof. Ryn found the creature creepy, though it seemed harmless enough.

Ryn wore a clean set of clothes, a brown linen shirt and woolen trousers, still with his leather boots. The dried blood stains could have been mud. He nodded to the stranger. "So, what did bring you to Sylphren Wood in the first place?" he asked.

Max shrugged. "Long story short," he said, "I'm a treasure hunter. I know, that sounds a bit grandiose, but it's the truth."

A treasure hunter? It sounded like something out of a story. "And what treasure do you hunt?"

"Runeforms mostly. And any Stone-laced objects forged before the Burning. They made stuff back then that no Weaver today can replicate."

Ryn's knowledge of history was spotty at best, but he had heard of the Burning. Approximately a thousand years ago, something had happened, something that tore down all existing governments, scattered peoples across the land, and destroyed every written record that existed at that time. What that something was, no one was sure, though many theories existed.

Ryn looked up at the bird-thing. "Is that where you got Corvus?" he asked. "You found him treasure hunting?"

"Yes. Most of what I acquire I sell, but I got kind of attached to the little guy."

Corvus squawked. "You found me!" it said.

Max nodded. "Yes, I did. I also kept these." Max reached up and drew his two blades from his back, unsheathing them in one fluid motion. The steel glistened in the pale morning light. Both weapons were strangely shaped. The longer blade he held in his left hand wasn't exactly a sword. The metal had been shaped into a four-sided rod, though it did taper into a stubby point. The shorter blade looked like a curved dagger or shortsword, except the cutting edge had jagged rectangular slots set along its length. "This is a bladecatcher," he said, brandishing the shorter weapon. Those slots did look perfect for snaring an enemy's sword. "And this is a bladebreaker." That name was also self-explanatory. The longer rectangular rod, a solid beam of steel with sharp edges, would easily shatter a thin blade swung against it. "Both are indestructible and never need sharpening."

"That's... amazing," Ryn said, genuinely impressed.

Max shrugged. He sheathed his blades before continuing. "Now, last night you spoke of a nearby village. Would that happen to be Aen's Hollow?"

Ryn nodded.

"Excellent. I have been seeking that village. I have it on good authority that there is a Runeform somewhere near Aen's Hollow."

"A Runeform? I've never heard of one."

"Well, you may have seen it and not known what it was. They don't all talk and move around like Corvus here. His type is actually rather rare. Those who know of its existence may not know to call it a Runeform. If it is here, it's likely been around for centuries. However well hidden it may be, it is having some effect on the village. Runeforms always do."

"Could... Could the Runeform be what attracted the Kobolds?"

Max bobbed his head from side to side as if considering the idea. "Possibly. I don't think it's likely though. I've been hearing rumors of Kobolds in Aldria for nearly a year now. If they were coming down for the Runeform, they would have gotten here sooner."

"Well, I can take you to the village at least. Maybe you'll be able to find it."

"How far is the walk?"

Ryn pointed to the southwest. "Only about a mile that way."

Ryn put the shovel back into the pig shed. Anya had still not returned, but the woods were massive, and he still didn't have the nerve to go off searching for her. Out of habit, Ryn grabbed the foraging satchel before they left, and the two men set off, walking silently at first. Corvus shadowed them, flitting from tree to tree.

"It's awful quiet here," Max said. He kept glancing to the left and right, scanning the trees. "Is that normal this time of year?"

"No," Ryn said. "These trees should be full of songbirds and squirrels. The woods got quiet a few days ago. Maybe those Kobolds scared all the animals off."

"Maybe. Still, stick with me and we'll be fine. If it's only three of them, I should be able to handle it." Max was certainly confident. His weapons looked formidable, and apparently, he could use Aether to enhance his speed and agility.

Ryn nodded. "The village should be just up ahead. I've been thinking it over, and I still can't think of anything there that could be a hidden Runeform."

"Don't tax your brain over that, kid. I have a knack for finding these things."

Ryn silently wondered if that "knack" was like Ryn's talent for finding silverbells.

As soon as the village came into view through the trees, Ryn could tell something was wrong. Aen's Hollow was a ramshackle collection of wooden buildings clustered around the village green. Three country roads connected the village to the outside world, each named for the town or village at the other end. Ashborne Road ran north, and Thorpe Road ran south, though they were really two sections of the same road, what the merchants called Sylphren Road, after the woods. No one, as far as Ryn knew, ever traveled west along the narrower Banam Road. The town of Banam lay the farthest away, across the Levent Hills in the neighboring kingdom of Mirkwald. The land west of the village was an open field, the trees having been cleared by the woodcutters. They worked systematically, clearing different sections of the woods at a time and always allowing trees to grow back before returning to a previously harvested section. East of town, Aen's Spring bubbled up into a deep pool.

Nobody moved among the houses or on the village green. The only sounds breaking the silence were the occasional grunts of mushroom pigs, kept in backyard pens. The concentration of animals made the village always smell like moldy hay and mud. Both men moved cautiously between the silent houses onto the green, glancing around corners as they went.

Max looked at Ryn. "Is this some kind of local celebration? A ritual day of silence?"

Ryn shook his head. "Something's wrong."

Corvus flew to the high steeple of the church, which stood at the edge of the green, and perched atop it. The village smithy and the tanner's stall both stood empty. Ryn spun in a slow circle, looking for anyone. Were they all just inside their houses? He moved toward the Sweetwater Inn, the largest building in Aen's Hollow and the only structure built of red brick.

He tried the wide double doors, but they were locked. Those doors were never locked in the daytime; he had never seen them closed except during winter. On a warm spring day like this one, the great room had to be stifling. All the windows they could see were shut and shuttered, as well. Ryn turned back toward Max, still on the green, and shrugged with his hands spread to show he had no idea what was going on. Max glanced around the silent village again, then strode up to the doors beside Ryn. He tried them as well, tugging more aggressively than Ryn had. Then he rapped his knuckles against the wood.

"Hello?" Max called in a loud voice. No one responded. "Any vacancies?" He continued banging on the door.

Ryn took a few steps away to look up at the windows on the second floor. Max kept banging on the door and shouting for service. Finally, a face did appear in one of the upper windows. Mr. Ansley, the squat innkeeper, frowned down at the green, apparently trying to see who was knocking on the door before deciding if he would open it. His eyes widened when he spotted Ryn. He opened the window, raising the glass up in its casement only wide enough to speak through, as if he feared someone might scamper up the wall to get in.

"Ryn, my boy, what are you doing here?" Mr. Ansley said.

Hearing the voice above, Max stopped banging and took a step back, craning his neck up to see Mr. Ansley's pink face in the window.

"What's going on, Mr. Ansley?" Ryn asked. "Where is everyone?"

"They're all in their houses with their doors locked, I suspect. You're not likely to see anyone out on the green until the Watchkeepers get here in a day or two. They've been sent for, I assure you."

"But what's happened?"

Mr. Ansley's eyes widened even further. "What, you haven't heard? Why, yesterday morning, the whole village awoke to the sound of screaming. Poor Angela Clemont's mother had found her girl at the edge of the wood, all slashed and cut up, murdered by some foul creatures. Then two of the lads who were out mushrooming never came back, Toran and Ban. We found what was left of them and their pigs."

Ryn frowned. He knew their names and faces, but he had not been close to Angela, Toran, or Ban. The two boys had often teased him for living in the woods with a witch. In truth, his gravest concern at that moment was that Anya may have suffered the same fate as the other mushroom pigs. Likely she had.

Mr. Ansley pressed his nose to the glass to peer down and get a good look at Max. "I'm sorry, sir," he said. "We've no rooms to let at the moment, and we'll not be serving meals until the murderous creatures are dealt with."

Max nodded. "Fair enough," he said.

"Listen, Ryn," Mr. Ansley continued. "These woods aren't safe right now. You best get back to Marla. Come back down to the village in a week or so. The Watchkeepers should have everything sorted by then."

"But Marla was…" The window shut with a snap before Ryn could say anything more. Mr. Ansley wasn't taking any chances, apparently.

Max frowned at Ryn. "I guess the Kobolds got here too."

Ryn nodded. "And it looks like you won't be able to ask anyone about that Runeform you're looking for either."

"Well, that may be just as well. People can be a little protective of their Runeforms, even if they don't know what they really are. This could be for the best. I get a chance to poke about without anyone asking questions."

"How would you start?"

Max turned in a slow circle, surveying the green again. "Well, normally inns are a good place to look for clues, when they're open. What is the name of this fine establishment, anyway? I don't see a sign."

"Apparently, they had one years ago, but it fell off, and no one felt the need to replace it. The Sweetwater is the only inn in town, after all."

"Sweetwater? Why do they call it that?"

"That's what it's always been called. I suppose it's because… Well, it's the spring."

Max walked closer to Ryn. "I know that look. It means you've just had an idea."

"Aen's Spring. It's famous around here because the water is so pure and tastes almost sweet. People say if you drink from it, it gives you good health and a long life." Ryn had thought that was just another superstition.

"That sounds like—"

"A Runeform! Could a spring be a Runeform?"

"There's only one way to find out. You're an excitable kid, huh? That's a good thing. I can tell you got the makings of a real treasure hunter."

"Come on, the spring is just over here."

Max followed Ryn back through the houses to the southeast corner of the village. Aen's Spring was a large pool of water ringed by mossy stones. It spilled over into the narrow Aen's River, which flowed east for several leagues before joining the River Aldria. The deep water looked slightly greenish, but it came out clear when scooped into a bucket. It all seemed perfectly natural.

Max stood at the edge of the pool, studying the water for a moment. Corvus perched on an overhanging tree branch. "Tell me more about this spring," Max said.

"I don't know what else to say. It's supposed to be very deep, but no one knows how deep."

"Has no one ever tried swimming to the bottom?"

Ryn laughed. "Of course not. Swimming in the pool is forbidden. It's said that anyone who does will be cursed with bad luck. Do you think that part is true?"

"Not a chance, kid. No, that's exactly the sort of rumor some olden-time person would start to keep future generations from finding their Runeform. I've heard rumors like that a thousand times. That usually means you're looking in the right place, and I've certainly never been cursed. I bet if we swam down to the bottom of that pool, we would find some sort of Runeform that filters the water somehow. If it really does improve your health, it would be quite valuable. I'll give you a cut, of course."

Ryn glanced around. The nearest houses were several paces away, their doors locked and windows shuttered. "Are you talking about just stealing it?" Ryn said.

"Not in so many words, kids. How can it be stealing, if no one even knows it's here?"

Ryn ran a hand over the back of his neck. He looked down at his own shadowy reflection in the calm pool. "I don't know. It doesn't seem right. The whole village gets its water from this spring. What if we mess it up?"

Max put a hand on Ryn's shoulder. "That won't happen, kid. I've drank from the streams around here, and from the pump at your place. The water tastes perfectly fine to me. It's not like this spring will suddenly turn to poison if we remove the Runeform. It's just adding a little something extra to the water. I doubt anyone will even be able to tell that it's gone."

Ryn couldn't meet Max's gaze. This didn't feel right.

Max leaned in closer. "Listen, Ryn, buddy, from where I'm standing, you don't owe these people anything. Where were they when the Kobolds attacked you? And poor Marla? I hate to bring it up, kid, I really do, but just think about it. You heard what the innkeeper said. That Angela girl was killed early yesterday morning. You weren't attacked till midday. Why did no one come to check on you or your aunt?"

Ryn frowned. He hadn't thought about that.

"They made sure to send riders down south to find the Watchkeepers, but why did no one even think to send a warning to you and your aunt? Maybe they could have stopped what happened."

"I don't know. They were scared. They still are."

"They weren't too scared to send people out into the woods to find those missing boys. Yet no one walked twenty minutes up the path to check in on the village herbalists? I'll tell you why. They don't care. I know it's hard to hear, kid, but they don't care about you, and they didn't care about Marla. What do you really owe these people?"

Ryn turned away from Max, but he couldn't argue with him. Max was right. Sure, the villagers kept their distance from Marla, but Ryn always believed that they respected her for the invaluable service she performed for the community. Did they though? When the village kids called Marla a witch and shunned Ryn, did their parents ever do anything about it? They let it happen. They whispered that Marla was a Root Weaver, but what was a Root Weaver to a bunch of superstitious backwoods peasants, but just another kind of witch?

The boy had been considering the idea of continuing Marla's work, serving as the village herbalist, but could he ever look any of them in the eye again after they left him and his aunt alone at the mercy of the Kobolds? No, his Etching had given him a second chance at life, and he wasn't about to waste it by making ointments and tinctures for these miserable villagers. He had to leave Aen's Hollow behind him for good. He knew how ignorant he was of the world outside the Sylphren Wood, but perhaps Max could help him. Either way, a little extra coin from helping the treasure hunter would aid him on his journey.

Ryn ran the sides of his hands across his eyes, wiping away the welling tears. He didn't know if those had fallen for Marla or for himself. He turned and looked up at Max. "All right," he said. "Let's steal the Runeform."

Max nodded solemnly. "It's the right call, kid." He looked down into the water. "Now we need to decide who will take the plunge. I'm happy to do it, but it might be a little tricky for me. I'm not a great diver, because my body just wants to float. It's a side effect of being an Aether Weaver."

Ryn peered into the depths, trying to make out the bottom. He could only see green rocks and shadows, distorted by the depths of the water. Aen's Spring held no fish, and frogs and insects never spawned there, another sign that it was no natural body of water. "I'm not the best swimmer, but I think I can do it. I'm willing to try."

Max smiled. "We'll make a treasure hunter out of you yet. The trick will be to grab one of these big stones before you jump in. The extra weight will sink you straight to the bottom."

"How will I know what it looks like?"

"You'll know. Trust me. It will be the only thing down there that looks manmade."

"What if it's down in one of those shadowy areas? I might not be able to see it."

"No worries. That's how Corvus earns his keep. Those glowing eyes come in handy in the dark."

"Corvus can swim?" Ryn looked up at the bird-thing, which was pretending to preen itself.

The creature squawked and cocked its head. "Corvus can't swim," it said.

"Nonsense," Max said, making a dismissive gesture and not looking at the Runeform. "Just give it a try, Ryn. If you don't find anything or get too tired, I'll take over."

Ryn nodded. He unslung his satchel, stripped off his shirt, and pulled off his boots, piling his items on the side of the pool. Max pried a mossy rock loose and handed it to Ryn when he was ready. The bank here was steep below the waterline, and a short hop away from the edge would position Ryn to sink most of the way down. He looked up at Corvus, who hadn't moved from the tree.

"Don't worry," Max said. "The bird will follow right behind you. Right, Corvus?" That last was directed to Corvus in a raised voice. The Runeform only squawked, but that must have been an agreement.

Ryn took a few deep breaths, filling his lungs. Cradling the rock in his arms, he extended a leg and took a jumping step into the water. The spring water stayed cool year-round, and the sudden change in temperature almost caused him to gasp and lose all his air. He sank quickly, descending into a world of hazy green shadows. His feet touched bottom. The rocks around him flashed to blue, and he looked up to see Corvus plummeting through the water, its cerulean eyes glowing like twin torches. The bird had its wings tucked in tight, kicking with its feet. Crows were not designed for swimming, yet Corvus somehow managed to flit about underwater with the same speed as a loon.

Ryn dropped the stone and started swimming, picking his way across the rocky bottom. Corvus swam in circles just above his head, illuminating some rocky openings and casting others in deeper shadows. None of the craggy holes he saw went very far. He knew he would run out of breath soon, but he pushed on. Finally, he found an opening that seemed to go down deeper than the others. Corvus shot past him into the hole, lighting up the depths with its eyes. There was definitely something down there.

Ryn used his hands to pull himself along the rocks while kicking with his legs. The hole narrowed the farther down it went, but Ryn had always been a scrawny kid. He wriggled through easily. The passage continued straight down, its bottom hidden in shadows even Corvus's eyes could not pierce. Ryn didn't need to go all the way down though. He could see a square-shaped stone with a large hole in its center wedged into the mouth of the spring. It looked like a frame for a window. It almost blended in with the surrounding rocks, but those edges were too smooth and straight to be a natural formation. He could make out faint lettering along the sides of the stone, but it wasn't an alphabet he knew. The opening through which the water flowed seemed to shimmer, almost like the surface of a pond, though that made no sense underwater. Corvus flitted in and out of that opening and seemed unaffected by it.

Ryn grabbed the edges of the stone frame and tried to pull it out. His lungs were starting to burn, but he wanted to get this on the first attempt. He felt a need to impress Max. He yanked, but the stone Runeform—if it was a Runeform—didn't budge. He braced his legs against the side of the opening and pulled again. The thing was wedged in tight. Maybe they could borrow a chisel from the blacksmith. Either way, it would take a second dive. If Ryn stayed down any longer, he would drown.

He planted his feet on the sides of the Runeform and kicked off, swimming up toward the surface. He kicked and paddled his arms with all his might, feeling his lungs about to burst. Corvus shot past him again and launched up out of the water. Ryn kept swimming and finally broke the surface, gasping for air and taking in several ragged breaths. The sensation was not unlike when he had woken up in the woods after being healed. He was on the far side of the pool from where he started, facing away from the village. He treaded water for a moment and sputtered.

"I found it!" he said, spinning around to face Max.

The treasure hunter was down on his knees, the edge of a sword against his throat. The sword was held by a tall woman in a gray tabard. Four other strangers in identical gray uniforms stood around the edge of the spring. Corvus flew in loops above the heads of the Watchkeepers but made no effort to aid Max. All eyes swiveled toward Ryn, still bobbing in the pool.

The woman with the sword arched an eyebrow. "Please," she said, "get out of the pond."

Chapter 6
A Broken Mast

SHILO LORN STOOD in the stern of her family's fishing sloop, watching the pursuing vessel draw nearer. Her father stood beside her, working the *Windlacer*'s tiller and calling out directions to her brothers to adjust the mainsail. The boom swung overhead to take better advantage of the wind.

Shilo looked to her father. He kept his eyes fixed ahead, scanning the water for signs of trouble and never glancing back, though he surely knew the raiders were gaining on them. Her younger brother Lou stood in the bow, scouting for shoals. Those were a real danger this close to shore. The rocky coast of Aldria raced by off the port side. Her three older brothers worked the rig.

Shilo took a step closer to her father. "What can I do, Papa?"

"Just keep out of the way!" he said.

He never barked orders in such a harsh tone like that, except in dire situations. Her father was a kind man most of the time. He had broad shoulders and callused hands. In the spring heat, he was bare-chested, as were her brothers. Years working in the sun had turned his skin a deeper shade of brown. To Shilo, he represented strength and stability, but even he could grow impatient with the girl's... shortcomings.

It hurt to hear it, but she knew she would only just get in the way. It seemed like she had spent more of her life on boats than on shore. She knew everything there was to know about sailing. She could rig the jib and the mainsail by herself, and she knew how to work the tiller and cast the nets, yet when she was actually out on the water, she just made too many mistakes. She couldn't be trusted, her older brothers said. Her parents were kinder. They always explained how tricky the seas were around Palmoor. The currents and winds in and around the Finger Isles could be hard to predict. Judge the waters poorly, and you could run aground. She had never wrecked the boat, fortunately, but when her hand was on the tiller, she always seemed to make the wrong calls. She had the knowledge and she had the experience, but there was a third factor, an intangible one, that she still lacked. Lou had tried explaining it to her once, saying you had to "feel" the boat. It was a given that he and her brothers would continue the family trade once Papa got too old, but Shilo would be of age soon, and she'd heard her parents talk of finding her a good husband. Whoever they tried to match her with, she knew he would not be a sailor.

Shilo's first and only solo outing, in the family's smaller dinghy, had nearly ended in disaster. Lou had gone with her, but she worked the tiller alone. True, a sudden squall had come up between them and the shore. Shilo tried to run around it, but they kept getting swept farther and farther out to sea. By the time she managed to reef the sail, they had been carried farther south than any sane sailor dared venture. She never told her family about that part, but they had drifted within sight of the Rune Lands. That grassy shoreline had filled Shilo with dread. No vessel that set out for the Rune

Lands ever returned. She took to the oars and rowed for as long and as far as she could, until that cursed coast was well beyond the horizon, before she dared hoist the sail again.

Now her whole family was in peril, though they couldn't blame her for this one. She glanced back astern, and the pursuing raiders were even closer. Their boat had a single triangular sail that made the vessel seem lopsided, but it was clearly built for speed. One of the pirates crouched at the tip of the bowsprit, a large spar designed for ramming. He wore a curved sword at his hip.

These raiders were likely part of the crew based out of the Lembalt Archipelago to the west, and it was an open secret that they worked as privateers for the Tamorine Empire. They rarely ventured this far east, however, and they had never been known to target fishing vessels. What did they want? The *Windlacer*'s hull was empty; they had only just reached their planned fishing grounds west of the Finger Isles when the raiders started bearing down on them, and even a full haul of sea trout shouldn't have interested pirates.

"They're getting closer, Papa," Shilo said. She could at least update him on the progress of the pursuit.

Her father groaned in frustration. "We just have to make it to port, and they'll break off. They wouldn't follow us into the harbor." He spoke with confidence, but Shilo knew her father well enough to hear the traces of doubt in his voice.

The westernmost of the Finger Isles came into view off the starboard bow. They didn't have far to go now, and the wind blew favorably out of the southwest. Still the other boat kept gaining on them. The man on the bowsprit looked at her. She met his gaze and refused to look away. He had a ruddy complexion and long black hair kept in a ponytail. He sneered at her and slowly drew his sword. Did they mean to board the *Windlacer*?

She could see four more pirates on the other vessel's deck, but they were all focused on maneuvering the boat closer. Her father and her brothers carried knives, not swords, but did this one pirate think he could take all five of them on? They would overpower the swordsman, but who would he wound first? Who would he kill?

Shilo glared back at the man as hard as she could. She hated these pirates. What gave them the right to terrorize her family? She felt her nails dig into her palms as she clenched her fists, but she didn't care. She wished she wasn't so useless. She couldn't sail, not when it mattered. Her father had taught her to throw a punch, but she knew she couldn't fight a grown man. She had always been a slight and slender girl. Still, she had to do something to help her family. Her arms began to tingle. The bowsprit inched closer. A few more feet and the man would be able to leap aboard. Shilo squared her stance. She would not run.

Suddenly, the swordsman leapt from his crouch and dashed forward along that narrow beam of wood. He jumped. Shilo didn't think he could have made it, but her eyes widened in horror as his feet thudded onto the deck. The man ignored her.

"Papa!" she said.

Her father turned to look, just as the man reached him. Papa's free hand shot to his waist where his knife hung. The man raised his arm. Rather than swing at Papa with his sword, the man brought his clenched fist and the butt of his weapon down on the side of Papa's head. Shilo stood frozen as she watched her father collapse onto the deck. His hand fell from the tiller, and the ship swerved to starboard. Her brothers looked back. The swordsman turned to face them. He continued to ignore Shilo, like she wasn't even there, like she was worthless.

She charged the man before she realized what she was doing, striking out with a right hook. She caught him in the ribs. A sudden flash of light blinded her. She heard a loud crash. She blinked to clear her vision. The man was gone. She'd felt him falling away from her fist. Across from her, a section of the wooden bulwark on the side of the ship had splintered and fallen away.

She stared at her fist. Her skin glowed with a strange pulsating light. She glanced to her right. The other boat was falling away, tacking hard against the wind. Whatever Shilo had just done convinced them to call off the pursuit. She also saw the swordsman, floating face down in the choppy sea. Somehow, her blow had launched him into the bulwark with enough force to break it. His sword lay on the deck. The raiders' ship angled toward the man, clearly intending to fish him out.

She looked to her brothers. They stared at her with identical expressions, eyes wide and mouths agape. The boat lurched again, and the boys started moving. Her eldest brother took the helm, and the other two checked on her father. Only Lou thought to check on his sister.

"What did you do, Shilo?" he said, staring at her still-glowing fist.

"I don't know," she said. "It just... happened."

A sudden noise like a loud peal of thunder drew all eyes toward the bow. It wasn't thunder. A massive crack had formed in the wooden mast.

They barely made it back to port.

Ryn sat, still dripping wet from his dive, on the floor of an iron cage. They'd let him put his shirt back on. His satchel and boots sat beside him. On the other side of the cage, Max had his hands over his face. They'd taken his weapons away but left him his own satchel, after searching both. They'd taken Ryn's knife and trowel as well, though those hardly qualified as weapons. The cage sat on the bed of a wagon. It had just enough room for them to lie stretched out, but they couldn't stand in it.

The five Watchkeepers stood a little ways off, discussing something. The wagon sat on the edge of the village, just south of the spring. Two brown horses stood hitched to it. Three other horses grazed nearby, cropping the grass with their legs hobbled. Ryn wondered what the punishment was for stealing a Runeform. Why had he let Max talk him into trying?

Max let out a long sigh. "Listen, kid," he said. "Let me do all the talking. I'll get you out of this. Technically, you did nothing wrong. Sure, you violated a local taboo by swimming in the spring, but that's not an actionable offense. It's a lucky thing you couldn't pull out the Runeform on your first go. She's coming over now, so keep quiet."

Ryn looked up. The woman with the sword had separated from the other four Watchkeepers and was striding toward the wagon. She wore the gray tabard over a pair of gray trousers and black boots. Her thin blade hung at her side. She was a little over average height and looked about the same age as Max. Rows of tight black braids ran across her scalp and hung down her back. The braids ended in beads that clinked musically as she walked. A blue pin on her chest shaped like a cresting wave flashed in the late morning light.

Her eyes were fixed on Max. She ignored Ryn for the moment. "We were on our way north, following rumors of Kobolds in Sylphren Wood, when we ran into a group of riders who directed us here to Aen's Hollow." Her voice was soft, almost friendly. She smiled. "We'd hoped to catch a Kobold in this cage, but it suits you just as well, Pavel Talvor."

Max returned the smile. "I'm afraid you have me mistaken for someone else."

She laughed. "Oh, I don't think so." She leaned in closer to the cage. "Just a friendly word of advice, if you ever manage to see the light of day again. If you want to remain inconspicuous, lose the ancient weapons and the talking bird."

Corvus sat perched in a nearby tree. The Watchkeepers had tried unsuccessfully to capture the winged Runeform, but it was too quick.

Max sighed. "Fine, you got me."

Ryn narrowed his eyes. "Your name is Pavel?"

Max, or rather Pavel, shrugged. "Yeah, it was my father's name, but I've never really liked it. I've always seen myself as more of a Max." He turned back to the Watchkeeper. "Listen, you can let the kid go. He hasn't broken any laws."

The woman's eyes swiveled to study Ryn. He probably looked like an oversized drowned rat to her. She was an attractive woman, with large eyes and a soft brown complexion. She kept her gaze on Ryn but spoke to Pavel. "Maybe not. Maybe he's just one of your marks, or maybe he's your protégé."

Pavel scoffed. "If you know who I am, then you know I always work alone."

The woman ignored the comment, still watching Ryn. "What's your name, kid?"

"Ryn."

"And your second name?"

"Oh. I don't have one."

A look of confusion crossed her face, and Ryn realized that what he'd said was odd. He knew the villagers of Aen's Hollow had second names. If Marla had one, he never knew it. Surely, he must have had a second name. Why had he never thought to ask Marla?

Why had she not simply told him? The woman had kept too many secrets. What other obvious things had she neglected to teach him?

The Watchkeeper didn't press him on the name. "Do you have any family around here, Ryn?"

"I lived with my aunt, but... No, I don't have anyone."

She nodded. "Listen, Ryn, I apologize in advance if you are just a rube, but we'll need to haul both of you down to Thorpe so we can sort this out. My name is Nyssa Lahmeer, I am an officer in the Watchkeepers, and I give you my word no harm will come to you while in my custody." She shifted her gaze to take in both Ryn and Pavel. "We'll head out as soon as we get this whole Kobold situation sorted."

Nyssa turned and strode back to the others, beads clinking as she went. She called out quick orders and the group dispersed. Nyssa and three of the others headed north, back toward the village. The fifth Watchkeeper, the only other woman in the group, stayed behind. Nyssa had ordered her to watch the prisoners, calling her Tabbot.

Tabbot, a short woman with red hair and an upturned nose, stood with her arms crossed, keeping her eyes on the iron cage, but she maintained her distance. After Nyssa and the others left, Pavel leaned his head back against the bars and closed his eyes. Ryn stared at him for several minutes before saying anything.

"A treasure hunter, you said? You're a thief, aren't you?"

Pavel didn't open his eyes. "Some would say that is a matter of semantics. I see myself more as a... liberator of antiquities."

Ryn shook his head. "You lied to me."

Pavel opened his eyes and stared sideways at Ryn. "Don't take it personal, kid. Lying is sort of a bad habit of mine."

Ryn glanced at Tabbot. She had turned to scan the tree line beyond the spring and didn't seem to be paying any heed to their conversation. "I don't suppose you could get us out of here?" he said to Pavel. "Weaver the bars or something."

"No can do, kid. For one, these bars are laced with Stone. That's one of the fun quirks of the Five Forces; if I tried adding Aether, it would only make the bars stronger. On top of that, Nyssa has us warded, so I couldn't summon up a lick of Aether if I tried."

"Warded?" Ryn remembered the pin on her tabard. "She's a Wave Weaver then."

"Yeah, we've found ourselves in the clutches of your basic Watchkeeper Pentad. They like to have one of each kind of Weaver in their units. That way, they can face any challenge, or so the rhetoric goes. Our new friend over there is a Root Weaver like you." He hooked a thumb at Tabbot.

The woman wore a small green pin on the front of her tabard. It was hard to tell from a distance, but it looked like a leaf. Ryn studied the woman more closely. As far as he knew, she was the first Root Weaver he'd ever seen. He wanted to talk to her, to ask her if she could teach him how to use his gift. If only he wasn't a prisoner. He doubted Watchkeepers were in the habit of giving lessons to suspected thieves.

Ryn sighed. It didn't look like they would be moving anytime soon, not with the rest of the Pentad out hunting Kobolds. He stretched out as best he could, using his satchel as a pillow. He had not slept well the night before. He had kept waking up, panting in the dark and straining to hear any sounds outside, but hearing nothing. He soon dozed off.

The woman, Tabbot, woke him around noon by banging on the side of the cage. She held an empty copper mug. She smiled when he opened his eyes. "Are you hungry yet?" she said.

Ryn nodded.

"I could eat," Pavel said. He sat in the same position, slumped against the bars with his eyes closed.

Tabbot slid each of them a small loaf of crusty bread and a wedge of white cheese through the bars of the cage. Ryn wolfed it down. He had not eaten in over a day, having lost his appetite after what happened to Marla. It was back now. Seeing how quickly he ate, Tabbot gave him another smaller piece of bread. Pavel seemed satisfied with what he'd been given, eating only some of it and sticking the rest in his satchel. Tabbot gave them each a copper mug filled with cool spring water. She made no attempt at conversation, so Ryn refrained from asking any of the hundred or so questions he had formulated.

After the meal, Ryn drifted off to sleep again. He awoke just as the setting sun touched the tops of the trees. Something was wrong. Corvus flew in a circle around the cage, squawking. The bird-thing could easily have fit through the iron bars, but it didn't. Pavel jolted awake a second after Ryn.

"Corvus," the thief said. "What's wrong?"

The bird kept circling and cawing, pausing only to say, "Everything's fine!" before flitting off out of view.

Pavel rose to a crouch, suddenly fully alert. Was the Runeform being sarcastic? Pavel reached instinctively for the blades on his back, but of course, they weren't there.

Tabbot came from around the side of the wagon where the horses were. Apparently, she had been tending to them. "What's all the noise about?" she said, directing the question at Pavel.

Pavel turned to her. His eyes widened. "Behind you!" he managed to say through a sputtering gasp.

Ryn saw a blur of movement loping up behind the Root Weaver, something short and gray. Tabbot spun around and then jumped back as the Kobold swung a spike-studded club at her. It might have been one of three Kobolds that attacked Ryn the day before, but it wasn't the one that stabbed him. The Kobold's club swung through the air, just missing the front of Tabbot's tabard, but the creature didn't stop. It lurched forward again, slashing with its free hand. Tabbot raised an arm instinctively, and the Kobold's claws rent the sleeve of her gray shirt. The Watchkeeper winced with pain, but she didn't stop there either. She raised one booted leg and kicked the Kobold square in its chest. The creature toppled over backward, dropping its club.

Tabbot ran back several steps, putting the edge of the wagon between her and the creature. Pavel leaned toward her, pressing his face against the iron bars. "Let me out," he said. "I can help you fight."

She glanced at the cage. The Kobold was climbing back to its feet. "Not a chance," Tabbot said. "You'll just run away." She paused. "That does give me an idea though."

"What?" Pavel asked, but she didn't respond. She completed her loop around the cage and darted off toward the other horses. The horses still in their traces for the wagon whinnied and tried shying away from the Kobold, but the wagon's brake was down, so they couldn't get away. "Um, please don't leave us here!" Pavel called after the Watchkeeper.

The creature picked up its club, eyeing Ryn and Pavel. It moved closer to the cage, apparently having forgotten about Tabbot. Pavel scooted back away from the creature, as far as he could inside the cage. Ryn stayed fixed in the half-crouch he'd risen to upon waking. Once again, he felt paralyzed in the presence of the creature. Its club was too bulky to fit between the bars, but it could reach inside with those claws. The creature walked right up to the side of the cage, studying Ryn with those yellowed eyes. If it recognized Ryn from the day before, that leathery face showed no hint of surprise at seeing him alive.

The Kobold moved past Ryn toward Pavel's side of the cage. It raised its club and pointed it at the thief. "Gris ick dewon?" it said in that gravelly inhuman voice. It leaned in closer, its hooked nose wrinkling as it sniffed the air.

Pavel took his eyes off the creature and looked at Ryn. His face was paler, but he spoke with confidence. "Curse me, but these things are ugly."

The Kobold growled and lunged toward the cage, stabbing with its clawed fingers. It stopped short, however, and lurched backward. A strange blue liquid seeped from its neck where the feathered shaft of an arrow had bloomed. Tabbot stood fifty paces away, back toward the spring, holding a curved bow. The creature staggered, turning toward Tabbot. She drew another arrow quickly. She had stabbed half a dozen arrows into the ground beside her. She drew the bow string back to her cheek and loosed the second bolt. It buried itself in the creature's chest, knocking it down for good.

Tabbot grabbed another arrow and spun toward the east. They could all hear something crashing through the woods toward them. Nyssa emerged from the undergrowth, followed by the other three members of her Pentad. Nyssa had her sword out, and the others had their own weapons. One carried a pair of daggers, and one held a wooden stave. The third man had a pair of iron cudgels that he held by perpendicular bars sticking out near one end.

The Watchkeepers closed the distance to the wagon quickly. They stood in a half circle looking down at the dead Kobold. Its dark blue blood seemed to boil as it made contact with the air.

Nyssa gestured back toward the forest. "We overtook a group of three making their way toward the village. We struck down the first two, but this one got away from us. I was hoping to take one alive, but they fought too savagely." Dark blue blood stained the tip of her sword.

Three dead Kobolds. At least someone had avenged Marla.

Nyssa saw the tears in Tabbot's sleeve. "Are you wounded?"

Tabbot raised her arm. "Oh, just a scratch," she said. Blood soaked her sleeve, but it didn't seem to be actively bleeding.

Nyssa frowned. She turned to Ryn. "You, boy, are there any Root Weavers in town?"

Ryn didn't understand the question, but then he remembered that a Root Weaver wasn't supposed to be able to heal herself. Ryn shook his head. "I don't—"

Pavel cut him off. "The kid is a Root Weaver, actually."

Tabbot arched an eyebrow. "Really?" she said.

Ryn shrugged. "Well, I think I am, but I only just found out about it. I don't actually know how to do anything."

"How did you find out then?" Tabbot asked.

"Well, I…"

Pavel interrupted him again. "It doesn't matter how he knows. The kid is a quick study. If you just show him the lacings, he'll be able to do it."

Nyssa scoffed. "You expect any of us to take your word on anything? We all know your history, Pavel Talvor."

Pavel grinned. "Fans of my work, are you?"

"Hardly."

Tabbot studied the cuts on her arm. "No, it's not deep," she said. "I can treat this with Rootbalm. You needn't trouble yourself, lad." She paused, seeming to consider something. "Though if you are a Root Weaver, I can show you the basics tomorrow, on our way to Thorpe."

One of the male Watchkeepers spoke up. "Should we really be teaching the prisoner how to Weave?" He wore a red flame-shaped pin.

Tabbot shrugged. "Why not, Mercer? It's not like he's a Flame Weaver. What's he going to do, heal us to death?"

Chapter 7
The Testing

JAYN ELDRAGOR, DAUGHTER of Anyse Eldragor, who was Fourth Pentarch of Aldria, lay on her bed and wept. The moment she had anticipated for as long as she could remember had ended in disaster. She hated herself for crying, but when all her plans for the future had suddenly unraveled, she didn't know what else to do.

Jayn's mother was a renowned Flame Weaver, a general in Aldria's Standing Army, and a member of the Pentarchy. All her life, Jayn had wanted to follow in her mother's footsteps. From the start, that had been Anyse's wish as well. As a member of the first echelon, Jayn had received the standard tutelage in history, mathematics, art, literature, and penmanship. In addition, she had trained in military strategy, hand-to-hand combat, fencing, and archery. She also learned to ride shortly after learning to walk.

Though not as tall as her mother, Jayn was slender but athletic, with sandy blonde hair and blue eyes. Her father assured Jayn that she would have no trouble finding a suitable husband when the time came. But finding a husband was not the first step she intended to take. No, first she would enlist in the Standing Army. With her natural intelligence and determination, she would rise quickly through the ranks. That had been the plan anyway. Few women made it far in the Standing Army, unless they were Flame Weavers. And Jayn Eldragor, it seemed, was not a Flame Weaver.

It made absolutely no sense. Both her parents were powerful Flame Weavers. All four of her grandparents had been Flame Weavers as well. Even her eight great-grandparents had been Weavers, though one, it was said, had been a Stone Weaver. The gift was not always passed down hereditarily, but Jayn had never doubted she had it.

She was still two years shy of being eligible to enlist, but having turned sixteen a month ago, she was old enough to be tested. She'd considered it a mere formality. She arose early that morning, the day she was to be tested. She smiled to herself as she selected her outfit from among the options her maid had laid out for her. She would dress the part. When Lord Stilton, who would be conducting the testing, arrived at her family's country estate in the hills above Appencourt, she received him in the front parlor, wearing a long red dress with slashes of yellow in the skirt and a red ribbon holding back her hair.

Jayn's mother wasn't home, having been called away on some political business, a common occurrence. Jayn's doting father hovered behind her as she sat on a sofa across from Lord Stilton. She frowned, glancing back at her father. She asked him to give them some privacy. She asked it sweetly, with a smile. Gelard Eldragor seldom ever refused his daughter's requests. Before he left, he said something that Jayn found rather strange at the time. "Don't worry," he said. "No matter the results, we will always be here for you." With that, her father left the room, though she knew he would stay in the hallway, just out of sight. One of the maids offered Lord Stilton some tea, and then they began.

The test for Flame was a simple one. Lord Stilton placed a stubby white candle before her on a low table, set out for just this occasion. The candle sat in a simple metal pan to catch the wax. He touched his thumb and forefinger to the wick. She couldn't see the lacings—it took training and practice to see another's workings—but she knew he was wielding Flame. His fingertips seemed to glow faintly, and then he took his hand away and the candle was lit.

He talked her through the visualization process. Jayn's mother had always refused to explain that part to her, knowing full well the girl would have tried Weaving well before she was old enough. It didn't seem especially complicated. He spoke of envisioning a flame, a fire glowing in her chest, and letting that flame grow to surround her entire body, before reaching out with her mind and touching the candle.

"Heat," Lord Stilton explained, "is a natural byproduct of Flame. Even the simplest lacing will warm the air around you. If done properly, the candle will glow brighter."

"Don't I need fuel?" Jayn asked. "A piece of wood or coal?"

Lord Stilton shook his head. "Fuel only serves to strengthen a Weaver's lacings. For this test, your body's own energy will be sufficient."

Jayn closed her eyes and concentrated, taking deep breaths in and out, as he had suggested. She pictured a flame glowing inside her chest. She saw it in her mind's eye. It seemed too simple. She could just as easily imagine a flying donkey glowing in her chest. She had to trust Lord Stilton though. He had been administering the test for decades.

She imagined that flame growing, spreading, and enveloping her body like a shield of light. She opened her eyes and focused all her attention on the candle. She'd pictured the fire perfectly in her mind, but she couldn't actually see anything. Shouldn't she be able to see the lacing around her? She didn't let it bother her. Maybe that part came with practice. She stared at that dancing ball of light atop the candle, watching the wax melt around it and drip down into the pan. She willed it to glow brighter. A minute passed, then another. After a full five minutes, she couldn't take it any longer.

"What am I doing wrong?" she said, looking up at Lord Stilton.

He smiled. "Not everyone gets it the first time. Let's start over from the top."

He explained it to her again, using the exact same words. She nodded along impatiently, and when he finished, she closed her eyes and pictured the flame. Nothing happened that time either. She shook her head without saying anything and started over on her own. After the third failed attempt, she grew nervous. She looked up at Lord Stilton, who was frowning now.

"This isn't working," she said. "Is there another test we could try?"

He hesitated before answering, seeming to choose his words carefully. "I'm afraid the test may have yielded its result, just not the one we were hoping for."

"No!" she said. He flinched. She moderated her tone. "I can do this. Let me try again."

He opened his mouth but then decided not to say anything. She closed her eyes and tried again. She rendered that imaginary flame in as much detail as she could, picturing each flickering tendril of fire. She tried different colored flames, mixing red, orange, yellow, and even blue. The candle diminished, the pool of wax around its base growing, yet the flame continued to glow at a steady and constant brightness. From the corner of her eye, she could see Lord Stilton squirming in his seat, but blessedly he said nothing to interrupt her. This dragged on for over an hour. Her face grew warmer, though it had nothing to do with Weaving. Her pale cheeks turned rosy with embarrassment. Hot tears welled up in her eyes. At that point, she was only going through the motions, barely visualizing anything, but she refused to give up, to acknowledge defeat. Finally, nothing remained of the candle but a blob of cooling wax, and its flame flickered and winked out. With that, the light inside her seemed to die as well.

She let out one quivering sob but stifled a second one. "Maybe…" she said, her voice faltering. "Maybe I'm still too young. Maybe we can try again in a month or two."

Lord Stilton shook his head. "I'm sorry, Jayn. You don't have it."

"But I must! Please let me try again."

Lord Stilton spoke slowly. "I've been watching you this whole time. Remember, a trained Weaver can see the lacings of another. It's true, some Weavers are so weak in the gift that they cannot make the candle glow, but I saw nothing around you. There is not a single spark of Flame in you."

Jayn couldn't contain the sob that time. She practically wailed.

Her father burst into the room. He'd been out in the hall for the entire hour. He must have known for some time that she had failed; a successful test would not have taken so long. He dropped to his knees beside her. "Sweetheart, please don't cry. We still love you. You're still my bright and beautiful girl."

She couldn't stand it any longer. She leapt from the sofa and fled the room. Her red-slippered feet pounded up the stairs, and she threw herself on her bed. Then she wept as she had not done in years. Her mother abhorred crying.

Her father came up and tried to comfort her. She yelled wordlessly at him, and he withdrew. She was in a daze, replaying the failed test over and over in her mind. She was still lying there when her mother arrived home that evening.

She heard her mother's voice on the stairs. "I'll speak with her." Jayn's father must have intercepted her at the door and broken the terrible news.

Jayn froze. Her mother's voice was icy and even as always. The woman seldom showed emotion, in complete contrast to Jayn's father. Jayn knew that her mother loved her, but Anyse Eldragor was a general first and foremost. She had been a general on the battlefield, she was a general in the Hall of the Assembly, and she was a general in her home. She was quick with praise when Jayn performed well, but she did not tolerate weakness.

Jayn had never failed her mother before, not like this. At that exact moment, she couldn't stand the idea of seeing her mother, of having to admit defeat and acknowledge that their plans for her future were ruined. She heard her mother's footsteps coming down the hall toward her bedroom. She wanted to run and hide, but that would have been childish. There was no running from the truth now. She stifled her sobs and swallowed, putting on as stoic a face as she could manage. She turned toward the open doorway and waited.

Her mother appeared, a stately woman in a high-necked dress, with streaks of white in her blonde hair. Anyse Eldragor's face was smooth, belying no emotions. Her eyes lingered on Jayn for only a moment before sweeping across the room. Her expression changed. She looked... puzzled. Anyse glanced back the way she had come. "Where is she?" she called to her husband.

Jayn frowned. Her bed stood only a few paces from the door, and she had not gotten under the sheets. She lay on the soft blue coverlet, her red skirt spread in a fan around her, fully visible. What did her mother mean?

"In her room," her father called from the foot of the stairs.

Her mother scanned the bedroom again, wrinkles forming on her brow. Jayn opened her mouth to speak, but then her mother left, moving down the hall, as if in search of her daughter.

"What?" Jayn said aloud, and the whispered word contained many questions. Was this her mother's response to her failure, pretending her daughter had disappeared? Would she refuse to acknowledge her presence now? No, her mother was too straightforward for such mind games, and she'd looked genuinely confused.

Jayn sat up and looked around the bedroom, as if it might hold any clues. She froze when her eyes landed on the large wooden vanity and the wide gilt mirror above it on the far side of the room. Something was off with the reflection. She could see her entire bed, but she could not see herself. Was it some strange trick of the light? She scrambled up and walked closer, though the empty mirror made her feel strangely dizzy, so she kept her eyes averted until she was right before the vanity. She looked up. Through the mirror she could see most of her room—the bed, the washstand, her long bookshelf lined with academic texts—but she could not see herself. Staring into the mirror gave her a strange feeling of vertigo, so she turned away.

She looked at her hands. They were as solid and substantial as ever. Her mother couldn't see her because she was invisible. How could she be invisible? That was the kind of thing only a Weaver could do, and Jayn Eldragor was no Weaver. She smiled with understanding. She was not a Flame Weaver, but she was a Weaver.

The wagon jostled south along the Thorpe Road, with Ryn and Pavel still in the cage. Two of the Watchkeepers rode on the bench, with the others on their own horses. Nyssa rode ahead of the group.

Ryn had learned each of the Watchkeepers' names, though they referred to each other only by their second names. They called Nyssa "Lahmeer" without a "Captain" or other title before it. Tabbot rode to the left of the wagon, while Brug, the group's Aether Weaver, rode to the right. Brug was a short man, shorter even than Ryn, but he made up for it with a constant scowl and a general swagger. The pin on his tabard was a white spiral. Clayborne the Stone Weaver and Mercer the Flame Weaver sat atop the wagon. Both men were tall, but Mercer was slender to Clayborne's broad shoulders. Mercer had light brown hair and a fairer complexion, while Clayborne was completely bald. Mercer looked like a soldier, while Clayborne looked like a blacksmith. The two men seemed the friendliest of the group, chatting amicably together as they rode along.

The group had been headed south for several hours, seeing no travelers as they went. They'd left behind the small farms clustered south of Aen's Hollow and would see nothing but trees for the two days it took to travel to Thorpe. Ryn watched the forest roll by, mostly oaks and maples. He didn't bother cataloging the weeds and wildflowers clustered along the verge of the dirt road, as he normally would. He felt despondent. First, he lost his aunt—and his pig—and now he was a prisoner. Why was this happening? Pavel had been right about one thing: Ryn technically hadn't done anything illegal. Ryn glared at Pavel, who was again leaning on the bars with his eyes closed. Why had he let the thief talk him into trying to steal the village's Runeform? The world was a dangerous place, he knew, and he couldn't be so quick to trust people.

The forest was still too quiet, and that worried Ryn. The Kobolds were dead. Shouldn't the birds have returned? The only sign of movement Ryn saw among the trees was the occasional glimpse of Corvus. The blue-eyed creature shadowed the caravan, keeping its distance. It seemed completely loyal to Pavel. From where had he stolen that thing? Nyssa had Pavel's curious weapons bundled up and tied behind her saddle.

The wagon lurched to a stop. The sun stood exactly overhead. No one spoke, but it quickly became clear the Watchkeepers had stopped for lunch. They dismounted and dug through their saddlebags. They filled feedbags with oats and strapped them to the five horses. Tabbot offered the prisoners another meal of bread and cheese. The Watchkeepers ate the same fare, though they added some stringy dried meat to the repast.

Ryn studied Tabbot's face as she handed him a cup of water, filled from a waterskin. She looked pale, especially around the mouth. "Can I see your arm?" Ryn asked.

Tabbot arched an eyebrow. "Why?"

"Well, I... I've trained as an herbalist. Maybe I can help."

Pavel cut in, holding up his own arm. "Yeah, the kid is great. He gave me a salve for my... sourthorn itch, was it? It's doing wonders for me."

Tabbot smiled. "I appreciate the concern." She paused, squinting at Ryn. "You know, with all the commotion yesterday, I never asked your name."

"Ryn."

"Ryn? Just Ryn?"

He nodded.

"Well, Ryn, I applied some Rootbalm last night, so the wound should be clearing up."

"Rootbalm? My aunt taught me every kind of medicine she knows, but I've never heard of Rootbalm."

"Your aunt must not be a Root Weaver then," Tabbot said. "Rootbalm is sort of a catch-all term. If you took one of the salves or tinctures you already know how to make and laced it with Root as you made it, you would get Rootbalm. All Watchkeepers carry some with them, since there might not always be a Root Weaver nearby when you're injured. It's also a sneaky way for a Root Weaver to be able to heal herself, though it doesn't work as quickly as lacing the wound directly. The balm took away the pain, and I should be healed in a day or two. Here, let me show you."

She had changed her torn shirt for a clean one. She undid the buttons at the cuff and rolled up the gray sleeve past her forearm. She frowned, seeing the wound. A clear shiny substance had been applied to the scratches, but the skin still looked red and irritated. Four black scabs ran across her arm where the claws had sliced her.

"Hmm," she said. "Perhaps I'll need to apply some more." She glanced southward, looking down the road. She seemed to be talking to herself now. "It's still a day and a half till Thorpe…" She turned back to Ryn. She looked concerned for a moment, but then she smiled. "Well, how about I give you a lesson in Root Weaving?"

Ryn smiled too. "I would like that."

"Lahmeer," Tabbot called to the group's leader. "Could you kindly remove your ward from the cage."

Mercer, still atop the wagon, scoffed. Nyssa rose from where she had been sitting on a log beside Brug. "And why would I want to do that?" Nyssa asked Tabbot.

"I want to test the boy, Ryn, to see if he can Weave."

Nyssa eyed Pavel, who had gone back to pretending to be asleep.

Tabbot made a dismissive gesture with a flick of her wrist. "Oh, the cage will still hold them. If the thief gets squirrely, you can poke at him with your sword."

Pavel opened one eye to glance at the female Watchkeepers, but then he closed it again.

Nyssa shrugged. "All right, but make it quick." She touched the side of the cage and then returned to her seat on the log, but she kept her eyes on the prisoners. That simple tap had apparently been enough to remove her ward that prevented Weaving.

Tabbot stepped quickly, moving to the edge of the forest. She plucked a single leaf from an oak tree and returned to the wagon. She held the leaf up for Ryn to see. The broad leaf was divided into several round lobes. Tabbot placed her fingers at the top of the leaf and carefully ripped it along the stem, stopping when the tear reached about an inch in length. She stuck the leaf between the bars, handing it to Ryn.

"Hold it like this," she said, cupping her hands together. "This is the test for Root. If you follow my instructions, you will be able to mend the leaf."

Ryn stared at the torn leaf in his hands. Could he really do that? Although, if Pavel had it right, he had already healed much more complex injuries to himself. He looked at Tabbot.

She nodded, seeing that he was ready. "The key to any Weaving is visualization. We use words like Root and Flame, but those are just metaphors, imprecise analogies that attempt to describe how the Five Forces work and interact. Root is really the force of growth, but a tree is a helpful metaphor. Like a tree, you must draw your strength from the world around you. Close your eyes and breathe. Breathe intentionally, focusing as you draw the air in and out. Imagine a seed inside of you, in the pit of your stomach. Imagine it sprouting and growing. Send out your roots and draw the energy in. Then send out your branches and direct the energy into the leaf."

Ryn closed his eyes. He breathed in and out, slowly. He had been breathing like this when he lay on the ground bleeding out. He tried not to think about that, driving away the images of himself wounded in the woods, of Marla down in the root cellar. He focused on the idea of a seed. He made it an acorn, like the seed of the oak leaf he held. He pictured it floating in a void. The acorn started off brown, but it suddenly shifted to a vibrant green, which somehow felt right, so he left it that color. It was just an image in his head, but somehow it felt tangible. It wasn't just in his mind, but it was, as she'd said, in the pit of his stomach.

He imagined the seed sprouting, sending out roots. The roots grew rapidly, spreading out around him. The image seemed to have a mind of its own. He meant for the roots to grow slowly, but they shot out and thickened like the woody roots of a century-old tree. The tree grew upward too, the trunk rising and shooting branches out all around.

His eyes opened, and the world around him had turned green. A distinct wall of green light tinted everything in front of him. The thing he had only just imagined was also somehow visible now. It wasn't exactly like a tree or anything solid. Instead, streaks of green light had formed around him, bending and twisting together. When taken as a whole, the shapes seemed to suggest the outline of a tree. The roots spread out below him, stretching from one side of the road to the other. The trunk of light rose up through the bottom of the wagon and enveloped him. From the corner of his eye, he saw Pavel staring, mouth agape. He felt the eyes of the other Watchkeepers on him too. Could they see it?

He pushed those thoughts away, knowing somehow that if he lost his concentration, the whole tree would vanish. The branches were growing and spreading out haphazardly in all directions, so he focused on guiding them, growing them out toward the leaf in his hands. The tips of a dozen different glowing branches touched the leaf. He felt the leaf, and not just with his hands. He felt the wound where Tabbot had torn it. He drew some unseen energy up through those still-expanding roots and guided it into the leaf. The rip began knitting itself back together. Tiny green fibers sprouted from either side of the tear and interlaced themselves. The wound closed up and disappeared like it had never been there. His whole body tingled. It felt strangely good. He didn't want to let it go just yet. That energy still flowed into the leaf. Suddenly, white tendrils shot out from the base of the broken stem, wriggling like worms. Ryn gasped and dropped the leaf, and the whole imaginary-yet-real tree vanished.

Tabbot reached her hand between the bars and carefully picked up the leaf. They both could see that it had started to send out its own roots from the stem. "Impressive," she said.

"You could see that?" Ryn said. "You saw the tree?"

She nodded. "With practice, you can learn to see the lacings of others as well."

Nyssa cleared her throat and stood again. "Well, good job, Ryn," she said. "If you end up not being a thief, perhaps you could consider a career in the Watchkeepers." She looked at her companions. "Let's get moving."

Tabbot frowned. "Oh, are you sure? With a result like that... I've never seen such a strong gifting. I'd love to run him through a few more exercises."

Nyssa shook her head. "You can teach all you want when we make camp tonight. We keep moving, and the ward goes back up."

Pavel looked scandalized. "What?" he said. "Did you see even a puff of Aether out of me? We don't need a shield."

Nyssa ignored him. She touched the cage again, her fingers lingering for a few seconds this time. Ryn saw and felt nothing, but

Pavel's sigh meant the ward was back up. Tabbot looked concerned again, but she said nothing. The party got moving, this time with Brug and Tabbot on the wagon and Mercer and Clayborne mounted. Nyssa still led the way on her brown mare. For the sake of the wagon, they advanced at a walk. Ryn tried throughout the day to visualize the tree again. He could picture an acorn in his mind just fine, but it never turned green or started growing on its own. Nyssa's ward was effective.

Chapter 8
Dowsing and Healing

THALIA MOLDO STOOD before the Rigel fountain. The sun lay half-concealed behind the two-story buildings to the west. All the businesses around the square, including the redsmith's shop, were shuttered for the evening, but she had time yet before she would need to worry about footpads. While the more enterprising criminals operated out of Falport across the river, Rigel had its share of second-rate thieves. Thalia glanced around, checking the square for pedestrians. This part of town held few homes and no inns, so it was not unusual for the streets to be empty after business hours.

The day after tomorrow, she would begin her training with Master Caston. She still wasn't sure if she would actually join the Watchkeepers, but she needed to understand her Etching. She saw now its great potential, but she still was not certain how she could best utilize it. For the next few weeks, she would be spending most of her time inside the Watchkeepers' Citadel. She didn't know when or if she would ever return to Master Foster's shop. This would be her last opportunity for a while to study the Rigel fountain, and she wanted to try one more time to ask it a question.

She had a great deal of questions, most of which she knew the Runeform would not answer. *Should I join the Watchkeepers?* The fountain never gave advice and would remain silent if asked such a question. *If I join the Watchkeepers, will I…* That line of questioning was out as well. Rigel ignored hypotheticals. The Runeform only dealt in facts, though amazingly, it seemed capable of reading the future—when it decided to actually answer the question put before it, instead of providing a nonsensical, seemingly unrelated response.

Once, Thalia had overheard a question from the wife of a Mirkwalder merchant. Apparently, the woman had accompanied her husband on a voyage down from Nuzibah. While in Falport, she had discovered she was pregnant. Her question to Rigel: "Will I have a healthy child?" The Runeform's response: "You will bear a hearty son." That was a clear-cut answer, with the added detail that her child would be a boy. Thalia never learned if the fountain's prediction came true. Thalia never saw the woman again, as she likely returned with her husband to Mirkwald shortly after asking the question.

She had witnessed—or heard about through town gossip—dozens of other similarly straightforward answers, mostly given to questioners from distant places. People had been told the names of their future spouses, the locations of lost family heirlooms, and whether or not planned enterprises would prosper.

One incident would always stick out to her. About a year ago, she had been closing up shop when a shabbily dressed young man with a haunted look in his eyes approached the fountain. His question was simple but unsettling: "When will I die?" Rigel's response: "Your life will end in forty-seven years, seventeen days, six hours, and eleven minutes." In response, the man only nodded and ambled away. Thalia could not see his face to know how he received the news. She always wondered what had prompted the man to ask such a question. Thalia was far too frightened to consider making such a query herself.

Mostly, the answers did not make sense, or rather, the Runeform seemed to answer a different question, one that the questioner did not ask or even know. She remembered her first question and the strange response about something being in the "third well." She also could not forget that Scholar, Mina, asking about dinner and receiving that ominous response about "the Rivening," whatever that was.

Chances were, she would get an answer like that no matter what she asked. Still, she was here now. She needed to ask a simple question about her future. She thought about her ambitions. If she did join the Watchkeepers, it would only be a means to an end, a way to receive training in the craft she most aspired to master.

She cleared her throat and said, "Rigel." The fountain's impish face sprung to life and stared down at her. "Will I ever be a master bladesmith?"

Immediately, the fountain spoke in that resonant almost-human voice: "YOU MUST TRUST THE BOY WHO SAVES YOUR LIFE."

Thalia frowned. Another puzzling answer. Was Raef's theory right? Was this an answer to someone else's question? Was this the answer to the question she was *supposed* to ask? She knew dozens of boys, the apprentices to Rigel's other master craftsmen, but none had ever saved her life. If this was some prophecy intended for her, then she would not know who the boy was until after her life had been in danger, and there was no telling where that danger would come from. She sighed and started for home, wondering if she would ever bother to ask this frustrating fountain a question again.

***

An hour before sunset, the Watchkeepers' caravan pulled off into a clearing along the Thorpe Road. Nyssa Lahmeer and her Pentad were clearly experienced travelers, and it only took them half an hour to make camp. They unhitched and unsaddled the horses, wiped them down, fed them, and looped their reins around sturdy tree branches, before spreading out their bedrolls in a ring beside the wagon. Ryn and Pavel would spend another night inside the cage. They ate another dinner of bread and cheese, with more meat for the Watchkeepers and water for everyone. The night was warm, but they built a fire anyway. Fires were good at keeping predators away. Brug and Clayborne loped off in opposite directions down the road, apparently to keep a watch. Mercer tended the fire. Tabbot asked Nyssa to lower the ward. Ryn had watched the Root Weaver apply another coating of Rootbalm to her wound. She still looked pale, and her face seemed strained around the eyes. Ryn said nothing. The rest of the Watchkeepers seemed oblivious to Tabbot's pain. They must have assumed the Rootbalm would be sufficient.

Tabbot smiled, and when she spoke, she sounded genuinely fine. "Now, healing a wound or illness in a human is far more complicated than fixing a leaf. Before you can do that, you must first be able to Dowse."

Ryn nodded, though he had no idea what that meant.

She held up the waterskin she had been using to fill their cups. "Imagine you had a waterskin," she said, "and this waterskin had a leak in it. You could start by applying patches all around it at random, and eventually you would plug the leak, but that would not be efficient, and all those extra patches could weaken the waterskin. No, you would first need to carefully examine the skin and test to see precisely where the hole was. Then you could patch it. This is a good metaphor for Dowsing, though it is not a physical examination. Not all injuries can be seen with the naked eye. Some are internal. I want you to practice Dowsing on your infamous friend here." She gestured toward Pavel.

Pavel spit out the bit of bread he'd been chewing on. "Hang on," he said. "I didn't consent to that."

Tabbot scoffed. "There's nothing to worry about. Dowsing is harmless."

Ryn looked to Pavel. "After the mess you got me into, the least you could do is let me practice on you."

Pavel sighed. "Fine, but if you find out I'm dying of some hidden, incurable disease, you just keep that information to yourself, mind. I'd rather not know."

Ryn nodded.

Tabbot stepped closer to the bars. "Start by visualizing that tree again. It doesn't need to be quite so big as the one you made last time. Send out the roots, but this time, don't draw any energy in. You don't need to transfer any energy to Dowse. Send out the branches toward Mr. Talvor and envelop him in the lacing. Reach out with your mind. What you feel will be overwhelming at first. It takes time to learn to process and sort the sensations. Give it a try, but make sure you transfer no energy into him."

Ryn looked to Pavel again.

The thief frowned. "Don't go rearranging my insides now," he said. "I've grown rather accustomed to their current configuration."

Ryn closed his eyes. With the ward down, the green seed sprung quickly to life. He opened his eyes and sent out the roots. It was strange that the others could see those curvy streaks of green light, somehow made only from his mind. He hoped he would be able to see their lacings soon. He deliberately arrested the roots' growth once they reached a few feet in length. Then he raised the trunk up around himself, but he stopped the branches from sprouting in haphazard directions. He sent them all toward Pavel, who closed his eyes and flinched as the splinters of green light enveloped him. Ryn held them in place, weaving the branches into a dense thicket, but he was mindful not to draw any of that mysterious energy out of the ground.

At first, he felt nothing, but then a wave of sensations flooded into his mind. He couldn't make any sense of them. It was like when he connected with the leaf and could feel it in his mind, but this tangled web of impressions was far more complicated. He tried focusing on a single thread, unraveling it from the bundle. *Pavel's neck is sore.* Somehow, he knew that. Ryn's neck was fine, but at the same time, he felt a ghost of soreness and knew it belonged to Pavel, who had been leaning too long against the bars. He found another thread. *Pavel is hungry.* Why was he not eating all his dinner then? He'd stashed half the food in his bag again.

Ryn began to see an order in the tangle. Each distinct thread corresponded to some part of Pavel's anatomy, though most made no sense. The human body was incredibly complex, and Ryn knew far less about its makeup than he knew about plants. These bits here seemed to do with Pavel's digestion, and those over there connected to the circulation of his blood, but he could only guess at most of it. A quivering mass of white at the center of the bundle seemed to be Pavel's mind, his consciousness.

Ryn also realized that he could sense whether each part was functioning as it should be and which parts were out of balance. The bulk of that tangle seemed to glow green in his mind, vibrating in sync. A few parts of it had a yellow tinge and pulsated more erratically. The threads connected to his neck and his hunger were like that, which was why they had stood out at first. Ryn found another yellow thread.

"I've found it," he said with a gasp. "I've found the scratch on his arm. It's… vibrating out of sync with the rest of him. I think I can fix it." He started to draw energy up through his roots.

"No," Tabbot said. "You must stop immediately."

He'd never heard such intensity in her voice before. He glanced at her.

She shook her head. "It can be dangerous to run before you are ready."

Pavel had pushed himself back against the bars, eyeing Ryn uncomfortably. "Listen to the lady," he said.

Ryn sighed and let the whole tree disappear. "I really think I could have done it though."

Tabbot's voice softened again. She offered a knowing smile. "You are a quick learner. I know you wish to discover the full extent of your gift. This is natural. But to wield Root on another person can be dangerous. If you don't know what you are doing, you can make an injury worse, not better. I'm sure when your aunt taught you herbalism, she did not let you begin by simply mixing plants together at random and imbibing the results."

Ryn nodded. There were just as many useless or poisonous plants in the woods as beneficial ones, and mixing some ingredients together made them more salubrious, while other combinations had adverse effects. Herbalism came naturally to him now after all these years, but it was a complicated craft. Now it seemed as if he were starting all over by learning how to Weave.

"Still," Tabbot said. "I suppose Mr. Talvor has suffered from sourthorn itch long enough. I can mend that, and if you focus, perhaps you can see my lacings." She hesitated, then turned to Nyssa, still at the fire with Mercer. "If that's all right?"

Nyssa frowned. "You sure have taken a keen interest in the kid," she said. "He has potential, I'll give you that, but I think you've shown him enough for now. He is still a prisoner after all."

Tabbot wrung her hands. Why did she seem so worried again? She nodded slowly. "As you wish, Lahmeer."

She offered Ryn a sad smile and turned away. She started toward the fire, but she never made it. She faltered when taking a step and then collapsed. Mercer and Nyssa jumped up and rushed over to her, turning her onto her back. She had passed out.

"What happened to her?" Mercer said.

"I don't know," Nyssa said. "You know I'm no good at Dowsing."

Mercer scoffed. "Me neither."

Dowsing? Ryn remembered Pavel's confusing description of the Five Forces from two days ago. He said Flame and Wave were complimentary to Root, which meant these two must have been able to do some Root Weaving as well.

Before either Watchkeeper got the chance to try any lacings, a commotion to the north drew everyone's attention. The setting sun had just dipped below the horizon, and in the fading twilight, they could see five figures running down the Thorpe Road toward their camp. The creatures were short and squat, with pointed ears and steel weapons gleaming in their hands.

Pavel groaned. "Not again," he said.

"Blast the stars," Mercer said, an oath Ryn had never heard before. "How did they get past Brug?" Suddenly, he held a pair of daggers in his hands. He must have kept them up his sleeves.

Nyssa rose, turning south. "Clayborne!" she called. "We need you in camp!"

"Can you shield us?" Mercer asked. His voice remained calm. He planted himself between the unconscious Tabbot and the advancing Kobolds. His hands started to glow, seemingly lit from within, like a flame beneath a thin lampshade.

"There's no time," Nyssa said, drawing her blade. She took up position beside Mercer.

Two of the charging Kobolds held curved shortswords, like the one that had stabbed Ryn. Two others held hatchets, and the fifth carried an oversized knife with a serrated edge. They all wore those brown trousers and vests, made of some coarse material. Despite their girth and their short legs, they came on quickly, their oversized clawed feet thumping along the hardpacked road. They kept no order as they ran, and two of the creatures surged ahead of the group. They made straight for Mercer and Nyssa.

Nyssa used her long blade to keep her foe at a distance, slashing at it anytime it tried to swing its hatchet. Mercer, on the other hand, let his hatchet-wielding attacker get in close. The Flame Weaver's daggers had large quillons, and he used one blade to stop the swinging axe while stabbing with the other. Both Kobolds were bleeding now, but that didn't stop their frenzied assault. The three slower creatures would soon catch up and join the fight.

Ryn glanced both ways up and down the road. He saw no further movement from the north. The creatures must have ambushed Brug, the Aether Weaver, before he could shout any warning. To the south, Clayborne, the tall and burly Stone Weaver came running up the road, holding those two iron cudgels.

Mercer continued grappling with his foe, slashing its arms and chest with his daggers. He jumped back a step, raised his knee, and planted a kick squarely in the Kobold's chest. The creature flew backwards, colliding with its companion, who had just come up behind it. Both creatures fell to the ground in a tangled mess. The injured Kobold's companion showed it no mercy, hacking at it with its weapon and shoving it aside. Nyssa scored a finishing blow against her attacker, slashing its throat with the tip of her blade. She spun, parrying a lunge from the Kobold with the oversized knife.

The fifth Kobold did not throw itself into the fight. It skirted around the edge of the fray, perhaps looking for an opening or a weakness to exploit. It seemed to consider Tabbot, still lying in the road, but then those beady eyes saw the cage, with Pavel and Ryn still inside. Its lipless mouth widened into a sneer or a smile as it dashed toward the wagon. The creature made straight for Pavel, stabbing through the bars with its sword. Pavel threw himself against the bars on the far side of the cage, and the blade stopped barely an inch short of reaching him. The sword's cross guard stopped it from extending farther into the cage, and the creature didn't seem to realize it could simply rotate the sword to penetrate further. It stabbed again and again, ramming the hilt against the bars. Ryn also pressed himself against the wall, away from the creature, but it was ignoring him for now.

The creature pulled the sword back and began circling clockwise around the wagon. Ryn heard the horses whinnying with fear, struggling to pull their reins free from where they were tied. As the Kobold circled, Pavel shifted around the cage, trying to keep his distance from the monster. Pavel threw himself against Ryn, squeezing him into the bars. Ryn groaned, but he could not fault the thief for his squirming in the name of self-preservation.

The Kobold was now on the south side of the wagon, and it seemed so intent on finding a way to reach Pavel with its blade, that it didn't hear Clayborne trotting up behind it. The muscular Stone Weaver swung one cudgel down onto the creature's head. Ryn heard its skull crack as it fell to the ground, dropping its sword. Clayborne glanced at the prisoners huddled together in the cage, gave a friendly nod, and rounded the wagon to join his fellow

Watchkeepers. The fight was over though. Nyssa and Mercer had each felled their second attacker.

Nyssa surveyed the carnage, grimacing as she clutched a hand to her side. One of the Kobolds must have nicked her with a blade or a claw. She looked at Mercer and pointed north with her chin. "Go check on Brug," she said. "I don't like that we haven't heard from him."

Mercer nodded and started loping north into the dark.

Clayborne crouched beside Tabbot. "What happened?" he asked.

Nyssa shook her head. "I don't know. She just collapsed, right before the Kobolds attacked."

Clayborne pressed two fingers to the Root Weaver's neck. "Her pulse is faint," he said.

Suddenly, another noise shattered the silence of the still woods, the sound of a crow cawing, but it was no crow. Corvus the Runeform swooped into the camp, its cerulean eyes glowing like torches. It flew in a circle around the wagon, squawking the whole time.

Pavel rolled his eyes. "Oh, stifle it," he said. "You're a little too late with the warning this time."

Corvus didn't stop. More movement to the north signaled the return of Mercer. His hands glowed with a steady white light now, as if he carried a pair of lanterns. He held the daggers still but advanced at a walk. Nyssa looked toward him, expectantly. The Flame Weaver's shadowed face looked grim as he slowly shook his head. The creatures had gotten to Brug.

Mercer was about a hundred feet from the camp when the woods erupted with the sound of bodies thrashing through the undergrowth. Mercer raised an arm, his glowing hand illuminating the trees. A dozen more Kobolds emerged directly beside him.

"Mercer!" Nyssa called. "Fall back to me!"

The Flame Weaver broke into a sprint before his commander had finished giving the order. He moved quickly, outpacing the stocky Kobolds.

Pavel threw himself against the cage, rattling the bars. "Let me out!" he said. "I can help you fight. You can't take them all on."

Clayborne, rising to his feet, glanced back at the cage. He seemed to be considering it.

Ryn barely heard the thief's request. He watched Mercer's flight from the pack of monsters. Ryn remembered what had happened when he'd turned his back on Kobolds before. "Look out!" he shouted, but it was too late.

One Kobold threw its sword like a javelin, catching Mercer in the back. He fell forward with a grunt. The injured Flame Weaver rolled onto his side. The blade, wedged deep in his back, must have missed his spine. Mercer raised his daggers, and although he threw from an awkward angle, both hurled blades flew true. Two Kobolds fell backward, hands flying to their necks, trying in vain to stop the blue blood fountaining from their throats. Mercer made a noise. It almost sounded like a chuckle. Then the pack was upon him, hacking with their blades and stabbing with their claws.

"No!" Nyssa yelled, the anguish plain in her voice.

Clayborne grunted. He ran to the back of the wagon, where a sturdy lock held the cage's door shut. Setting his cudgels on the edge of the wagon, he took the lock in both hands. He must have applied some Weaving, as the lock snapped open. Without another glance at the prisoners, he took up his cudgels and ran to join Nyssa, still standing before Tabbot, her bloodied sword at the ready. Mercer had delayed the mob only a few seconds, and then the ten Kobolds still standing were advancing toward the two remaining Watchkeepers.

Pavel lunged for the door as soon as Clayborne popped the padlock. He stuck his fingers through the bars and lifted the lock from the latch, letting it fall to the ground. He threw open the door and jumped out. He glanced at the Watchkeepers, who had their backs to him now, and the approaching Kobolds. Then he jumped again. He must have applied a lacing of Aether to himself, as that leap took him clear to the top of the wagon. Ryn heard the thief's feet hit the top of the cage, though the thud was softer than it should have been. At some point, Corvus had stopped cawing and flown off again. Pavel ran along the top of the cage and jumped down onto the far side of the wagon. Ryn watched him, thinking at first the thief intended to run away after all, but Pavel made for the horses. He was going to get his weapons.

Ryn eyed the open door of the cage. He knew he would be of little help in this fight, but the cage could not protect him now. He crawled on his hands and knees to the entrance and jumped out. He almost collapsed when his legs hit the ground. He had been in the cage for a full two days, unable to stand. Using the side of the wagon to keep himself upright, Ryn hobbled around to the far side of the cage, watching the fight through two sets of bars.

Nyssa and Clayborne fought frantically. Clearly, they'd been trained to fight multiple assailants at once, but they wouldn't hold out long against ten armed monsters. Five of the Kobolds had gone for Nyssa, while the other five attacked Clayborne. Ryn had never seen armed combat before, but he could see clear differences in the way the humans and the Kobolds fought. The creatures stayed clumped together, rather than fanning out in a circle, as they probably should have. They got in each other's way so much that they couldn't all strike out at once. Their attacks seemed haphazard as well.

Meanwhile, the Watchkeepers flowed smoothly from one movement to the next, but they could only react to the onslaught of blows, constantly on the defensive. Nyssa seemed to struggle the most, gripping her sword with both hands. From this angle, Ryn couldn't see the wound she had taken in her side, but it seemed to be slowing her down. Clayborne deflected attacks as well as he could with his cudgels, but he'd sustained a few cuts to his forearms and a slash to his leg. The Watchkeepers would not last much longer.

Ryn looked toward the horses, but he could not see Pavel. Had he taken his weapons back and then fled? Ryn turned back to the fight, just in time to see Pavel emerge from the bushes. The Aether Weaver surged forward, his movements a blur. He held the rectangular bladebreaker in his left hand and the slotted bladecatcher in his right. He attacked the Kobolds from behind, stabbing out with the pointed tip of the bladebreaker. He ran along the line, spreading out the stabs among as many Kobolds as he could. He was trying to draw their attention away from the Watchkeepers.

The punctured Kobolds snarled, half of them turning to face Pavel. The thief jumped back a pace and took up a defensive posture, raising both weapons. Three of the creatures continued to slice at Clayborne, while Nyssa had only two to deal with now. The remaining five bore down on Pavel.

Like the Watchkeepers had been forced to do, Pavel only used his blades defensively, though Ryn soon realized that was the perfect position for him. His weapons were designed to disarm his foes. A Kobold lunged at Pavel with a long dagger, and he parried with the bladecatcher. The blade caught in a slot of the weapon. Pavel twisted his wrist and wrenched the dagger from the Kobold's hand. Then Pavel danced back again. He moved around the pack in a circle. The Kobolds were still bunched together, so only one could attack him at a time. A creature swung its sword at Pavel, and he parried with the bladebreaker this time. True to its name, the rod of steel held, while the Kobold's sword shattered. The creature recoiled then threw itself at Pavel, stabbing with the fractured stub of its sword. He parried with the bladecatcher and disarmed another creature. Pavel deftly deflected or dodged each attack, moving with Aether-enhanced speed. He managed a few counterattacks, lashing out with his bladebreaker like a switch. One Kobold crumpled after a blow to the head.

The tide looked to be turning in favor of the humans. Nyssa and Clayborne each felled one of the creatures, and the seven Kobolds still standing were all bleeding or limping from hits. Ryn edged around the wagon, closer to the melee. He felt useless. He had never been in a real fight before and didn't know how to wield a weapon. He saw a sword at his feet, dropped by the first Kobold Clayborne had killed. He bent and picked it up. He felt the weight of it in his hand. It was lighter than he thought it would be. Would he be able to do any good in this fight? Or would he just get in the way?

Two more Kobolds fell. The remaining five stood pressed together, with Nyssa and Clayborne on one side and Pavel on the other. The Watchkeepers were on the offensive now. The creatures eyed the woods, perhaps hoping to flee. Pavel gave them no chance, dancing back and forth, his blades a whirl of movement.

Ryn froze, sensing a presence behind him, that same force he'd felt two days ago, the first time he encountered these creatures. He spun around. This Kobold stood taller than the others, a head taller than Ryn. Its wideset bloodshot eyes stared down at him. It wore a full set of armor, made from some kind of black leather, complete with greaves and bracers, though no helmet covered its bulbous head. It carried a full-sized curved sword, the kind Ryn thought was called a scimitar. A long scar ran diagonally across the creature's face, crossing between its eyes and down one side of its hooked nose. Ryn still held a sword, but he could not raise it, feeling once again paralyzed with fear.

The oversized Kobold did not raise its sword either. It leaned in closer to Ryn and sniffed, its nose crinkling. It eyed Ryn up and down. He couldn't even breathe. If this thing killed him outright, Ryn doubted his body would be able to heal itself. The Kobold raised its eyes, watching its remaining soldiers falling at the hands of the humans—surely this thing had to be some kind of commander. Its face and eyes showed no emotion. Slowly, almost leisurely, it turned and walked around the wagon, ignoring Ryn completely. A sigh escaped from Ryn's mouth, but he didn't understand it. Why did it spare him? Did the creature simply conclude that Ryn was not a threat? It made no sense.

Suddenly, Ryn realized what the giant Kobold was about to do. It strode directly toward the Watchkeepers, who had their backs to it. Only three of the regular Kobolds remained, fighting one-on-one with each of the humans. Ryn opened his mouth, but only a hoarse rasp escaped. Fear had dried his throat. He coughed and managed to yell, "Look out! There's another one."

Nyssa slashed her opponent, sending it sprawling backwards. She spun around, hearing Ryn's shout. Her eyes widened upon seeing the towering black-clad Kobold. She held her sword only in her right hand now. She had taken more hits, and her left hand was clenched to a fresh wound in her side. Nysa's surprise delayed her only a second, and then she swung her sword at the beast. The creature's own blade shot up with lightning speed. The steel clashed against Nyssa's sword with such strength that her arm bent backward, her weapon flying from her hand. The creature lunged forward, slashing her across the chest with the claws of its left hand. Nyssa fell, toppled over by the force of the second blow.

Clayborne, hearing his commander's anguished cry, threw his weight against his opponent, sending the smaller Kobold staggering back. Then the Stone Weaver spun to confront the new arrival. The large Kobold moved with the speed and grace of a serpent, lunging with its blade. Clayborne brought his cudgels up to block, but he was a hair too slow. The Kobold's steel caught him directly in the chest. The cudgels slammed uselessly against the sword. In one final act of defiance, Clayborne hooked his cudgels around the blade, locking it up. It would take the Kobold a moment to free its sword.

Pavel used that moment, jumping over the head of his last opponent in a massive Aether-enhanced leap. He stabbed down with the tip of his bladebreaker. The large Kobold saw him descending from above. It bent unnaturally at the waist to dodge the attack. Pavel landed directly in front of it, his stabbing lunge passing through the air between the creature's torso and its raised left arm. The creature pressed its arm to its side, trapping Pavel's weapon. Pavel raised his notched bladecatcher to hack at the Kobold's arm. The creature's hand shot up, catching the blade. It hissed as the bladecatcher sliced into its palm. That wound didn't stop it though.

Still gripping the blade, the Kobold wrenched the weapon from Pavel's hand. It threw the bladecatcher off into the woods. Then it struck Pavel in the chest with that wounded hand. Pavel groaned with pain. It looked like an open-palmed punch at first, but Ryn saw as he got closer that the Kobold had stabbed its clawed fingernails into Pavel. Ryn had been running toward the fight since he'd first called out the warning, but the creature had moved so quickly.

The Kobold shoved Pavel hard, sending him backward into Clayborne. Both men fell down, with Clayborne sliding off the monster's blade. Pavel managed to hold onto his bladebreaker, pulling it loose from the Kobold's armpit. The creature stared down at Pavel, who lay panting beside Clayborne's motionless body. It raised its sword and swung it down toward the thief. Pavel barely raised his bladebreaker in time, clutching it with both hands now. The Kobold's sword did not shatter. The impact of steel on steel rang out through the night, sending out a shower of blue sparks.

Ryn stopped a few paces short of the creature, momentarily blinded by the sudden flash of light. He didn't get any closer. Attacking the monster would be useless.

Though Nyssa and Pavel still lay moaning in pain, the creature seemed to be done with them now. It turned its attention to the two smaller Kobolds, the last ones still standing. The shorter creatures regarded the armored one with something akin to fear. The closest one, with cuts up and down its arms, raised its open palms toward its apparent leader. "Gree sorry," it said in its gravelly voice.

The armored Kobold said nothing. It surged gracefully across the road, weaving through the scattered bodies of its soldiers. The two shorter creatures turned to run. The leader caught the first one quickly, swinging that curved sword and taking its head clean off. It leapt over the falling body. The last Kobold looked like it might escape its commander's wrath. It headed for the darkness of the tree line. The black-clad Kobold raised its empty hand toward its prey and flexed its fingers. The fleeing soldier stopped suddenly, as if frozen in place. It cried out in a wordless panic but seemed incapable of taking another step forward. The larger Kobold walked casually toward it, then plunged its sword into the creature's back until the tip burst through its chest. Using its foot, the leader pushed the dead Kobold from its blade.

It glanced back at the carnage spread across the Thorpe Road. Some seventeen Kobolds lay dead, their foaming blue blood turning the earth to mud. Of the humans, only Nyssa and Pavel were still moving, though all they could do was clutch at their wounds. Ryn stood rooted to the ground, the shortsword hanging uselessly in his hand. The nearby campfire bathed the scene in flickering orange light and shadow. The creature seemed to smile. Then it turned and disappeared into the night.

Ryn dropped the sword. What was that thing? How had it stopped the last soldier? Was the armored Kobold... a Weaver? It seemed impossible, but it had to be. And why, when it slaughtered its own soldiers, had it left Ryn standing? He was completely unharmed.

Ryn snapped out of the daze, realizing that some of the humans were still alive. He ran to Nyssa, who was the closest, crouching down at her side. Bloodstains ran up and down her sleeves and marred her tabard. The biggest tears were those claw marks across her chest, just below her throat. She stared up at him in confusion, no doubt wondering why he was still standing.

Ryn raised a hand but didn't know what to do with it. No individual wound looked life-threatening, but with so many cuts, she was in danger. If he had the right supplies, he could clean and bind the wounds, but... "Maybe I can heal you," he said. "I can try."

Nyssa scrunched up her eyes from the pain, but she shook her head. "No," she said. "Check on Tabbot first."

Ryn looked over at Tabbot. She had not stirred since passing out. Of course. She was the Root Weaver. If Ryn could heal her, she could help save the others. He moved quickly to her side. He closed his eyes, remembering the method for Dowsing. The green seed formed in his stomach. He spread out the roots and enveloped Tabbot with the branches. He reached out, trying to sense that bundle of impressions. It wasn't working. He felt something, but it wasn't like before with Pavel; it was a blank void.

He swallowed, looking over his shoulder at Nyssa. "I think... I think it's too late."

Nyssa sighed. "I can hang on a little longer," she said. "Try to help the others first."

Ryn moved to where Pavel and Clayborne lay side-by-side. He knew Mercer was dead, and he suspected Clayborne was as well. He was right. The Stone Weaver's glazed eyes stared up at the night sky. A pool of blood enveloped his chest and head. Ryn didn't need to Dowse him.

Pavel was still breathing, though he seemed to have passed out. He'd received a few minor cuts in his fight against the five Kobold soldiers, but the claw wounds to his chest were more concerning. With each beat of his heart, more blood seeped out from those punctures. He would be dead soon if Ryn couldn't heal him.

Ryn closed his eyes, struggling to control his breathing. His own heart raced, knowing that the time was short. It took him three tries to summon the seed. He didn't bother to constrain it this time. The roots shot out, covering and spreading beyond the battlefield. The trunk rose, towering above his head, sending out a canopy of branches. He concentrated a dozen of those branches toward Pavel. The mass of sensations sprung into Ryn's mind. Many of the quivering systems pulsed with a yellow light, and several lit up a brilliant red. Ryn somehow knew those corresponded to the more grievous injuries.

Ryn didn't know what to do next. Was it simply a matter of directing energy into those red and yellow threads? He had to try something. He drew in energy. He could sense the forest around him, the trees, the shrubs, the weeds, and the wildflowers on the margin of the road. He knew they were providing the energy he needed. He tried directing the flow to only the reddest threads, but the energy burst out, like water from a ruptured skin, overpowering his constraints and flooding into Pavel. The thief's eyes shot open. He gasped and then he screamed.

Ryn halted the flow but didn't release the imagined tree. He glanced at Nyssa. "What am I doing wrong?"

She coughed. Her voice sounded feeble. She would need urgent attention soon. "You… You healed his fatigue, not his wounds. He can feel his pain more than he could before."

"Curse me," Ryn said, borrowing an oath he'd learned from Pavel.

He tried again. The flow was too powerful to constrain to a single thread, but he found that if he divided it, he could touch all the red and yellow pieces at once, leaving the green threads alone. He sensed they were vibrating too quickly. He focused on slowing them, matching their pulses to the healthy threads. Gradually, the red and yellow parts turned green. Ryn looked at Pavel's chest again. Tan skin showed through the tears in his shirt where the rends had been. His breathing had slowed to a normal rate, and he lay on his back, staring in bewilderment at Ryn.

"I did it," Ryn said. "I healed him."

Nyssa didn't respond. He turned toward her. Her eyes had shut. Ryn reached out with his lacings. He didn't even think to move closer. She lay within the reach of his spreading roots and branches. He Dowsed her quickly. Her bundle of impressions was similar to Pavel's and yet distinctly different, like a unique fingerprint. Far more of her threads were strobing red. She had concealed the extent of the wounds in her side. Injured as she was, she had still told him to help the others first. The white glow of her mind at the center of the mass flickered. Instinctively, he knew she was on the edge of death. He unleashed the full flood of energy, barely managing to guide it toward the red and yellow areas. It took longer, but each part gradually turned green. Nyssa awoke with a gasp. Ryn released the massive spectral tree. Then he collapsed.

Chapter 9
Choices for a Future

SHILO LORN SAT at the end of her family's narrow wooden dock, dangling her bare feet over the water. She watched her wavering reflection in the blue sea. Her tightly curled hair hung in ringlets just past her shoulders. She wore loose trousers rolled up past her knees and a red linen shirt with the sleeves up. Most of her clothes were hand-me-downs from her older brothers. She owned a handful of dresses for feast days, though she never liked to wear them.

The fishing village of Palmoor spread out around the bay to either side of her. The southern coastline folded inward here like the pleat of a skirt, forming a small bay, sheltered from the sea winds by a jutting piece of land to the west. The Palmoor watchtower sat atop the cliffs there. A squat white building, the tower housed a brazier and a mirror used to signal ships. Few trading vessels bothered to stop in Palmoor, though shipping lanes passed right by the harbor. Traffic between the larger ports of Nadell to the northwest and Falport to the east always hugged the coastline, preferring the narrow channel between Palmoor and the Finger Isles, rather than sailing too far south. All sailors gave the Rune Lands a wide berth.

The morning sun hung low in the eastern sky. The *Windlacer*, moored to her left, cast a long shadow over Shilo and the family's dinghy, moored to the other side of the dock. In the larger ports, Shilo had heard, their docks were separate from the town, but this was not the case in Palmoor. All the fishing families had their own piers, built directly in front of their homes and scattered haphazardly around the inlet. A network of wooden boardwalks crisscrossed the village. All the houses sat on wooden stilts. The tide changes were dramatic here, so building out on the water prevented boats from getting stranded in the muck. At high tide the village was flooded, and at low tide a muddy expanse stretched beneath the raised houses and boardwalks. Shilo's mother always said Palmoor was blessed by the stars, because the people here would never starve. Even when fishing grew scarce, they could simply dig for clams and catch crabs right beneath their piers.

The tide was up now, and Shilo could see dark shapes moving in the shadows of her family's dock and boats. Most of those were whiskerfish, which had a decent taste but were not popular outside of Palmoor. She looked up at the *Windlacer*. Their neighbors had always said it was too grand a name for a simple fishing vessel, but Shilo's father had named it, and she was proud of their boat. It was in a sorry state now, with the sails and rigging all taken down and the mast removed. Her brothers were hard at work making a replacement for the cracked mast down at the village's communal shipyard.

Shilo looked at her hands. She still couldn't believe she had done that. Her fingers were calloused from working with ropes, wood, and nets, but she had the smallest hands in her family. Even her little brother Lou's mitts dwarfed hers. Yet she'd sent a grown man flying with a single punch. The explanation was simple: She had manifested a gifting as a Flame Weaver, which meant her days at sea had come to an end.

The dock groaned and swayed. Shilo glanced back to see her Papa walking toward her. She looked back down at her own reflection. His image appeared beside hers, and he squeezed in next to her, sitting on the edge of the dock. From the corner of her eye, she saw him extend his hand, palm up. Reluctantly, she held out her hand, and his large fingers engulfed hers. Papa's broad shoulders and powerful hands had always embodied strength and stability in her mind. Yet, now, if she could learn to control her gift, she would be the stronger one. It made her want to laugh, but she did not. Instead, she sat and stared at the water. Papa said nothing. He was a patient man.

At last, Shilo sighed. "I am sorry, Papa," she said.

"Hmm," he said after a moment's consideration. "What do you have to be sorry for? You are sorry for saving my life and the lives of your brothers?"

She shook her head. "You and the boys could have fought those pirates. I almost sunk the *Windlacer*."

"Ah, but you didn't. A boat can be replaced, but none of my children can."

"I didn't even know what I was doing. It just… happened."

He fell silent for a few moments. Finally, he said, "You know I am a Wave Weaver, yes?"

She nodded. "Yes, Papa." She'd always known he had the gift, but as far as she knew, he never used it.

"Well, truth be told, I am useless at Weaving. I'm probably the weakest Weaver there is. Even the simplest of wards were a struggle for me. I gave up even trying years ago, before I was married."

She looked at her father. She had never known that part. He was looking out at the sea now.

"It does help me to be a better fisherman, though. All Wave Weavers have an affinity for the water. Why do you think your old man is so good at navigating currents and predicting the weather?"

She shrugged. "Experience, I thought."

"That helps too. But there is something to be said for natural talent. We had your older brothers tested, but none of them have the gift. Your mother and I think Lou might have it. The boy took to the water like a fish. He's not old enough for the testing though."

Shilo frowned. She knew why she had never been tested for Wave. She had no affinity for the sea. Perhaps she now knew why.

Papa squeezed her hand. "I know you've been hard on yourself lately, for not being as good of a sailor as you would like. It is good that this happened. We now know where your true talents lie. That Etching of yours is truly powerful. You will be a great Flame Weaver."

Shilo kept her eyes on the horizon. She spoke in a quiet voice. "I never wanted to be a Weaver. I only ever wanted to be a fisherman like you, Papa."

He clicked his tongue. "Ah, the world has enough fishermen. I'll tell you what it doesn't have though."

"What?"

"Shilo Lorn."

She rolled her eyes.

"You are destined for greatness, my daughter."

"What will I even do? I've never even considered life away from the water."

"Well, you must figure that out for yourself. Very few are born with strong giftings like yours, and it can open many doors for you. You could go to Lon's Watch and become a Scholar. You are a smart girl, after all. Many Flame Weavers do join the Standing Army, of course. You are certainly brave enough for that. Or you could join the Watchkeepers. Your heart of compassion would serve you well there."

"That's a lot of options."

"Well, take all the time you need to decide." He paused. "While you do though, I'm afraid you must stay shore bound. What happened was not your fault. Flame Weaving is fueled by dried wood or coal. But the *Windlacer*, well, she is all wood."

Shilo nodded. Until she learned to control her power, she would be an even greater liability at sea. She looked at her free hand. She wanted to understand her gift, though she was a little afraid of it. "Whatever I do," she said, "I want to find a way to help people."

Shilo and her father sat in silence, watching the undulating sea as the tide slowly ebbed.

Ryn awoke in the gray morning light. The air hung thick and warm around him. A faint breeze carried a putrid smell. Someone had moved him to one of the bedrolls near the wagon. The campfire was now a smoldering bed of ashes, but an even larger blaze had been kindled further up the road. The heat and the smell emanated from that bonfire. Ryn's head felt fuzzy, and he lay staring at the gray sky for another minute.

A number of sounds echoed in the periphery of his awareness. Suddenly, he realized what they were and what they meant. Birdsong. The woods, which had stood silent for nearly a week, now echoed with the trills and warbles of birds. He picked out the calls of wrens and orange-bellied robins, mixed with the screeches of jays.

He sat up, taking his bearings. Nyssa and Pavel moved around the camp, readying the horses. While he'd slept through the night, they had been busy cleaning up the battlefield. He gazed again at the bonfire, built in the center of the road a hundred paces away. Leaned against the flaming pile of wood were over a dozen charred and lumpy forms, the bodies of the Kobolds. That explained the smell. It took Ryn a moment to discover what had become of the four slain Watchkeepers, but then he spotted four large bundles made from blankets and bedrolls piled in the wagon's iron cage. Ryn sat up. He saw a ceramic canteen had been placed beside his bedroll. He drank greedily from it.

Seeing that Ryn was awake, Pavel came over and looked down at him. "How are you feeling, kid?" The thief had changed his ruined black shirt for a gray one, which had to have come from a dead Watchkeeper's wardrobe. He wore his shoulder harness with his two blades sheathed and his satchel slung over his shoulder. He dug his hand into the bag and pulled out a chunk of bread, which he shoved into his mouth. He seemed to have regained an appetite.

"I'm all right," Ryn said. He watched as Pavel followed up the bread with a large piece of cheese.

Noticing Ryn's stare, Pavel grinned around a mouthful of food. Swallowing, he said, "I forget how little you know sometimes. This is how an Aether Weaver refuels. I can't drain energy from the forest like you can."

The quickly rising sun illuminated the dead trees lining the road on both sides. Shriveled black vegetation clung to the verge of the woods. Ryn must have killed these plants when he healed Nyssa and Pavel. Periodically, a bird would alight on one of the desiccated tree branches, and even that little added weight was enough for the limbs to snap and fall to the ground. Those occasional thuds added to the general din. Forest sounds had always just been background noise to Ryn, but they seemed gratingly loud now after so many days of silence. He hoped that meant whatever Kobolds were still alive were no longer in the area. The thought of that tall black-clad monster sent a chill up his spine.

Nyssa appeared from around the side of the wagon. She'd just finished hitching up the two horses that would pull it. She leaned against the side closest to Ryn and sighed. Her face and her slumping shoulders showed clear signs of weariness. A sleepless night moving bodies—including those of her fallen comrades—had taken its toll. Ryn sat up fully, crossing his legs. She regarded him and Pavel with a level look.

"The question becomes," she said, "what do I do with the two of you?"

Pavel crossed his arms and cocked his head. "Do you still intend to see us tried in Thorpe?"

Nyssa shrugged. "I consider that a lost cause at this point. You have me at a disadvantage, since Aether trumps Wave. The way you were leaping about last night, I doubt I could catch you if I tried."

"We are agreed on that point," Pavel said.

Ryn studied the thief from the corner of his eye. Why was Pavel still here? After the way Pavel had manipulated Ryn, he had assumed that the man only did things that aligned with his own self-interest. Fighting the Kobolds could be attributed to self-preservation, but why had he not slipped away once the fighting was over?

"I have a proposition," Nyssa said. "I think we can come to a mutually beneficial arrangement. But first, I have a few questions. Primarily, I need to know why the Kobolds didn't touch you." She leveled that question and a finger at Ryn. "I've heard some sketchy reports of humans working with the Kobolds, but I've never put much faith in them."

Ryn shook his head. "I don't know why they didn't kill me. I certainly don't work for them."

"I think I might know why," Pavel said.

Ryn and Nyssa looked to him.

"Tell her about your Etching, kid, and how it first manifested."

In a few sentences, Ryn related the story of his first encounter with the Kobolds, getting injured, and waking up healed. Once he got going, he told her everything, including the death of Marla and meeting Pavel and Corvus. He even explained why they'd found him in the spring and how Pavel had talked him into trying to steal the Runeform. Pavel looked away and shifted his feet uncomfortably at that part, but he didn't interrupt.

Nyssa nodded along as she listened, an unreadable expression on her face. When Ryn finished, she seemed to mull it over for a moment. "Self-healing," she said, "and the fact that it seemed to happen automatically... That's a powerful Etching." She looked back at Pavel. "But it doesn't explain why the Kobolds wouldn't try to kill him this time."

"Well, consider what happened to your Root Weaver... to Tabbot," Pavel said.

She frowned.

"She collapsed before the Kobolds attacked. Her only injury was that scratch on her arm. That's what killed her."

Nyssa slowly nodded. "Poison," she said. "The creatures' claws must be poisoned, and somehow it's resistant to Rootbalm."

"Right. Now twice when we've been attacked and I was locked in that cage with Ryn, one of the Kobolds went after me, but they ignored the kid. This is just speculation, but the kid got scratched too the first time around. They carry weapons, but those creatures go out of their way to get their claws into you. They know if their blades can't kill you, the poison eventually will. It must work pretty quick too. I think Tabbot only made it a full day because of the Rootbalm. That's why the big one didn't bother to finish us off last night. We were already dead as far as he was concerned."

"She must have known," Nyssa said. "Tabbot must have known something was wrong with her and that she might not make it to Thorpe. That's why she was so eager to train Ryn. She must have hoped he would be able to heal her." She slowly shook her head and added under her breath, "Why didn't she tell me…"

That made sense to Ryn. He remembered all those nervous looks and hasty glances to the south. The Root Weaver's death laid heaviest on him. The men had mostly ignored him, but she had gone out of her way to treat him with kindness and teach him to Weave. He wondered how Nyssa must be feeling. How long had her Pentad been together? They must have formed close bonds, and now she was the only one left. Ryn wished he could have used his gift to save the others.

Nyssa looked back at Pavel. "Are you saying the Kobolds last night knew that Ryn had already been scratched? How?"

Pavel shrugged. "Clearly Ryn's Etching was able to purge the poison, or else he wouldn't still be breathing, but perhaps there's still a trace of it in him. Maybe the Kobolds can smell it or sense it somehow. They all ignored Tabbot as well, and she was still breathing when the attacks started."

Nyssa sighed. "It's as good an explanation as any, I suppose. Ryn doesn't strike me as the kind of person who would work with the Kobolds anyway. I don't know what sort of lowlife would, but it's not him. If you're right, then hopefully you and I don't need to worry about another attack either. I don't feel like I'm dying, so Ryn must have purged the poison from us too."

Pavel nodded in agreement. When Ryn Dowsed them, he had not detected anything that felt like poison, but he barely understood what he was doing at the time, and he had not examined each of the red threads in any detail.

Nyssa looked back and forth between Pavel and Ryn, studying their faces. "I suppose I'm just going to have to trust you two," she said. She looked at the bundled bodies in the back of her wagon. "I have to transport them to the Thorpe outpost and make a full report. The Kobolds are here in greater numbers than we anticipated. We still know so little about them and their motives. Three years ago, I thought they were only myths. We can either part ways here, or you two can come with me to Thorpe."

Pavel scratched his chin. "Look, Nyssa, I truly do sympathize for what happened to your men. That's why I stayed and helped you... clean up. And I needed to keep an eye on the kid." He jerked his head toward Ryn. "But in all seriousness, why would I possibly hand myself over to the Watchkeepers?"

"A fair question. You certainly could run and take Ryn with you if you like. I'd advise keeping a low profile. You are still a wanted man, and I will have to mention you in my report. That will make the Watchkeepers even more keen to track you down, not only to see you stand trial but also for your firsthand testimony of Kobold activities."

He shrugged. "That's not so bad. If they want an interview, I can use that as leverage, should they ever catch up to me."

"Yes, you certainly could keep running. You are talented at it. But if you come with me, I can offer you something far more worthwhile: a fresh start."

Pavel laughed. "Not likely. What, I tell them what I know about the Kobolds, and they just forget about my... alleged crimes?"

"There's a little bit more to the arrangement, but I've seen the higher-ups make deals with men who had far more illustrious criminal careers than you, Pavel Talvor. If I can't get you amnesty, then I promise I'll help you break out of custody myself."

"So, what's the catch then? What's that 'little bit more'?"

"Oh, you'd have to enlist with the Watchkeepers."

Pavel laughed louder this time. "You're joking! Me, join the Gray Guard?"

"I know, it would be a change, but just think it over." She turned to Ryn. "It would be a great opportunity for you too. From what you've told me, it doesn't sound like there's much left for you in these woods, and they won't be safe until we can send up a whole legion of Watchkeepers. If you want to help people, if you want to use your gift to make a difference, join the Watchkeepers."

Ryn stared up at her, not sure what to think. For the last few days, he hadn't thought about much beyond surviving. He wondered what had happened in Aen's Hollow. Had more Kobolds attacked the village? He had to get out of here, and Nyssa gave him that chance. He knew little about the Watchkeepers, other than that they helped keep peace in Aldria. The Standing Army dealt with external threats, like raids from Tamor or Silgaria, while the Gray Guard, as he'd sometimes heard them called, dealt with internal issues, which apparently included Kobolds. Part of him never wanted to see another Kobold again, but another part of him wanted to find a way to fight back. The Watchkeepers were Weavers, but they knew how to use weapons as well. If he could get that kind of training, he could fight too. He wouldn't be helpless. He wouldn't have to just stand by and watch good men and women be slaughtered. He didn't know what Pavel would say, but he knew his answer.

Chapter 10
Negotiations

JAYN ELDRAGOR SAT with her mother in the front parlor of the family's country estate, the same room where she had failed her test for Flame. She had since taken the test for Wave and passed. It wasn't the gift she or her mother had been hoping for, but she was a Weaver. She still had a bright future; she just needed a new trajectory.

Her mother sipped her tea from a delicate porcelain cup. Everyone always remarked over how much Jayn resembled her mother, but she lacked Anyse Eldragor's poise and presence. When Anyse Eldragor walked into a room, she commanded it, drawing everyone's attention with a look. The maids and footmen were all a little afraid of her. In her mother's presence, Jayn was still a child. The woman had high cheekbones and piercing blue eyes, while the girl had a rounder face, still puffed with what her mother called "baby fat," and paler, nearly gray eyes.

Anyse Eldragor wore an elegant black dress, cinched at the waist, with a straight neckline. Jayn's parents were to have dinner that evening with their neighbors, the Larkens. Lord Rory Larken was an influential member of the Hall of the Assembly. She'd squeezed in this appointment with her daughter between a visit to Appencourt and the dinner. Jayn had been informed of the meeting via her maid.

Jayn wore a simple blue dress, hemmed at the knees, with short puffy sleeves. She'd been wearing a lot of blue lately, and not merely because it complemented her eyes. She knew this talk would be about her future. Jayn had come to a decision on that topic, but she doubted her mother's new vision would match hers. No, this would not be a meeting, but a negotiation. Jayn was not sat across from her mother, but General Anyse Eldragor, Fourth Pentarch of Aldria, and the girl would need to keep her wits about her to win this confrontation.

Anyse Eldragor set down her teacup. "Now, Jayn," she said, "I know you have always wished to enlist in the Standing Army."

"Yes, Mother," Jayn said. She would be polite and listen, waiting for the right opening.

"Certainly, you still could. Very few Wave Weavers enlist, but it is not unheard of. Eloise Munroe, who was Fourth Pentarch before me, she had a son who enlisted. He was a Wave Weaver and served our country admirably. However, the Army does not seek out that kind of skill. In effect, you would be on the same footing as a non-Weaver."

Jayn nodded. When it came to Weavers, the Standing Army was only interested in Flame and Root Weavers. Root Weavers made excellent medics, but Flame Weavers were more highly prized. Even an average Flame Weaver was as good as ten regular soldiers. The gift was too rare for any nation to construct an entire army solely from Weavers, so most soldiers couldn't wield any of the Five Forces. The ungifted rarely advanced high up the ranks, however.

"No," Anyse continued, "you must accept that you have manifested as a Wave Weaver. I admit, it came as a surprise to your father and me. We haven't a single Wave Weaver in our lineage, but these things do happen. Given this new reality, I'm afraid your talents would not be properly utilized in the Army."

"Yes, Mother."

It hurt to hear, but Jayn had accepted this fact as well. She consoled herself by remembering that the Army was only ever meant to be a steppingstone. The ultimate goal was still election to the Hall of the Assembly and then appointment to the Pentarchy. There were many paths that could take her there, though she hated that she would never experience the rush of commanding soldiers in battle.

"Indeed," her mother continued, "there are many far more promising options for a talented Wave Weaver. Lady Kairn assures me that you tested well above average, and that peculiar Etching of yours points to that as well."

It had taken some convincing to get her parents to believe that Jayn had turned herself invisible. She didn't yet know how to do it on command.

"Consider your possibilities here in Appencourt. The Hall of the Assembly always has need of Wardens, and you could make many political connections that way. Alternatively, you could join the Appencourt Guild and receive training there. They provide an invaluable service to the people. Then there is the city guard. The captain of the guard himself is a Wave Weaver and well respected in the city."

Jayn nodded, pretending to mull over each option. Her mother made it seem like each one had merit, but Jayn knew that Anyse

Eldragor had already decided on the correct path for her daughter. It worried Jayn that her mother had not even mentioned Jayn's new preference. This would not be easy, but she wasn't about to give up.

"Personally, I believe the Guild is your best option," her mother said. "It will allow you to mix with all echelons and make a name for yourself in the business world. Many former Pentarchs were Guildsmen."

Jayn's heart sank, but she didn't let it show on her face. Of everything she thought her mother might pick, that was the worst. A career making the same wards against thieves over and over for the same shops and homes? Sure, it would be lucrative, and she could gain reputation in the capital, but joining the Guild sounded so banal and tedious compared to the Army. Jayn still had a chance. She would test how well her mother had trained her in diplomacy and military strategy.

General Anyse Eldragor smiled, a political smile that never touched her eyes. "What do you think, Jayn?"

Jayn did her best to pause and look thoughtful before responding. "Yes, Mother, I too have been considering how best to utilize my gift." *Never answer a direct question in a political debate*, her mother's own advice echoed in her head. "There is certainly much to be gained by joining the Appencourt Guild. It would be a productive way to serve our nation." *In a negotiation, conceding the validity of your opponent's claims encourages cooperation.* "I feel it is the obligation of the first echelon to improve the lives of those beneath them. That's why I had hoped to join the Standing Army, not to seek glory, but to serve and defend all of Aldria." *Find common ground where you can.* "The Army would have afforded me the opportunity to see more of our great country, beyond the walls of Appencourt. You are an inspiration to me, Mother, and if I hope to be as great of a Pentarch as you someday, I need to learn everything I can about our land." *Flattery never hurts*, and Jayn was telling the truth. "I fear that by joining the Guild, I would be narrowing my focus too much. Yes, I would understand the ways and the needs of the capital, but Aldria is more than just Appencourt. A good Pentarch must understand the needs of the Sylphren woodcutters and how they differ from the needs of the coastal fishermen or the Flint Hills coalminers. I believe a posting outside the capital would ultimately be more beneficial."

Her mother nodded, considering. "Well put, Jayn. And what would you suggest, if not the Guild?"

Jayn kept her voice even. This was a crucial step. "Well, Mother, if I wanted to learn more about Aldria's people, its culture, and its history, as well as Weaving, then perhaps the best place to do that would be the Academy of the Ways."

Her mother's eyebrows rose a fraction of an inch, her only sign of surprise. "The Scholars? That is a novel idea. However, you must consider the drawbacks to such a path. While the Scholars' work has benefited our nation, the Scholars themselves are far too removed from the world. You know they consider themselves as independent from Aldria. They believe politics to be beneath them. No, I'm afraid if you aspire to join the Hall of the Assembly, joining the Academy of the Ways will not get you there."

Jayn hid her smile by taking a sip from her own teacup. *Your first proposal should never be your true goal. Give your opponent something you know they'll say no to, and it will be easier to get the yes for what you really want.* Jayn carefully set down her teacup, nodding. "You raise a valid point, Mother. Simply acquiring knowledge is not enough. I need practical, real-world experiences. I need to be out in the republic, interacting with all manner of people." She took a deep breath. She hoped it would seem like the idea had only just come to her. "What about… What if I joined the Watchkeepers? They train in all Five Forces and provide a direct service to the entire nation. I would have to wait two more years to join the Army, but I could enlist with the Watchkeepers as early as tomorrow. In many ways, it would give me a head start."

General Anyse Eldragor took another sip of tea and slowly nodded. "That is an idea worth considering."

Jayn knew the negotiations weren't over yet, but that was as close to a "yes" as one could get from the Fourth Pentarch of Aldria in the first round.

"Can you see it now?" Pavel asked.

Ryn shook his head. He could see nothing emanating from Pavel.

They were waiting in a windowless interior room of the Thorpe Watchkeeper outpost. Nyssa had left them in there over an hour ago, while she debriefed the outpost's commander about the Kobolds. It took them a full day of traveling after the slaughter on the road to reach the town of Thorpe, a fishing community on the shores of massive Lake Lagdo. Ryn had not seen much of the town, as they'd arrived after sunset and headed directly for the outpost. The part of town they had passed through consisted entirely of brick buildings with slate roofs, while the Watchkeeper outpost was a two-story stone structure. Candles mounted on copper-backed sconces illuminated the small room, furnished only with uncomfortable wooden chairs and a round oak table. The door had not been locked, but the outpost commander had made it clear they were not to leave until told otherwise.

To pass the time, Pavel attempted to teach Ryn how to view another's Weaving. His explanation had been muddled and confusing. It had something to do with opening yourself up to the possibility of seeing things that were not there, which made absolutely no sense to Ryn. Pavel stood in a corner of the room, away from the chairs and table. Wielding Aether had nothing to do with visualizing a tree of course. Instead, a swirling mass of white lights apparently encircled Pavel.

The thief scratched his chin. He looked to be in need of a shave. "Maybe it's better if you see it in use." Without warning, Pavel jumped into the air, tucked himself into a ball, executed a backflip, and landed on his feet. He raised his arms overhead in a flourish of showmanship.

Ryn frowned. "A couple years ago, a pair of acrobats passed through Aen's Hollow, performing for coins on the village green. They could do tricks like that, but they weren't Aether Weavers."

"Well, we're in a confined space. I can't do anything too spectacular in here."

"Do you have an Etching?"

Pavel shook his head. "No, not everybody gets those. My ability is pretty mediocre, but it's always served me well in my profession."

"As a thief?"

Pavel scoffed. "Treasure hunter, kid. If I have broken any laws, I've never been convicted for it, so I am technically an innocent man, but I guess you're on Nyssa's side now, huh? All it takes is a pretty face and you turn your back on your friend?"

"I never said you were my friend. I hardly know you."

"Well, like it or not, Nyssa has roped us together, so there's no getting rid of me now."

"You could have left. Why did you decide to come along?"

Pavel shrugged. "The lady made a good point. The Gray Guard had my number, and they would have caught up to me eventually.

It beats a jail cell, and they don't keep you forever. I just need to put in my time, get a clean slate, and then I'm back on the road."

"Back to stealing, you mean?"

"Back to adventuring."

Ryn frowned. Pavel was certainly confident and had a charismatic likability, but something about him bothered Ryn. The thief was hiding something.

The door opened with a wooden groan, and Ryn turned toward it. From the corner of his eye, he saw a flicker of white light around Pavel. He glanced back but it was gone. Nyssa entered the room, followed by Commander Lucen Nohl. The head of the Thorpe Outpost was a stout balding man in his middle years. He wore the red pin of a Flame Weaver. He nodded to Ryn and Pavel.

"Are you boys serious in your commitment to join the Watchkeepers?" he asked.

"Yes... sir," Ryn said. Pavel only nodded.

"Then here is the deal. You will accompany Captain Nyssa Lahmeer to Falport to officially enlist and begin training with the Watchkeepers. You will serve for a minimum of five years. Do so and you will not be held responsible for any past... transgressions."

Ryn frowned. He had not broken any laws. Still, joining the Watchkeepers did seem like the best course of action. Nyssa had explained the organization on the ride to Thorpe. They would teach him to use his gift, and they would train him to fight. He wanted to learn how to defend himself even more than he wanted to learn how to Weave. Though he had managed to save Nyssa and Pavel, he still felt entirely too helpless. Another thought came to him. "What about Aen's Hollow?" he asked.

"I've already dispatched all available Pentads into the Sylphren Wood," Lucen said. "I'm confident they will be able to drive out however many Kobolds remain. Don't worry about your village.

It's far more vital that you go with Nyssa to deliver her report to the Citadel."

Ryn nodded.

Pavel cleared his throat. "What about my… belongings?" The thief had been forced to surrender his blades at the outpost.

Lucen nodded. "Wherever you dug those up, no one seems to have reported them missing. Provisionally, we're willing to let you keep them, though that will change if their provenance is proven to be illicit."

Corvus had not followed Pavel into Thorpe, and Ryn did not know if Nyssa had mentioned the Runeform in her report.

Pavel smiled. "I have a right to those weapons under the Law of Salvage. They were recovered from unmarked barrows that predate the Burning."

Ryn did not know what that meant, and Lucen didn't seem convinced. "Well," the man said, "then it shouldn't be a problem. It's a shame the Law of Salvage cannot be applied to all of your alleged acquisitions."

"Alleged being the key word."

Lucen nodded. He turned to go but paused. "Let me make myself clear, Pavel Talvor. If you do not hold to this agreement in good faith or if you 'salvage' anything else while in the employ of the Watchkeepers, then the deal is off and you will be jailed."

Pavel nodded. "On my honor, I promise to serve honorably and faithfully for five years. I am grateful for the opportunity."

Lucen seemed satisfied with that and left. Nyssa remained, studying Pavel with narrowed eyes. She had washed the travel grime and dirt from her face and hands, but a puffiness under her eyes and her sagging shoulders revealed the strain of the past two days.

"I'm taking a chance here with you two," she said. "Don't make me regret it."

Ryn sat awkwardly in the saddle atop a dappled mare. Before yesterday, he had never ridden a horse. He'd had plenty of time to practice on the long ride to Thorpe, but he was still far from confident and already becoming sore. Ryn, Nyssa, and Pavel had been outfitted with different horses after spending the night in the Watchkeeper barracks. They also had a fourth animal, a stout mule, which carried provisions and bedrolls. It walked placidly along behind Nyssa's tall black gelding, a line running from her saddle to the mule's bridle. Pavel rode behind her on another gelding, a brown one with white splotches. Ryn took up the rear, and his horse seemed content to follow the others without much guidance from him.

Ryn and Pavel wore gray Watchkeeper shirts and breeches, though without the tabards. They would get those in Falport, but something else would be required to earn the pins that marked Cadets. Pavel wore his shoulder harnesses, the bladecatcher and bladebreaker forming an X on his back. Ryn wore his aunt's satchel, though he hadn't had a chance to refill the ceramic canisters. His knife and his trowel hung at his side. He felt glad knowing his training as an herbalist would still aid him as a Root Weaver. He wondered how Marla would feel about all this. He shook his head. He tried not to dwell on his losses too much, though the gruesome scene in the root cellar had appeared more than once in his troubled dreams the night before. He yawned and patted the mare's neck. He did not know the horse's name but had privately taken to calling her Foxfeathers.

They rode south along the hardpacked road out of Thorpe. The early morning sun cast long shadows across the rolling Koathing Plains to the east. The Sylphren Wood came to an abrupt end at Thorpe, though a few copses still dotted the landscape. Here and there rocky ridges emerged from the soil to run for a few hundred paces before plunging back into the dirt. The plains were far from barren, however; a dense layer of heath covered most of it, along with squat bushes and sprawling purple heather and red snakevine. It was beautiful, though wholly different from the cluttered and ancient woods Ryn thought of as home.

The road clung to the banks of Lake Lagdo, and though the sprawling town of Thorpe had fallen from view, this part of the lake was still clustered with small red and green fishing boats, trawling the lake with large nets. They rode at a steady pace without talking for most of the morning. Nyssa wore a brave face, but Ryn caught glimpses of the strain behind that mask from time to time. She was still grieving the loss of her Pentad, but having a new mission to focus on seemed to help. Even the usually loquacious Pavel kept silent, though his head stayed on a swivel as they rode, and Ryn didn't think he was merely taking in the scenery.

Ryn, a good ten years younger than his traveling companions, lacked the confidence to strike up a conversation, though he was brimming with questions about Weaving and what to expect in Falport. It would take them at least a week of traveling to reach the Watchkeepers' Citadel. There would be time for questions later.

So, the morning passed in silence, as did their stop for lunch and water. Toward evening, the lake fell away as the road curved slightly to the east. At their pace, Nyssa informed them, it would take another two days of riding to reach the next town, a place at the intersection of two major roadways called Fivewells. For the first time, Ryn realized how sparsely populated this corner of Aldria was. He knew most of the wood and coal coming from the north was put aboard boats in Thorpe and floated down to Nadell, but enough traffic traveled this road to surely justify at least a few inns along the way. On top of that, why were there two days of empty road between Aen's Hollow and Thorpe? Today they had passed by a handful of isolated homesteads and through the stony ruins of ancient villages, but that was it. The region seemed too empty, like a whole host of people had gone missing. A thousand years on, had the land still not fully recovered from the Burning? More questions he could not ask now.

They stopped to make camp with an hour of daylight left. Nyssa led them off the roadway a short distance, reining in her gelding once they reached a ridge that curved around in a nearly complete circle. It was like a hollowed-out hill, sheltering a miniature valley in its center, accessible only through a gap a few paces wide where the two ends of the curving rock failed to connect. Ryn saw its usefulness as a campsite, and indeed a heap of ashes stood at the center of the dirt bowl, the accumulated remnants of previous travelers' fires. The steep rocky walls protected them from the chilly night winds, the last vestige of winter, and while a dedicated assailant could climb up over the ridge, they could not do so without making noise.

Ryn managed to dismount without falling. He watched and imitated what Nyssa and Pavel did in unsaddling and tending to the horses. They fitted the horses and the mule with oat-filled feedbags, built a fire, and ate their dinner largely in silence.

Afterward, Pavel stood and stretched. The sun had set by then. The only sound besides the wind was the gentle thrumming of crickets. He looked down at Nyssa, who sat staring into the flickering fire. "Are you going to put up that shield of yours?" he asked.

She nodded. "In a minute."

Ryn looked back and forth between the two of them. "What sort of shield?" he asked.

Pavel cocked his head, as if in question, but then seemed to answer it on his own. "Ah," he said, "I guess you were pretty much out of it the last time. She set one up that night we spent on the road after…" He coughed. "Nyssa here has an Etching."

Nyssa shrugged. "Shields are one of the most common sorts of Etching among Wave Weavers, and any of them can make a shield by Blending in Stone. And a few well-placed lacings of Aether could easily unravel it."

"Yeah, but I haven't seen any shields as strong as yours." He turned to Ryn and grinned. "Once she has that set up, it'll be like a brick wall. If there are any Kobolds this far south, they'll smack right into it if they try climbing in here."

A faint smile crossed her lips as she looked up at the thief. "You're worried about Kobolds? They couldn't possibly be this far south. We'd know if they were. And besides, if your theory is correct, we won't have to worry either way. We're already poisoned, as far as they're concerned."

He shrugged. "Better safe than dead, I always say. It could be that faint trace of poison that protected Ryn will eventually fade from our systems. I stand by my hypothesis, but I'm not eager to test it either."

Nyssa held her waterskin up to Pavel. "If it will help you sleep, I'll set the shield, but I'll need some more water. There should be a stream a hundred paces south of here. You can't miss it."

Pavel hesitated, glancing out through the opening in the rocky circle into the night. Then he nodded, took up the waterskin, and set out on his own. Nyssa watched him go until he disappeared from sight. Then her gaze returned to the fire.

Ryn wondered why she needed water, but it soon made sense to him. "Water is how you refuel, isn't it?" he asked.

She nodded, glancing at him. "Yes. Unlike the other three forces, Wave and Aether Weavers, like Pavel and me, cannot use external fuels. The food that would go to fueling his body gets burned up by Aether when he exerts himself too much, and Wave draws the very moisture from my body. In many ways, it is the trickiest force to wield. You can't use it haphazardly, or you'll endanger your health. Many of the lacings, like my shield, take a minute or two to create. Given time and preparation, it can be formidable, but in the heat of battle, it is often useless."

"That's why you've trained with the sword as well, right?"

"Every Watchkeeper learns to fight without Weaving. To rely too much on your gift is a mistake. Even though you can drain the plants around you as fuel, Root Weaving still takes its toll on your body. There is a limit, and when you reach it, you'll have only your own physical strength to defend yourself."

Ryn nodded. He must have gone over his limit the other night when he healed Nyssa and Pavel. That's why he collapsed.

Nyssa stood up and walked closer to Ryn. She gestured for him to stand too. They were about equal in height. "I'm a poor Root Weaver," she said, "but it is complementary to Wave, so I can show you a thing or two while we are on the road. We don't need to wait till Falport to begin your training."

Ryn nodded. "All right," he said.

"First, I think we should try to get a better understanding of your Etching. Give me your knife."

His eyebrows rose. "Why?" he asked, taking a step back.

She said nothing and merely stood with her hand extended and a look on her face that showed she expected to be obeyed. Reluctantly, he pulled his knife from his belt and held it out to her. She took the knife with one hand but grabbed his wrist with the other. "Hold still," she said.

Before Ryn could ask what she was doing, Nyssa pressed the edge of the knife against the palm of his hand and made a shallow cut. He winced, jerking his hand away. She pulled a handkerchief from her shirt pocket and held it out to him, her expression calm, as if she had just done something completely normal.

"What was that for?" he asked, looking at the line of blood welling up in his palm. It stung but was only a minor wound.

When he did not take the proffered handkerchief, she seemed to grow impatient. She handed him back his knife, then grabbed his wounded hand, wrapping the gray cloth around it and tying the ends together. A dark stain began to form on the improvised bandage.

"We have to test your Etching," she said. "If you are going to heal yourself, you need an injury."

He scoffed. "I don't know how I did that. It was only the one time. Maybe it only activated because my life was in danger. You have no way of knowing this will work."

She shrugged. "That's why we're testing it. It's just a scratch. Keep checking the wound and let me know the moment it heals, if it does."

"Fine, but just ask me next time. You want to know how my Etching works? How do you think I feel? And why did you cut my hand? There are so many less painful places."

"You're right," she said, seeming to concede a little. "I'm sorry."

He sighed, putting away his knife and sitting back near the fire. He cradled his wounded hand with his other one. The cut on his palm pulsed slightly but the pain had diminished. He was still annoyed Nyssa had done it without asking, but he was also genuinely curious to see what would happen now. He glanced at Nyssa. "Should I visualize the seed and the tree?" he asked.

She shook her head. "We can try that another time. I want to see first if we can get it to work automatically."

He nodded. He could tell by the dull throbbing that the wound was still there. By the time they bedded down for the night, the bleeding had stopped, but that was just normal clotting. The wound had not yet healed as he drifted off to sleep.

Chapter 11
Fivewells

WHEN RYN AWOKE in the gray light of morning, his hand had healed. He peeled off the blood-stained cloth to reveal a smooth, unblemished palm. He wasn't sure when during the night it had happened. He vaguely remembered waking up once, troubled by some shadowy nightmare involving Kobolds and squealing pigs. He'd been too groggy then to check his bandage. He'd drifted back to sleep soon enough, dimly aware of the sounds of crickets and someone sobbing.

He realized now that had been Nyssa. By the light of dawn, she seemed fine, bustling about preparing breakfast. Pavel was still sound asleep in his bedroll, snoring faintly. Corvus stood in the dirt beside him, pecking at something on the ground. Apparently, the Runeform had returned sometime in the night, having disappeared right before they entered Thorpe. Ryn wondered where the creature had been. He didn't have to wonder what had caused Nyssa to cry. The loss of her fellow Watchkeepers was still a fresh wound. He didn't know how she was able to put up such a brave front in the daytime.

Seeing him awake, she paused in her work to offer a smile. He held up his healed hand to show her. She nodded. "Very nice," she said.

"I wonder if it only works when I'm asleep?" Ryn said. "The first time, I passed out pretty quickly after I was wounded."

"We'll have to keep testing. Give yourself another cut, and we'll see if it heals as we ride."

Ryn sighed. It made sense, but he still wouldn't enjoy it. He fetched his knife out from his belt, lying with his satchel by his bedroll. He chose a spot on the back of his forearm, far less sensitive than his palm and easy to monitor. He made a shallow cut. Holding the soiled handkerchief to it for a minute staunched the bleeding, leaving a thin red line that stung only a little and was easy enough to ignore.

They soon struck camp and were back on the road. Ryn was still sore and stiff from the previous day's ride, but he found a puffblossom bush near the stream when he went to refill his waterskin. If he'd had a kettle, he could have made a proper tea out of it, but just chewing the leaves helped alleviate sore muscles. He filled two canisters of his satchel with extra leaves.

The hardpacked road wended south across the rolling plains, arcing slightly to the east. To the west, a forest arose, though it never came within a few hundred paces of the roadway. If the woods had a name, Ryn didn't know it. They saw little on the second day out of Thorpe, beyond the occasional small farm nestled among the ridges. The farmers out sowing their fields barely looked up as Ryn and his companions rode past. Travelers were common enough on this road, but perhaps the locals would have taken more notice if they'd spotted the strange bird-like creature perched on Pavel's shoulder.

When the sun reached its zenith, they stopped to rest the horses and eat. As he scrambled off his horse, Ryn noticed the red mark on his arm had vanished. He'd been checking it periodically throughout the day, riding with his sleeve rolled up. He'd seen no progress in healing, but now suddenly it was gone. He frowned. Such a minor cut, and yet it had taken about six hours to heal. He knew even that was miraculous, but it wasn't very practical.

He shared his concerns with Nyssa. She shrugged. "From what you told me of the first time it activated and the severity of your wounds then, your Etching had to have worked much quicker. You would have bled out in minutes. It probably healed you as soon as you passed out, and then you slept for a couple hours while your body regained its energy. Maybe the rate at which you heal is proportional to the severity of the injury. A minor cut is no threat to your life, so healing it is a lower priority."

Corvus, who'd been perching on the pommel of Pavel's saddle, squawked. "You should stab him!" the bird said.

Nyssa and Ryn glanced at the Runeform. That was the first time all day it had spoken. Pavel grinned at the creature's suggestion. Nyssa shook her head. "Let's not risk anything serious, at least not until we're at the Citadel with other Root Weavers around."

Ryn frowned. "Thanks," he said, worried that she had apparently already considered the idea of seriously wounding him to test his Etching.

They continued on their journey, stopping at sunset to spend another night on the plains. The sky grew cloudy to the east, but thankfully it never rained. Ryn had cut himself again after lunch. He had a small scar on his left arm from his own brush with a sourthorn bush years ago. Curious to see what would happen, he made the fresh cut along that scar. It only took two hours that time to heal, and when it did, the old scar vanished.

He felt tired that evening, but no more than he expected to be after the third straight day of riding. His Etching seemed to use little energy to stitch up his small cuts. It didn't use any fuel either; he'd seen no sudden decay in the surrounding heath, and the cuttings in his satchel had not turned to dust. He'd recognized several helpful plants throughout the day and taken the time to restock his canisters. He had seen no foxfeathers, however; they didn't seem to grow here.

He continued his routine through the next day as well. Every time his cut healed, he made another one, alternating arms. Some he made deeper and had to bandage to staunch the bleeding. He timed the healing as best he could. He felt no sensations when the wounds did heal. One moment they were there, and the next they were gone. He had not actually seen it happen. The times varied with no apparent pattern. It took anywhere from half an hour to six full hours, and the size of the wound had no correlation to how long it took to heal.

Nyssa assured him all Weavers could learn to wield their Etchings deliberately, though he would likely need to work with a master Root Weaver to learn that skill. She herself had no problem creating her powerful Etching shields, though it did take a solid minute.

That second evening outside of Thorpe, Pavel and Ryn had played around with the shield. Apparently, Pavel could see it, marked by a thin line of blue light running in a circle around their camp. Ryn saw nothing, but he could touch it. It felt almost like glass, though his hands slid off it and couldn't find a firm purchase when he tried to push against it. Throwing his weight against the invisible wall caused him to rebound in the same way jumping into a tree would. While the shield was up, no one could cross it from the inside or the outside. It made an effective wall and an effective prison. Pavel assured Ryn he could destroy it from either side with a few lacings of Aether, but he didn't because the shield took a lot out of Nyssa, and he didn't want her to have to create one again needlessly. Every time she put the shield up, Nyssa took long sips from her waterskin to rehydrate herself. Strangely, Corvus could flit back and forth through the shield with no effect on either the lacings or the Runeform. Neither Nyssa nor Pavel knew how the creature managed that, but then again, no one even knew how Runeforms had been made in the first place.

The travelers spoke little during the three days it took to reach Fivewells from Thorpe. Ryn, who had never spent this much time with anyone beside his aunt and Anya—and his long-dead, half-remembered parents—still felt awkward and shy around the two adults and made few attempts at conversation. Nyssa seemed like a serious and quiet person, or at least the loss of her Pentad had made her one. Pavel had also become less talkative since Thorpe. Perhaps he was regretting his decision to join the Watchkeepers and was looking for a chance to escape.

Signs of human habitation increased the closer they got to Fivewells, as did traffic on the road. They overtook a few wagons carrying wood and coal from the north. Those shipments had left before the trouble with the Kobolds started. Finally, on the evening of the third day, with the sun hanging low in the west, as the road crested a gentle hill, the town of Fivewells came into view.

Two intersecting roads cut the town into four sections, and each quarter was larger than all of Aen's Hollow. Thorpe had been a large town as well, but Ryn had seen little of it, arriving after dark and departing early the next day. The streets of this town bustled with people, more than he had ever remembered seeing in one place, even on a Market Day. The buildings, all of stone or brick, were larger too, many reaching two or three stories in height. The noise seemed deafening after the comparative silence of the open road.

Nyssa led them to the center of the town. People moved quickly through the streets, on their way home or to one of the town's several taverns. Few were on horseback, but the three travelers in Watchkeeper gray attracted little attention, though Corvus garnered a few stares from those who noticed him perched on Pavel's shoulder. Fivewells saw a lot of traffic, positioned along two of Aldria's busiest thoroughfares. The roads west and south led to coastal ports, and the eastern road ran directly to the capital, Appencourt, after passing through Savo.

A large open square dominated the center of town, what in smaller villages might be called the green, but the trampling of hundreds of feet each day prevented anything green from growing here, except a narrow band of grass around the round stone well at the center of the open space. Nyssa reined in her gelding and scanned the square. Four different inns stood in each of the four corners, and she was apparently deciding which one looked more favorable.

Pavel, however, steered his mount toward the well. Ryn allowed his mare to follow. The structure looked quite simple, built out of river rocks and cemented together by some gray mortar. A conical wooden roof covered the well, and a few people stood beside it, waiting their turn to fill their buckets, using a rope and pulley to move a strange-looking stone vessel up and down the well.

Pavel gestured around the square. "In each corner of the town there is another well, making five total. Hence the name."

Ryn nodded, watching a middle-aged woman fill her bucket. The water sparkled in the fading evening light.

"It may not look it," Pavel said, "but this well is actually a Runeform."

Ryn glanced sideways at the thief to see if he was serious.

Pavel nodded. "All five wells are. More than a thousand years and they've never run dry, never been destroyed. Wars over the centuries have razed this town half a dozen times, but the wells still stand. Each time the town was destroyed, the wells attracted new settlements. Fivewells is the name of the Runeform more than it is the name of the town."

"Wow," Ryn said. "What do they do?"

He shrugged. "As far as anyone knows, they're just wells. They probably purify the water, not unlike that Runeform in Aen's Hollow."

Pavel's knowledge of this place implied he had been here before, which raised a question. "Have you ever tried stealing one of these wells?" Ryn asked.

Pavel laughed. He turned his horse to ride back toward Nyssa. As he did, he muttered, as if to himself, "They're impossible to move."

When they got back to Nyssa, Pavel pointed to the inn at the northwest corner of the square. "If you're not sure where we should spend the night," he said, "I've always liked that place."

Nyssa narrowed her eyes. She seemed to be wondering whether Pavel's endorsement meant they shouldn't stay there, but eventually she shrugged and squeezed her knees to get her horse back in motion. They headed for Pavel's inn, a redbrick three-story building, with light and music pouring out from the swinging double doors. A painted sign above the entrance read, "The Sixth

Well," and depicted liquid flowing from a large barrel into a glass mug.

Nyssa made arrangements for the horses and the mule to be stabled in the barn behind the inn and for rooms, while Pavel led Ryn to a booth in a corner near the bar. Corvus had flown off again at some point. The Runeform didn't seem to like going inside buildings much.

A pair of musicians, a man and a woman in matching red outfits, sat in chairs on a small wooden stage at the center of the great room. The woman played a dulcimer, while the man played a flute, and their light, rollicking tune floated on the air above the din of the evening crowd. Ryn recognized it as the melody to a song called "The King's Five Crowns," which was a mainstay of feast day performances back in Aen's Hollow. Locals in dull brown and red clothes and more richly garbed merchants filled the tables and booths spread across the wooden floor. A dozen barmaids flitted between the tables and the bar, where a tall, somber-looking man poured the drinks and scowled at everyone. The barkeep did nothing to spoil the festive mood, however.

From where they sat in their booth, Ryn and Pavel could overhear a conversation between two older men leaning against the bar.

"I'm telling you it's true," the first man said. He had a scraggly white beard and slurred his words.

"And I'm telling you, it's hogwash," said his companion, a younger black-haired man whose bushy eyebrows drew together as he squinted. "Kobolds is just a nursery tale."

Ryn perked up at hearing the familiar word. Pavel didn't look at the pair and kept running his eyes across the entire room, but he did lean in closer.

"My cousin saw a pair of them out on the plains, roasting rabbits over a cookfire," the first man said.

"Your cousin is a drunkard," the second man said. He spoke in a steadier voice than his friend but still slurred a little.

"Ah, but then, how do you explain what we heard from that rider today? He said the whole Sylphren Wood is overrun with the creatures."

Ryn frowned. No riders had overtaken them on the journey down from Thorpe, at least not that he had seen. Of course, one may have passed in the night while they were camping away from the road. If the Kobolds really were on the Koathing Plains too, that would be a problem.

The younger man remained unconvinced. He scoffed. "Bah, I don't care how many people says they seen one. That don't change the fact Kobolds is a myth. Next, you'll be saying we have Wave Sprites coming up out of the wells!"

The first man made a sound of disgust. "There's a difference between Kobolds and Sprites! Everyone knows Sprites aren't real, but Kobolds? Why, up in Silgaria, they got more of them than they do people, so I've heard."

The second man only shook his head. Suddenly, he stood up straighter. "Say! Isn't your cousin the same moon-brained fool who said he saw a Drake swoop out of the sky and steal his milk cow?" He broke into a raucous laugh, and his companion grew red in the face.

Nyssa slid into the booth across from Ryn and Pavel. "You two are sharing a room tonight," she said. "They only had two open."

Pavel nodded. "It beats sleeping on the ground." He sighed wearily. "I'm looking forward to a real mattress. They got good goose-down ones here."

Ryn cleared his throat and gestured toward the men at the bar, who had moved on to another topic of conversation. "We heard someone may have seen Kobolds out on the plains."

Nyssa nodded. "When I mentioned to the innkeeper we were down from the north, he told me all about the rumors. Seems news of Aen's Hollow has overtaken us."

"Do you think they could really be this far south?" Ryn managed to keep panic from his voice.

She shrugged. "Three years ago, as far as anyone knew, Kobolds were just a myth. Then they started appearing up in the Coldreach Mountains. There were also unconfirmed sightings across the border in Mirkwald, in the Ever Wood, but rumors of monsters are always coming out of the Ever Wood. Up until now, the Kobolds have not done much. They've been mostly hiding, trying to keep their presence in Aldria a secret, I think. Never have they attacked unprovoked like they're doing now. That's part of why we were taken so much by surprise." A shadow seemed to pass over her face as she thought back to the slaughter on the road.

Ryn coughed. "The other day you mentioned that there might be people working with the Kobolds. What did you mean by that?"

She shrugged. "Just rumors. People have supposedly been witnessed conversing with them a few times. Our best theory has been that the Kobolds are looking for something, but we have no idea what."

Ryn frowned. People conversing with Kobolds? He remembered the strange, garbled things he'd heard the Kobolds saying, and the question they'd asked on two separate occasions, once about him and once about Pavel. "I think..." he began, not sure how to say this or if he even should. He swallowed and kept going. "I think they're looking for... someone. I heard them asking a question, and I didn't understand the words at first, but I think what they were saying was, 'Is it...' or is he... 'the one.'"

Pavel's eyes widened. "That's what it said to us? When we were in the cage?"

"I think so. One of them asked the same question when they found me the first time."

Nyssa studied her two traveling companions with narrowed eyes. Finally, she sighed. "You may be right. We still don't know who they're looking for or why, but every little piece of intelligence helps." She paused before continuing. "There's more. Not about the Kobolds, but another bit of news I heard. Apparently, the day before yesterday, an entire squadron of the Standing Army passed through here heading west."

Pavel frowned. "Toward the border?"

She nodded. "Nothing has happened yet, but apparently Tamor has been amassing its forces across the Mirkwald River near Nadell. I'm sure they're calling it a 'training exercise,' but Aldria had to respond and increase its own troops on the border."

Two barmaids approached, one depositing bowls of steaming stew and the other plopping down glass mugs of ale. Nyssa smiled in thanks. Pavel dug into the stew right away, slurping it up by the spoonful. It did smell and look appetizing, with large chunks of yellow potatoes and stringy beef. Ryn didn't touch it, or the drink. He never cared much for the taste of alcohol, and he wanted to hear more of what Nyssa had to say.

He knew only a little about Tamor. Aldria had once been part of Tamor, up until about two hundred years ago, when they broke off and formed an independent nation, ruled by the Hall of the Assembly and the Pentarchy, rather than a king, though remnants of the former monarchy could still be found in the names of plants—like king's lances and queen's barrels—and in their name for the language they spoke, the King's Tongue. They also still called gold coins "crowns." Tamor had not forgotten the ancient arrangement either, and many believed they still longed to re-conquer Aldria. Tensions had been high for two centuries, with the occasional skirmish, but never an all-out war.

The Watchkeeper took a long sip from her glass before she continued. "In all likelihood, nothing will happen, but I don't like the timing. Skirmishes with Tamor are the last thing we need right now. I've also heard reports of increasing attacks on merchant vessels by the Lembalt raiders. We need to make it to Falport as soon as we can. The sooner Aldria can deal with the Kobold threat, the sooner we can turn our full attention to Tamor."

Pavel cleared his throat, wiping broth from his chin with a cloth napkin. "Do you know any shortcuts?" he said.

"Actually, yes," Nyssa said with a nod. She spread her own rectangular napkin out on the oak table. "We're here in Fivewells," she said, pointing to one corner of the napkin. She then pointed to the opposite corner. "There's Falport. Normally we would take the road south to Palmoor, and then along the coast." Putting her finger back in Fivewells, she traced a line down one edge and then along the next. The sides of the napkin represented roads. "Or we could go east to Savo, and then south along the river. Both routes take about the same amount of time. However, we could shave off a couple days by going this way." She put her finger back in Fivewells and moved it diagonally across the cloth in a straight line to Falport.

"Is there a road that way?" Ryn asked.

Nyssa shook her head. "No. I admit it is a little risky. Nobody lives out there, so if a horse throws a shoe—or one of us—we'll be on our own. This route will take us straight through the South Forest, but that's nothing like the Sylphren, and you can move through it quickly. If all goes well, we'll be in Falport in five, maybe four days. We've still got plenty of provisions, and I'll restock us before we head out in the morning." She looked at the two of them, apparently seeking their input on her plan.

Pavel only shrugged. "You're the boss," he said.

Ryn nodded. He didn't know enough about Aldria's geography to offer any real feedback on the plan.

Nyssa finally seemed to notice the stew in front of her. "Right," she said, picking up her spoon. "Well, eat up and rest up tonight. We've a long few days ahead of us."

Chapter 12
Through the Forest

NYSSA LAHMEER AWOKE, feeling more rested than she had in days. She had not slept well since the disaster in the Sylphren Wood. She pushed away thoughts of her Pentad, as tears rose unbidden in the corners of her eyes. She had served with each of them for many years, but she would have to mourn them later. The mission always came first, and Commandant Lahey needed to be informed of the growing Kobold threat.

Groaning, she rose from her bed and stretched. She filled a cup from a glistening pitcher on the fireplace mantel and drank it down in several gulps. The fire had died down to faintly glowing embers, but the room was still warm.

She drifted over to the window, overlooking Fivewells' main square. The sun, just beginning to rise, lightened the eastern sky. A few lingering stars shone between the clouds to the west. Several people were already up and moving through the town, but a lone figure near the well caught her attention, a tall man with shaggy black hair and a pair of strange blades strapped across his back. He stood with his back to the inn, but she didn't need to see his face.

Frowning, she quickly dressed, pulling on her boots but leaving off her Watchkeeper tabard. She downed another glass of water and paused only to rearrange her braids, using the warped and cracked mirror near the washstand. She hurried down the empty staircase, across the dark great room, and out the front door. Pavel Talvor did not turn as she came up behind him.

She cleared her throat. "Figuring out how to steal it?" she asked.

He flinched slightly but glanced over his shoulder with a casual smile. The handsome thief was certainly charming, but Nyssa was nowhere close to trusting him. She had first suggested the deal to him largely out of desperation, and she had been surprised when he so readily agreed to it. He seemed intent on honoring his commitment, but she still awoke each morning expecting him to have vanished in the night.

Turning back to the well, he shook his head. "Only admiring, I promise."

She moved up beside him so she could see his face. He had taken the opportunity to shave sometime in the night, as his chin was now free of black stubble. "You're up early," she said. "Not thinking of disappearing, are you?"

He shook his head again. "You'll not be rid of me that easily, Nyssa Lahmeer."

They stood in silence for a time, both staring at the well. After a minute, Pavel looked up and to the southeast. "This is the last push to Falport, I suppose," he said. "I'm not exactly looking forward to that, to be honest."

She studied his profile. "Honesty? From what I know of your reputation, that's not exactly your strong suit."

The ghost of a smile crossed his lips. "What can I say, Nyssa Lahmeer, you've inspired me to be a better man."

She scoffed. "Don't go soft on me. If the Kobolds really have made it this far south, we'll need our wits about us in the South Forest. Like you said, we can't assume our previous poisoning will keep us safe."

"You don't have to remind me."

He fell silent again but clearly had more to say. She stayed quiet. He glanced at her for only a moment. When he spoke, it was in a quiet voice.

"Have you composed your report for the Citadel yet?"

"Why do you ask?"

"I'm just wondering if you're going to give the... full account. I keep thinking about that big Kobold with the black armor. We've been avoiding the topic. The kid couldn't see it, but I know you did. How do you think the Watchkeeper commandant will respond to the news that the Kobolds have Weavers?"

She frowned, remembering that monster who had so easily defeated her. The Kobolds, though hideous, had never inspired fear in her, but that one... She knew it was different the moment she saw it. Its face held an intelligence and a cold hatred unmatched by its shorter brethren. She remembered when it turned on its soldiers, striking them down for apparently not dispatching the humans faster. One had tried to flee, but the leader had held out its hand and *something* had shot out and wrapped around the other Kobold, holding it in place.

"I'm not even sure..." she began. "What kind of lacing was that? It looked..."

"Black." The word came out as a whisper.

She nodded. So, he had seen it too. To a Weaver, lacings seemed to glow with a different colored light, depending on their source. Wave was blue; Aether, white; Root, green; Flame, red; and Stone, yellow. What the Kobold wielded, however, wasn't even light, but a swirling mass of shadows. The lacing it used took only a moment. The shadows seemed to rise from the ground, encircling its body, before erupting from its chest, flowing in the direction it pointed.

She shivered in the cool dawn air. As the sun rose, the shadows fled, gathering into long silhouettes beside the well, Pavel, and Nyssa. Another shadow swept across the square, small and quick. Nyssa flinched as a black bird settled atop the roof of the well, but it was not a bird.

Corvus squawked a greeting to Pavel and tilted its head to look at Nyssa. She shook her head. Nyssa didn't understand why Pavel kept the thing around. Now seemed like a good time to ask though, and it would move the conversation away from that horrible Kobold and its twisted Weaving. She gestured to the Runeform. "Why do you keep that thing?" she asked. "A flying, talking Runeform? You could make a fortune selling it to the right buyer."

Pavel laughed and shook his head. "I could never sell Corvus," he said.

"Never!" the Runeform squawked. It spoke in a harsh, grating voice that somehow seemed appropriate for a creation imitating a crow.

"I've sold most of what I've... salvaged." He coughed, moving quickly on from the topic of his thievery. "I keep anything that catches my fancy though." He reached back and touched the handles of his blades, to give an example. "Besides, Corvus seems to have... imprinted on me. I don't think I could get rid of him."

Nyssa shook her head. "Does it ever say anything useful?" The Runeform had said little in her presence, though she had noted several times over the previous few days that when Pavel and the creature were alone together, too far away for her to overhear, Corvus spoke a lot more. She'd seen the two of them seeming to have actual conversations, though she couldn't possibly guess what they talked about.

Pavel shrugged. "He's a little shy around people, but Corvus is actually a wonderful conversationalist. You've just got to know how to talk to him."

Nyssa nodded, studying the bird. In the bright morning light, she could barely see the blue glow of its eyes. A woman approached to draw water from the well, and she completely ignored the creature, no doubt assuming it to be just a crow. More and more people bustled about the square. Nyssa turned back to look at the inn. "I suppose we should get ready. Will you make sure Ryn is up?"

It took about an hour to restock their saddlebags, eat a hasty breakfast in the now much more subdued but still crowded great room, and collect their mounts from the stable. Nyssa led them along the eastern road toward Savo for a short distance, before cutting off the road and into the South Forest. She had traversed these woods many times before, taking the shortcut on missions with her Pentad, so she knew they would not get lost.

Tall pine trees, spaced out like columns, made up the bulk of the vegetation here, and the dense layer of brown pine needles along the forest floor from the previous autumn and winter kept little else from growing. Plus, the ground ran relatively level, so the horses navigated the woods with ease, though there was always the danger of hidden divots or badger holes beneath the ground cover. One wrong step and they would be down a horse. Nyssa kept the party to a walk. Anything faster would be dangerous and unsustainable for the four or five days it would take them to reach Rigel, across the river from Falport.

She glanced back at the others as she rode, making sure they were keeping up. The thief rode in the rear today, Corvus perched on his shoulder. Ryn kept close to the mule, which trailed behind Nyssa on a lead. The boy was still awkward in the saddle, but she no longer feared he would fall out. She still had her doubts about Pavel, but Ryn seemed to be a sweet kid. He had a bandage around his arm from where he'd made a fresh cut that morning. The pale, scrawny youth reminded her of many another Watchkeeper recruit, eager to learn and more than a little naïve. With his Etching and his powerful gifting, he would be a great addition to the Watchkeepers.

She pushed the horses and the two men as hard as she dared, and they crossed through the South Forest in just four days. Thankfully, those four days were uneventful. They saw no other people and no signs of Kobolds. She awoke each morning grateful for the sound of birdsong in the trees, remembering how eerily quiet the Sylphren Wood had been.

They spent most of the days in companionable silence, focusing on navigating between the trees or following the occasional game trail. Small streams crisscrossed the wood. They were easy to ford and kept their waterskins full. For some reason, Pavel kept his distance from her. He was agreeable and shared in the tasks of setting up and breaking down camp, but he spoke little, slipping off into the woods more and more to have private conversations with his Runeform. She tried not to worry overmuch about the thief, using most of the spare hours when they rested at noon and in the evenings to give what instruction she could to Ryn. The boy was desperate to learn.

He definitely had talent and picked things up quickly. With her limited gifting in Root, she ran out of things to teach him long before they reached Rigel. He got more control over his vis-ualizations, creating lacings appropriate to his task rather than the massive oak trees he'd formed at first. She let him practice Dowsing on her, and each night she would make small cuts on her arms for him to heal. He faithfully made sure his own arms were never without a wound and reported to her every time they healed.

Each time they stopped, he would search the sparse under-growth for plants he recognized, taking cuttings here and there and adding them to his collection. He laughed excitedly on the first night when he found a scraggly little bush he called "foxfeather." Apparently, it held very useful properties for an herbalist. He begged her to teach him how to make Rootbalm, but she told him he'd have to wait till they reached the Citadel for that. She'd never mastered that skill.

The boy's greatest outburst of excitement came on the second evening, in the heart of the South Forest. He jumped up and down, pointing at the forest floor where she had just laid her shield. She was taking no chances. "I can see it!" he said, pointing directly to the thin blue line of light that encircled their campsite. That impressed Nyssa the most. Little more than a week had passed since the boy first learned he was a Weaver, and already he could see the lacings of others.

He spent the rest of that evening begging Nyssa and Pavel to use their Weaving so he could see it. The boy's innocent excitement roused the strangely reserved Pavel, who for that evening became his normal outgoing self again—what Nyssa assumed to be his normal self, anyway. The thief put on quite a show, lacing his arms and legs with swirling white Aether. Nyssa had to let down her shield so he could move freely among the trees. He leapt high into the air, turning impossible flips or kicking off the tree trunks to bound higher and higher. He scrambled effortlessly to the top of a towering pine before dropping to the ground, using a common Aether lacing to cushion his landing.

Ryn was delighted. He could see everything now. He marveled at the differences between the forces, not just in color. Aether was made of swirling bands of light that never stayed still, while Wave was more solid, capable of holding to straight lines and right angles and never flickering. She showed him a couple small wards, needing to reserve energy to remake the shield before they slept. She made a small circle on the ground and told him to step across it. That ward filled anyone who entered it with a sudden sense of unease. It wouldn't stop a determined person, but it was great at repelling wild animals. A line along the ground marked the boundary of the ward, and the air above it shimmered with a faint rippling that always reminded Nyssa of the surface of a pond. Wave lacings were subtle, and while any Weaver could see a ward easily enough, if he were distracted or in a hurry, he could miss it.

Soon even Pavel grew tired of performing, and he had to scarf down a second dinner before bed. Thankfully, that was the most exciting night they passed in the forest. Toward evening on the fourth day, they emerged suddenly from the woods, finding the road that ran along the coast between Palmoor and Rigel. Far to the south across a grassy field and a narrow strip of beach, they could see the shimmering band of blue that was the Morro Ocean. Ryn stared at it in amazement, but they had no time for sightseeing. They joined the flow of traffic along the road, and the sprawling bridge town of Rigel soon came into view.

Ryn gaped at everything as they rode into town, which anywhere else would have been called a city. The buildings, few with less than three stories, were built wall to wall along the cobblestone roads. Crowds of people milled about, many of them foreigners. These sights were all too familiar to Nyssa, and normally she felt relieved to pass through Rigel, the first sign that she was almost home. The barracks of the Watchkeepers' Citadel were the only home she had known for fifteen years. This time, however, she did not feel any sense of peace riding through Falport's overgrown bridge town. She dreaded the report she would have to make, the painful memories she would have to relive.

Pavel pushed his horse up beside her, despite the crowded streets. For some reason, he was smiling. She arched an eyebrow. "What do you want?" she asked.

His smile didn't waver. "I know we are on somewhat of an urgent mission," he said, "but this is Rigel, is it not?"

She nodded.

"Is there any chance we could make a brief stop, before we report to the Citadel?"

"A detour?"

"The fountain. The famous one. I would love to see it. From my understanding, it would only be a slight detour."

"You mean the Runeform?"

"Yes, the Runeform. From what I've heard, it's too big to move, if that's what you're worried about."

She laughed. "Oh, yes, it is definitely too big. Like the wells."

He nodded. "Does it really answer any question you ask it?"

"It does, and it doesn't."

"Yes, I've heard that bit too. So, what do you think?"

She opened her mouth to say no, but then she hesitated. They had an hour yet of sunlight. A warm evening breeze blew in from the sea, carrying the calls of gulls. It would be a brief diversion, but it would mean a little more time before she had to face the commandant and speak again of what happened in the Sylphren Wood. Plus, another thought occurred to her. She glanced at the thief. "What question do you want to ask it?"

His grin broadened. "If you want to know, you'll have to take me to the fountain."

She sighed but nodded. "Very well, but this will be a quick detour."

"You're the best."

She didn't respond but heeled her horse forward, taking the lead again. Pavel fell back beside Ryn. She could hear snatches of their conversation as they rode on. Pavel explained where they were going and how the fountain worked. He seemed to enjoy taking on the role of the knowledgeable adventurer, lecturing the sheltered youth on the ways of the world.

Nyssa led them through a series of turns, heading for the square that housed the Rigel fountain. She'd heard every rumor and theory about it, living in Falport as long as she had, but she had never asked the fountain a question herself. She had never thought of a question that couldn't be answered more reliably elsewhere.

Soon the fountain came into view. In this part of Rigel, the streets were mostly deserted. Only one of the storefronts facing the square remained open. The raised shutter revealed a modest smithy, apparently specializing in copper. A boy in a leather apron swept the interior of the shop. He stopped and looked with interest as the three gray-clad travelers rode up to the fountain.

Pavel took his horse in a circle all around the three-tiered stone structure, admiring it. He pulled to a stop in front of the side with the face of a man on top. Apparently, he knew enough to know where the voice came from. He cleared his throat but looked sideways at Ryn and Nyssa. The boy leaned forward in his saddle, staring up at the fountain, but Nyssa kept her eyes on the thief. He offered her a sheepish grin. "I don't suppose I could get a little privacy?" he asked.

She scoffed. "Not a chance. Now, hurry up. If you're going to ask it a question, you're going to have to do it now."

He nodded. "Very well." He looked up at the stone face. "Rigel," he said. The face sprung to life, looking down at him with its strangely lifelike gray face and faintly glowing eyes. Ryn gasped.

Suddenly, Corvus flew from Pavel's shoulder with a squawk, disappearing over the rooftops. Pavel's mouth hung open, apparently just as surprised as Nyssa by the creature's sudden departure. He started to say something but stopped himself, looking back at the fountain. He had already activated it, and it would take anything he said now as his question. He shot a sideways glance at Nyssa, shrugged, and said, "*Ish sigern kunn prim?*"

The Runeform spoke as soon as he finished the unintelligible question. "WHAT YOU HAVE SEEN WILL COME TO PASS. YOU CANNOT ALTER OR ESCAPE IT."

Pavel and Nyssa frowned, likely for two different reasons.

"What was that?" Nyssa asked. "Silgarian?"

Pavel winced. "You don't speak it, do you?"

"Unfortunately, no. You really didn't want me to know your question, huh?"

He shrugged. "It was a personal issue."

"And did the answer make any sense?"

He shook his head.

"It usually doesn't with this thing."

He sighed. "Right, well, let's go join the Watchkeepers."

Nyssa watched the flickering firelight as she sipped her tea. The past two hours had been a blur, reporting to the Citadel, handing off Pavel and Ryn as new recruits, and delivering her full report to Commandant Lahey and his Council of Masters. She'd managed to hold back any tears as she spoke of the slaughter of her Pentad. She now sat before a cozy fire in the private study of Mistress Agia Bellos, her longtime friend and mentor.

Agia offered a sympathetic smile, sitting opposite Nyssa in a matching overstuffed armchair. They'd spent many an evening together in these chairs. "Losing a member of your Pentad is never easy," the master Wave Weaver said, "and to lose all four..."

Nyssa nodded. She could not stop tears from gathering in the corners of her eyes this time. "I will be all right," she said, though she knew Agia would see through that lie. "I just need to get back out there. We need to strike hard against these Kobolds."

Agia frowned. She stared into the fireplace for a while before responding. "Rest assured, Nyssa, the Watchkeepers will be bringing their full resources to bear in dealing with this threat." She hesitated before continuing. "But your place is not on the frontlines right now."

Nyssa could not hide her scowl or keep the bitterness from her voice. "What do you mean? I now know more about fighting these creatures than anyone in the organization. I can..." She trailed off, doubting the conviction of her own words.

In the end, she had left out the part about seeing the lead Kobold Weaving. She had described the creature, its armor, and how it seemed to be in command of the smaller creatures, but she had not mentioned those swirling black shadows. She wasn't entirely sure why. Maybe it was because she knew she would be met with skepticism and disbelief. Despite confirmation from Pavel, she still doubted herself whether she had really seen what she thought she had. The council would not have accepted it as truth without independent confirmation from other Watchkeepers anyway. Nyssa knew even Agia would have doubted her. Agia would likely have attributed it to the great trauma of watching her own men get struck down, or the result of the fatal poison that had been coursing through her veins at the time. Nyssa glanced sideways at her old friend, whose long hair was now entirely gray.

Agia's sympathetic smile returned. "Everything you have told us will be passed on to the Pentads we dispatch to support the Thorpe outpost. Every effort will be made to contain and eliminate the threat."

Nyssa nodded. "When can I expect to be reassigned? Are there any Pentads with an opening for a Wave Weaver?"

Agia shook her head. "We'll not be reassigning you just yet. You need time to recover, to process what you experienced."

Nyssa shook her own head, more emphatically. "No," she said, "you can't stable me."

"You don't see it yet, but you are in no condition to leave Falport right now."

"Well, if you expect me to just sit on my hands, then I have to tell you, that will make me go crazy more than anything. I will process the loss in my own time, but I can't do it just sitting alone in my room. I'll fall to pieces if you make me do that, and I won't be good for anything."

"There's plenty to be done here in the Citadel. You can help me with my classes."

"Teaching? I'm no master."

"You've been with us for fifteen years, Nyssa. You were my best student, and I'll wager you know more about Wave Weaving than anyone in the Watchkeepers, except for me, of course." She gave a sly smile.

Nyssa stared into the fire, considering. "I've never given much thought to teaching. I'm not sure I have the patience for it, to be honest."

"Nyssa Lahmeer," Agia said, her tone suddenly chiding. The Wave master was quick to offer a sympathetic shoulder to lean on, but she had always been a strict teacher, with no patience for anything she considered foolishness. "No one on the council will approve your reassignment in your current condition, so reconcile yourself to the idea that you will not be leaving Falport anytime soon. You yourself said you must be kept busy, so unless you'd rather squander your considerable talents being assigned to full-time guard duty, then I would suggest you promptly take me up on my offer."

Nyssa's eyebrows rose. It had been years since she'd earned a reprimand from Agia Bellos, but the Wave master still had form. She cleared her throat. "Yes, Mistress Bellos."

"Besides," Agia continued, her voice softening, "we have a new recruit who I think could truly benefit from your mentoring. She is a headstrong girl who reminds me a lot of how you were at her age."

Nyssa frowned. "Sounds like I have my work cut out for me, then."

Agia laughed, the sound dissolving all remaining tension from the room. "Oh, yes," she said. "On top of all that, she's the daughter of a Pentarch. She's been here only a week but has mastered the basics, and we'll be adding her to a training Pentad tomorrow. As the stars would have it, we were only lacking a Root and an Aether Weaver."

"You mean the two recruits I just brought in?"

"Yes, given what you've told us, we will be waiving the preliminary training for those two. The infamous Pavel Talvor already knows enough of Aether to get himself in trouble, and given young Ryn's background in herbalism and the lessons he's already had, he shouldn't have any trouble getting up to speed in a training Pentad."

Nyssa smiled. "If I'm sticking around anyway, it will be interesting to watch that group's progress. Tell me more about this headstrong Wave Weaver."

They spoke well into the night, talking of the new training group and of Nyssa's own training at the Citadel, a simpler time before she had known much loss.

Chapter 13
The Training Pentad

THALIA MOLDO TAPPED a length of copper rhythmically with her hammer, forcing it into a circle. She'd wrapped it around a bar of steel to get the shape right, but now she was finishing it on the wooden work bench. She alternatingly tapped the ends of the almost-circle until they touched. Normally, she would need to use crimping or brazing to join the two ends, but she had an easier way of doing that now. She set down her hammer and held the ring loosely in her calloused hands.

It turned out her luck Etching worked the way many Stone Etchings did. Anytime she worked metal now, she could sense faint lacings of Stone leaking out from the palms of her hands into the material she shaped. By concentration, she could stop it, which would allow her to create normal, unlaced pieces. She had also learned a few other lacings from Master Caston. She employed one now to join the two ends.

She concentrated, and before her eyes lines of yellow light radiated from her hands. Since joining the Watchkeepers, she had seen examples of all other kinds of Weaving, and besides Wave, the rest seemed messy and chaotic compared to Stone. The yellow lines grew at sharp angles to one another, bending and splitting as they did, forming a complicated pattern, but the light never flickered or wavered. Master Caston said the patterns mirrored the way certain crystals grew within caves.

Metal, rock—any solid material, really—all had an underlying invisible structure, what Master Caston called a matrix, that helped it keep its rigid shape. Stone Weavers could manipulate those matrices and overlay their own. Some materials were simpler than others and could only be altered so much. Gemstones and crystals had the most complex matrices, for reasons she did not yet understand, which is why they were used in more advanced Stone lacings. The lacing she used now was the most basic one, and copper could handle it easily.

She overlayed her crystalline network of light onto the copper ring, and it faded into the metal, though her eyes were now trained to see the faint shimmer that lingered just below the surface of the reddish metal, a sign to any Weaver that it held a lacing. She studied her work, examining the ring with a nearby loupe. The two ends had completely fused, leaving not even a seam. The ring looked to have been cast in a mold from molten copper. This was the same lacing that held the walls of Falport together and made them nearly indestructible.

She set the ring aside in a wooden box that had been designated specifically for her. Master Rohan had painted it with the white image of a skull to warn off anyone from taking anything she placed in it, though she doubted there was anyone still in the Citadel who did not know of her Etching. The box was also probably not necessary for another reason. Through nearly two weeks of experimenting, they had determined that her luck-laced pieces

185

only seemed to activate when Thalia directly handed them to someone else.

Thalia looked around the massive Watchkeeper smithy. Though the space was alive with movement, noise, and heat, it seemed almost quiet that morning, compared to the usual hubbub. Many of the Weavers who worked there in their spare time had left Falport at first light. She still had not been told where they were going. It had something to do with a report brought in by three travelers who had arrived the evening before. Three was an odd number, she thought, as Watchkeepers generally traveled in groups of five. Others who would normally be in the Citadel were half a day's ride to the east, holed up in a previously abandoned outpost, weathering the effects of her handiwork. The Stone Weavers who worked with Master Caston had been among the first to volunteer to test her Etching.

For the first three days, only Master Caston himself had tested her gift. Just as with her unsuspecting customers, he experienced exceptional luck. Apparently, there was always a bit of chance involved in the more advanced enchantments. The same lacings would produce varying results in terms of strength, longevity, and the severity of the recoil. While wearing a copper ring Thalia had made, Master Caston created lacings that were stronger than anything he'd ever made before, he claimed. On top of that, he'd negotiated a favorable deal with the Falport jewelers' guild for a cache of valuable gemstones.

He'd also been struck with inspiration in the middle of the night for a way to improve the fleet foot enchantment, an advanced and complicated lacing that required Blending Aether with Stone. With the exception of innate Etchings, all the really interesting enchantments required such a Blending. To show his gratitude, Master Caston had gifted her a pair of enchanted leather shoes, which would allow her to run for longer than normal. She hadn't had many opportunities to run, though, spending most of her days in the smithy and her nights in a bunk in the Recruit Barracks. She had much to learn, even beyond Weaving.

After a busy day and a half of luck, Master Caston rode out alone to weather the recoil. He'd sent some Watchkeepers to clean up the old, abandoned outpost ahead of him. He holed himself up in a barracks with some food, water, and a book to read. Sometime in the night, a storm swept through, knocking a tree down in such a way that it wedged itself against the only door, trapping him inside. On top of that, rats got into the room and ate most of his food. Fortunately, he had instructed the Watchkeepers helping him to keep their distance for a day and then return to check on him. They freed him from the room, and he was otherwise unharmed, if a little hungry.

After that successful trial run, the experimentation truly took off. Every day started with Thalia crafting different luck-laced items, using different materials and techniques, and even adding in other basic enchantments the Watchkeepers taught her. Nothing seemed to affect the results much. This morning, Thalia was back to copper. She felt a special affinity to the metal, after two years as a redsmith's apprentice.

A dozen test subjects were at the outpost now, and more would leave the Citadel today as their luck expired. Knowing the recoil was coming helped them deal with it. The misfortunes so far ranged from freak injuries, to animal attacks, to a caved-in roof in one of the barracks. They'd made sure to include Root Weavers in the test groups to deal with the injuries, and no one was regretting their participation yet. Master Caston had joked that they would need to rebuild the entire outpost before long. Many of the Watchkeepers left in the smithy wore her luck-laced jewelry—the subjects didn't have to keep the items on them, except to know when they broke, and rings and necklaces were easier to carry around than frying pans and kettles. None of the test subjects had been sent west on that sudden urgent mission, however; Master Caston wanted to limit experimentation to within the Watchkeeper compound, for now.

Thalia looked up as someone approached her workbench.

"Good morning, Thalia," Master Caston said.

She smiled and returned his greeting. She'd found the Stone master to be a patient teacher and a decent man.

"I'm glad to see you are hard at work this morning. You are a diligent student."

"There's just so much to learn," she said, looking around at all the varied work being done. She wanted to master it all.

He chuckled. "You are young. You have plenty of time." He hesitated before continuing. "On that note, I came to ask you if you are still certain you wish to officially enlist with the Watchkeepers. Remember, there will be no hard feelings if you would rather take your impressive talents elsewhere."

She nodded. "I have considered my options. On the practical side, I want to be able to help support my mother. The Watchkeeper pay is more than enough for that. Beyond that, I want to make things that are useful and actually help people. I don't want to enchant trinkets for some first-echelon lord just so he can make more money. I'd rather use my talents to help the Watchkeepers protect Aldria."

His smile broadened. "I am glad to hear it. I've recommended you for the next Training Pentad, and a slot has opened up today."

"Today? But I've only just started. Do you really think I'm ready?"

"The preliminary training is only just to familiarize you with the basic building blocks of Weaving. Your training with Master

Foster put you ahead of many new recruits who have never even held a hammer. Trust me, you are ready." He glanced at the skull-marked box. "And if you are worried about our experiments, those can continue while you complete your Watchkeeper training."

She slowly nodded. "Well, when can I meet the others?"

Ryn and Pavel stood waiting in a chamber within the towering black Citadel at the heart of the Watchkeepers' compound. Ryn adjusted the gray tabard he'd been given that morning. Things seemed to be moving quickly now that they were in Falport, especially after a mostly tedious week spent on the road. They'd been housed in the same room, part of the men's barracks. Corvus had not reappeared after its sudden flight when they stopped at the Rigel fountain, but that didn't seem to bother Pavel. The thief leaned against a table set up at the center of the room, playing with the gray sleeves of his shirt. They seemed a little short for his arms.

The door opened and Nyssa entered, followed by a green-clad servant carrying a large leather-bound book. They had not seen her since the night before, when she handed them off to another servant and then went to deliver her report. Pavel straightened up, clicked his heels together, and saluted. "Captain Lahmeer," he said.

Nyssa arched an eyebrow. Pavel had spoken in a deep voice with far too much pomp, showing that he wasn't being serious. She chose to ignore the sarcasm, nodding to Pavel and then Ryn. "You two clean up nicely," she said.

Ryn grinned. "We were told we would be meeting our training group soon?"

She nodded. "Yes, the others will be here shortly. You'll be training with a Pentad containing one of each kind of Weaver. It's how we do things here. First, we just have one more piece of business to take care of."

The servant, a middle-aged man with deep creases around his mouth, set the book on the table. Atop it rested a small wooden box, from which he produced an ink bottle, a pen, and a blotter. The servant flipped the book open. It contained a series of entries written in a small, cramped hand. He traced his finger along the page to the last entry. He looked up, glancing between Ryn and Pavel. Finally, his heavy-lidded eyes settled on Ryn. "Are you..." He glanced back at the book. "Ryn?"

Ryn nodded. "Yes, sir," he said. He felt a little strange, addressing a servant formally, but he had never actually been anywhere that employed real servants before, so he wasn't sure how he was supposed to treat them.

The man nodded. "It seems when you were registered last night, the clerk did not note your second name?" Though he didn't phrase it as a question, he did seem to be asking one.

Ryn cleared his throat. "Actually, I don't have a second name. Or, probably I do, but I don't know it."

The servant swung his head around to stare at Nyssa, seeking confirmation.

She smiled. "He's telling the truth, I believe, as strange as it sounds."

The man sighed, swinging his head back around to Ryn. "Well, that simply will not do, I'm afraid. Everyone registered with the Watchkeepers must have a second name."

Ryn glanced at Nyssa, not sure how to respond.

"Well," she said, "you will simply have to give yourself a second name. Would that work?"

The servant shrugged. "It's unorthodox, but I suppose, under the circumstances, we can allow that."

"Great," Nyssa said. "What name would you like, Ryn?"

Pavel leaned in, as if to whisper confidentially, but he spoke loud enough for Nyssa to hear. "I can help you out, kid. I'm great at coming up with pseudonyms."

Nyssa scoffed. "Uh-huh, and what name were you using when I apprehended you in Aen's Hollow?"

Pavel frowned. "Max," he said quietly.

"Max what?"

He coughed and said under his breath, "Max Aetherstorm."

Nyssa laughed. The servant cleared his throat, tapping on the book with his index finger, clearly impatient. Nyssa nodded to him, then looked back at Ryn. "I would come up with your own name, Ryn."

Ryn thought it over for a moment. An impatient glare from the servant forced him to go with the first name that came to his mind. "Silverbell," he said.

The man frowned but decided not to comment. He quickly jotted the name down in the register. Pavel gave Ryn a reassuring nod, approving of the name.

The door opened again, and another servant led three women in Watchkeeper gray into the room. Nyssa smiled and said, "Well, Pavel Talvor and Ryn Silverbell, let me introduce you to the rest of your Training Pentad."

Ryn looked at each of the women. They all seemed to be about his age, but they were very different from one another in appearance.

The first woman, or girl really, was shorter than the others, with pale skin and straight blonde hair hanging past her shoulders. Nyssa introduced her as Jayn Eldragor, a Wave Weaver. Jayn nodded to the men, keeping her face even. Her features were small but not quite delicate. She had a way of carrying herself that made her seem taller than she actually was.

Next to her was Shilo Lorn, a Flame Weaver. Her hair hung about her head in curly black ringlets. She had large dark eyes and full lips that parted in a shy smile as she regarded the two men.

Towering over the other two was Thalia Moldo, the Stone Weaver, who stood several inches taller than Ryn. Beneath her gray tabard she wore a sleeveless shirt, exposing toned, muscular arms. Her beige complexion was midway between Jayn's and Shilo's, and her long wavy hair hung in two braids over her shoulders. She smiled as well and even extended her hand to Ryn and Pavel. Ryn found her handshake lighter than he expected. His arms looked scrawny compared to hers.

Pavel grinned at the girls in a way he no doubt thought was charming, but then he turned deliberately toward Nyssa and whispered. "They're all a bit young, aren't they?"

Nyssa laughed. "Get used to it, Talvor," she said. "Truth be told, you're about a decade older than our average recruit. No offense."

Pavel shrugged, glancing back at the three girls. "That's all right," he said. "I enjoy mentoring the youths of the next generation."

Jayn Eldragor scoffed and stepped forward. She seemed especially petite before the lanky thief, but she gazed up at him with confidence. "Pavel Talvor, is it? The word around the Citadel is that you only enlisted to avoid prison time. That's hardly the sort of mentoring I came to Falport to receive."

Pavel's grin didn't waver. "Oh, you might just be surprised at what I have to offer, Miss Eldragor. Say, you wouldn't happen to be related to Anyse Eldragor, Fourth Pentarch of Aldria, would you?"

Jayn stiffened. "She's my mother, actually, but what's that to you?"

Pavel laughed. "Well, well, you're practically royalty then. With no offense to the Gray Guards, I think you will find that you are the one out of place here."

Jayn did not respond but seemed to grow about a foot taller as she glared up at Pavel. Ryn glanced at the others. Pavel and Jayn clearly had the largest personalities of the group. Shilo Lorn folded her arms across her chest and kept her eyes on the floor, clearly uncomfortable but too reticent to speak. Thalia Moldo also seemed on the shy side, but she reluctantly took a step forward and cleared her throat. "Let's take it back a step," she said. "We've all only just met, and my understanding is we will have to work together closely during training. I think we should at least try to start off on cordial terms."

Nyssa stepped forward as well, placing herself between Pavel and Jayn. "Moldo is correct," she said. "In order to succeed as Watchkeepers, you must learn to work together as a team. For the foreseeable future, you five are stuck with each other." She glanced up at Pavel and down at Jayn. "Can you two play nicely now?"

Jayn suddenly broke into a smile. "Of course, Captain Lahmeer." She leveled a look at Pavel that belied her suddenly airy tone. "I've learned enough of diplomacy from my mother, the Fourth Pentarch, that I can work with just about anyone if I must." She extended a hand to Pavel.

Not to be outdone, Pavel opted not to shake her right hand with his, but instead he cupped it with his left hand, gave a flourishing bow, and bent as if to kiss it. He stopped short, looking up at her. "I would be honored to serve alongside you, your majesty."

Jayn recoiled, withdrawing her hand. Her smile faltered, but she glanced at Nyssa and retained it. "Right," she said.

Nyssa frowned at Pavel. She gave her head a quick shake as if to clear away a thought and then addressed the whole group. "Well, then," she said. "Your training will officially start tomorrow morning. In the meantime, it is about noon, so why don't you all head to the dining hall? You can break bread together and get to know each other a little better."

Jayn gave a curt nod. "Very well, Captain Lahmeer." She turned quickly and made her way toward the door, clearly expecting the others to follow. Shilo and Thalia exchanged a glance that conveyed some meaning Ryn didn't quite grasp. Thalia shrugged, and the girls fell in line behind Jayn. Ryn and Pavel took up the rear.

The two men had visited the dining hall the night before and that morning, but Ryn was still glad to have someone to follow. The compound was massive, larger than Aen's Hollow and with far more buildings, and he felt it would be some time before he knew his way around. The dining hall was in another part of the main Citadel, so Jayn led them through several hallways and down a flight of stairs to the ground floor. Despite the ornate exterior, the corridors of the Citadel were simple and unadorned, the floors, walls, and ceilings all composed of smooth black stone fitted together somehow without seams. As if to compensate for the dark interior, the Watchkeepers had laid bright floor runners in alternating hues of red, blue, green, yellow, and white. Evenly spaced silver-backed sconces reflected light from strange lanterns that held bright orbs of light that didn't flicker the way a torch or a candle would.

Pavel grabbed Ryn's arm and slowed down, putting space between them and the three girls. "They're all too young for my tastes," Pavel whispered, this time quietly enough that no one else could hear, "but do you fancy any of them?"

Ryn felt his cheeks redden. There had been a few girls in Aen's Hollow he'd found attractive, but given his status as an outsider, he knew better than to ever have tried courting any of them. His fellow recruits were about his age and certainly not unattractive, but... He shook his head. "That's not what we're here for, Pavel," he whispered.

Pavel scoffed. "Fair enough," he said. "Why did you join up anyway? You know, they didn't really have enough back in Thorpe to charge you with anything."

"I'm here... to learn how to Weave." There was more to it than that, but he wasn't feeling very solicitous toward the former thief just then.

They reached the dining hall, a long rectangular room at the front of the Citadel. High arched windows along two sides overlooked the lush green yards of the compound. An opening above a counter along one wall gave access to the kitchens. Cooks set wooden trays of food out for the Watchkeepers filing past. This was the fullest he had seen the dining hall, but after a few minutes in line, they all sat down together at one end of a long table.

The food here was decent, if a little under-seasoned. The noon meal consisted of a hearty broth of chicken and red beans, alongside some yeasty bread rolls. The five recruits ate and talked, introducing themselves in turn.

Jayn said little about herself, other than to explain she had grown up in and around Appencourt. She acknowledged that her mother was the Fourth Pentarch, but she didn't want the others to treat her any differently because of it. Ryn wondered how much of her swaggering confidence was an act, much like Pavel's seemed to be.

Pavel gave the girls the usual line about being a treasure hunter, who specialized in salvaging Runeforms and ancient Weaver-made objects. Thalia perked up when he mentioned his weapons, and he agreed to show them to her sometime. They were stashed in his dorm, as recruits weren't allowed to carry weapons inside the compound. Ryn didn't feel the need to correct Pavel about the real nature of his former occupation. If Jayn had already heard rumors of the truth, then the others soon would.

Shilo and Thalia were more forthcoming about their pasts. Shilo seemed shy but didn't appear to have anything to hide. She talked about her life as the daughter of a fisherman down in Palmoor and explained what had happened when her Etching manifested. Jayn, who had been cool and disinterested for most of the conversation, leaned in and asked a few questions, apparently eager to know more about the Flame Weaver's ability that had sent a man flying overboard and drained enough energy to crack a boat's mast.

Thalia described her life in Rigel, how she had trained as a redsmith's apprentice, and how she really aspired to be a blade-smith like her father. That explained her interest in Pavel's laced weapons. Pavel in turn grew excited when she mentioned her hometown and questioned her about the Rigel fountain. She didn't tell him anything he didn't already know, though she seemed reticent to speak about it. Pavel didn't press her. Thalia wasn't exactly outgoing, but she appeared comfortable speaking when needed. Even Pavel and Jayn looked impressed when she told them about her Etching, which somehow gave people increased luck.

Finally, all eyes swiveled to Ryn. The girls looked at him anyway; Pavel was busy using his roll to sop up the last bits of food from his wooden bowl. Ryn had remained quiet during the whole conversation. He'd grown comfortable around Pavel and Nyssa, traveling with them alone for so long, but now he had been forced into company with three new strangers. Three young women. He felt his face reddening and silently cursed Pavel for introducing that idea into his mind. He tried to fight it, but all through the meal he'd found himself wondering which of the three ladies he found most attractive.

Thalia leaned forward, offering a reassuring smile. She was seated opposite him. "You don't need to share anything you're not comfortable with," she said. "We just want to know who you are."

He nodded. "Well, I'm from up north, near Aen's Hollow."

"Where's that?" Jayn asked. She sat beside Ryn on the bench.

"It's up in the Sylphren Wood," Ryn said. "I lived there with my aunt. She was an herbalist. She taught me everything she knew. If any of you ever get sick, I know how to treat just about anything."

Shilo and Thalia smiled at the offer, but Jayn just laughed. "Thanks," she said, "but any Root Weaver can treat sickness, without herbalism."

Ryn dropped his gaze, feeling foolish.

Thalia shot the Wave Weaver a glance. "You've been here long enough, Jayn, that you should know Watchkeepers should never rely too much on Weaving."

Jayn frowned, but she seemed determined to keep her word to Nyssa that she would be civil.

Thalia gave Ryn an encouraging look. "And what made you want to join the Watchkeepers?"

Ryn frowned. He didn't want to share his recent trauma with these strangers, but he knew they would find out eventually. He wasn't sure how to start. "Have you heard of Kobolds?" he said.

Jayn laughed again. He was anticipating that response. "Like from the fairy tales?"

Ryn didn't know how to reply to that, but Pavel suddenly leaned forward from his seat on the end of the table. He glared at Jayn. "Listen here, Miss fancy britches, I know we are supposed to be playing nice, but if you could step down from your Golden Lands pedestal for a moment and stop pretending like you already know everything there is to know, you might actually learn something." Jayn gasped, opening her mouth to protest, but Pavel didn't give her a chance and kept right on talking. "Kobolds are absolutely real, and you should thank your guiding star you have the luxury of not believing in them. Why do you think half the Weavers in this place left in such a hurry this morning?"

Thalia's eyes widened. She spoke up before Jayn had a chance to recover from the barrage of words. "That was you two? You were the ones who came in last night with that report that has the entire Citadel on edge?"

Pavel nodded. "Us and Captain Lahmeer." He glared at Jayn. "Why don't you ask her if Kobolds are real? But before you do, you should know that Kobolds slaughtered her entire Pentad not a week gone. They would have killed her and me too if not for the kid here." He hooked a finger at Ryn. "He may not look it, but this kid is about the finest Root Weaver you will ever meet."

Thalia and Shilo regarded Ryn with a new look of respect. Jayn glared at the table. Apparently mention of Nyssa was enough to cow her, or she realized she didn't know enough yet to argue. Thalia suddenly frowned, her eyes searching Ryn's. "You spoke about your aunt in the past tense. Did she...?"

Ryn nodded. "The Kobolds... They invaded the Sylphren Wood in force. No one knows why yet."

Ryn had his arms resting on the table. Thalia reached across and squeezed his hand. Her fingers felt rough, no doubt from her work as a smith's apprentice, but he appreciated the gesture. He was glad no one pressed him further for information. He knew he would need to tell them more and explain his Etching eventually, but everything still felt too fresh for him to go into detail readily. A silence fell over the group.

Finally, Shilo of all people cleared her throat. She'd spoken barely more than Ryn had. "I think," she said, apparently overcoming her shyness, "that there is something we all have in common. I think that we are all here because we want to use these gifts of ours to do something good. To help others." She nodded to Thalia. "To help Aldria," she said to Jayn. "And to make the world a safer place." She gave a slight smile to Ryn.

Slowly, they all nodded, even Jayn.

"Well said, Miss Lorn," Pavel said. He glanced at Jayn. "I'm sorry, Eldragor. I know I can't fault you for not knowing what you don't know."

"I'm sorry too," Jayn said after a moment's hesitation, though her eyes were on Ryn.

The group fell silent again. Pavel sighed, perhaps feeling responsible. He put on an air of cheerfulness. "All right, it's time we start acting like a team. Everyone put your hands in the middle." Pavel stuck his hand out over the table. The girls gave him questioning looks. "Come on, this is good for morale. Everyone put your hands in the middle."

The others each reluctantly extended a hand over the table.

"All right," Pavel said. "Now make a fist and stick your pinky out. Come on, this is how all the Watchkeepers do it."

"I don't think so," Thalia said, but she laughed as she did it.

Pavel wrapped his fist around Shilo's extended pinky. "Now everyone lock in, like this."

Jayn hesitated but then wrapped her small hand around Pavel's pinky. Ryn followed their example, taking hold of Jayn's finger as

Thalia took his, locking in between him and Shilo. Their fists made a small circle in the center of the table.

"All right," Pavel said, "now everyone shout 'Pentad' on three. One, two, three, Pentad!"

No one shouted with him, but the others laughed, and even Jayn smiled along.

Chapter 14
The First Day

RYN STOOD WITH THE REST of his Training Pentad in a paved courtyard behind the main Citadel early the next day. The morning sun had not yet crested the high city wall to their backs, so they stood in shadows as they listened to Mistress Agia Bellos, a Wave Weaver, deliver her welcoming address.

"Just by making it to this point," she said, "each of you can already count yourselves among the elite Weavers of Aldria. The Scholars tell us that only one in five children is born with the gift, and affinity in the Five Forces is evenly distributed between that twenty percent. That means, for example, that only one in twenty-five people will manifest as Wave Weavers, but many of those are too weak to do anything productive with the gift. Each of you has been deemed strongly gifted enough to join the Watchkeepers, which puts your talents at more like one in a hundred. Some of you could have used your rare gifting to join a Guild, which, frankly, would be more lucrative. Others could have joined the Standing Army and defended our borders. In choosing to join the

Watchkeepers, you chose to protect this nation from all internal threats. Few wish to acknowledge it, but the greatest threat to the internal peace of Aldria comes from those Weavers who lack the noble aspirations each of you displays. Some rogue Weavers choose to use their gifts to abuse and exploit others. Once you have completed your training, your Pentad will be deployed anywhere you are needed within Aldria to combat the corrupt Weavers and anyone else who seeks to exploit the weak and vulnerable." Mistress Bellos hesitated. Her speech so far had seemed well-rehearsed, no doubt from frequent such addresses. Now a look of concern crossed her face, and she looked at each of the five gray-clad Recruits. When she spoke again, her tone was more conversational than oratorical. "That's the speech I have given every new Pentad before you. Believe me, rogue Weavers are still an ever-present threat to Aldria, but by now everyone within the Citadel has learned of the recent Kobold incursion into the Sylphren Wood. Some of you witnessed it firsthand. I don't mean to cause alarm. We have deployed dozens of Pentads to meet the threat, and they are working with a unit of the Standing Army. However, I would be remiss if I did not say that even you may someday find yourselves facing the Kobolds in combat once you have completed your training."

She paused to gauge the impact of her words on her listeners. Ryn kept his chin up, meeting her gaze. He did not look at the others. She continued her speech, seeming to slip back into the scripted part. "Trust that we will do everything in our power to prepare you for the threats you will face. Before any of you will engage in Weaver-to-Weaver combat, you must first master your affinity and learn to Blend it with the complementary forces. Your three morning classes will focus on those areas. After lunch, you will train in combat and weaponry. Each day of training will end with the Gauntlet. For now, don't worry about that. You have a long day ahead of you."

Ryn nodded. The girls, who had each been in the Citadel for a week or two before his arrival, had filled him in on the basic outline after lunch the day before. He would be training with the master Root Weaver and learning to Blend Root with Flame and Wave.

Mistress Bellos gestured to a green-clad servant standing nearby holding a small stack of papers. He was the same man who had asked Ryn for his second name yesterday. "Giles here has the schedule for each of you," she said. "You will be challenged and you will be tested, but face each day with determination and perseverance, and you will succeed." She nodded, signaling the end of her speech. "I will see some of you shortly."

She dismissed them with a wave of her hand, turned, and walked off across the courtyard. Giles handed a scrap of paper to each of them. The five recruits compared their schedules before splitting off to their separate destinations. Shilo left alone, heading for her independent lesson with the resident master Flame Weaver. Thalia and Pavel went to the smithy to receive a lesson from Master Rohan Caston on how to Blend Aether and Stone.

That left Ryn with the headstrong Jayn Eldragor. She nodded to him before leading the way toward the greenhouses, where they were to meet with the master Root Weaver. He fell in step beside her. Despite her shorter legs, Jayn strode purposefully across the yard, and Ryn did not need to alter his gait to stay in sync with her. She glanced at him once or twice but made no effort at conversation. Her fair hair and complexion would not have stood out in Aen's Hollow, but everything else about her would have. Her straight-backed posture and the way she carried her chin conveyed a confidence he had never seen in a girl her age.

Ryn cleared his throat. He knew he should make an effort to be friendly if they were going to be training together, but he didn't know where to start with her. She seemed to come from a completely different world. "So," he said. She answered with only a glance, so he continued. "Are you like, some kind of princess then?"

The straight line of her mouth curved into a slight smirk. She shook her head. "You really are from out in the woods, huh?"

He shrugged. They had not slowed their brisk pace.

She shook her head, keeping her eyes forward as she spoke to him. "Aldria is not a monarchy." She said it as if she were explaining that the sky was blue. "Yes, my mother is the Fourth Pentarch, appointed by the Hall of the Assembly, but her political power does not extend to me. If she were to step down, the Hall would appoint someone else to the position. One might suppose that I have a measure of influence because I have my mother's ear, but anyone who would suppose that does not know my mother."

Ryn nodded. "She sounds like my aunt."

For some reason, that seemed to amuse Jayn greatly. Rather than respond to his comment, however, she continued her own line of thought, speaking as if musing aloud. "It's true my mother's position has afforded me the best education that can be got in Aldria, but anyone with sufficient means could do the same. That's what makes Aldria a true republic."

Ryn nodded. Then he made a decision. Jayn clearly already considered him to be a simple country rube, so there was no use dissembling. He was here to learn after all, so he needn't try to hide his ignorance. "I know we're a republic," he said, "but what exactly does that mean?"

She stopped, turning fully to face him. She studied him with a puzzled look. Then she shook her head and resumed walking. He didn't know what to make of that, but she did launch into a hasty explanation. "The Hall of the Assembly. Every single member is elected by a general vote of the citizenry."

Ryn frowned. "I've never voted. And I don't think my aunt ever did, either." He wondered how he could be expected to select someone to make decisions in such a faraway place as Appencourt.

Jayn scoffed. "Well, perhaps not, all the way out in the Sylphren Wood. Did that little village of yours not have any government officials?"

He shrugged. "Just the tax collector, I suppose." In all the fairy tales, tax collectors were depicted as greedy, evil men, but Mr. Thrudow in Aen's Hollow had a decent reputation, his only sign of any wealth being that he alone in the village owned a horse that wasn't used for farm work.

"Well, likely then the county seat is in the nearest town. For the Sylphren Wood, I believe that would be Thorpe. That's where the vote would be held, every five years."

Ryn scoffed. "Thorpe? That's three days away on foot. I'm sure no one in Aen's Hollow ever traveled that far just to vote between strangers."

Jayn shrugged. "It's not a perfect system, but what is? It ensures at least some of the citizenry have a say. It certainly makes us better than Tamor, where the emperor can oppress the people however he sees fit."

Jayn's political lesson came to an abrupt end as they arrived at the greenhouses, large, impressive buildings made of glass and metal. Through the fogged windows, Ryn could see a menagerie of verdant plants. He recognized barely half of them, and most of those he had only seen in Marla's illustrated book. He did not get a chance to explore the greenhouses that day, however. Mistress Gwen Hinter stood outside waiting for them. She nodded in greeting, introduced herself, and led them to a shed that stood apart from the five greenhouses.

Mistress Hinter was of a height with Jayn, though much rounder. She wore a voluminous green robe, rather than the gray uniform of the Watchkeepers, though she did have the leaf sigil pinned to her chest. A messy bun barely contained her frizzy brown hair, and when she spoke, delicate wrinkles spread out from the corners of her narrowed eyes. The shed they entered was larger than Marla's cottage and appointed with everything an herbalist might ever need. Shelves lined all four walls, crammed with mortars, bowls, vials, and plenty of things Ryn did not recognize. Drying racks suspended from the ceiling contained more clumps of herbs than Ryn could harvest in a week of foraging and in greater variety than the entire Sylphren Wood held. An oaken table at the center of the room provided plenty of work surface, though it currently stood bare, save for a white chicken in a wire cage.

Ryn cocked an eyebrow at the chicken, at a loss to understand its presence here. He glanced at Mistress Hinter. Here was yet another stranger he would have to get to know. He wondered how he would be able to keep them all straight in his mind. She seemed rather friendly.

She spread her arms and smiled at each of them. "Well, my darlings," she said, her voice deep but not unfeminine. "Are we ready to begin?"

Ryn only nodded. Jayn glanced around the shed with an appraising look. "Are there no other students?" she asked.

Mistress Hinter shook her head. "Not at the moment. You lucky ducklings will get all of my attention for the next hour."

Jayn seemed surprised at that. "Is that… typical?" she asked.

Mistress Hinter nodded. "Oh, it's not uncommon at all. I'm sure Agia gave you her speech this morning about how rare Weavers of your caliber are. We typically only graduate a handful of Pentads in a year. The Watchkeepers favor quality over quantity, and our methods work. A well-trained Pentad is a formidable unit, you will soon find. Now, if you have no other questions, shall we begin?"

Jayn nodded.

"This will be your first lesson on Blending Wave and Root. Just as roots take in water for nourishment, so Root subsumes Wave. Root is the force of growth, and Wave is the force of stability. Together they make a potent combination." She had been speaking to both of them, but now she looked Ryn directly in the eye. "Ryn, I am told that you have already used your gifting to heal others, including some rather life-threatening wounds."

He nodded. "Yes, ma'am."

She frowned and gave a slight shake of her head, though she continued in her amiable tone. "You performed admirably, given the circumstances, but one should not be forced to run before he can walk. Now that you are here, you will not be doing any more healing without permission and supervision. Do you understand?"

He nodded again. He wondered if she knew about the practice lessons Nyssa had given him, when she cut her own arms and let him heal her, but he decided it was best not to mention it if Mistress Hinter didn't already know.

"Good," she said. "Given your experience, perhaps you have felt the frustration of only being able to help after the damage has been done."

He remembered the regret he'd felt realizing that Tabbot and the others had died before he could heal them.

"This is where Wave comes in. Wave Weavers create wards, and Root Weavers heal. When you combine the two together, what do you get?"

Jayn's hand shot up. Mistress Hinter arched an eyebrow at that. Jayn lowered her hand with a sheepish grin and fought to contain her eagerness. "Wards on a person?" she asked.

Mistress Hinter nodded with an indulgent smile. "Very good, Jayn. There are many ways to blend these two forces, but it essentially boils down to the placing of wards not in a defined area but on a living being. Properly planned and placed wards can prevent someone from being injured in the first place."

Ryn's eyes widened. Neither Pavel nor Nyssa had told him much about Blending, both advising him to only focus on Root, so he had only been able to speculate about its potential. He glanced at the table. "A living being?" he said. "You mean, like a chicken?"

Mistress Hinter nodded to him now. "Indeed. Hetty here will be our test subject this morning." She gestured grandly to the white hen in the cage.

It was so obvious that Ryn didn't know how he had not realized it before. He had only ever considered Root's potential to heal humans, but of course it would work just as well on animals and even plants, as the testing had shown.

Mistress Hinter seemed to understand something of what had just passed through his mind by the dumbfounded look on his face. She only smiled and continued with the lesson. "We'll start with each of you only using your respective giftings and working together to Blend them. However, you will eventually practice wielding both forces, individually and then together. How well you can do so remains to be seen. Jayn, you will have it the hardest, as Root is the most difficult for other Weavers to learn. Very few Wave and Flame Weavers have any competency in healing."

Jayn only nodded, but the flinty set of her jaw made it clear she intended to be one of those few.

Mistress Hinter then explained the ward she intended to demonstrate, though most of the explanation went over Ryn's head. She spoke briskly and did not check that they were following along. She made it clear that they would not be expected to do this today. Then she set the ward. She closed her eyes for a bare moment before opening them again. That instance of concentration was all it took to conjure her tree. It sprung up quickly around her, though the spectral streaks of green light did not form any kind of tree he had seen before. The roots were shallow, the trunk long and slightly curved. It bore no branches but massive fan-like leaves at its crown. Then lines of blue suddenly swirled at her feet. Nyssa had explained to him that while Root started in the pit of one's stomach, Wave formed at the balls of one's feet. Both Ryn and Jayn's jaws dropped as they watched her wield two forces simultaneously.

The solid lines of blue traveled up the base of the tree, melting into the green and turning it a color he had first seen two days ago when they'd come in sight of the ocean. Suddenly laden with massive round fruit, the sea green tree bent toward the silent hen in the cage. Light dripped from the leaves and disappeared into the chicken, which seemed oblivious to the whole spectacle. The light around Mistress Hinter faded and disappeared. The hen clucked softly and cocked its head at the three people staring at it. The only sign it had been laced was faint gleams of green almost like iridescence on its feathers.

Jayn spoke first. "What did you do?" she asked, almost managing to hide the awe in her voice.

"A simple deflection ward," Mistress Hinter said. "Tomorrow, I'll let the two of you practice making it together." Jayn grinned in anticipation, but Mistress Hinter's smile and voice took on a merry edge. "*If* you can catch Hetty before our hour is up."

With no further explanation, the master Weaver flipped open the latch on the hen's cage. As if on cue, Hetty hopped out, fluttered off the table, and ran through the open door. Ryn and Jayn exchanged confused looks. Mistress Hinter placed her hands on her ample hips. "Well, go on!" she said.

Ryn looked back to Jayn with a broad grin, but the Fourth Pentarch's daughter had set her jaw again and nodded seriously. "Yes, ma'am," she said and ran out the door.

Ryn had no choice but to follow, though he felt foolish. This was not how he expected his first lesson with the Watchkeepers to go. Something had seemed strange about the chicken as it darted from the shed, and now that Ryn saw it in full daylight, he knew what it was. The chicken appeared... blurry. As it ran toward the greenhouses, no faster than a normal chicken, a strange afterimage trailed behind it like the ghost of another chicken dogging its heels. Ryn's eyes couldn't focus on it and actually seemed to slide off it to the surrounding grass. Jayn quickly closed the distance in a full sprint and bent to lunge at the chicken with her hands. She seemed to connect with the bird's round body, but it kept going, and she clutched at nothing but the air.

She looked back at Ryn, baring her teeth as she groaned. "Come on!" she said.

He realized he was standing still. With a nod, he took off running. The hen ran along the side of one of the greenhouses, and Ryn dashed around the other way, hoping to circle around and take it by surprise. It almost worked. At the backside of the greenhouse, he found Hetty running straight toward him. The bird stopped and that strange doubled image caught up to it, forming one whole chicken for a moment. Then it spun to run the other way. Ryn grabbed at it. He felt the brush of feathers, but the hen somehow slipped his grasp.

This continued for several minutes, with Ryn and Jayn taking it in turns to lunge at the chicken. Hetty did not try fleeing the compound but stayed near the greenhouses. When it got far enough away from them, it would stop to peck casually at the ground. They tried approaching it slowly, but as soon as either got within grabbing distance, the bird would take off running or flap its wings and hop out of reach.

Jayn gritted her teeth, focusing solely on the bird, her round cheeks reddened from the exertion. Ryn felt his face flush as well, but more from embarrassment. Several green-pinned Watch-keepers had emerged from the greenhouses and other nearby sheds to watch the two new recruits chase the chicken. From their wry grins and joking comments, Ryn deduced that they had all faced Mistress Hinter's chicken challenge on their first day of training as well.

After another unsuccessful grab, Jayn grunted in frustration, stopping to catch her breath. Mistress Hinter leaned against the side of her shed, watching them with her arms crossed. They had to be close to running out of time. Jayn waved her arm at Ryn. "Come on and quit your panting," she said.

Ryn swallowed, his mouth dry from the running, but he only nodded. The pair redoubled their effort, running at the bird simultaneously from two different directions. This caused the bird to squawk in agitation, but they still couldn't get a firm grip on it. It reminded Ryn of trying to catch fish bare-handed in a stream, a childhood game at which he had never succeeded.

Ryn closed in on the bird once again, and it turned a sharp angle and darted toward Jayn. Ryn turned to follow, but the bird zagged again. In their blind pursuit, the two Weavers had lost sight of each other, until they collided. Both fell backwards, sprawling on the ground, as the onlookers erupted in laughter.

Jayn sat up, her face crimson as she glared at Ryn. "You clumsy buffoon!" she said.

He offered a sheepish grin. He climbed to his feet and extended a hand to help her up. She ignored it and stood on her own. He looked at the hen, standing not ten paces away, pecking at the ground. "This isn't working," he said.

He expected a mocking retort, but Jayn only sighed and nodded. She seemed completely unaware of the crowd they had gathered, narrowing her eyes at Hetty. He admired her ability to do that, focusing single-mindedly on the task at hand with seemingly no regard for how stupid they looked. Perhaps she was being too single-minded.

"We need a new strategy," he said. "We have to get around that ward."

She considered it, then seemed to brighten. "The ward... She called it a deflection ward. Think. If you put that on a soldier and sent him into battle... Well, he would be a hard target to hit."

"It's like... the bird's not where it's supposed to be."

"Exactly. Let's try this. Don't reach for where the chicken is but where it's going to be."

He nodded. It was a good idea in theory but harder to do in practice. His mind told him exactly where the chicken was and seemed to rebel at the idea of missing on purpose. After a few more failed passes, Jayn finally got a good grip on the bird. She reached out, snatching at the air in front of it, and then suddenly it was there, caught by the nape of its neck in her small fist. Hetty still almost got away. Jayn wrapped her arms around the bird, hugging it to her chest, but it kept squirming, and she couldn't keep a firm grip on it, as if it really were a slimy fish instead of a feathery bird. It got its wings free and flapped up and out of her arms.

Ryn almost made a blunder that would have forced them to start over, but he stopped his lunge short, snatching at the air directly in front of Jayn instead of at the bird. He made contact with that squirming mass of feathers as it materialized in his grip. He hugged it to himself, even pressing his face down against it, heedless if it might try pecking at him. Jayn reached up and grabbed hold of the bird as well. It felt as if they were struggling to detain a drunken brawler rather than one small chicken. Finally, Hetty quieted, clucking softly in his arms. He relaxed enough to hear the cheering, as the gathered crowd of Watchkeepers hooted and hollered. Despite their jesting before, they seemed genuinely impressed now.

Mistress Hinter ambled over to retrieve the bird. "Well done," she said. Ryn felt slightly guilty as he saw Hetty's ruffled and torn feathers. He had not considered its safety as he wrestled with it. At a touch, Mistress Hinter dissolved the ward around the bird. Then she summoned her strange tree for a moment to drape one broad leaf over the chicken, healing in a moment whatever damage he and Jayn had done. She regarded the two panting recruits. "That may have seemed like a silly game, but it was an important first lesson. When your foe is not a chicken but a rogue Weaver, you will need quickness, not only physical but also mental." She looked first to Jayn. "Now, you will need to hurry so you will not be late for your lessons with Captain Lahmeer."

"Captain Lahmeer?" Jayn asked. She seemed to have recovered her poise, though Ryn was still out of breath. "I thought I was to train with Mistress Bellos?"

Mistress Hinter took on a sterner tone. "Your lessons on Stone Blending will be with Mistress Bellos, but your one-on-one instruction will be with Captain Lahmeer. You will find more success if you simply do as you are told without so many questions. Not all instructors here are as patient as I."

"Understood." Jayn gave Ryn a simple nod in farewell and hurried off away from the greenhouses.

Ryn dug the scrap of paper from his pocket to see where his next lesson would be. "No need to check," Mistress Hinter said. "You stay here with me."

The hour that followed was an in-depth lesson on how to create Rootbalm. "Whatever else we do," Mistress Hinter said, "we will start each session making Rootbalm. The Watchkeepers can never have too much." He quickly got the hang of it. They used as the basis an ointment for relieving swelling, a simple combination of two plants he had read about but never seen in person. One ground easily into a sticky pulp. He asked many questions about where they were found and how they were harvested. These sorts of questions, Mistress Hinter was happy to answer. "Rarely do I have students who come in with such extensive knowledge of herbalism already," she said. Lacing the ointment involved visualizing the tree and then depositing some small part of it into the medicine. A seed made the most sense, though she was quick to remind him that it was still just a mental metaphor and not at all what was really happening. He nodded as if he understood. He dropped a flashing green acorn into the mortar, imbuing the white mixture with hints of spectral green light, visible only to him and other Weavers. She had him repeat the exercise half a dozen times before the hour was up. She had to warn him several times to draw energy only from himself. The materials they worked with and the plants hanging overhead could all be used as fuel, but doing so would ruin them for other purposes. When the hour was up, she gave him careful directions to the location of his next lesson.

Master Jalen Nox conducted his classes in a spacious stone structure behind the stables. The smell of manure and hay wafted in through the open windows. Training dummies, made of wood or cloth stuffed with straw, lined one of the long walls. Ryn caught up with Shilo at the entrance. She had had her first lesson up there before going to train with Pavel and the Aether master. Her face shone with beads of perspiration from whatever she had done in her first two lessons. Ryn knew he looked just as tired. His woolen shirt, still damp with sweat, clung to his back.

The Master Flame Weaver was not tall for a man, shorter even than Ryn, but he was solidly built, his broad shoulders straining under a short-sleeved gray shirt. Bristly black stubble covered his square head. He stood barefoot on the stony floor of his dojo, worn smooth and glossy by decades of training. He greeted them with a stern nod. "Welcome back, Shilo," he said. "And you must be Ryn?" He spoke in a soft voice, almost devoid of emotion.

"Yes, sir," Ryn said.

"I hear you have quite the remarkable Etching, though the Council is still at a loss as to how to properly test its limits. They were too overly concerned with your safety to consider my suggestions."

Ryn smirked, assuming it to be a joke, but Master Nox's bland expression showed no hint of humor. Ryn glanced at Shilo, who stood rigidly at attention. She had more experience with this man, so Ryn decided to follow her example.

Master Nox continued. "Still, yours appears to be a rather promising Pentad. Shilo here has already gained a degree of mastery of her Etching." He gestured to the corner of the room, where the splintered remnants of several training dummies lay in a pile. "We are still working on... moderating her strength."

Shilo lowered her eyes, as if embarrassed.

"Today's lesson will be something neither of you have done before. To the uninitiated, it may seem odd that Flame and Root are complementary forces. It is easy to understand that Flame subsumes Root, just as wood fuels a fire's growth, but how can you Blend the two? Flame is the force of chaos and destruction, while Root is about healing and restoration, correct? Well, while Flame is best utilized in combat, it is not an inherently violent force. Flame is about energy, amplifying the energy found in all living things. On its own, this energy cannot escape the body, except in the most rudimentary of ways, through a punch or as a tiny spark to light a candle or dry kindling. Root, on the other hand, is always directed outward, used to restore the energy of others. Blending the two then enables one to transfer energy from one source to another.

"When you think of it that way, as the power of transference, the possibilities are endless. Sure, some still use it aggressively, sapping strength from their foes. However, it can be used constructively. When Root is used alone to heal fatigue, it is really only a masking of weariness. Real rest will still eventually be required. However, Blending can be used to transfer real vitality from a well-rested man into an exhausted one, allowing the two to share the burden and continue moving. Because such things involve tampering with actual life forces, it will be several weeks before either of you is allowed to attempt such a lacing. However, there are many other ways to transfer energy. We will start with one of the most basic and practical ones."

Master Nox led them to one of the walls, opposite the training dummies. Here, as in most rooms within the Watchkeeper compound, glass lanterns containing those strange balls of light provided illumination. Ryn had concluded on his first day that the light was produced through Weaving, but he had not had a chance to ask how. Master Nox showed them.

He blinked and suddenly a mass of swirling red light surrounded him. The light of Flame shone brighter than any of the other forces, though it did not reflect off the bare stone walls as a true light would. This apparition existed somehow only in the minds of the Weavers who perceived it. Master Nox's hands began to glow. Ryn was reminded of Mercer's glowing hands that chaotic night in the woods. "Illumination is a simple lacing," Master Nox said. "By Blending in Root, it can be externalized." Suddenly, a mass of shimmering green vines emerged from his torso. They spread down his arms, disappearing into the red flames that swirled around his hands and tinging the light orange. The internal light beneath his skin concentrated into his palms and then emerged as two perfectly round balls of luminescence hovering in the air. By some internal will, he caused them to float up to the ceiling.

Despite her attempts at military stiffness, Shilo could not help but gape in awe. Ryn openly grinned. "Once you two master this technique, lamplighting around the compound will be added to your chore rotations," Master Nox said. They had been given a reprieve the first day, but each new day of lessons would begin with an hour of early morning chores. "Let's try working together now."

Master Nox walked them through the process of Blending the forces between two people. For beginners, physical touch helped. He took their right arms and showed them how to make the connection. They did not hold hands but instead grasped each other's forearms. Ryn was too focused on the task at hand to be overly distracted by making such prolonged physical contact with a girl. Shilo barely seemed to notice; hers was the more difficult half of the Blending.

Ryn kept his oak tree small. Nothing green grew within the stone dojo, so he could only use his own energy as fuel. He sent the branches along his arm, extending them toward Shilo. He did not

Dowse her or do anything really. The swirling Flame lacings around her leapt to meet his branches, pulling them in. On their first attempt, the sudden jerk broke his concentration and the tree vanished. He mumbled an apology and they tried again. He had to keep the tree growing at a constant and steady rate to keep her flames from coming too far down his arm. He felt his energy flowing around him and away like standing in a strong river current.

Shilo's task was immensely more complicated. She had to take in an additional force she had never used before, channeling it through her body and into the palm of her free hand. After what felt like several minutes of concentration, a flickering orb finally emerged. She gasped in wonder, losing her own concentration and extinguishing the Flame lacings around her.

Ryn wasn't prepared for that. He was still feeding her Root, so for a moment, with nowhere else to go, the branches surged up her arm and around her. He Dowsed her then for a split second, the collection of sensations that made up her being appearing briefly in his mind's eye. The shock of that broke his own concentration. He flushed with embarrassment, as if he had accidentally seen some hidden part of her, but Shilo didn't seem to notice. Her dark eyes glittered in the flickering light of the orb that still hovered above her hand. It was only half the size of Master Nox's and did not maintain a persistent glow. After less than a minute it dimmed and winked out. Shilo did not seem disappointed by the meager results. She turned to Master Nox with a broad grin. His blank countenance remained unchanged, but he did nod in approval.

"Very good for your first attempt," he said. "Once mastered, both of you should be able to create orbs that last on their own for up to a week. Now try again."

Before the hour was up, they had made four more orbs of light, each bigger and steadier than the last, and sent them floating up against the ceiling alongside the two Master Nox had made. The Flame master finally dismissed them for lunch. Ryn's stomach growled in anticipation, and he plodded wearily down the stairs. It wasn't just a physical tiredness that overtook him but a fatigue he had never felt before, as if he had overstrained his brain. This was the drain Weavers felt when they approached the limit of their abilities.

Shilo had to be just as worn out, but she bubbled with excitement over the orbs they'd created. This overcame her usual shyness, and she chatted happily with Ryn as they crossed the yard to the towering black Citadel. Her solo session with Master Nox had focused mainly on controlling her explosive Etching, in case she needed to incapacitate someone without doing major bodily harm. She spoke briefly of her training with Pavel and the Aether master. Flame and Aether were both inwardly focused, so Blending the two allowed the user to improve their bodies in new and interesting ways. Shilo had spent that lesson feeding Pavel Flame while he wove a lacing to increase his tolerance of heat. He tested its effectiveness by holding his hand over a burning candle.

The way Pavel cradled and favored his singed hand at lunch showed the lacing had not been completely effective. Ryn almost offered to heal it before remembering the injunction Mistress Hinter had placed against doing such a thing. Pavel ate heartily, going back up for seconds, and Jayn downed several glasses of water. Ryn and the other two girls scarfed down their meals as well, though it did not have quite the same restorative effect on them. The group spoke briefly of their individual and paired experiences, though neither Jayn nor Ryn mentioned the chicken chase. Ryn groaned as they filed back out into the yard, realizing the day was only halfway over.

Chapter 15
The Gauntlet

THE AFTERNOON LESSONS were a chaotic affair. Their schedules listed it simply as "Fitness and Weapons Training." When the five recruits reached the large open field at the far back corner of the compound, where the two massive city walls came together, they found dozens of gray-clad men and women training. Apparently, physical conditioning and weapons practice was an ongoing pursuit for all Watchkeepers, not just the Training Pentads. A large swath was set aside for archers and their practice targets, while several round stone platforms served as dueling arenas. Some practiced with staves, wooden or blunted swords, and various other weapons, while others dueled using the Five Forces.

In one ring, two young women faced off, one swathed in swirling red light, and the other in white. The Flame Weaver's hands and bare feet glowed as she attempted to strike the Aether Weaver, who deftly dodged each attempt with graceful, sweeping movements. Pavel and Jayn stood and watched the fight with fascination, but Ryn, Thalia, and Shilo were drawn to another ring, where an even stranger fight took place.

A few days ago, Ryn would only have seen a man and a woman engaged in a strange sort of dance, standing five paces apart and staring intently at one another while making subtle movements with their hands and feet. Now, with his Weaver-awakened eyes, Ryn saw a kaleidoscope of movement and light surrounding the pair. Concentric circles of blue Wave surrounded the man, forming shields or wards of some kind. The woman attacked him with volleys of Aether. Each time Ryn had seen Pavel Weaving, white light had flowed from the crown of his head down to encircle his body. Aether could only enhance its user and not others, the former thief had said, but it also somehow counteracted Wave. That was how the female Weaver used it now. Streaks of white light poured seemingly from her eyes and lanced outward to attack the Wave Weaver's shields.

Some of the Aether made it through, shattering the blue rings, but the Wave Weaver slid his feet across the ground in small sweeping movements to create more Wave circles. He also fought back against the Aether attacks. Vines of green Root burst from his midsection, swinging wildly like cows' tails. Root trumps Aether, Pavel had once told Ryn. He saw now what the thief had meant by that. Anywhere green and white collided, the Aether simply vanished, like so much smoke dissipating in the air.

The attacking Aether Weaver seemed to be winning the duel, dispelling the blue rings faster than the Wave Weaver could replace them. Suddenly, a massive limb of green Root emerged from the defender's back, circling in a wide arc toward the Aether Weaver. Perhaps he hoped she would be too focused on guiding her streaks of Aether through the tangle of Root to notice. Ryn wondered what the man hoped to do if the curving arc of green managed to reach her, but it never did.

The woman saw it, and she flung her hand out toward it. From the palm of her hand, lines of yellow light emerged, bending and splitting at right angles to form a complex web of tessellation. Thalia gasped at the sight of it. The mass of green vines withered on contact, shriveling and disappearing in a moment. Such was the force of the counterattack that all Root disappeared from around the defender. A final volley of unimpeded Aether surged from the attacker, wiping away all the Wave shields. The white light blew past the man, though it could not even ruffle his shaggy brown hair the way a true wind would.

Still, the destruction of the Wave shields must have signaled the end of the duel. The Wave Weaver bent over, placing his hands on his knees and panting as if he'd just run a footrace. Sweat glistened on both their foreheads. The woman staggered as she took a few steps forward. The man smiled good-naturedly as they shook hands.

"I had no idea Stone could…" Thalia said, speaking to herself and not finishing the thought aloud.

So that yellow light had been Stone. Ryn had not seen it wielded before. He didn't know it had any uses besides enchanting weapons and armor. Apparently, neither had Thalia. What would that surge of Root have done, had the woman not deflected it? Which force trumped Stone? A hundred questions bloomed in Ryn's mind as he realized just how complex the Five Forces and their interactions really were. He shook his head in bewilderment and glanced at Thalia, doing a double take when he saw another woman standing close beside her.

This woman, just as tall as Thalia but slimmer, had not been watching the duel but studying Ryn and his companions. She wore the gray Watchkeeper tabard over divided skirts rather than trousers. Her skin resembled leather, both in color and in its apparent texture. She kept her gray hair in a tidy bun, and she studied the recruits with dark intelligent eyes set into a lean, almost skeletal face. Her prominent nose reminded Ryn of an eagle's beak.

"Mistress Whitcomb," Shilo said, recognizing the woman.

The woman nodded. "Training Pentad," she said, "gather to me."

The clear command in her voice drew the attention of Pavel and Jayn, who had still been watching the other duel. As they moved closer, Ryn glanced back at Shilo.

Shilo shrugged. "Mistress Whitcomb took an interest in my Etching when I first arrived."

Mistress Lane Whitcomb, as Ryn would soon learn, oversaw the training and conditioning of all recruits. She looked at each member of Ryn's Pentad in turn before speaking. "Don't get too excited about what you see here," she said, gesturing toward the surrounding arenas. "It will be some weeks before any of you are allowed to wield the Five Forces against each other, even in training."

Ryn nodded. Jayn and Shilo muttered, "Yes, ma'am."

Thalia followed her agreement by saying, "May I ask a question, though? You're a Stone Weaver?"

Mistress Whitcomb nodded. Ryn noticed the yellow pin on her tabard. "Was that the question?" she asked.

"No, I just... Well, I wanted to know what that lacing was." Thalia gestured to the duelists, who were now walking away from the raised platform, chatting amicably.

Mistress Whitcomb nodded, a small smile spreading across her weathered face. She seemed to understand not just Thalia's question but all the other questions behind it. "You will learn it all in due time, the positive as well as the negative interactions between the Five Forces. Stone consumes Root, just as a blade hews through wood. Aether consumes Wave, just as all life consumes water to live. And in turn, Root consumes Aether, just as a stand of trees breaks the wind."

"Trees break the wind?" Ryn heard himself asking, the skepticism clear in his voice.

Mistress Whitcomb only shrugged. "Remember, these are all just analogies created by men to explain the interactions between the Five Forces. You could also ask why Aether destroys Wave. Why are they not complementary? Does not water enhance life? Do not storm winds whip up the waves into powerful waterspouts? Yet you saw that Wave vanishes on contact with Aether, so we must use the best metaphor we can to describe the real interactions."

Despite her gruff exterior, Mistress Whitcomb seemed willing to answer their novice questions. This emboldened Ryn. He cleared his throat and asked his own nagging question. "Could the Wave Weaver have countered the Stone in turn with... Flame?" At this point, he was only guessing at what trumped Stone.

He was glad that Mistress Whitcomb did not rebuff the question. "Perhaps, though very few Weavers ever gain competency with the forces that are not complementary to their innate gifting. He would also have had to give up on his Wave shields." In answer to Ryn's questioning look, she added, "A Weaver cannot wield more than two forces at the same time." She held out her open palms. "We say this is because a Weaver only has two hands. That is just another analogy, but an important one to learn."

She considered each of them again before continuing. "Now, I suggest you reserve any other questions you might have about the Five Forces for a later time. In fact, you will not be doing any

Weaving with me today. Any Watchkeeper who has ever been in the field will tell you that there comes a point when you reach your limit and can no longer rely on the gift. At that point, you are no different from any man, and only your wits, your strength, and your stamina can aid you then. It is my job to ensure each of you attains a certain degree of physical fitness and competency with a weapon that best suits you. We will start with conditioning."

Conditioning, as near as Ryn could figure, meant running. Mistress Whitcomb set them a course that took them along the perimeter of the entire Watchkeeper compound. She had them run it twice before allowing them a brief respite to catch their breath and drink from the water pump. It seemed to take Ryn longer than the others to catch his breath. He had not had many reasons to run in the Sylphren Wood. Mistress Whitcomb gave them each another appraising look before sending them off to train with different weapons. She had apparently been given a detailed report on each of them.

"Pavel Talvor," she said. "I've heard of your salvaged blades. I'd love to take a look at them sometime, if you'd permit me." Pavel only nodded. "In the meantime, head over there and find yourself a sparring partner." She gestured toward where several Weavers were practicing with wooden training swords. "We'll see how much technique you've picked up over your years spent as a rogue."

Ryn frowned at that, reminded of Mistress Bellos' speech about the dangers of rogue Weavers. Well, Pavel must certainly have been one if he'd used his Aether Weaving to help him steal. Pavel only grinned and loped off toward the swordsmen. Mistress Whitcomb turned her attention to Shilo and Thalia, who stood close to each other. The two seemed to have formed a quick friendship, which did not extend to the other girl in their group.

Jayn stood off to the side with her arms crossed, looking haughty as usual.

"The fisherwoman and the redsmith's apprentice," Mistress Whitcomb continued. "Both professions call for strong hands, I reckon. I'll start you two off with quarterstaffs. It may not be as glamorous as a sword, but the staff is an excellent weapon. If you know what you are doing, you can take down even the greatest swordsman."

She gave them quick directions on who to see for lessons, before turning to Jayn. "Jayn Eldragor, I understand you are already adept in several weapons. Which do you figure is your best?"

"The sword, ma'am," Jayn replied without hesitation.

Mistress Whitcomb frowned and shook her head. "No, that won't do. You're athletic enough, but you don't have the reach. A sword is no practical weapon for someone of your size."

Jayn flushed but managed to keep her tone even. "I… had hoped to be a Flame Weaver."

"Yes, I am aware of that. Had that been your gifting, you could have been a swordswoman, but the stars were not in it. What else can you do?"

"I am… competent with a bow."

Mistress Whitcomb nodded. "Yes, that is a weapon far more suited for a Wave Weaver. Head to the range and find a spare bow. I will see how competent you are in a moment."

That left Ryn. Mistress Whitcomb looked him over once again, with a slight frown this time. "The herbalist," she said. "You're a scrawny one. I'd like to put you on the bow too, but you'll need to build some muscle first. The Root Weaver is arguably the most important member of a Pentad, so you cannot be at the forefront of a brawl. Your Pentad must learn to protect you, because you are the one who will heal them once the fight is over."

Ryn tried to keep his back straight and his chin up. "I'd still like to learn," he said.

Her frown disappeared into a smile. "Oh, you will. No Weaver can be completely defenseless. I think I'll put you on knives. Most opponents will outreach you, but you can exploit that if you get in close. Knives are handy in tight spaces, and I'll teach you how to throw them."

Mistress Whitcomb walked him through the basics of knife throwing, setting him up with a set of well-balanced steel knives and a large wooden target board. The technique was more complicated than he would have thought. She explained that while the knives could be thrown straight like darts, he would get more range and accuracy by hurling them so that they spun end over end. However, if a spinning knife struck its target with anything other than the tip, it did little damage. While the angle and power of the throw mattered, the key factor was distance. He could stand neither too close nor too far away from the target. Hitting the stationary wooden target proved easy enough, as she showed him exactly where to plant his feet to get the desired range. However, he quickly realized how tricky this would be in a real fight, when your opponent could not be trusted to stand a set number of paces away from you. By the end of the training session, his arm was sore from the repeated over-the-shoulder gesture.

After getting him started, Mistress Whitcomb moved about the training yard, checking on the others and periodically returning to critique his throws. Finally, she gathered them all up, congratulated them on their efforts, and dismissed them after giving them directions to the final session of their day, what she and the other instructors had referred to only as "the Gauntlet" with no elaboration.

Nyssa Lahmeer stood waiting for them outside a building that looked like a tin shed enlarged to an enormous scale. She smiled as she took in their weary countenances.

"Captain Lahmeer," Jayn said with a formal nod. Ryn wondered how their one-on-one training session had gone that morning.

"Welcome, recruits," Nyssa said. "Are you ready for the Gauntlet?"

Pavel sighed. "If I'm being honest," he said, "I don't think I am. I feel pretty exhausted, both physically and… Weaver-ly."

Nyssa's grin broadened. "Yeah, that's… sort of the point. Follow me."

She led them through a narrow door set into the corrugated wall near the corner. The interior did appear to be one expansive room, but Ryn could not see much of it. Overhead, the sloping ceiling, reinforced by exposed metal beams and struts, disappeared into the dimly lit darkness. They stood in a space partitioned by ten-foot black walls, apparently built of the same material as the Watchkeepers' main Citadel. Once Nyssa closed the door behind them, the only illumination came from two Weaver lights suspended on either side of the entrance. The only other features in the room were a black door set into the opposite wall and a tapestry hanging to their left. That side and the wall behind them were the tin outer walls of the building, while the remaining two walls were of the ancient-looking black stone.

Ryn stepped closer to the tapestry and quickly puzzled out what it depicted. The hanging displayed a visual representation of the Five Forces and their interactions. Spaced evenly in a circle were five gray boxes, each emblazoned with a different symbol: a green leaf, a red flame, a white swirl, a yellow mountain, and a blue wave. A circle of white lines connected the five symbols, showing how each force could be fed into the next through Blending. The lines were fatter on one end and narrowed toward the other, indicating direction. Those relationships were easy to understand: Root subsumes Wave, Flame subsumes Root, Aether subsumes Flame, Stone subsumes Aether, and Wave subsumes Stone.

Ryn's head started to spin as he turned his attention to the center of the circle, where crisscrossing black lines showed the negative relations between the Five Forces. He suddenly understood how complicated it actually was. The intersecting lines narrowed toward the force that canceled out its opposite. Root destroys Aether, Aether destroys Wave, Wave destroys…

Nyssa cleared her throat to get their attention. Ryn wasn't the only one studying the tapestry. Of the Pentad members, only Jayn had come in already understanding the complexities of the Five Forces, as she had lived her whole life in expectation of manifesting a gift.

"Now then," Nyssa continued, once she had everyone's attention. "Allow me to explain this test." She gestured toward the opposite door. "The Gauntlet is designed to test a Pentad's ability to work together as a unit, but I must warn you: You will not pass it today." She paused to make sure they understood the significance of that statement.

Pavel quirked an eyebrow, and Jayn opened her mouth to speak, but Nyssa cut her off.

"Some of the chambers within this room will require techniques you simply have not learned yet. You must still try. Every training day will end with another run at the Gauntlet. You will attempt to pass it, room by room, until an attendant—today that is me—decides you have put in enough effort to allow you to quit. Now, go ahead and ask the question."

Pavel was the first to get it out. "Why are we starting this now if we don't stand a chance of finishing it?"

Nyssa nodded in understanding. "There are a number of reasons. If nothing else, it is a good exercise in teamwork. In the field, there may come a time when your Pentad faces an insurmountable obstacle."

Her gaze, which had been sweeping back and forth across the five of them, now lingered on the two men. Ryn and undoubtedly Pavel knew what she meant. They had learned through Jayn that Nyssa had opted to stay in the compound to help teach the recruits rather than find a new Pentad. Likely the choice was not entirely her own.

Nyssa's voice held a certain tightness as she continued. "Even when you face impossible odds, you cannot hesitate for even a moment. An attempt must still be made. You might surprise yourselves. Moreover, this exercise will force you to think strategically, to find creative ways to use your gifts. Each chamber beyond this door contains a specific obstacle. Your attendant will explain the nature of the challenge, but we will not tell you the solution. Before we begin, there are a few key rules to remember. Some of the obstacles were constructed using Runeforms and are thus indestructible, but some rely on simple lacings of Wave and other forces. You are not to tamper with or destroy any lacings in place here. Brute force is not the solution to any of the challenges. For example, in each room, you must respect the 'ceiling' and not rise above it." She gestured upward and Ryn finally noticed the shimmering streaks of blue separating their small chamber from the rest of the building. A lacing of Wave kept them from merely scaling the sides. Nyssa nodded toward Pavel. "Your Aether Weaver could easily destroy it, but your goal is not to find a shortcut. Are there any questions before we begin?"

Jayn spoke up. "If I understand correctly, you are saying we have not yet been taught all the techniques needed to pass this test, but we must attempt it anyway. When precisely can we expect to have learned enough to succeed?"

"I cannot give you an exact day. There is a difference between knowing the techniques and being able to apply them effectively. I can tell you that no Pentad has ever completed the Gauntlet in less than a month, but almost all finish within the six months allotted for training."

Ryn had learned that he and the others would spend half a year training in Falport before spending a minimum of four and a half years in the field. After five years they could "re-up" their service or leave the organization, as Pavel intended to do. Yesterday, the prospect of training for six months had daunted Ryn, but now it seemed like hardly enough time to learn everything there was to know about Weaving.

No one else seemed to have a question. Nyssa nodded and gestured toward the black door. Jayn led the way, her back straight and chin up as always. Now that Ryn was beginning to know the three young ladies of his Pentad, even their walks seemed to characterize them. Jayn's pace bordered on a militant march, while Thalia, the muscular redsmith's apprentice, plodded solidly along, her chin level. Shilo, who moved just ahead of Ryn as they filed through the door, walked with a peculiar rolling gait, apparently adapted to the swaying deck of a ship, and she kept her eyes downcast more often than not.

The second chamber was no wider than the first but much longer. The six Weavers found themselves crowded into a space that extended about five paces before the floor fell away into a seemingly endless pit. As their eyes adjusted to the dim light, they saw the drop was only about twenty feet. An iron ladder led down into the black-stone sublevel. On the opposite side of the room, a good fifty paces away, another ladder led up to a second platform and a door. A black-stone wall bisected the pit, rising not quite to the level of either platform. The obstacle here was clear. To get to the other side they must scale the wall in the middle.

The group looked to Nyssa for instruction, but she kept moving to the right, toward the encasing black wall. She climbed up another iron ladder mounted there, passing smoothly through the shimmering "ceiling" of Wave. Whatever that barrier was, it wasn't a shield. Perhaps Jayn could discern its function. Nyssa stood atop the ten-foot wall and looked down at them. The walls separating each chamber of the Gauntlet were surprisingly thick, providing ample space to stand. Ryn guessed she would stay up there, following the group's progress from room to room without actually having to take on the obstacles herself.

They didn't make it past the first room that day. Nyssa explained the obvious, that they must scale the wall, and she offered them a few words of advice. "One cannot Weave forever, so you must all make the best use of what is a limited resource. You are all tired, and that is part of the challenge. Silverbell here does know how to mask fatigue, but doing so would only drain him further, and you cannot leave him behind." Ryn felt strange being referred to by a second name he'd only just made up yesterday. "You must move through the course together. Now begin."

The five recruits descended the ladder into the pit and crossed to the wall, which rose about twenty feet from the floor. The wall presented a completely smooth surface without any visible seams. Ryn looked to the others. His limited experience with the group told him that either Pavel or Jayn would take charge, yet both regarded the obstacle with similarly irritated expressions, and neither opted to speak. Perhaps the knowledge that they were guaranteed to fail made them reluctant to try.

After a few seconds of silence, Thalia cleared her throat. She spoke hesitantly at first, but her voice gained confidence as she continued. "Look, let's at least make an attempt here, if only because Captain Lahmeer won't let us leave until we do. This first obstacle doesn't seem too bad." The others nodded, and she pressed on. "Now I know I'm starting with the obvious here, but let's just reason through it together. This obstacle is clearly best suited for an Aether Weaver, right, Pavel?"

The former thief nodded. "Of course. I could hop it no problem, but the rest of you…"

"Right. Now Shilo and I stand the best chance of picking up Aether, but obviously we're not there yet."

Ryn tried to recall the tapestry from the other room. Aether fit between Stone and Flame on the wheel, making them complementary forces. Then he thought about how he had Weaved Root into Shilo earlier that day, and he spoke up, addressing his question to Thalia. "Could Pavel feed his Aether to us somehow?"

Thalia shook her head, and she spoke with patience as she answered, rather than annoyance at his ignorance, as Jayn surely would have. "No, Aether Weavers can only lace themselves. Even when Pavel and I practiced Blending this morning, he fed Aether directly into the metal I worked, rather than through me."

Pavel touched the wall. "It's all bound together with Stone lacings. Couldn't you make a hole, Moldo?"

It took Ryn a second to remember that Moldo was Thalia's second name. He squinted at the wall, and in the dim light, he could just make out the flickering bits of yellow that revealed the presence of a Stone enchantment.

Thalia Moldo shook her head. "We can't destroy any lacings we find, remember?"

Pavel shrugged. "We're just brainstorming here."

Thalia stepped back as if to get a better view of the wall in its entirety. "Let's just try it. How about you do hop up there, Pavel, and maybe you can help the rest of us over without any Weaving."

Pavel wagged his head from side to side as if deliberating. "Yeah, all right."

Without further discussion, he moved to one of the corners. As he did, streaks of white flashed from the crown of his head and enveloped his body. Though Ryn and the others could see it, the bands of Aether weren't true lights and offered no illumination to the dim pit. Down here, the lacings appeared a dingy gray rather than the pure white they would be in full daylight.

Apparently, Pavel could not scamper up a completely smooth surface in the same way that Ryn had seen him climb the rough-barked trees in the South Forest, but Pavel used the corner to his advantage. He jumped and pushed off one wall with his hands, before swiftly turning to push off the adjoining wall. In that way, he seemed to ricochet upward, like a fast-thrown ball careening from wall to wall. In a moment, he was atop the narrow barrier, balancing like an acrobat. He started moving back toward the center where the others waited, but then he stopped.

"Actually, the corner might aid the rest of you," he said, gesturing for them to approach. The group gathered in the corner. Pavel lay flat on his belly and reached his left arm down toward them.

"Stand back," Thalia said, and they cleared a space for her. She took a running jump and tried to seize Pavel's hand, but she banged into the wall several feet short of reaching him. She sighed, but she wasn't ready to give up. "Well, I can give each of you a boost to reach Pavel, and then once you are up, you can drop down to the other side."

Jayn sighed, finally breaking her silence. "Sure, but then how will you get over? Remember, we can't leave anyone behind."

"I know, but let's just try and see how far we can get."

Jayn shrugged in response. Thalia looked at each of the others in turn, sizing them up. Her gaze settled on Ryn. "Give me a hand, and we'll boost the other two up first."

They started with Jayn. She and Shilo were both slender, but Jayn stood several inches shorter. Ryn imitated Thalia's form, cupping his hands to take one of Jayn's feet. The blonde Wave Weaver placed her hands atop their heads, and they boosted her up. Jayn reached up toward Pavel and they grasped each other's forearms. Ryn and Thalia boosted her higher, and she scrambled up and onto Pavel's back. The Aether Weaver groaned as Jayn dug her knees into him. She moved to a spot further down the wall and lowered herself down the other side. They heard a muffled thud as her feet hit the ground. Then they hoisted Shilo up in like manner.

Ryn and Thalia were left appraising each other. She stood several inches taller, and Ryn's arms looked especially scrawny compared to hers. She clearly was the heavier one, but Ryn had no desire to acknowledge that. He had limited experience with women but knew they tended to be sensitive about their weight.

Thalia seemed to sense his dilemma. She smiled and said, "Come on, Ryn, you can hop up on my shoulders."

He nodded and she crouched down into a squat, facing the wall. Careful of where he placed his hands and feet, Ryn climbed up on her shoulders. She reached up and took hold of his ankles, then slowly rose from her crouch. Pavel's face was already beaded in sweat from helping the girls over, but he quickly had Ryn up and down the other side. That side of the pit seemed darker, and Shilo and Jayn were shadowy figures beside him.

Over an hour passed before Thalia admitted defeat. For a while, Ryn could only stand there and listen to Thalia's attempts to scramble up the side of the wall to reach Pavel's dangling arm. They'd already known that wouldn't work, but no one said anything. Eventually, Pavel was the one to suggest they try a new tactic. Thalia thought it over for a moment, and then another idea seemed to come to her. "Ryn," she called, her voice muffled through the wall, "can you come back over?"

Pavel shifted his position atop the wall, and Shilo and Jayn worked together to boost Ryn up, and soon he was back where he'd started. Thalia looked at him and then up at Pavel. She addressed the Aether Weaver. "If Ryn could boost me up, do you think you could hold onto my arms and leave me sort of dangling?"

Pavel mulled it over. He gestured over his shoulder. "Maybe if Jayn got up on Shilo's shoulders and held onto my ankles, we could make kind of a human chain?"

They tried it, though Ryn wasn't entirely sure how this new plan would work. Once Shilo and Jayn were in position, Pavel shifted until he had his legs down one side and his arms down the other. Then it was Thalia's turn to climb on Ryn's shoulders. That must have been why she had selected him to return. His knees buckled as he took her full weight. No one could call her fat, but she was certainly well-muscled. It took most of his remaining energy to stand up. She took hold of Pavel's arms, and he took some of her weight. Ryn ducked back down and shifted free of her dangling legs.

Ryn looked up at the pair of them. Swirling white Aether once again encircled Pavel, which must have aided him in holding onto Thalia. Ryn frowned. "Now what?" he asked.

Thalia laughed, and her voice sounded muffled again with her face pressed against the wall. "Climb me."

"Climb you?" Ryn asked, incredulous. He studied the dangling Stone Weaver. Below her straining arms and broad shoulders, everything seemed made of soft curves. Where could he even put his hands?

"Make it quick, kid," Pavel said, tension in his voice, though his grip on Thalia's forearms seemed sure.

"Don't worry about it," Thalia said, seeming to read Ryn's mind again. "Just try."

Ryn was red in the face before it was all over, for a number of reasons. Her shoulders were the only place he could safely put his hands. He took a running start, jumped up, and managed to grab on there. He flailed against her back until he managed to get a leg hooked around her. Pavel groaned from the added weight but didn't let go. Ryn heard some noises from the girls on the other side but didn't have time to worry about that. He tried not to focus on Thalia's physical proximity as he shimmied up her back toward Pavel, who was also going red in the face, if only from the strain.

Clambering up Pavel posed its own dilemma, with no clear place to take hold. Ryn wedged a knee into Thalia's shoulder, reached up, and grabbed the back of Pavel's belt. This proved a mistake. Pulling on Pavel shifted his weight. Jayn cried out as Pavel's legs slipped from her grip. Ryn fell, pulling Thalia down on top of himself. Pavel used his Aether to kick off the wall and land well away from them on his feet. Then his knees gave out and he fell to the floor.

Pavel lay groaning and looked up to Nyssa. "I give up," he said.

Nyssa had watched them silently the whole while. She nodded. "Yes, I think that is enough for today." She knelt down and pressed an unseen button or switch. A concealed door swung open in the climbing wall, allowing Shilo and Jayn to cross back to their side. The two girls helped Thalia up off of Ryn. The five weary Weavers climbed up the ladder and trudged out of the building that housed the Gauntlet. Their first day ended with a quiet dinner and early retirement to their dormitories.

Chapter 16
The Second Day

THALIA SMILED TO HERSELF as she swept the smooth stone floor. Sweeping all the corridors on the third level of the Citadel was the first chore on her morning rotation that second day of Watchkeeper training. The hallways of the Citadel covered far more space than Master Foster's redsmith shop, but the mechanics of cleaning were the same. The easy chore allowed her to focus on the day ahead. She eagerly awaited the afternoon session when she could take a second run at the Gauntlet.

She'd awoken that morning knowing the solution to the climbing wall. She managed to keep it to herself as she and the other girls dressed. She, Shilo, and Jayn had been moved into a shared room when their Training Pentad had formed. However, as soon as they met up with Ryn and Pavel at breakfast, she had to share her news.

"Our mistake," she told the group, "was trying to use Weaving to solve the problem first. The instructors keep telling us that we cannot rely too heavily on the gift, and I think the Gauntlet is meant to teach us that as well. I don't know why I couldn't see this yesterday, but the key is not to put Pavel atop the wall, but to keep him on the ground until the end."

"Of course," Jayn said, her eyes widening. "He's the only one who can climb the wall unaided, so we leave him for last instead of you."

"Good idea," Shilo said, smiling at Thalia. Ryn smiled as well, and Pavel nodded in agreement.

So, Thalia still felt elated as she mindlessly swept the floor. She wondered what chores the others had drawn. She couldn't envision high-society Jayn doing any kind of menial work, yet that girl was clearly determined to succeed as a Watchkeeper, so no doubt she would grit her teeth and bear it. Of the Training Pentad, Thalia liked Shilo best so far. A friendship had bloomed naturally between them, perhaps because they were both the daughters of tradesmen or knew how to work at honest labor. They did their best to include Jayn, but the Fourth Pentarch's daughter seemed to hold herself deliberately aloof. Perhaps she would mellow over time.

The two men in the group, despite having traveled to Falport together, seemed to have little in common. Ryn, who was of an age with her, seemed sweet, if shy. Stone and Root were opposing forces, so she didn't see much of him during the day, but she did feel some kinship with Ryn after learning of his aunt's death. The loss of her father was a wound that had not and would never fully heal. She still didn't know what to make of Pavel.

A chime from somewhere down the hall signaled the end of the hour just as she finished sweeping the last bit of dust into a wide metal dustpan. The Watchkeeper compound held more clocks than any place she'd ever been. An ingenious Stone lacing kept them ticking along without ever having to be wound. The green-liveried servant who had been moving up and down the floors supervising the recruits and cadets appeared, took Thalia's broom, and excused her to hurry on to her first lesson.

Thalia thought of Pavel again as she crossed the grassy yard toward their joint lesson at the Watchkeepers' forge. She'd never had much tolerance for men of his disposition. That arrogant, self-assured swagger always rankled her. A few of the apprentices back in Rigel would put on airs like that sometimes, and she'd learned to put them in their places, but those were mere boys, and Pavel was a man full grown. If the rumors could be believed, he had earned some reputation as a thief, which did nothing to endear him to Thalia. Their Training Pentad was supposed to learn to trust one another, but she didn't know if she could ever fully trust a man like him. Jayn was a prickly one, but she at least seemed to be here for the right reasons.

Spring days grew warm indeed in southern Aldria, and Thalia worked up a good lather during her first two sessions, both in the smithy. Her lesson working with Pavel proved more agreeable than she'd anticipated. She hammered out copper rings, while Pavel fed a steady stream of Aether into the metal. They'd practiced a similar exercise the day before, but Master Caston told them they must master this enchantment before moving on to the next one.

Enchanted jewelry, armor, and weapons sounded wonderful in the abstract, and every hero in every legend always had some powerfully laced object. However, the Watchkeepers preferred to focus on the practical. The stronger the enchantment, the greater the recoil. Experiencing a powerful recoil at the wrong moment while on mission could prove disastrous. Most Watchkeepers opted not to take that risk, despite the benefits a powerful lacing could offer. Instead, most Weavers preferred "low-level" enchantments that provided a modest boost with hardly any recoil.

Thalia had tried moderating her luck Etching to level out the extreme highs and lows, but she had not been successful. That was the way of things with Etchings sometimes, Master Caston had explained, but she'd had more success with common enchantments, such as the one that would help a blade keep its edge. The basic Blending that Thalia and Pavel practiced now would imbue the ring's wearer with greater physical endurance in exchange for a modest increase in appetite. The slight boost in stamina could make a difference in the field, and most Watchkeepers wore something marked with the "lasting lacing," as Master Caston called it.

Branching yellow light poured slowly from Thalia's hands into the ring. The lacing required careful control to not overdo it, as she bent the fractal lines into a specific pattern. A strong lasting enchantment could enable someone to run all the way to Appencourt, assuming they didn't collapse from hunger first. Yesterday, Pavel had spoken little while they worked. He'd never employed Aether in such a manner before, and it required much concentration. When his puffs of white light flowed into the ring, the network of yellow Stone mellowed into a softer color, like desert sand. Today, he seemed more confident in his task and spoke freely as they worked.

"Are you adding any luck to this one?" he asked.

She shook her head. "The luck only comes when I want it to now."

"I would love to experiment with one of your lucky rings sometime." He spoke casually, with no hint of avarice in his voice.

She shook her head again. "Master Caston is handling the testing for my Etching, and he would never let a recruit participate."

"Of course," Pavel said, "but eventually they will send our Pentad out into the field, and surely by then they will trust you to manage your own Etching."

"I suppose, but the recoil can be severe, so we can't use it too liberally."

"Nevertheless, it's a remarkable gift, maybe even more impressive than what Ryn can do. I've heard tales of ancient artifacts that granted luck, but I'd never given them much credence. It's a wonderful conceit for a minstrel. No matter how dire the situation the hero finds himself in, he can always luck his way out thanks to his enchanted sash or sandals."

"Until a tree falls on him two days later." Thalia paused. Pavel's comment about ancient artifacts had reminded her of his alleged former profession. "Master Caston keeps a strict inventory of my work, just so you know."

Pavel scoffed. "Hah, how little you all must think of me. But don't worry, I do intend to take this fresh start seriously." Almost to himself he added, "Besides, I've heard the luck will only activate if you give me the ring."

Thalia looked at him then, but he kept his eyes focused on his work. She didn't remember sharing that detail with the group. Clearly, he had been asking around about her Etching. Did he have something nefarious in mind, or was he simply curious? Before she could speculate further, Pavel changed the topic, asking her about her life back in Rigel. He had many questions about the town's namesake Runeform.

Despite her suspicions toward the Aether Weaver, Thalia found herself enjoying the conversation toward the end of their hour together. He spoke little and asked insightful questions, and she found herself relating stories from her apprenticeship and some of the stranger questions and answers she'd heard at the Rigel fountain. She knew men like Pavel could wield charm as a weapon, but that knowledge didn't make her completely immune to its effects.

When their lesson ended, he shook her hand, said, "It's been a pleasure," and sauntered off to his next appointment. Master Caston allowed her a few minutes to drink from the pump that stood at the edge of the smithy, before she began her solo lesson with him, a now familiar routine of practicing the simple lacings that didn't require Aether. Eventually, she would be taught to wield Aether herself, assuming Master Caston's faith in her abilities had not been misplaced. She wondered what she would be able to create then.

Soon her time in the smithy came to an end, and she headed for her next lesson with Jayn and the master Wave Weaver. Part of her wished Shilo and Ryn had been the ones with gifts complementary to hers.

Wave Mistress Agia Bellos had a different instructional approach than Master Caston. Rather than walking Jayn and Thalia through the lacings one step at a time and insisting they show mastery before moving on, she took more of a rapid-fire approach. Her standards were no lower than Caston's, and she was just as strict, but she walked the girls through the basics for each lacing and fully expected them to practice and perfect it on their own time.

Yesterday, they had just barely managed to create an alarm ward, but today they would move onto something new. A Wave Weaver could sense when someone crossed the perimeter of certain wards, but Blending in Stone produced an audible sound that anyone could hear. Setting up such wards on homes and businesses was among the most common services offered by Guilds. They'd also received preliminary instruction on creating shields. Captain Lahmeer's Etching allowed her to create a shield using only Wave, while other Weavers needed to mix in Stone to create one. Some Etchings were like that, while others, such as Thalia's luck and

Ryn's self-healing, were unique and could not be replicated. Today, Mistress Bellos started them on something completely different: an enshrouding ward.

"Once Jayn masters her invisibility Etching, this may be far less useful, but it's good practice nevertheless," Mistress Bellos said. She held her lessons in a spacious, mostly empty room on the second floor of one of the compound's outbuildings. "And of course, it's also far more useful at night."

Eventually, Thalia would also try her hand at wielding Wave, but for now she only had to feed Jayn a steady stream of Stone, just as Pavel had aided her in the smithy. Physical contact helped beginners, so Thalia stood behind Jayn with her hands on the shorter girl's shoulders. The fractal lines of yellow flowed through Jayn and merged with her lacings, tinting the light a deeper shade of royal blue. It still seemed strange to Thalia that Wave originated from the soles of one's feet. Jayn stood with her right foot a step ahead of her left, and from the toe of her gray boot, two blue lines appeared. The lines spread in opposite directions but then arced around and joined together, forming a perfect circle. The ward was barely wide enough for a person to stand in, but novices had an easier time starting small, according to Mistress Bellos. A circle was also the easiest shape.

The room was well illuminated by natural sunlight streaming in through a window, as well as several wall-mounted Weaver lights, created by a clever Blending of Root and Flame, but within Jayn's ward that light began to dim. A haziness spread across the stone floor, like a shadow without a source. Something almost like a cloud, though completely black, gradually appeared and thickened within the blue ring. It condensed until it formed a perfect half-sphere of darkness.

The way the girls stood was not conducive to conversation, so they spoke little, though Jayn had plenty of questions for the Wave mistress. "I see how this could help conceal someone in the dark, but could those within such a ward see anything?"

"Within this one, you would see nothing," Mistress Bellos said, "but Nyssa or I can show you the technique to create a sort of double layer within the ward. In my field days, I would sometimes build such a shroud around our camp. From within, we could enjoy the light and warmth of the campfire without giving our position away. No one can see in, but no one can see out either, like being placed under an overturned bowl, so it can leave you vulnerable. That is another reason your invisibility ward should prove superior, especially if it can conceal others."

Jayn nodded. She focused her attention on "setting" the ward, allowing it to hold without her active manipulation. Depending on the strength of the ward, one could last unattended for days or even weeks. Silently, Mistress Bellos handed her a large waterskin, knowing the thirst Jayn's Weaving would produce.

Jayn took a long sip and wiped her mouth before launching into her next question. "You know, Mistress Bellos, that I had hoped to manifest as a Flame Weaver like my mother, but I am coming to appreciate all that Wave has to offer." She took another long draught before handing the skin back. "However, it still seems like such a weakness that any half-trained Aether Weaver can destroy anything I can build."

Mistress Bellos nodded, a rare smile crossing her face. "True, but consider what I told your Pentad about the rarity of the gift. The vast majority of people you encounter will not be Aether Weavers of any training. The Weaver must also know that the ward is there if she wishes to destroy it. Aether consumes Wave, but that is the way of the Five Forces. They exist in perfect balance.

Consider how the Flame Weavers you so admire can be equally unmanned by any half-trained Wave Weaver." Mistress Bellos subtly shifted her feet, and a thick blue line of Wave shot out from beneath her. It ran straight across the floor and up the opposite wall until it reached one of the Weaver lights. The glowing orb vanished, leaving only an empty glass casing.

Jayn gasped. "Amazing! I have wondered about Wave's usefulness in direct combat. Why don't our enemies employ Wave Weavers against the Standing Army?"

"Oh, they surely could. In the War of Secession, Weavers of all stripes fought on both sides, but Aldria has not seen true warfare in generations. The simple reality is that Tamor prefers to risk few of its Weavers in border skirmishes, using regular soldiers as fodder instead."

Jayn nodded, her cheeks tinged red, as if perhaps embarrassed to learn something she felt she should have already known.

Mistress Bellos, if she noticed, chose to ignore it. She moved brusquely along. "Now, if we can set politics aside, I would like to see another shroud." She glanced toward the window. "Yes, make this one a rectangle and block off that side of the room. I don't want to see a single ray of sunlight."

"Yes, Mistress," Jayn said and sprung gamely to the task.

Though Thalia's contribution required no mental acuity, she still felt drained by the time the lunch hour struck. The reunited Pentad spoke little in the dining hall, every one of them eating with the relish of a spent Aether Weaver. Still, even another round of swinging a staff against wooden targets under Mistress Whitcomb's supervision could not dampen her spirits as the time for another run at the Gauntlet drew ever closer. Wielding a staff somehow seemed to employ completely different muscles than swinging a hammer.

Once again Nyssa Lahmeer awaited them outside the large warehouse-like structure that housed the Gauntlet. "You will cycle through different attendants," she told the group, "but I wanted to see a better showing after yesterday's disappointment."

Despite the barb from Nyssa, Thalia's group smiled. They were all eager to try her solution to the wall. They made short work of it. Thalia volunteered to lie astride the wall and help the others over. First, Pavel climbed up to give her a hand, while Ryn and Shilo boosted her. Once Thalia was in place, Pavel hopped back down, and he and Ryn gave Jayn and Shilo boosts, while Thalia handed them over. The two girls dropped to the far side to await the others. Ryn climbed atop Pavel's shoulders, and Thalia helped him over. She noticed again how the pale Root Weaver's cheeks flushed red. She herself thought little of the close scrambling, having played many a rough and tumble game with her young apprentice friends in Rigel. Once Ryn was over, Thalia shifted her position, lowering herself as far as she could with her arms before dropping down. Shilo touched her shoulder to steady her as she landed. Thalia thanked her with a smile. A moment later, Pavel came plummeting over the side wreathed in white swirls. He landed easily on his feet, flourished with his hands, and gave a cry of triumph like a showman.

The group filed up the ladder, ready to take on the next challenge. In the back of her mind, Thalia recalled that no one had ever finished the Gauntlet in less than a month, but she tried not to think about that. The black door swung shut behind them, plunging the group from dim light into complete darkness. Nyssa had not climbed down from her position atop the dividing wall. She had preceded the group into the next chamber, but looking up, Thalia saw no sign of her, or anything else for that matter.

"It's a shrouding ward," Jayn said.

They heard Nyssa's disembodied voice from up to the right. "Lorn and Silverbell, I recommend you provide your Pentad with some illumination." Nyssa always used their second names, though not all the instructors did so.

"Ryn?" Shilo said.

There was some jostling as the two Weavers moved to find each other in the dark. Thalia blinked as an orb of light suddenly bloomed into existence. Ryn and Shilo stood clasping forearms, as he fed her tendrils of green Root. She used that to form the Weaver light, which hovered above her free hand. After a few seconds, Ryn cut off the flow of Root and released Shilo's arm.

Shilo seemed a little embarrassed to be the center of the group's attention. "Master Nox has had us practicing for the past two days," she said by way of explanation.

"Well done," Pavel said, already turning to survey the new chamber.

Ten feet overhead a rippling black fog shrouded out all outside light. Nyssa stood above the ward, which meant she could not see the Pentad below her feet. Still, she seemed to know they had made the light. "Cross to the other side of the room, and you will find a lock."

Shilo led the way, holding the light aloft, and the others followed. They had to take a few turns to reach the end, as several thin stone walls zigzagged through the room, forming almost a maze, though it was an easily solvable one. Every square inch of the walls was covered in tiny engravings. The symbols appeared to be random. Some were recognizable numbers and letters, while others were runes from a foreign alphabet.

At the end of the simple maze, they found the lock. It was not a kind Thalia had ever seen before, though it somewhat resembled a gigantic combination lock. Five wheel-shaped dials were embedded into the black wall, numbered zero through nine. Five familiar symbols were engraved above the dials: the mountain, the wave, the leaf, the flame, and the spiral.

Jayn called up to Nyssa. "How do we solve the lock?"

"Study the walls and you will find the combination."

The group waited, but that seemed to be the end of Nyssa's explanation. Pavel stood studying the lock, but all other eyes swiveled to Thalia. How had she become the leader? Still, she didn't want to let them down. She cleared her throat. "Right, well, let's assess our resources again. Shilo, how many of those lights can you make?"

The Flame Weaver grimaced. "Just one at a time, and I haven't learned how to fix them in place yet. If I let this one go, it would just float up to the ceiling." She looked up. "And probably through it."

Jayn nodded. "Or it would be destroyed by the ward."

"Not a problem," Thalia said, trying to stay upbeat. "You'll have to lead the way, and we'll take it one wall at a time until we find the combination."

"How will we know we've found it?" Ryn asked.

"I'm not sure, but there has to be some identifying mark."

It took them some time to find the best arrangement. Eventually, they had Shilo stand in the middle of the corridor formed by the maze walls, her arm and the Weaver light held up above her head. The others spread out around her, two to a side, studying the walls. It wasn't the easiest process, since they had to contend with their own obscuring shadows, but it seemed the most efficient with only one light source.

After about five minutes, Jayn found the first clue. "Look here," she said, pointing to her section of wall. On closer inspection, what first looked to be an unknown rune was actually a flame with the number seven etched in the center.

"Brilliant," Pavel said. They were still near enough to the dials, that he could sprint back without Shilo needing to follow. He pulled down on the dial below the flame symbol, stopping it at the seven. Nothing seemed to happen, but they still had four other symbols to find.

"Now we know what we are looking for," Thalia said as Pavel rejoined the group.

"Yeah," the Aether Weaver said, "and next time this room will be a breeze, since we'll know the combination."

From somewhere above them Nyssa laughed. "The combination will be different tomorrow, Talvor."

Ryn's forehead wrinkled. "How is that possible?"

"It's a Runeform," Thalia guessed and then knew it must be true. "Somehow this whole thing is a Runeform puzzle."

"Yes," Nyssa said, "and if you don't hurry, the solution might change before you finish."

They redoubled their efforts, and since they knew what symbols to look for now, they moved faster. Still, it took them ages to find all five numbers. The runes and symbols extended all the way to the floor. For most of the group, the task was merely tedious, but it took a toll on Shilo, who needed to sustain their light source. Twice, her orb flickered and winked out, and she and Ryn had to fumble in the dark to find each other, so he could supply the Root she needed. Thalia was amused to notice that clasping arms with Shilo also made Ryn blush.

Shilo also struggled to keep her hand held up. As her hand swayed, the light wobbled, and after the second blackout, Jayn suggested someone help her. Ryn was the obvious candidate, and so Shilo rested her elbow on the Root Weaver's shoulder, and he did his best to hold her forearm up and keep the light steady. Even his ears flushed pink from that prolonged contact.

They eventually found the last symbol and dialed in the combination. For a moment nothing happened, and Thalia worried the first symbols they'd found had shifted. Then a concealed door slid open, and the room flooded with light. Shilo's orb had gradually dimmed as she labored, so the sudden change in brightness nearly blinded them. They stumbled through the doorway to find the next challenge.

Fire filled one half of the room, but it was clearly not normal flames. Looking up, they could once again see the high metal ceiling overhead and Nyssa standing atop the wall. The Gauntlet had started in the corner of the larger structure and followed along one of the metal exterior walls. Now they had reached the next corner and had to turn to face the new obstacle. A rectangular structure the color of sandstone had been affixed midway across the room, connecting to the tin wall on one side and the ten-foot black dividing wall on the other, just below the shimmering blue "ceiling" of Wave. Flames poured from the bottom of this structure, clearly another Runeform, like jets shooting from a fountain, to form a curtain of fire.

Thalia held her hands out toward the gushing flames and took a step closer. She felt no heat, when her experience around forges told her it should have been palpable. That much sustained fire should also have melted the exterior wall or singed the stone floor. "Is it an illusion?" she asked.

"It's real," Nyssa said, "but it's not conventional fire. Touching it will cause no permanent harm, but it will be painful."

"Another Runeform," Pavel said, and his eyes seemed to twinkle in the firelight.

Nyssa gave more detailed instructions for this challenge. "Only one of you need cross through the flames. A lever on the other side will disable the Runeform. This obstacle is a test of Weaving, not bravery. While you could leap through the fire and bear the brunt of the pain it will cause, I cannot accept that as a solution. Therefore, let me suggest two courses of action." She pointed to Pavel. "Talvor has been learning a Flame Blending that can shield him from heat. It would work even on these flames."

It dawned on Thalia that all the separate training her group had been receiving was designed in part to help them complete the Gauntlet.

Shilo shook her head. "I don't have the energy left to help him with that."

Under his breath, Pavel added, "And I haven't quite mastered that one."

Nyssa nodded. "It's good to know your limits. Your training is designed to stretch you and help you grow faster, but there is no benefit in going too far. Doing so could put you in the infirmary for a day or more, which would hinder you and your Pentad."

Ryn nodded at that, and the look that crossed his face told Thalia that he had some experience with pushing himself too far.

"Another option then is a shield. Mistress Bellos has instructed Eldragor and Moldo on the basic technique, and it would repel these flames."

Thalia and Jayn locked gazes. Thalia knew more than any of the others the limits of Jayn's wards, yet the petite Wave Weaver set her jaw and betrayed no doubt in her own abilities. Reluctantly, Thalia assented. "Let's try."

She stood behind Jayn and placed her hands on the girl's shoulders. So far the Gauntlet had required neither of them to Weave, so she felt that stamina at least would not be an issue here.

She fed the branches of Stone into Jayn and allowed her to wield it as she chose. The curving lines of the shield's base emerged from her feet and disappeared into the flames. The silent, heatless fire began to part as the dome formed. Its shimmering surface fluctuated back and forth between a rippling pond and a complex tessellation of geometric shapes.

Jayn did her best to enlarge the wedge in the flames that her shield created. Eventually, a space large enough for someone to crawl through emerged, though the shield wasn't perfect. Occasional gouts of flame broke through and filled the space below before deflecting away again.

Thalia glanced back at the others. Shilo had sunk to her knees from exhaustion, and Pavel was far too gangly. That left only Ryn. She hated to have to ask him, but she spoke anyway. "Ryn, do you think you can crawl through the gap?"

Ryn balked at the idea, his eyes fixed on the uncertain narrow passage. "I can try," he said, hiding most of the fear from his voice.

Jayn gritted her teeth in concentration and enlarged the shield a little more. Slowly, Ryn stepped closer, crouching down to get in front of Jayn without blocking her view. He hesitated but began inching closer to the opening.

Jayn sighed. "Wait," she said, and Thalia felt her let go. The shield collapsed and fire rushed in to fill the gap. Ryn fell back against Jayn's legs. She addressed her explanation to Nyssa. "You told us we would face challenges we are not yet prepared for. This is one of them. I cannot safely maintain this shield. Not yet." She spoke in a level, almost emotionless voice.

Nyssa studied her for a moment before nodding. "Understood." She gestured toward the exit. "Proceed to the dining hall. We are well past the dinner hour, but food will have been set aside for you."

Jayn led the way out and did not look back at the others. Reluctantly, Thalia followed behind. She was disappointed but decided it was the right call. She was a little surprised that Jayn had given up. Was the stuck-up Wave Weaver actually concerned about exposing Ryn to potential pain? Still, Thalia knew it was better not to force it. They still had time if they wanted to break the record.

Chapter 17
The Wheel

JAYN ELDRAGOR AND SHILO LORN labored to carry a full water pail up the narrow stone steps. Underground pipes supplied water to most of the Watchkeepers' compound, except in the oldest buildings. Of all the chores Jayn had rotated through so far, she enjoyed this one the least. She imagined she had lived a disciplined life in her mother's home, but this first week of Watchkeeper training seemed interminable. Though she had been schooled in basic combat and horsemanship, most of her education had focused on her mind and not her body. On top of the physical demands of training, Weaving required a peculiar mental exertion that left her feeling drained at the end of each day. Despite sharing a room for the first time in her life and lying in a narrow bunk much less comfortable than her bed at home, Jayn had no problem sinking into the oblivion of sleep each night.

The two girls reached the top of the stairs, hauled their bucket down a short corridor, and turned into a small room. With labored grunts they hoisted the bucket and tipped it into a large wooden barrel. Why this room needed water, Jayn hadn't a clue. Part of her suspected some of these chores were mindless busywork, but she was loath to ask. It still rankled her that they were expected to throw themselves against the Gauntlet each afternoon, when Captain Lahmeer and the others knew full well they were not yet trained enough to pass.

Jayn sighed as they turned back toward the stairs. Shilo hooked her arm through the handle of the empty bucket and let it hang from her shoulder. "At least the first week is nearly over," she said.

Jayn mumbled an agreement. Tomorrow, the sixth day of the week, the recruits would be given a lighter schedule. In the morning, they would have an extended round of chores, while the afternoon would be given over to pursuits of their own choosing, so long as those pursuits aided their growth as a Watchkeeper. Options were primarily limited to independent practice in Weaving or weapons training. Recruits from rougher backgrounds could also obtain tutoring in grammar or arithmetic. Then would come blessed Sunday, a day reserved for quiet contemplation and leisure. Jayn intended to stay in bed as long as she reasonably could.

Jayn glanced sideways at Shilo as the girls descended the stairs. The pair had shared few conversations over the course of the week, in part because they had no joint lessons. Despite their disparate backgrounds, they did have some things in common. She knew Shilo had lived her whole life in expectation of following in her fisherman father's profession, and her unexpected man-ifestation of Flame had ended all that. Jayn well knew that kind of disappointment, yet something about the fisherman's daughter still irked her. Jayn didn't think it was a matter of simple jealousy.

Sure, Shilo was a Flame Weaver, the very gifting Jayn had long coveted, but Jayn was not that petty. Still, she often wished Shilo behaved in a manner more becoming of a Flame Weaver. Granted, all the Flame Weavers Jayn knew were members of the Standing Army and cut from a similar cloth, but did Shilo have to be so hesitant and unsure of herself? The girl could send grown men flying with a single punch. Where was her confidence? Where was her pride in her abilities? What Jayn would do for such an Etching…

Perhaps she was being unfair to Shilo. As the pair crossed the lawn back to the pump, Jayn cleared her throat and attempted conversation. "So what do you make of Ryn?" She thought that comment might be taken the wrong way and felt the need to add, "We both have lessons with him, I believe."

Shilo shrugged. "He's a straightforward guy. He kind of reminds me of my kid brother Lou."

"Yeah, he does seem to be more boy than man."

Shilo laughed. "Well, I didn't mean it in a bad way. Truth be told, I still feel like a kid most of the time." She looked around at the expansive grounds. "I still half-expect each day someone will tell me there's been a mistake and I shouldn't be here."

Jayn frowned. She'd bemoaned the girl's lack of confidence, but maybe she could help with that. "Listen, Shilo, you deserve to be here as much as any of us. I've heard the other Watchkeepers talking about what you can do with your punches. They all seem very impressed." That overheard praise had needled at Jayn, but she wouldn't acknowledge that here.

Shilo grinned. "Thanks, Jayn. It might sound a little pitiful, but I guess I'm just not used to actually being good at something."

"Well, get used to it. My mother says the key to success is to find the thing you do best and then get better at it."

"I suppose that's true." They walked on in silence for a moment, and then Shilo added, "You know, that's not the first pearl of wisdom I've heard you quote from your mother. I think I might like to meet her someday, though I think I'd also be a little afraid of her."

They both shared a laugh at that. "You'd be a wise woman then," Jayn said. "Anyse Eldragor is not for the faint of heart."

They made two more trips with the bucket before the hour was up. The girls parted amicably, and Jayn headed toward the greenhouses to meet Ryn and Mistress Hinter. She stretched her sore arms as she went, again looking forward to Sunday's rest.

Mistress Hinter, a frumpy older woman with a raspy voice, seemed to delight in exposing her pupils to needless embarrassment. Today's lesson was no exception. Ryn did the bulk of the work, incorporating her flows of Wave into his lacings, but the peculiar way Root worked also required her to be the test subject.

After the humiliating chicken chase, Mistress Hinter had begun to actually teach them. Today's lesson involved a more advanced version of the deflection ward. Ryn stood behind Jayn with his hands on her shoulders. The interchange of Weaving created a peculiar sensation in Jayn. Ryn summoned his tree of green light, and the roots spread to entangle Jayn's feet. She fed a steady stream of Wave into them. It reminded her of filling her cupped hands from the tap and letting the water drip out between her fingers. She let it flow, not too quickly and not too slowly. The Blended lacings traveled through Ryn, along his arms, and back into Jayn, though she had no control over it.

A traditional Wave ward covered a defined area and could not be affixed to a living thing, but a Wave-enhanced Root lacing could. Looking down at herself, Jayn could see tendrils of sea-green light snaking over her skin and clothes. It tingled.

"Very good, Ryn," Mistress Hinter said. "Next week, I will show you how to set it in place, but for now maintain the connection, and keep your head down!"

They were outside on the open grass today. Mistress Hinter had moved them out of the shed, as Ryn had trouble controlling his tendency to suck the life out of any surrounding plants. A few dead spots on the lawn marked his more recent failures to use only his own energy. Mistress Hinter kept assuring him that the grass was tough and would recover.

A table near the Root mistress held an array of wooden blocks, like the kind infants play with. With a look bordering on glee, Mistress Hinter selected a block and lobbed it toward Jayn. She watched it arcing toward her face and fought hard not to blink or flinch. The lacing worked. The block curved away at the last moment, plopping harmlessly in the grass, though Jayn felt the wind of its passage beside her ear.

"Well done," Mistress Hinter said. "Just remember, there is a limit to what this ward can deflect. A determined opponent with a blade can still push through it and stab you. Now, let's see how long you can keep it up."

Jayn could only stand there as Mistress Hinter hurled a barrage of blocks. Some made contact as they brushed past her arms or legs, but the deflection shield slowed their momentum to the point of harmlessness. Jayn decided it was better to close her eyes, pretending to herself that it was only so she could concentrate better on releasing the lines of Wave.

Jayn's eyes shot open as a wooden block caught her squarely in the chest. Mistress Hinter did nothing to hide her smile.

"Sorry," Ryn mumbled behind her, "it slipped…"

Jayn gritted her teeth. "Just concentrate."

Before the hour was up, Mistress Hinter landed two more hits. Jayn took a block to the stomach and another to her shoulder. If she'd been hit in the face, she surely would have turned and struck Ryn in retaliation. The boy apologized each time, but she clenched her fists and ignored him. That first blow to her chest would likely leave a bruise, and the one to the stomach had nearly knocked the wind out of her. Finally, the lesson ended, and she headed for her next session without any word of parting to Ryn. She took a few steadying breathes as she made her way to the training room that Captain Nyssa Lahmeer and Mistress Agia Bellos shared.

Jayn still wasn't sure why the traditional training format had been altered for her. Why was Captain Lahmeer giving her instructions in Wave instead of the master? As the daughter of the Fourth Pentarch, she sometimes received more favorable treatment. She didn't expect it, of course, and often she did not want it, but she had become accustomed to it. However, this passing her off to Captain Lahmeer seemed more like a snub than anything. Perhaps it was politics and not about her personally. Maybe Commandant Lahey disliked some political stance of her mother's. People in power were often more petty than one expected. Still, Jayn would not be cowed. The Watchkeepers were only a steppingstone to the Pentarchy, but she had to succeed here if she wanted to take the next step.

Despite all that, Jayn did admire Captain Lahmeer. She was a competent and exacting teacher, who reminded Jayn of some of her best tutors back home, although sometimes during their lessons, Captain Lahmeer would get a vacant look and lose focus.

There were two awkward moments in that day's lesson. The first came as Jayn practiced expanding the size of her wards. Captain Lahmeer cocked her head as she studied Jayn's lacings, and her beaded braids clinked musically. "Your wards have improved greatly," she said, "but I hear you have not used the shield Blending for the Gauntlet's wall of fire?"

The Training Pentad had cleared that obstacle on their third day of training, using Pavel's Flame-enhanced heat resistance then and again on the fourth day. They'd had a different attendant both days.

Jayn nodded. "Pavel felt confident in his lacings."

"And you did not?"

She shrugged. "It... still seemed risky."

"Remember, part of Weaving is believing you can do it. The lacings we can see are nothing more than an external manifestation of an internal visualization. They are entirely a product of the mind. If you believe the shield will hold, then it will. If you doubt it, it will fail."

Jayn studied her feet and kept her voice level. "Yes, Captain."

Nyssa continued to study her. "Tell me, if you could set the shield and pass through the wall of fire yourself, would you?"

Jayn nodded, adding a moment later, "I would."

"So you fear exposing Ryn to the flames?"

Jayn didn't know how to respond. Did she? After the hits she'd taken today, she felt she wouldn't mind sending the incompetent Root Weaver through the wall of fire now.

Nyssa continued before Jayn could form an appropriate response. "I know you had hoped to be an officer in the Standing Army, so you surely know an officer cannot be afraid to send her men into danger. You must have faith in your battle plan and trust your soldiers to do their part."

"Yes, Captain," Jayn said through gritted teeth.

"Now, release your ward and let's take another run at unlocking your Etching."

Jayn's Etching was another source of frustration. She could quickly learn any of the Wave lacings Captain Lahmeer and Mistress Bellos threw at her, but invisibility eluded her. The embarrassing truth was she had not yet replicated it since that first manifestation in her bedroom. Another round of failed attempts prompted the second awkward conversation that morning.

"Jayn," Captain Lahmeer said, surprising her by using her first name. "There is one aspect of Etchings we have not yet talked about. It may be the key to unlocking yours." She paused, seeming to choose her words carefully. "Not always, but sometimes, an Etching will manifest in moments of great need. Your other Pentad members with Etchings, have they shared their stories with you?"

Jayn nodded, wondering where this was going.

"Consider Ryn Silverbell's case. He manifested the ability to heal himself only after being grievously wounded by the Kobolds. Or Shilo Lorn. Her Etching manifested from a desire to defend her father's boat from those pirates. We don't know how or why this happens; perhaps a Scholar could tell you. You haven't told me much about the day your Etching manifested. I know *how* it happened, but if we can understand *why* it happened, that might be the key to unlocking it."

Why it happened? Jayn compared her story to Ryn's and Shilo's, and she did not like the obvious conclusion. A moment of great need? The others had been facing down monsters and pirates, while she had been sobbing in her room after failing the test for Flame. What was her great need? To hide from her mother. And that's why she turned invisible? It was too childish a reason, too cowardly. Jayn Eldragor was not a coward. She imagined people years hence asking her how she got her Etching and recoiled at the idea.

She shook her head and lied. "It was just a normal day." She paused. "What about Thalia Moldo? Her Etching had no connection to need."

Captain Lahmeer seemed intent on peering into her soul. Jayn averted her eyes. After a moment, Captain Lahmeer shook her head and said, "Correct. Like I said, it is only sometimes the case." She hesitated, seemed to decide something, and then launched into her own story without preamble. "My Etching first manifested when I was about your age. I lived with my mother in this muddy little slum on the outskirts of Farhaven. I had a run-in with some older boys from the neighborhood." She shook her head. "I still don't know what prompted it. I'd known them my whole life. We played in the streets together when we were younger. One of the boys had an older brother who'd just been discharged from the Army. He wasn't a Weaver, just a foot soldier, and there were plenty of rumors about why he'd been booted. Anyway, he took those boys under his wing and must have filled their minds with dark ideas. Or maybe they just finally noticed I was becoming a woman. I went out one evening to get water from the cistern, and they all came at me at once. I ran, but they were faster. They cornered me in a blind alley. I knew what they wanted, but I couldn't get away, so I just threw up my hands... and I made a shield so strong none of them could batter their way through it. Eventually, they just gave up. I screamed, but no one came. That's the sort of neighborhood it was. Anyway, I told my mother, and within a week, she'd scraped together enough coin to buy me passage on a wagon train to Falport."

Jayn could not meet Captain Lahmeer's gaze. She wanted to say she was sorry for her but bit back those useless words. "I'm glad you were able to protect yourself."

"So am I. My Etching may have saved my life that day, and it certainly opened a door to a better one. I feel no shame for how it happened."

Jayn wriggled under the captain's unflinching stare. She took a coward's way out. "Thank you for sharing that. I will... consider what you have said. Perhaps I can find what triggered my Etching." *A lack of spine*, she told herself.

Nyssa's words stayed with her through the third session of the day with Mistress Bellos and Thalia. She could barely focus on her lacings, earning several rebukes from the Wave mistress. She spoke little to the others at lunch. During afternoon conditioning, she managed to regain some focus. She'd always enjoyed running, and she was a competent archer, though the bow was not her first choice.

By the time her Training Pentad gathered to face the Gauntlet, she had managed to put aside the humiliating origins of her Etching, if only because the obstacle course filled her with a different sort of dread. They passed quickly through the first two obstacles. The climbing wall barely required any Weaving, and Shilo now had more mastery over her Weaver lights. She'd learned to attach them to walls, so she and Ryn moved quickly through the room, affixing a dozen different orbs. They paused only to make sure the lights wouldn't obscure any clues. Then all five Weavers spread out and swept the room, finding the new combination within a quarter of an hour.

In the third chamber, Shilo and Pavel clasped forearms to form their heat-resistant lacing. "Wait," Jayn said suddenly. She'd been thinking about what Nyssa had told her, before they discussed her Etching. An officer cannot be afraid to send her men into danger. But, her mother would have said, an officer should never send her men into danger she would not face herself. She looked up at the attendant standing over them. He was a middle-aged Root Weaver she had seen working in the greenhouses, though she could not recall his name. "Would a deflection shield work for this challenge?" she asked him.

"Sure," he said. He spoke with the drawling accent of the Flint Hills. "A strong one would do the trick."

She turned on Ryn. The scrawny boy's eyes widened. "We only just learned that today," he said.

"It held well enough."

"I haven't learned how to set it yet."

"Setting is easy. I can show you that. Remember, Weaving is all about believing you can do it. Do you believe?"

She saw him swallow before speaking. "Yes."

A few minutes later, he had the shield set, and she stood facing the curtain of fire. An image of a single flickering candle flashed through her mind. She had not moved that flame, but these would part. She just had to believe this would work.

She took a step forward and then another. She closed her eyes, but only against the brightness. She felt nothing as she passed through it. She opened her eyes to find herself alone on the far side, unharmed. She turned and triggered the lever mounted to the wall that would stop the flames. She smiled to herself as she led the others into the next room.

This was their third time facing the fourth chamber, and they'd cleared it twice before. An elaborate metal blacksmith's puzzle occupied the center of the room. The objective was simple enough. The interlocking metal rings and other intricate shapes were affixed to the floor by a chain, and the key to the next room was attached to one of the pieces. They had only to separate it. This too was a Runeform puzzle, so the solution changed daily.

The obstacle was designed to test their Stone Weaver, so Thalia led the way. She could not use lacings to pull the pieces apart, but infusing the whole thing with a network of Stone allowed her to better understand how the pieces hooked together and which could be removed. Jayn didn't quite understand it, but she imagined it was similar to how a Root Weaver could Dowse the human body. The large puzzle required multiple sets of hands to manipulate, so Thalia talked the others through it, telling them where to lift, twist, or squeeze.

Soon enough, they had the key loose, and they filed into the fifth chamber, the one that had stumped them for the past two days. The first time they had reached this room, their attendant, a bubbly young Aether Weaver, had explained that this numbered among the toughest challenges in the whole Gauntlet. It posed a major stumbling block for all Training Pentads.

The obstacle was simple enough in theory. A metal pillar stood at the center of the room. A ring made of smooth gray stone encircled its base. Five stubby arms extended from the stone ring. It reminded Jayn somewhat of a five-spoked wheel without an outer rim. Shilo had compared it to a starfish. Inscribed on the end of each arm was one of five familiar symbols. Each node only responded when touched by lacings of the corresponding force. All five Weavers needed to activate their designated nodes to awaken the Runeform. When activated, the ring began to rise. The goal was to move the ring to the top of the pillar, which would open the next door.

Two things complicated this challenge. For one, they were not allowed to touch the ring and had to extend their lacings outward while standing a certain distance from the pillar. The boundary was marked by a red circle painted on the floor. The other complication was how the ring moved. It slid upward along grooves carved into the pillar. The grooves did not run straight but rather curved around the pillar like the colorful stripes on a candy stick, causing the ring to rotate as it rose.

This twisting was only a problem because of the arrangement of the nodes. They did not follow the traditional pattern, where one complementary force flowed into the next. Instead, the progression went from Wave, to Flame, to Stone, to Root, to Aether. The Pentad spread themselves out around the red circle. Jayn stood between Shilo and Pavel, who both wielded forces that opposed Wave. If any part of her lacings brushed against theirs, one would be destroyed, and the ring would fall back to the ground. Each Weaver faced the same dilemma, forced to work in between opposing forces. The five had to work in unison, applying the same level of power and moving in a circle as the ring turned. It was like dancing around a bizarre Springday Pole, where the ribbons disappeared if they touched each other.

Jayn found the challenge simple enough, but the others struggled. Her gifting gave her an advantage here, of course. Wave started along the ground and did not arc through the air like the others' giftings. As Captain Lahmeer had explained, Wave Weaving was all about defining a boundary and then allowing Wave to fill it like water poured into a vessel. Jayn sent out two lines of blue light, set so close together that they appeared to be one. She stopped just short of reaching the node, which rested on the floor. The air above her narrow lacing filled with shimmering light, like a single sheet of water sliding over the edge of a manmade water feature. She extended it high enough that it could maintain contact with the wheel all the way to the top. She did not form a specific ward but merely created the space for one. By not giving any intentionality to the lacing, she could keep it fluid and shift it with her as she circled around the pillar.

Jayn's thin lacing posed no danger to her neighbors, but they couldn't say the same. Just as air and fire could not be as easily constrained as water, Aether and Flame could not be kept to a narrow beam of light. Pavel had some control, but Shilo's flickering red lines often spread farther than she intended and had shattered themselves against Jayn's sedate wall more than once. Pavel and Shilo also struggled because their typical lacings encompassed only themselves. They were unused to extending the force out so far.

Ryn had perhaps the second-best level of control, after Jayn. His Root lacing still formed as a squat tree around him, but the green tendrils he sent out were more like thin vines than branches. Thalia had other issues. Stone refused to travel in a straight line; her lacings, though slender, would bend, split, and spread as they extended from her hands. She tried to contain the refraction along a vertical axis, but she couldn't keep it from spreading horizontally. Ryn and Shilo shifted away from her to give her the space she needed, but that only pushed them closer to Pavel and Jayn's lacings.

Once the others had set their lacings in place, Jayn allowed hers to inch forward, activating the final node. They began their plodding dance. Their lacings somehow seemed to stick to the nodes once they activated. If it turned too quickly, it would take those fixed ends with it, wrapping them against each other so that they winked out. They kept their input to the bare minimum, producing a gradual rise and turn, making progress tedious and painstaking. After a few false starts, they suddenly seemed to find the right rhythm. They kept their distance and circled the pillar. Seconds and then minutes crawled by, and still the stone rose. It approached the halfway point, farther than they'd ever taken it.

From the corner of her eye, Jayn could see that Thalia's lacing was becoming a problem. The higher the stone rose, the further she had to extend her lacings. Each strand of Stone split as it spread, and then split again, making its growth exponential. Shilo picked up her pace to put more space between her lacings and the yellow light. Ryn slowed down. A wobbling burst of red Flame licked against Jayn's wall, just as a stray gust of Pavel's Aether entangled itself in Ryn's vines. Two lacings winked out, and the stone Runeform spun its way down the pillar, landing with a thud.

Jayn clenched her fists, turned, and stormed a few paces away from the others. She fought to control her breathing. The mounting frustrations of the day and the week threatened to overwhelm her. The others sighed or made their own sounds of disappointment. Pavel may have muttered an oath.

After a few moments of silence, Thalia spoke up. "That was good," she said, forced cheerfulness in her voice. "We've never made it that far before. I think we're all getting better at controlling our lacings."

Jayn scowled. What was Thalia talking about? Didn't she see it was her fault they had failed?

Thalia continued. "We have time for another try, I think. If we don't get it this time, then maybe tomorrow during our free period we can find a way to practice together."

For a long time after that day, Jayn would wonder what made her snap. Maybe it was the pressure. Maybe it was her newfound shame about her Etching. Maybe it was just the sound of Thalia's voice. Jayn spun and began uttering the regrettable words that would rob her of any meaningful sleep that weekend. "When exactly did you become our leader, Thalia?"

Thalia's jaw hung open. Jayn had done nothing to mask the venom in her voice. The broad-shouldered Stone Weaver stammered a response. "I wasn't trying to be the leader, but, well, someone had to step up, and I didn't see you doing it."

Jayn scoffed. She could no longer stop herself. "Why would I? Who would want to lead this miserable lot?"

"Jayn, don't—" Shilo started to say, but Jayn turned on her.

"Oh, spare me, Shilo. You haven't the backbone to stand up to me. Do you really think you can be a Flame Weaver after washing out as a *fisherman*? I used to think we had something in common, but now I realize you've been a failure your whole life, while I've only failed the once."

Shilo's jaw dropped now too. Ryn looked equally aghast, while Pavel wore the beginnings of a stupid grin.

Jayn pressed on. "And don't even get me started on the so-called men of our group. Ryn's too dumb to even know his own second name, and he's just as incompetent. Thanks for the bruises this morning, by the way."

The boy worked his lips but could muster no reply.

"Well done," Pavel sneered. "Am I next?"

She glanced at him. "Why are you even here? Who in their right mind would let a common criminal join the Watchkeepers? My mother says men like you are not even to be trusted with the chamber pot."

"Oh, your mother needn't worry about me. If the Eldragor family possessed anything of real value, I would have taken it by now. And that's including daughters."

"Hah, you deceive yourself. I've caught you ogling me. I'm sure you'd just love to—"

"Oh, you flatter *yourself*. You couldn't pay me to, not even for every grubbing crown in your family coffers—"

"Enough!" Thalia shouted, stepping between Jayn and Pavel. "This helps no one." The brawny Stone Weaver squared her shoulders and towered over Jayn, as if daring her to say anything more.

Jayn wouldn't be intimidated. She considered her options for another attack. Thalia's size was an obvious target, but that seemed... petty. She was being petty and childish, Jayn realized, and the heat went out of her. She glanced up at their attendant, who stood with his arms crossed and shaking his head. "I quit," she said only to him. She headed toward the exit.

"Jayn, wait," Thalia called after her, her voice softened.

Jayn paused in the doorway. She didn't look back. "Leave it alone," she said. "You're all just... cowards." She knew as she said it that she included herself in that statement.

Chapter 18
The Sea Docks

SHILO LORN MADE HER WAY across the green lawns of the Watchkeepers' compound, heading toward Master Nox's dojo. Though Thalia had suggested the Pentad use their afternoon free period to train together, no one had spoken further of the idea after Jayn's explosive tantrum. Shilo and Thalia had returned to the room after a later dinner to find Jayn already in bed, and Jayn was already up and out of the room by the time Shilo awoke to the morning chimes.

Shilo labored alone through her morning chore assignments. She didn't see any of the others in the dining hall at noon, but she ate quickly, before heading out to meet Master Nox. Yesterday, the Flame expert had asked her to see him at the start of her free period, though he had not offered an explanation.

She saw few others as she made her way across the lawn. Life on a fishing vessel did not conform to the traditional seven-day work cycle, but she knew the sixth day of the week, Moonday, was traditionally reserved for running errands and completing household tasks that may have been neglected during the five days of labor. In concession to this, the Watchkeepers gave recruits a lighter schedule, and most cadets and officers could leave the compound to attend to their own business. Moonday night was the prime time for social engagements.

Shilo climbed the stone steps to Master Nox's room. She found him kneeling on the ground and piecing some much-abused wooden training dummies back together. To her surprise, she saw branching lines of yellow light extend from his hands and reattach a dummy's head with a Stone lacing. He looked up and broke into a rare smile upon seeing the shocked look on her face.

"I'm just a novice with Stone," he said, "but it comes in handy from time to time."

Shilo knew she would eventually be trained in Aether and Root, but the Watchkeeper training regimen would not bother with showing her Stone or Wave. Very few Weavers achieved success with the forces that opposed their innate gifting, and perhaps the structure of a Pentad made it unnecessary. Thalia was the designated Stone Weaver, and in a pinch Jayn or Pavel could also cover that skillset, once they'd been trained, just as Pavel and Ryn might someday be able to throw Flame-laced punches.

She snapped out of her contemplation, realizing she had not responded to Master Nox's words. "It's still very impressive, sir."

He shrugged, wiped his hands on his gray trousers, and stood. Shilo and the Flame master were of a height, though he was broad and well-muscled. She had no qualms about being alone with the man. Her training sessions with him the past five days had given her no reason to fear him. He spoke with the authority of a man who clearly expected his orders to be obeyed, yet most of the time he seemed dispassionate to the point of boredom.

"So," he said, "you're probably wondering why I asked you to stop by."

"Yes, sir."

"I want to run a few tests, outside of our usual training regimen. It's about your Etching."

"Sir?" She wondered if he was still dissatisfied with her ability to scale back the strength of her punches. Her heart sank as she envisioned an exhausting afternoon of rote drills.

Something in her voice or expression must have conveyed her fear. He made a dismissive hand gesture and said, "It's nothing bad, but as we trained together this past week, I've noticed your Etching has a few... unusual properties. I have a theory, and I want to test it. I want to sort this out today because I may need to revise your training plan for next week."

She wasn't quite sure what he meant, but she nodded and said, "Yes, sir."

He led her to the center of the room, where he had laid out some equipment for his tests. He'd set several objects on a wooden table, though she could not fathom their purpose. Before they got close enough to study the table in detail, he stopped short and gestured to a wooden weapon stand. The stand stood empty, and she had assumed he'd placed it in the center of the room only as part of his tidying up. Instead, it was the focus of their first test. Master Nox extended his hands and expertly wove strands of Root and Flame to form a Weaver light. Shilo had seen him wield three different forces with casual ease. She wondered if she would ever attain such mastery.

Master Nox affixed his light to the top of the stand and stood aside. "Use your Etching and punch this," he said. "I do not mean the stand, but the light. Don't try to punch through it, but aim to make contact, as if punching something solid."

She studied the glowing orb. He'd selected the weapons rack because placing a light atop it put it at the perfect height for her. What would happen when she hit it? Would she destroy it? What would this test prove? She liked Master Nox well enough, but she wasn't yet comfortable with asking questions, so she kept them to herself and readied her Etching.

She'd learned the normal way Flame Weavers enhanced their bodies to give themselves preternatural strength, and though her Etching employed nearly identical lacings, it felt distinctly different in a way she could not describe. Her hands began to glow as if lit from within. The way Master Nox had explained it, glowing was a natural byproduct of powerful Flame lacings. Her Etching began like a simple light lacing, as the glow preceded the strength and perhaps even caused it. The Etching also sent a unique tingling sensation coursing through her body.

She took a deep breath, released it, and then drew another. Using the technique Master Nox had taught her, she drew her fist back with the thumb turned up. She took a step forward, rotated her fist as she threw the punch, and exhaled all at the same time. Punching the light felt like punching air, yet it produced an effect. The Weaver light flared in size and brightness, nearly blinding her. The release of energy lasted less than a second, and then the orb shrank back to its normal size and radiance.

Shilo blinked, a glowing white afterimage floating before her eyes, and the room seemed dim after the sudden flareup. "What was that?" she asked.

"Energy," Master Nox said. A hint of genuine excitement edged into his normally bland tone. "As you know, Flame can channel and enhance the body's natural energies. The standard lacings that any Flame Weaver in the Standing Army would know use the energy of motion, what the Scholars called dynamic energy.

In the same way that a bow can impart far more speed and power to an arrow than if a man were to simply throw it, so Flame can increase the strength of a thrown fist. This is present in your Etching, but I believe there is another sort of energy at play. Your hair is what first caught my attention."

"My hair?" she asked, completely lost by his explanation.

"You haven't noticed?"

Confused, she reached up and patted her hair. Her tightly curled ringlets gave her hair a great deal of volume that she'd never tried to tame. Her mother wore her hair the same way. As she felt the edges, Shilo found that her hair now stood up far more than usual. Some women in her fishing village liked to comb their hair out until it stood in great puffy cloud shapes, and her hair now reminded her a little of that.

Master Nox nodded when he saw she understood. "Every time you use your Etching, strands of your hair seem to rise up on their own."

"What causes it?"

"Let's try another test first."

He led her now to the table, which seemed set more for a meal than any Weaver experiment. Metal forks, spoons, and other implements lay scattered around a large ceramic bowl. Master Nox had filled the bowl to the brim with water, and Shilo's eyes widened as she leaned over and saw what else it held. A tiny orange fish, like the kind bred for ornamental ponds, swam slow circles inside the bowl. She raised an eyebrow, but Master Nox offered no explanation.

"I want you to create your Etching again, but you won't be punching anything," he said. "Once the lacing is in place, I want you to slowly extend your hand until you just touch the surface of the water."

"What's going to happen?" she had to ask.

"Just trust me. I can't say for sure until we try."

Reluctantly, she obeyed. She summoned the lacing again, waves of Flame flowing from her chest and into her arms. Cautiously, she lowered her glowing fist into the bowl until the cool water lapped against her knuckles. She felt a sudden flash of heat and thought she saw a tiny spark of light in the water. She pulled her hand back. The little orange fish bobbed at the surface of the bowl, belly-up.

"What happened?" she asked, her voice rising. "Did I kill it?"

"Yes, but don't worry about that," Master Nox said, unrestrained enthusiasm in his voice now. "I'll explain everything, but please do one more thing for me. One more test and then we'll know for sure."

She sighed. She'd managed to retain the lacing, so her hands still glowed. "What is it?"

"Very simple." He moved his hand across the table to demonstrate. "Just wave your open hand over the metal here. Get as close as you can, but don't touch anything."

Shilo obeyed, wondering what bizarre results this test would produce. She almost wasn't surprised when the fork she waved her hand over twitched. As she moved her hand, the effect became apparent. All the loose bits of metal responded as if drawn to her. The largest pieces barely reacted, but a tiny length of wire rose and nearly stood on its end.

"Am I... like a magnet?" she asked. Once in her childhood a traveling exhibit of curiosities had passed through Palmoor, and one man had demonstrated how a magnetic rock could draw metal to itself.

"In a sense. That plus what happened to the water tells me what we're probably dealing with here. Your Etching uses more than just dynamic energy. There's another sort of energy we scarcely understand, though some trace of it must exist in living things if you are able to manipulate it. We believe it is connected to magnetism, but it is also found in lightning."

"Lightning?"

"Yes, a bolt of lightning contains heat and light but something else as well. If you've ever walked in stockinged feet across a dense rug and then touched a bit of metal, you've felt a tiny fraction of what lightning imparts."

She looked back at the dead fish, wondering what to make of all this. She felt no sorrow for the little thing, as the killing of fish was her family profession, though it did seem a waste. The tiny creature would be a meager meal for even a cat. Then she had a darker thought. She met Master Nox's gaze. "Do you think... I've never really been sure, but the day those raiders attacked my family's boat... Do you think I killed that man?"

He sighed, as if her question had deflated his elevated mood. "It's very possible. I can't say for sure. Some men when struck by lightning recover within minutes. Others drop dead on the spot."

She frowned. She was no stranger to lightning, having seen many a summer storm roll in off the sea. Did she really wield that kind of power? She moved through the rest of her time with Master Nox as if in a daze. Eventually, she would be taught to spar with other Flame Weavers, and Master Nox warned her that she would likely never be able to use her Etching in such practices. He admonished her to never use it unless fighting for her life. Unless she was willing to kill her opponent.

Soon he shooed her out, saying he would need time to rework his plans for training her. She had a couple hours yet remaining on her free period, but she simply wandered the compound for the remainder of the time. If anyone asked her, she would say she was walking for conditioning, but no one confronted her. She shied away from the crowds at Mistress Whitcomb's training yard and spent her time in contemplation. Her Etching could kill. Probably it had.

She'd accepted early on that Flame was primarily used in combat, but a talented Flame Weaver could disable her opponent without doing permanent harm. That would be the goal in most field assignments, to apprehend criminals and rogue Weavers so they could face justice, not to kill. She had not asked for such a deadly power. If Kobolds continued to pose a threat to Aldria, would she be sent to fight and kill them? She still hardly believed that such creatures even existed. Could she really be a hunter? A killer? Objectively, she knew fishing was a form of hunting, yet it seemed gentle and mundane compared to the thought of chasing down and slaying humanoid monsters with her fists. A chill ran up her spine. She resolved not to dwell on it. She had months yet of training before she would ever face an assignment outside the stone walls of the compound. Perhaps she and Master Nox could still find a way to control her Etching.

By the time she shook herself from her daze, the sun hung low over the city. She turned her tracks toward the dining hall, finding the rest of her Pentad at what had become their usual spot. Even Jayn was there, picking discontentedly at her roast beef and potatoes. Shilo set her tray down at the end. Thalia and Ryn nodded to her but continued in their conversation, apparently about religion.

"I don't get it," Ryn was saying as Shilo walked up. "People in Aen's Hollow worship the Maker, but no one ever talks about the stars like that."

Thalia shrugged. "I don't go in for it much myself. The Rigel temple is very traditional. They never mention star guides."

"In Aen's Hollow, they call it a church, not a temple."

"They mean the same thing. I think a temple is just larger."

"But what do people think the stars do for them exactly?"

"It's always a bit vague, but basically they're meant to have a positive influence on people. That's why you hear things like 'blessed by the stars.' People don't really pray to the stars, but they will say things like 'thank the stars' or even 'bless the stars.'"

"Or blast the stars," Pavel added helpfully around a mouthful of food.

Thalia frowned at the oath but continued good-naturedly. "That too. Most of the time people don't really mean the actual stars when they say those things. It's just... something people say."

Ryn nodded, though he didn't seem too satisfied by the explanation.

Shilo leaned into the lull. "What brought this topic up?" Her mother used those star-referencing expressions, but Shilo had never put much stock in them. Her father said stars could guide a sailor across the sea at night, but not beyond that.

Thalia thought back for a moment. "Well, we were discussing our plans for tomorrow. I said I'd be going over to Rigel for Sunday service, but no one seemed too keen to join me."

Pavel scoffed. "I can think of much better uses for a Sunday morning."

Shilo smiled, not at Pavel's comment but at Thalia's offer. She was the only true local in their Pentad and had the luxury to visit home on the weekend. It was kind of her to include the others. "I'd love to go," she said and genuinely meant it.

Ryn spoke up then. "I'll go too. I mean, I wasn't opposed to the idea..." He stammered to a stop.

Shilo guessed at what he meant. He wouldn't set out alone with Thalia if they were the only two going. She exchanged a glance with Thalia and could tell the dark-haired Stone Weaver also understood.

"Great," Thalia said, smoothing over the awkwardness. "Sure you won't reconsider, Pavel?"

"Quite sure," he said, though without any malice.

Thalia seemed to hesitate and took a deep breath before turning to Jayn. "How about you, Jayn?"

Jayn met her gaze for a moment before returning her eyes to her plate. She shook her head. "My family is... non-practicing." Shilo could tell that the meaning of that word was lost on Ryn. Before anyone could respond, Jayn said, "Excuse me." She stood, gathered her tray of mostly uneaten food, and left.

An awkward silence hovered over the table for a while, but eventually it broke, and the conversation moved to other topics, mostly reflections on their first week of Watchkeeper training and how it differed from their expectations. Even Pavel participated. Before they parted for the evening, Shilo, Thalia, and Ryn made plans to meet early the next day and walk over to Rigel together.

Once again Jayn was already in bed as Shilo and Thalia joined her in their shared room. She stayed abed as the other two rose and dressed early the next day, though she was clearly only pretending to be asleep. She had not mustered the slightest apology after her rude outburst two days ago, and Shilo and Thalia had decided she probably would not. The two girls had resolved to simply let it go and move forward, if Jayn would let them. Shilo had only brothers and made few female friends growing up, so she was unaccustomed to the stormy waters that seemed to swirl around women living together. She and Thalia had become fast friends, and she was grateful for that. She wondered if she would ever call Jayn a friend.

Shilo and Thalia slipped out the door, shutting it gently behind them. They turned to find Captain Nyssa Lahmeer standing in the hallway that ran the length of the women's barracks.

"Captain?" Thalia said. Shilo had not yet found her tongue.

"Good morning, Moldo. Lorn." Nyssa nodded to them. "You're off early this morning."

"We're headed to Rigel," Thalia said, answering the unasked question. "Sunday service at my family's temple."

"Will Eldragor be joining you?"

"No, ma'am."

"She's… still in bed." Shilo managed to say. For some reason, Nyssa intimidated her. Perhaps it was her exact, military bearing.

"Well, I will have to rouse her then. You ladies enjoy your morning." It was a clear dismissal.

Thalia returned the pleasantry and led the way down the hall. Behind them, Shilo heard Nyssa knock on the door to their room and then enter without waiting for a response, shutting the door firmly behind her. The girls exchanged a significant look as they continued walking.

"She came for Jayn." Shilo stated the obvious.

"It didn't seem like a social call," Thalia said. Nyssa had worn the gray uniform and tabard of a Watchkeeper.

"Maybe she heard about her little outburst during the Gauntlet on Foamsday."

"I think it likely. That certainly wasn't Jayn's finest moment, but training has put us all under a lot of pressure."

"You're putting it generously." She thought a moment longer. "Or maybe it's a private lesson." She'd told the others last night about her private session with Master Nox and how her Etching seemed to have something to do with lightning and magnets.

"Perhaps, but I don't think a lesson would be carried out at the crack of dawn in her bedroom."

Shilo laughed. "Fair enough."

"Still, let's not bring it up later if Jayn doesn't. I think it would only further ruffle her."

Shilo agreed, and they hustled on. They found Ryn waiting for them at the compound's surprisingly small front gate. He'd clearly combed his hair but still wore the gray recruit uniform. Perhaps he had no other clothes. Shilo wore a long brown skirt, the only one she'd brought with her, and a loose cotton shirt, which was a hand-me-down from her older brother, but it was in good condition and passable as a female garment. Thalia wore a sleeveless blue dress with little flowers picked out in the design.

The guards passed them through the gate, and Shilo and Ryn fell in step behind Thalia as she led them through the empty morning streets of Falport. The trio exchanged a few comments but spoke little during the long walk across the city, over the river, and into Rigel. As they strolled, foot and cart traffic picked up with the wakening city, though it never reached its weekday volume.

Despite their early departure, they arrived just after the service started and slipped into an empty back pew. The service lasted barely an hour, featuring several droning songs and a teaching by a middle-aged man in black robes who was not a gifted orator. Several times in her life, often while sailing with her family on a clear day with strong winds, she had felt and shared in what many called the Maker's joy at his own creation, but she had never once experienced that presence while sitting through a stuffy temple service. It always filled her with a strange sort of melancholy.

After the service, they met Thalia's mother, a friendly older woman with gray streaks lacing her long black hair, who was dwarfed by her daughter. Thalia must have inherited her height from her swordsmith father. Mrs. Moldo invited them all over for lunch. Thalia's family home stood in a quiet street just off a main thoroughfare, in a respectable if sleepy neighborhood. The three-story home was grander than any Shilo had ever been inside, and she was sure that was the case for Ryn as well, judging by the way he gawked at everything.

The family seemed to have come down in the world since buying this grand home, as Shilo only saw one servant, and Mrs. Moldo served out the lunch herself, a modest repast consisting of cold meat and bread, alongside a sweet herbal tea. Shilo did her best to make conversation, as Ryn said very little. His only real contribution was in asking what herbs comprised the tea.

Thalia and her mother did most of the talking. Thalia gave her the broad strokes of Watchkeeper training so far, focusing on what she'd learned and glossing over any struggles or challenges. It was exactly the way Shilo would have described it to her family, if any of them could make the journey to visit her. Thalia's mother supplied her with updates on her married sisters and the rest of the extended family.

The sun stood high overhead by the time they left the Moldo home. Thalia's mother told them more than once they were always welcome to visit. Thalia smiled as she turned to look back at the others, who followed her like obedient ducklings. "I hope that wasn't too boring."

Shilo and Ryn spoke over each other as they assured her that they had had a lovely time.

Thalia looked up at the cloudless sky. "We still have half a day of freedom," she said. "I don't want to go back to the compound just yet."

"Me neither," Shilo said, as Ryn chimed in his agreement.

"Well, what do you two want to do?" They had just reached the foot of the long stone bridge across the River Aldria, and as she spoke, Thalia gestured to the towering walls of Falport that stretched before them. "I'm partial to Rigel, but there's plenty to see in Falport."

Ryn shrugged. "I'm still getting used to being in such a big city. I wouldn't know where to begin. I don't even think I could find my way back to the Citadel from here."

Thalia and Shilo both laughed, though in truth, Shilo wasn't sure she could find her way back either. Thalia turned her gaze to Shilo. "You decide," she said. "Where do we want to go?"

They were crossing the bridge now, which had no railing save for a series of black bollards and chains. Still, the bridge was wider than the deck of the *Windlacer*, and it gave her no pause. The scent of brine and the sound of gulls blew in on a southerly wind, and she had her answer, though she wondered how the others would respond.

"Well, it may sound silly, but I would like to see the docks," she said, adding a moment later, "if no one objects."

"Sure," Thalia said, smiling at the idea. "We'll head down to the Sea Docks. They have a greater variety of ships there than you are like to see anywhere else in the world." She had correctly guessed why the docks interested Shilo.

Ryn nodded in agreement, and they continued along the bridge. Shilo couldn't keep herself from beaming, feeling grateful for friends such as these. Her smile wavered as they crossed under the portcullis and a petite blonde girl rose from a bench to intercept them.

"Jayn?" Thalia said. It was a greeting and a question, though not an unfriendly one.

Jayn seemed nervous, though she attempted to look friendly. She wore her gray uniform. "I wasn't sure where in Rigel you were going," she said, "but I figured you had to come back this way."

"You were waiting for us?" This from Ryn, who sounded incredulous.

Jayn forced a smile, though it came across more as a wince. "I wanted to apologize to each of you, and I thought it best not to wait." She took a deep breath. "I am sorry for the way I behaved during training. I spoke in anger, and it is not how I wish to comport myself. I would like for us to function as a… cohesive Training Pentad."

Shilo knew exactly where this rehearsed speech was coming from. That must have been some rebuke Nyssa had delivered. This going out to meet them was probably the captain's idea as well.

Thalia was the first to break the stunned silence. "Thank you, Jayn," she said, using measured and correct words. "I accept your apology."

Shilo and Ryn mumbled their agreement. Jayn had been looking more through them than at them as she fumbled through her apology. Now she actually regarded each of them, biting her lip and clearly unsure what to do now.

A pregnant silence hung over the group, despite the bustle of traffic coming and going off the bridge. Shilo found herself speaking, if only to break the quiet. "Well, we were on our way to visit the Sea Docks. You are welcome to join us."

Jayn seemed to mull the offer over. Finally, she nodded. "Sure." She averted her eyes, and a sheepish look came over her face. "Actually, I've never been all the way down to the sea."

"Really?" Ryn said. "But you're so… Well, you're you!"

Jayn covered her mouth and laughed. It was the first genuine laugh Shilo had ever heard from her. "Truthfully, Falport here is the farthest I've ever been outside of Appencourt."

"Well," Thalia said, "that's a thing we all have in common then. Being farther from home, I mean." Shilo felt the wall Jayn kept between them begin to soften, and perhaps Thalia sensed that too. "I feel like we should all do Pavel's stupid handshake now," she said.

The others laughed, but no one actually objected, so the four of them locked their hands together by the little fingers and shook. They must have looked strange, with two in uniform and two in Sunday clothes, but Shilo found she didn't care. Thalia led the way, chatting with Jayn, and Shilo and Ryn fell in step behind. Ryn never talked much under the best circumstances, but Shilo found the long silences companionable rather than awkward. She couldn't say why.

As it turned out, the four of them did have a good time together that afternoon. Shilo felt a passing pang of guilt that Pavel had been excluded, but perhaps that was for the best. His biting sarcasm might have spoiled their mood, and he was just enough years older than them to make a difference. Less than two years separated these four, and the oldest amongst them barely qualified as adults. So for one afternoon, perhaps the last such afternoon any of them would ever experience, they were carefree youths exploring a large and prosperous city.

The Sea Docks on the southside of Falport were massive. A dozen separate piers made of cut white stone spanned an area several times larger than her home village. Even more wooden pilings stretched out to the east and west beyond the main dock, probably housing mostly local vessels. Two of the stone piers extended twice as far out into the calm waters as the others. Even at low tide, the water there was deep enough for even the largest vessels to tie off. Two massive Maer ships were moored there, making all others seem like toy boats by comparison. The towering three-tiered Tallsails were sea-going ships, capable of crossing the vast Morro Ocean to the exotic continent beyond for trade goods.

They also saw plenty of Iscernaen junks, with their bright multihued sails, and some of the shallow-drafted Mirkwalder vessels, built more for river travel than the open seas. Most did their trading in Nadell or Lembalt, but a few risked the journey along the coast to reach the richer markets of the east. Shilo had seen plenty such vessels sail past Palmoor, hugging the shore, though they never docked in her village, unless out of great need.

In addition to all the foreign ships, they saw many exotic strangers, and Jayn and Thalia helped the others identify their ports of origin by their unusual garb. They saw many Iscernaens, clad in garishly colored silks, and more somberly dressed pale-skinned Mirkwalders, as well as swaggering Maer merchants, identifiable by their sun-darkened skin and light-colored eyes. Maer men and women wore loose trousers and tight vests that exposed most of their stomachs. They even saw a few hulking Silgarian mercenaries supervising the unloading of what must have been a very valuable cargo. Trade never stopped, even on Sundays. Overhead, even the skies were crowded, as swarms of gulls circled for scraps. These were the same black-headed gulls that haunted Palmoor, though Shilo spied a few white hawk gulls spiraling above the others. Those larger gulls primarily hunted other birds, and sailors were of two minds as to whether they represented good or bad omens.

Jayn seemed to enjoy the sights and idle conversation as much as the rest of them, and when they stopped in a small dockside café, she treated them all to tea and dainty fruit-filled pastries. It was a truly lovely afternoon, and Shilo felt quite content as they filed out of the café, intent on returning to the barracks before the westward hanging sun could set.

Suddenly, a bird swooped down toward them, causing Shilo to reflexively throw up her hands. It wasn't a seabird but a common crow. It alighted on a streetlamp and squawked at them.

Ryn gasped, looking up at the creature as if he recognized it. Apparently, he did. With his next breath, he said, "Corvus?"

Chapter 19
The Fish Docks

RYN GAWKED UP at the blue-eyed creature. "Corvus?" he asked. "What are you doing here?"

"You know that bird?" Shilo asked.

"That's no bird," Thalia said. She'd been the first to understand the significance of those glowing eyes, the metallic blue feathers, and the hinged talons.

Ryn looked back at his three companions. Their expressions ranged from amusement to confusion. "Corvus is a Runeform," he explained. "He belongs to Pavel, but I haven't seen him since the day we reached the city."

"Ryn!" the bird-thing suddenly cawed. "Ryn! Ryn!"

Corvus had never addressed Ryn by name, and it sent a cold shiver up his spine.

"It can talk?" Jayn sounded shocked.

"Yeah, but he almost never says anything useful," Ryn said. To the bird he added, "What do you want, Corvus? Where have you been?"

The Runeform tilted its head, studying Ryn. He could read no emotion in those cerulean eyes, and yet it still unnerved him. After a long pause it squawked, "Everything's fine!" Then it took off, spiraling away through the air. The noisy gulls overhead seemed to ignore Corvus.

"That was odd," Thalia said. She looked to the others. "I guess we should head back now."

Ryn stood rooted to the ground. The Runeform's words summoned up dark memories that seemed a lifetime ago, though it was a matter of weeks.

Thalia touched his arm. "Are you all right?"

"No, something's wrong. The last time Corvus said that… Well, we were being attacked by Kobolds."

"And it said everything was fine?" Jayn asked.

"I think… Well, it's very strange, but I think Corvus likes to be sarcastic," Ryn said.

Shilo scoffed. "Clearly it is Pavel's pet then," she said. "Do you think he sent it here to find us?"

"I'm not sure," Ryn said. "Corvus seems to have a mind of its own. It doesn't like going in buildings. It flew off over a week ago when Pavel talked to that fountain in Rigel."

"He talked to the fountain?" Thalia asked. "What was his question?"

"I'm not sure. He asked it in a foreign language."

Thalia seemed to have a number of follow-up questions but decided to save them for later. "Well, we'll have to ask Pavel about it."

The bird-thing had vanished into the darkening sky, so there didn't seem to be much they could do except head back to the Citadel. The crowds along the docks forced them into a single-file line, so Ryn fell in behind the girls. He could hear snatches of conversation as Thalia explained everything she knew about the Rigel fountain to Shilo. Jayn seemed to already be familiar with that particular Runeform.

Ryn let out a contented sigh, reflecting on the afternoon. It had been, in all likelihood, the best day of his life. He'd never had friends before, and it made him giddy with excitement. No longer was he the outcast, the shunned changeling boy living alone in the woods with a witch. Now he was Ryn Silverbell, a gifted and promising Root Weaver and a Watchkeeper in training. He thanked the Maker, and if he believed in it, he would have thanked the stars as well.

And he had three young ladies he considered his friends. Even Jayn. Early into their training together, he had decided that friendship would be his goal, despite Pavel's insipient question about which one he fancied. They would all have to work together for at least six months, and possibly five years if the Watchkeepers decided they would continue to function well in the field. Ryn didn't know much, but he knew romance could be messy and complicated in such dynamics. On top of that, he had absolutely no idea how to initiate a romantic courtship. Though he was slightly older than them, Shilo and Thalia seemed to regard him as something of a kid brother, and he was content to fill that role. Jayn seemed to hold him in a similar regard in that she frequently found him annoying. He shook his head and tried to focus on his simple enjoyment of the evening. He decided that if his relationship with any of the girls was going to change into something more, it would be up to her to initiate that.

They passed through the massive southern gates back into Falport proper. The broad entrance seemed built for even ships to enter. As they did, Corvus suddenly returned, swooping low and nearly raking Ryn's heads with its talons. The behavior was identical to the way flesh-and-blood crows would mob perceived threats. Here it seemed intended to get Ryn's attention.

Corvus alighted on a second-story balcony overhanging the street. "Nothing to see," he cawed.

"What do you want?" Ryn asked, beginning to get annoyed. The Runeform had never behaved this way before.

Without a reply, it flew away but only traveled the distance of about a hundred paces before settling on a streetlamp. It cocked its head, looking back at them.

Thalia glanced back at Ryn. "Does he want us to follow him?"

He shrugged. "It's possible."

Thalia led the way toward the bird-thing. The others spoke little, but clearly their curiosity had also been piqued. When they reached the intersection where Corvus waited, it flitted away again, heading west and away from the Watchkeepers' compound. It landed on the eaves of a rooftop. It was definitely trying to lead them somewhere. Wordlessly, the four Weavers turned and followed after it.

Ryn lost track of how many turnings they made. The city had an unusual zigzagging layout. Corvus kept always just ahead of them, waiting till they nearly reached its perch, before flying to the next post, though it never left their line of sight. Around them, the streets grew quieter, as most residents retired for the evening. No one seemed to notice the four young people pursuing a crow through the streets. The setting sun painted the western sky orange and yellow.

Corvus led them into a broad open space in the heart of the city. The cobblestone square surrounded a walled-off structure with four pointed towers rising above the crenellations. On their way to the Sea Docks, Thalia had identified it as the Magistrate's Palace, the seat of civil government in Falport. The square was completely empty, save for scattered bits of rubbish, likely the remains of a Moonday market. Though Corvus briefly landed atop the battlements, the palace was not their final destination. He continued winding his way north and west, and Ryn and the others dutifully followed.

Surprisingly soon after leaving the palace square, they entered a more rundown and seedy part of the city. Here foot traffic increased, as laborers and a few well-dressed patrons shuffled in and out of bars and taverns. Trash littered the streets, and the rank smell of sewage was ever-present. Women in ragged low-cut dresses loitered outside a red-brick establishment with a bawdy painted sign. They smiled at Ryn, and he did his best to ignore them. He'd heard of such places existing in cities but had no desire to experience one. Not for the first time, he wondered where Corvus was taking them. Overhead a few feeble stars appeared in the darkening sky.

The girls bunched together as they walked, all clearly uncomfortable being in this part of town. Ryn felt somehow responsible for this turn of events. He wanted to suggest they turn around and forget all about the cursed Runeform and its merry chase. But he couldn't. Corvus had addressed him by name, and that naming bound him in some way to follow the creature. He told himself that they were all Weavers and could protect themselves if needed. Shilo could knock anyone out with a punch, though she seemed to forget that herself. She cringed and shrunk behind Thalia's shoulder as a passing drunkard leered at her. The man struggled to stay on his feet, so he posed no real threat.

Corvus led them to what appeared to be the most respectable tavern in that quarter, which wasn't saying much. It sat back aways from the street and had its own little courtyard with round tables and chairs. The raucous sounds of carousing and light poured from the open doorway, but only one patron had opted to sit outside. He sat slumped over a table, apparently unconscious. It seemed a foolish thing to do in the city. Ryn knew the night was the domain of footpads and cutpurses. Corvus plopped directly onto the man's table, nearly upsetting an empty bottle. The bird-thing cocked its head at the man and then released a series of loud caws. The man grumbled, stirring to wakefulness.

"Pavel?" Thalia was the first to recognize him.

Pavel opened bleary eyes and blinked at them. His lanky black hair framed and obscured his face. He sat up with a groan, rubbed the sleep from his eyes, and hefted his bottle to see if it held any more drink. Those preparations completed, he turned to regard his fellow Pentad members. "What do you want?" he said. Surprisingly, he did not slur his words.

"We followed Corvus here," Ryn said.

"Corvus?" He looked at the Runeform as if only now recognizing it. "What for?" he asked it.

The creature only looked up at him, tilting its head from side to side.

"Hmm," Pavel said. "Well, lead them somewhere else now." He lowered his head back to the table.

Ryn heard Jayn sigh in annoyance. Did Corvus really just lead them all the way across the city to find Pavel? Were they meant to help him stumble back to the barracks? Ryn had no desire to do that. If Pavel wanted to drink himself sodden, he could find his own way back.

"Go to sleep!" Corvus crowed and flew from the table.

Ryn assumed Pavel would heed that advice, but at the Runeform's admonition, he jerked upright. He squinted after the fleeing creature. His chair toppled over as he staggered to his feet. He made no effort to right it.

"Where are you going?" Jayn asked, disgust evident in her voice.

"I don't know," Pavel said, his tone prosaic, as he followed after the bird-thing.

Ryn and the girls exchanged glances. Thalia shrugged, and they all fell in behind Pavel. Jayn muttered a protest but then seemed to decide she'd rather not set off on her own in such a grimy neighborhood. Ryn had trouble seeing the Runeform now, a dark shape flitting through mostly unlit streets. Occasional glimpses of blue light were his only clues, yet Pavel never hesitated. He plodded along in unerring pursuit of the bird.

This whole thing still made no sense. The creature had intentionally collected Ryn and then Pavel to lead them on to some unknown third location. But why? And where were they headed? It was hard to read Pavel's response to Corvus' behavior. The drunken Aether Weaver stayed on his feet, but it seemed to take deliberate effort. Perhaps this was not unusual behavior for the Runeform, and Pavel had come to accept it.

Ryn had become disoriented in the meandering warrens of Falport and could no longer tell if they were still heading north-west. He guessed they were moving toward the river, and soon enough he could smell it. The River Aldria slowed to a crawl as it filtered through the marshy delta that Ryn had glimpsed from the Rigel Bridge. The musty scent of standing water and algae filled the air, as the entertainment district gave way to dark warehouses. Corvus now led them through narrow unpaved lanes built from layer upon layer of mud and matted straw. The city walls loomed suddenly before them.

Corvus darted through an opening in one of Falport's five gates. Based on Thalia's earlier description of the city's layout, this had to be the Fish Gate, leading out to the Fish Docks on the

River Aldria. The swampy delta prevented the ready passage of boats from river to sea, so cargoes making the transit had to be unloaded at one dock, ported across town by wagon, and then loaded onto a new vessel at the other docks. The thick wooden Fish Gates leaned on their hinges. They were neither securely shut nor invitingly open. Unless Corvus intended for them to buy passage up the river, this had to be their final stop. Curiously, the doors set into the wall on either side of the gate, leading into some kind of guard house, were securely shut, and no sentries had been posted.

Pavel turned back to the others. A single guttering lantern hung above the gates, and by its light, Pavel's face looked pale and alarmingly sober. "I think," he said, addressing only Ryn, "you'd best escort the ladies back to their barracks."

The others muttered their protest, but Jayn spoke the loudest. "No," she said. "You cannot send us away now."

Thalia raised a hand as if fearing another fight. "You forget," she told Pavel, "that Runeform came and collected us first."

"Hmm," he said. "There is that." He looked at each of them in turn. "I don't quite know what we will find here, but… keep your wits about you."

In the dark Ryn almost missed the waves of white that washed over Pavel. He turned and loped silently toward the gates. As the others moved to follow him, Ryn realized what Pavel had done. Their boots and shoes squelched through the permanently damp soil, but Pavel made not a sound as he ghosted through the Fish Gate. Of course, a thief would know such a lacing. Jayn followed after him, with Thalia on her heels. Shilo and Ryn trailed behind them. Both thought to glance back at the deserted streets before ducking through the gates.

The Fish Docks were composed entirely of wood, and the whole structure groaned and sighed as the floating piers bobbed on the river, which spread before them as a shimmering expanse of reflected moonlight. Not a glow of twilight remained on the horizon, and the moon had fully supplanted the sun to shine down in the black sky. Shilo and Ryn found the others squatting behind a large crate.

The dock workers seemed to have dropped everything as soon as their shifts ended, leaving a maze of crates, barrels, coiled ropes, and pallets of goods secured with netting scattered about the perimeter of the docks. Out amongst the pilings, a few dozen small boats floated at anchor or secured to a pier, but Ryn did not have to ask what had drawn the others' attention.

A medium-sized wooden vessel swayed against its mooring lines not fifty paces away from their location. It looked large for a rivercraft, though it was tiny compared to the behemoths they'd seen at the Sea Docks. A solitary lantern hung from its tall prow, illuminating a dozen sailors milling about above deck. The sailors looked strange, as they were all short but exceptionally broad. They wore heavy hooded cloaks that shadowed their faces even on this warm spring night.

Ryn glanced around, spying no other activity along the docks. Corvus had vanished entirely. Whatever it wanted them to see, this was it. Jayn leaned in to whisper something to Pavel, though Ryn couldn't hear it. Pavel placed his finger against his lips and turned to make sure the others understood his meaning. Ryn nodded. He had questions too but knew that no one in their group could answer them.

As they looked on, two more cloaked figures emerged from a small deckhouse. One sailor was just as broad as the others but much taller. Ryn guessed by his bulk that the man had to be a

Silgarian mercenary. They'd seen a few such men at the Sea Docks. Perhaps this was an entire crew of Silgarians, hired to protect some sensitive cargo. But why did Ryn and the others need to see this? The massive sailor's partner looked to be a man of normal proportions, though he looked child-sized compared to his companion. The two spoke together as they crossed the deck and swung themselves over the ship's railing and onto the docks. They conversed quietly and Ryn could not make out their speech. The big man and the other sailors all wore black cloaks, but the other man wore some lighter color. The night was too dim to make out the shade.

The two strangers seemed headed for the Fish Gate. Pavel motioned for the others to follow him. He ghosted to another shipping container further from the strangers' direct path but still close enough to observe them. The others followed slowly, moving in a crouch. They managed not to make much noise. Ryn hoped the shadows were deep enough to conceal them here as he crowded in with the others. They were packed shoulder-to-shoulder. The pounding in his ears subsided, and Ryn realized the sailors were now close enough to be understood.

The conversation seemed one-sided, with the regular-sized man doing most of the talking. "Don't misunderstand," he was saying, "we are grateful you have arrived safely. We know the risks you took in coming here, and we are grateful for your aid, Kalo."

The tall man, Kalo, only grunted, a low guttural noise.

"The only problem is... Well, my master believes it is not yet safe for you to enter the city. Several key elements are not yet in place, and we, uh, my master feels that your presence here must remain a secret."

Kalo grunted again.

The other man interpreted that as a sign of impatience. He raised his hands and made calming motions, like one might use to soothe a spooked horse. The cloak still shrouded the man's face, but his shirt sleeves appeared to be green with gold buttons at the cuffs. "Be patient, Kalo. It has taken us time to infiltrate the organization. We are moving now to secure the artifact. We just need a little more time." The two had reached a point directly opposite the Training Pentad's hiding place. The talkative man gestured back to the boat. "Please, will you head back up the river until we give you the signal?"

"Gree no tink so."

Ryn froze. A sensation like a block of ice formed in the pit of his stomach. There was no mistaking that rumbling animal voice. Kobolds had come to Falport, and that height meant he had to be the leader, the one with the black leather armor. As the creature continued his advance toward the Fish Gate, Ryn noticed a bulky shape at his waist that could have been a hanging scimitar. The man at his side, clearly a human, ran to catch up now, imploring Kalo to turn back, but Ryn could not focus on his words. He leaned back, unconsciously trying to distance himself from the monster but too paralyzed to run. One of the others grabbed his arm and squeezed it in a viselike grip. It had to be Pavel; only he could understand the significance of that voice. Whatever strength Pavel hoped to impart with that grip, it didn't work. Ryn's heart, which seemed to have nearly stopped, now pounded in his chest. He felt certain the creature could hear it. And maybe he could.

Kalo stopped suddenly short. The man with him took that as a good sign. "Yes, it would be much better if you returned to the boat."

Kalo made a snuffling sound, and Ryn knew he scented the air. Could the creature smell him? Or his fear? Kalo raised a clawed hand to silence the blathering man. Slowly, he began to turn around, back toward Ryn's hiding place. Pavel yanked his arm. "Go," Pavel whispered. He turned and scampered back along the docks on his hands and knees. Surprisingly, all three ladies followed him without protest. Perhaps they too could sense the evil radiating off of Kalo. Ryn had thought he'd sensed the Kobolds' dark presence back in the Sylphren Wood, and now that he had trained as a Weaver, he was certain of it. Somehow, he could sense the twisted lifeforce that ran through those creatures in the same way he could detect buried silverbells.

At the exact moment Pavel and the others broke from cover, Corvus had reappeared, a streaking dot of blue through the night. He croaked loudly and swooped low over the Kobold before darting away.

"It's just a bird," the man working with the Kobold said, clearly still intent on getting Kalo back aboard his boat. Judging by the man's continued protests, Kalo wasn't listening. Ryn had no chance to look back as he scrambled along the ground behind his friends, mentally urging them to move faster. His awareness of Kalo did not dim, and he knew the creature now moved steadily toward their position.

Pavel led them on a weaving route through the maze of cargo, though it was clearly too dark for him to have any idea where they were going. Indeed, the fleeing group soon came to a stop. Ryn nearly collided with Shilo. He lifted his head to see past her. Pavel had turned to regard them with wide eyes. He'd led them into a dead end. Towers of stacked goods rose on three sides. If they were to conceal themselves, they'd have to find a way to do it here. Climbing over the jumbled mess would make too much noise and could expose them to view. There was no telling how good a Kobold's night sight was.

Thalia turned on Jayn and grabbed her by both shoulders. "An enshrouding ward," she whispered. "That will conceal us."

"Right," Jayn said. "Everyone behind me." She turned toward Shilo and Ryn. They scrambled to get past her. Thalia and Pavel grabbed them and pulled them along. They landed in a cramped dogpile, but no one cared. Thalia leaned forward and placed her hands on Jayn's shoulders again, now from behind. For a moment, nothing happened.

This had to work. Kalo drew ever closer. Any second now he would round the corner and see their hiding place. If Jayn could not conceal them, he would find them. He would find them and he would kill them, not trusting his poison to finish the job this time. Ryn remembered how Kalo had lopped a subordinate's head clean off in the woods. Ryn's Etching could not save him from that.

Ryn could barely see the blue lines that extended from Jayn and looped back to encircle the Pentad. He saw a faint shimmer of Wave but no gathering cloud of darkness.

"Jayn," Thalia hissed. "That's not the lacing for a shroud."

"Shh!" Jayn said. "Trust me," she added in a whisper.

Then they had no more time to act or think. A massive shape appeared, blocking out the moonlight that poured into their narrow alley of boxes. Kalo raised his arms to push back his hood. Likely anticipating a gasp or scream, Pavel pressed a hand against Shilo's mouth. She did not resist. Neither man could safely reach Thalia or Jayn. Ryn hoped they would be too focused on their ward to be frightened.

The hood fell back, revealing that ugly leathery gray face, the bald head, the pointed ears, the hooked nose, the beady eyes, and even the bisecting scar. Ryn felt Shilo's body go absolutely still against him. Jayn and Thalia kept their eyes down, staring at the base of their ward, and gave no visible or audible reaction. Kalo swept his gaze across them, his face revealing no emotions, no hint of recognition. His nose wrinkled as he snuffed the air again.

Kalo's human companion appeared at his elbow. He'd thrown back his cloak in pursuit of the Kobold, though the hood still shadowed his face. He wore some sort of uniform. It looked familiar, but Ryn dared not even think in that moment and ignored the detail. The man gestured toward them. "See?" he said. "There's no one here."

Kalo's eyes roved all over their hiding place, but finally he nodded.

The man dared to take his arm and started pulling him away. "And if there had been someone," he said as they rounded the corner, "well, that would only further prove our need for caution."

None of them dared move until the man's imploring voice faded to a distant murmur. Ryn released his breath in a sigh. Shilo reached up and yanked Pavel's hand from her mouth, though she said nothing. An eternity seemed to pass before Ryn's mind began to function again. Jayn had used her invisibility Etching to conceal them. Thalia had tried to feed her Stone, but she hadn't used it. Still the girls did not break their positions, and Jayn held the shield. Hours seemed to pass, and no one relaxed until they saw the Kobolds' boat nosing its way back up the river. The shorter creatures used long poles to push against the current, while the towering Kalo stood in the bow, eyes fixed straight ahead.

Slowly, the boat faded into the night. Only then did Jayn release her invisibility ward. She fell back against Thalia, clearly exhausted, and the taller Stone Weaver wrapped her arms around Jayn in a comforting embrace. Ryn wished someone would hold him like that, though he doubted it would do anything to alleviate his fears. Pavel and Shilo extracted themselves from the tangle and climbed shakily to their feet.

"That man," Jayn said. "His uniform."

"Who do you mean?" Thalia asked, her tone as gentle as a mother comforting a child who had woken from a nightmare. "The man or the creature?"

"Didn't you see?" Jayn turned and looked up at the others. "His livery. I didn't recognize his voice, but that man is a servant of the Watchkeepers."

Chapter 20
The Missing Mirror

THE MAN WHO CALLED HIMSELF Pavel Talvor awoke with a groan. Not for the first time he reconsidered the wisdom of joining the Watchkeepers. He kept his eyes closed. He listened to the familiar sounds of Ryn rising and moving about their tiny, shared room. Five years, he told himself. Five years minus two weeks. Was it worth it?

The name Pavel Talvor had clearly outworn its usefulness. He'd carried it for too long, earned too much of a reputation. It was a sentimental name. Pavel had been his maternal grandfather's name. Talvor was the name of an ancient city-state, one of the first to emerge after the Burning, that perhaps fewer than a dozen people, mostly Scholars, knew had ever existed. Five years of service, and after that, no one would be looking for Pavel Talvor. Then, once he earned his discharge, Pavel Talvor would cease to exist. Other than that clean slate, he'd have little else to show for his five years. True, he had already picked up quite a few useful tricks, and if he could learn some Flame and Stone skills, well, those would surely come in handy someday. He could quickly turn a tidy profit, and he would need to. The bulk of his Watchkeeper wages would be garnished to compensate his so-called victims. Nyssa Lahmeer had failed to mention that in her little sales pitch.

Nyssa Lahmeer. Pavel smiled to himself and struggled out of his sheets. Each morning now began with that routine of deciding whether he had enough good reasons to get out of bed. He doubted he would ever get used to rising early, or the rigid weekly schedule of a Watchkeeper recruit.

The kid was dressed and out of the room by the time Pavel finished splashing his face with water from the washstand. Ryn had been jumpy and quiet—more so than usual—all week long after their Sunday night encounter with the Kobolds at the Fish Docks. Probably he still thought they should tell someone about what they saw and heard.

Prissy little Jayn Eldragor had been the first to suggest they keep quiet. They'd hashed it all out on the long walk back to the Citadel that night. "Remember what that servant said about infiltrating an organization?" Jayn had said. "He had to be talking about the Watchkeepers."

"It doesn't make any sense," Thalia said. "Why would humans be working with those creatures?"

"Nyssa told us about that," Ryn chimed in. "Well, she mentioned once that there were rumors of people and Kobolds working together. Right, Pavel?"

"I seem to recall something along those lines," Pavel said.

He'd heard similar rumors in Ashborne. That was right before he traveled south and ran into Ryn. He visited Ashborne while following a lead on the Five Crowns. That didn't pan out, and when he saw how spooked the townsfolk were and heard the rumors about how the Levent Hills were crawling with Kobolds, he thought better of sticking around. That business in Aen's Hollow had not been his first encounter with Kobolds. It seemed almost like they had shadowed him all the way down from the Coldreaches. They hadn't, of course.

He was just a treasure hunter, nobody special. Those creatures had no reason to be chasing him in particular across half of Aldria. Certainly, he wasn't responsible for what happened to Ryn's aunt and village. He did not bring that mess down on the kid. Those beasts would have spread south eventually. Pavel owed the kid nothing. He should have left Ryn to bury his aunt alone and kept right on south.

Still, he was here now. He needed to make the best of his last five years as Pavel Talvor. Even if those years included chores. He pulled his uniform on, ran a quick comb through his hair, and staggered down to breakfast. Ryn and the girls talked casually of inconsequential things, all purposefully avoiding the one thing they clearly wanted to talk about. Pavel swirled his porridge around in its wooden bowl, and his mind went back to that endless Sunday.

"We must tell someone," Shilo had said. The girl had a strong moral compass. Most of them did.

"Who can we trust?" Jayn countered. "Consider what we know. That servant mentioned a master. We must assume his master is also part of the Watchkeepers. But who is he? Just how many people are a part of this? What are their goals?" Jayn had the mind of a politician. She knew true north was not the only direction a compass could take you.

"Nyssa," Ryn offered. "Surely we could trust her. There's no way she would work with the Kobolds."

"Granted," Jayn said. "But what exactly do we tell her? We saw Kobolds at the docks, but then they left?"

"Someone could go looking for them," Thalia said. "We'd point them in the right direction at least."

"That river is not some murky provincial backwater," Jayn said. "It's the most heavily trafficked waterway in the whole country. If the Kobolds were hiding somewhere they could be found, they would have been by now. The Pentarchy has patrols running up and down the River Aldria to deter would-be brigands. I've heard that none of the Pentads we sent off to the Sylphren Wood have found a trace of the Kobolds that were there. Clearly, the creatures know how to avoid detection."

"We tell her about the servant then," Shilo said.

"Maybe if we could identify the servant that would be useful information," Jayn said. "Stop and think about it. Nyssa would believe us, but what would she do? She'd run it up the chain of command. And what would they do? The news is out about what happened in Aen's Hollow, and people are reporting Kobold sightings all over the republic. To Commandant Lahey, ours would just be another unsubstantiated report. We are just recruits after all, and some of us have less than sterling reputations." She deliberately avoided looking at Pavel.

"What about the artifact then?" Ryn said. "I heard the servant mention securing an artifact."

"But what artifact?" Jayn countered. "Maybe they mean a Runeform, of which the Watchkeepers have dozens stockpiled. Those are already strictly secured and accounted for. No, I can't see what actual good would come from reporting this. What it would do is alert whomever that servant's master is. That could be bad for us, or the conspirators might just go into hiding."

"What do you suggest then, princess?" Pavel couldn't keep quiet any longer. "Just pretend it never happened?"

"No. We watch and we listen. We may not have seen his face, but we all heard the servant's voice. It's beyond late. Let's get back to the compound, catch some sleep, and go about the week like nothing happened tonight. But keep an ear out. The first thing we must do is figure out who that servant was."

It took some convincing, but the group eventually agreed to Jayn's plan. Pavel had been on board from the beginning, but he kept that to himself. He knew Jayn would win the others over eventually, and he liked to see her sweat. He had no problem keeping secrets; it had become second nature by that point in his life.

He hadn't told any of them about his first encounters with Kobolds. He certainly hadn't told anyone about his quest to find the Five Crowns, the legendary artifacts Pavel's father had droned on about for all of Pavel's childhood. He never understood how a man could spend a lifetime researching ancient treasures but never go out looking for them. When Pavel came of age, he did just that. He changed his name and ran away from home. He'd made little headway in his search, chasing leads and rumors that always faded like mirages on the Silgarian tundra when he got too close, but he hadn't lost hope. When Nyssa took him to the Rigel fountain two weeks ago, he'd asked, "Where is the First Crown?" in Silgarian and received only a nonsensical reply. Admittedly, he had gotten sidetracked along the way, finding himself enmeshed in the underground market for rare Runeforms and other pre-Burning artifacts. He resolved to put all that behind him when he retired the name of Pavel Talvor. Sure, he'd do a few quick jobs first for ready cash. But after that, it would be back to his true calling, finding the Five Crowns. In five years.

After breakfast, Pavel went reluctantly to his morning chores and classes. He made conversation with any male servants he came across, putting on friendly airs but really just listening to the sound of their voices. He did enjoy those fleeting moments of espionage. Nearly a week had rolled by, and still none of them had identified the servant from the docks.

Pavel's assigned chore that morning was the asinine task of peeling potatoes in the kitchens. They had already ruled out the few male servants on the kitchen staff, so he peeled by rote and allowed his mind to wander. He wondered where Corvus was. The Runeform had not been himself for some time, and he refused to enter the Watchkeeper compound. Pavel knew Corvus would never abandon him completely. He'd exploited that bond more than once by selling Corvus off to wealthy collectors. He always warned the buyers to treat Corvus well, or he might not stick around. Then within a few weeks, the clever bird would slip away from his captors and fly unerringly back to Pavel. Corvus could take care of himself. Pavel wouldn't worry.

After chores, Pavel faced the equally dull task of feeding Aether to Thalia, as she worked on her little projects for Rohan Caston. For a while he had occupied their time together by running a confidence game on her to see if she would trust him with one of her luck charms, but two weeks in, he had mostly given up on that prospect. Caston had her well under his thumb, and the Stone master was a stickler for procedure.

After an hour in the sweltering smithy, he went to meet the Aether master, an unbearably chipper man named Trevor Flint. Flint was a lean and spry old-timer with a leathery face and a full head of white hair. He smiled entirely too much. For the first hour, they worked alongside Shilo. Pavel was still amazed by the lacings he could pull off with that girl feeding him Flame. Most of the Blendings focused on protecting the body, such as that nifty lacing that shielded him from fire, at least temporarily. He was eager to begin using Flame himself, but they wouldn't start those lessons for weeks yet.

Flint's training room was a specially designed stone chamber with thirty-foot ceilings. They needed a lot of room for the more acrobatic Aether lacings, and nothing could be made of wood, since they also worked with Flame. Flint brought in various equipment depending on the day's lessons. Pavel quirked an eyebrow when he strolled in to find a claw-footed bathtub in the center of the room.

"Are you trying to tell me something?" Pavel asked Flint. He lifted an arm and sniffed his pit.

Flint laughed. "Oh-ho, not at all, Mr. Talvor."

Pavel didn't like that Flint always called him "Mr. Talvor." He also didn't like the way the man laughed, but that annoyance was harder to explain.

Shilo slipped in behind them, and Flint began the lesson. He showed them an unusual lacing that could allow a Weaver to hold his breath underwater for a long time. Pavel could imagine some utility from such a lacing, but the practice was less than pleasant. Pavel had to climb into the tub fully clothed, while Shilo sat on the edge, her hands planted on his shoulders. Flame flowed from her chest into his body. He absorbed it into his swirling white Aether, giving his lacings a faint pink hue. As with any Aether lacing, he felt the power infuse his body. He became unusually aware of his lungs and his breathing.

"Good, Mr. Talvor," Flint said. "Now, Miss Lorn, please push him down and hold him under."

Shilo didn't hesitate to shove him down into the tub. Pavel sputtered but managed to hold the lacing in place. He closed his eyes and tried to concentrate. He was reminded of a ceremonial dunking he had witnessed once at some backwoods religious revival out east, the kind of place where people still spoke of the Shepherd-King. He didn't know how much time passed, but it couldn't have been more than a minute. Suddenly, he felt claustrophobic and his lungs began to burn. He flailed in the tub until Shilo finally let him up.

He wiped water from his face and scowled at her. "You're enjoying this too much," he told her. She struggled to hide her grin.

"Nonsense, Mr. Talvor," Flint said. "She is merely doing as told. You must try again. Concentrate, Mr. Talvor. I have told you every day for two weeks that you must focus. Try again."

On their third attempt, something clicked for Pavel. He stopped fighting it. Shilo kept her hands on his shoulders, but she didn't need to. He opened his eyes and looked up at the rippling surface of the water and the distorted world beyond. Then he let his eyes unfocus and he just drifted. He felt no discomfort. The lacing permeated every inch of his body, swirling in and out from his lungs. Long after he should have risen sputtering to the surface, the force sustained him. Aether. Air. Breath. Life. Somehow, the lacing kept him alive, taking over for whatever normal breathing did to maintain the body.

He didn't know how much time passed. Distantly he decided he liked it down here, and if Flint wanted to leave him in the tub for the entire hour, he would allow it. Eventually, he heard distorted voices overhead, and then Shilo was tapping him on the shoulder. Reluctantly, he sat up. He did not gasp for air but simply took a breath. Suddenly, his lungs were burning and he coughed.

"Slowly," Flint said. "You must give your body time to re-adjust."

Pavel tried to rise from the tub, but that made the room spin, and he slid back down.

"And you must listen," Flint said, placing a hand on his chest as if to hold him in place. "You may go, Miss Lorn."

Shilo nodded and slipped away, wiping her wet hands on the legs of her trousers.

Flint grinned down at him. "Take your time, Mr. Talvor. Then come join me when you are ready."

It took several minutes before Pavel could pull himself from the tub. He staggered over to where Flint stood on the far side of the room. His boots squelched and he dribbled water all across the floor. He didn't care. His head still spun a little.

Flint spoke without turning to face him. "Your problem is, Mr. Talvor, that you are not committed to being a Watchkeeper."

Pavel frowned. He thought he had won Flint over despite his concealed dislike for the man. "Sure I am," he said.

"You are a talented liar, Mr. Talvor, but you cannot lie to yourself." Flint kept his tone light and positive, despite the weight of his words.

"Where's this coming from?" Pavel gestured back at the tub. "I think I pretty much mastered that lacing, didn't I?"

Flint nodded. "True. You surprised me, but that is only the first step. Your problem is that you spend too much time in your head, too much time planning out your next step. I think in the tub just now, you learned to get out of your head and just exist in the moment."

"Sure, I can see that."

"I've decided I must help you take the next step. Get out of your head, exist in the moment, and act."

"Get out of my head and act? What, without thinking?"

"Oh, you must think, but only think of what you must do in that moment. Do not think about how it will make you look or how it will affect your carefully crafted persona. Think without regard for all the plates you keep spinning."

"All right, and how will I do that?"

"Simple. You must find a way to hit me."

"Hit you?"

"We will spar. You may employ any lacing you know."

"Can I change first? I'm soaking wet."

"Do as I do." Aether surrounded Flint's body, weaving a pattern Pavel had not seen before. The flickering lines formed tight spiraling channels all over him. Pavel was a quick study. He summoned a similar lacing. Flint pointed out a few flaws, and Pavel corrected them. "Good, Mr. Talvor. Now spin." Flint raised one leg and whirled like a top on the toe of his other foot. Pavel could see how the lacings unraveled around him, aiding in his spin. He quickly guessed the purpose of this technique.

Pavel spun. The Aether pulled him around in a dizzying gyre, like being caught in a tornado. The lacings slid between him and the beads of water clinging to his skin and clothes, prying them loose and flinging them away. The lacing unraveled and he staggered to a stop. Once again, the room spun, but he was now completely dry. He smiled. "That's an excellent trick."

"Yes, Mr. Talvor, but it shall not aid you in our sparring. Assume another lacing and let's begin. If you can land a solid hit anywhere on my body, I will dismiss you to lunch early."

The offer was enough incentive for any Aether Weaver. Already, he felt the beginnings of hunger pangs in the pit of his stomach. Light suffused his body. Flint summoned a similar lacing. Pavel tried for a quick jab. Flint flowed easily away, leaving Pavel striking at air. In the blink of an eye, Flint shifted on the balls of his feet, surged forward, and landed a solid punch in Pavel's stomach. Pavel staggered back, wincing. He sneered. "You're not pulling any punches, are you, Flint?"

"Master Flint," he said, his pleasant tone once again in contrast with his words. "I will teach you to call me that before our hour is over."

Pavel tried in earnest then, but they didn't call Flint a master without reason. Pavel wasn't the only Aether Weaver in his line of work, and he'd had a few rivals over the years, though it had never come to a physical fight—which was not to say he never fought anyone, but always he had danced circles around his foes, striking with impunity.

Pavel rose to the balls of his feet and glided forward, striking out with his hands and feet but always missing. Flint didn't even look like he was trying. He kept that stupid grin plastered to his face as he melted away. He landed several blows on Pavel, using only open-handed slaps now, just to show he could. Pavel seethed. He made no effort to dodge or deflect Flint's attacks, focusing solely on his offense.

They flowed in a violent dance around the training room. One end housed several pillars and platforms. Flint scampered his way to the top of the tallest pillar, balancing on one foot. Pavel stopped his advance. He stared up at the Aether master, contemplating a route of attack.

"Come on, Mr. Talvor," Flint said. Clearly, he knew how the title irked Pavel. "You are not even trying."

"Oh, I think I am," Pavel said. Now that he'd stopped moving, he had to pant to catch his breath.

"Stop holding back. You must *want* to succeed."

Pavel gritted his teeth and launched into another attack. Flint proved unassailable from his lofty perch. First Pavel had to bounce his way up the surrounding platforms, giving the master plenty of time to prepare. He easily evaded Pavel and began striking back with more force, sending Pavel flying more than once. Instinctively, Pavel's Aether cushioned each fall, but he knew he would be sore tomorrow. He staggered to his feet after one particularly bad stumble that sent him sprawling all the way back down to the ground.

"Focus, Mr. Talvor!" Flint called down. He repeated his advice, now with a hint of frustration that Pavel still didn't seem to be listening. "Exist in the moment. Stop holding back."

Pavel grunted. Was he holding back? Sure. Holding back, keeping secrets, that was his nature. He concealed and lied about many things, even when he didn't have to. He held back his full knowledge of the Kobolds. He told no one of his true quest in life. In an offhand comment, he'd told the kid he didn't have an Etching, and now he concealed that too, even from the man who was trying to teach him Aether. Was that it? Could the master tell he was holding back in the exercise of his gifting? He had no real reason to keep that secret. Pavel smiled.

The flow of Aether around his body changed. He called his Etching Featherweight. His body grew lighter, almost weightless. He rose to the balls of his feet, and even they seemed to barely touch the ground. It wasn't flying, but it was the closest thing. He flowed forward, taking the most direct path to Flint. He reached the base of Flint's pillar, jumped, and leaned back. He placed one foot against the pillar, and then another. He ran up the vertical surface just as easily as he could have run up the Gauntlet's climbing wall. He couldn't run forever; eventually, gravity would reclaim him, but not soon enough.

He saw a moment of surprise on Flint's face, but then the master launched his own attack. He threw himself off the pillar directly toward Pavel, allowing gravity to aid his descent. Pavel had anticipated it. He altered his trajectory. He swung around the side, spiraling around the pillar. Flint now fell through empty air, and Pavel completed his loop, placing himself suddenly above Flint. He leapt from the pillar, planted a foot squarely in Flint's back, and pushed off into the air again.

Flint landed flat on his stomach, though his own Aether cushioned the landing. He was back on his feet before Pavel glided smoothly to the ground. Surprisingly, he still smiled.

"Well done, Mr. Talvor. So, that's what you were keeping to yourself."

Pavel shrugged. "You were right, I have been holding back."

"I am glad you are beginning to trust me. Now you must also trust your fellow recruits. Each member of your Pentad has something to offer the group. Even you."

Pavel decided to ignore the slight. "I will try." He turned to go but stopped. Without looking back, he said, "Thank you, Master Flint."

Pavel found his chance to help his Pentad that afternoon. They breezed through the first four rooms of the Gauntlet, and now they were back at the wheel, the obstacle that had stumped them for days. Everyone had gotten better at constraining their lacings, but the twisting action still thwarted them. The wheel had already fallen twice, and they were on track for another failure. Their attendant was the same disinterested Root Weaver from last week.

Pavel reflected on Master Flint's words. What would it look like here to exist in the moment? Was Pavel actually trying to succeed, or was he merely going through the motions, letting the younger members take the lead? The wheel was a puzzle and not an overly complicated one. The ancients who built the Runeforms seemed to love puzzles, and he had cracked several over his years of treasure hunting. When the obvious solution didn't work, you had to come at the puzzle a different way.

The group released a collective sigh as Thalia's lacings once again collided with Shilo's, sending the wheel spiraling back down to the base of its pillar. Those two had it the hardest; Stone and Flame simply could not be constrained to a narrow beam. The group had come to terms with this, and no one blamed either girl for not trying hard enough.

"The problem," Pavel said, "is we keep crossing our lacings."

"Wow, Pavel," Jayn said. "You're a genius."

Pavel ignored the sarcasm. Jayn had gotten a lot better at controlling her acid tongue, though he didn't really mind her temper. The other kids were pleasant to the point of blandness, and she kept things interesting. He continued his line of reasoning. "Crossing the streams is only a problem because of how we are positioned, each sandwiched between opposing forces. Maybe the key is changing our positions."

"How?" Jayn asked. "We can't move the nodes."

"No, but we can move ourselves. Can you just humor me for a second? I want to try something."

The others exchanged confused glances. Pavel knew he was acting out of character here. Finally, Thalia, who had stumbled her way into being the unofficial leader of their Pentad, shrugged her broad shoulders. "Sure, Pavel. Tell us what to do. It's not like we're getting anywhere with our current approach."

Pavel nodded. He evaluated the others, considering their strengths and weaknesses, as well as the configuration of the Five Forces. He'd never paid much attention to anything aside from Aether, but the way the forces interacted and fit together was itself a kind of puzzle.

In his mind, he took it one step at a time, and each next step flowed logically from the last. He gave directions as they came to him. "Ryn and Jayn, you clearly have the most control, which makes sense, since Root and Wave are almost always directed outward. Switch places."

Reluctantly they did. Ryn didn't question it, but Jayn couldn't help herself. "How can we reach our nodes now?" she asked.

"You can't reach them in a straight line, but you can curve your lacings. They will cross through each other, but that won't matter. They don't cancel out."

"But his Root will absorb my Wave. And you're still in our way."

"It will absorb some, but you should be able to force your way through. And you'll be curving behind me. You shouldn't get anywhere near my Aether. Step further back if you need to. We can't cross this red circle on the floor, but that doesn't mean we need to be crowded around it. We have a whole room to work with."

Jayn had no protests then. She and Ryn moved back away from the circle. It freed up a lot of space.

"Good," Pavel said. "Actually, we can give ourselves even more room. Shilo, scoot down closer to Ryn, and Thalia, move toward Jayn. Stand right in front of them if you want."

They obeyed. This new configuration seemed a lot better. Instead of a circle, the young Weavers were almost in a straight line now, with the wheel in the middle. Thalia and Shilo now had plenty of room for their rangy lacings. Coming at their nodes from a steep angle instead of head on reduced their chances of colliding with each other. And they were now positioned near Weavers with complementary forces.

"Let's try it now," Pavel said. He glanced at Jayn and Ryn. "Remember to give me a wide berth. This might be harder for you two, but it helps the rest of us."

"No, this might actually work," Jayn said. "Captain Lahmeer told me earlier today that most Wave Weavers only create domes and boxes, but that limit is set by their imaginations. Wards can conform to any shape. Ryn, go as high as you can with your lacings. Instead of making a rectangular wall, I can build a sloping one that starts low and rises gradually. Then we don't even have to worry about overlap."

"Brilliant," Pavel said without an ounce of sarcasm. "Now we're thinking in three dimensions. This will work."

He had never been able to deliver a good pep talk, but nevertheless, his team went at the challenge with a renewed resolve. Unintentionally, he seemed to have given himself the easiest task. He stood directly in front of the node with the white swirl. Still, he kept his lacing as narrow as possible. It required barely any contact to activate. He couldn't see what was going on behind his back, but he trusted Ryn and Jayn to do their part. Beyond the wheel, he could see the blobs of Flame and maze of Stone, but they had plenty of room to work with.

The wheel rose and turned on its corkscrew track, and he moved to follow it. It spun faster now than on their previous plodding attempts, so he picked up his pace. The others did likewise. If any overlap occurred, it involved complementary forces. In a matter of minutes, the wheel reached the top of its pillar, a small chime sounded, and the next door slid open. It seemed so painfully easy now!

The others could not contain themselves. They cheered and even applauded. It felt good, Pavel admitted, despite how ultimately pointless it was. It lacked the reward of cracking the lock on an ancient barrow. Sure, another intriguing Runeform likely awaited them in the next chamber, but it wasn't like they could take it. Later, he would find that thought ironic.

Their bored attendant standing atop the wall nodded in approval. "A novel approach," he said, "but effective. Head into the next room. That one will also require a bit of an explanation, but I'll tell you once we're over there."

He started along the wall top, but the Training Pentad beat him through the door in their eagerness to continue the challenge. The next chamber was slightly smaller than the previous one. On the far side, the outline of the next locked door was clearly visible, but apart from that, the room stood completely empty. Pavel could detect no signs of any Runeforms or any lacings apart from the Wave ceiling above them. The others exchanged confused glances. A long moment of silence followed.

Pavel looked up at their attendant, who was staring down into the room with a look of pure bewilderment. "Something wrong?" Pavel asked.

"Something, well, something's missing," the attendant said. "The mirror is supposed to be right there." He jabbed a finger at the center of the room.

"A mirror?" Jayn asked.

"Yeah, it's a Runeform, and it's part of the challenge, but it's not here."

"What did the Runeform do?" Jayn pressed.

"It showed you—well, it doesn't matter right now, because it's not here. Maybe someone borrowed it, but this has never happened before. What would someone want the mirror for? I'm sorry, but we have to end the Gauntlet here today. Please make your way out. I'm going to get this sorted." The man clearly fought to keep panic from his voice. He turned and trotted off toward the exit without waiting to see if they would comply.

The Training Pentad didn't budge. They exchanged meaningful looks; clearly, they were all thinking the same thing. Shilo said it aloud. "A missing Runeform. That must be the artifact they wanted." She didn't need to explain who "they" were.

"That's not the only thing," Jayn said. "Tell them what happened this morning, Thalia."

"We don't really know what happened." Thalia retorted.

Jayn scoffed. "She wanted me to wait to tell you, since she wasn't sure. But I am, and clearly now we should have said something." She gestured to the empty chamber.

"We don't know when this happened. We're the only group running the Gauntlet right now."

"We know it was sometime this week, if this is the artifact they were trying to secure."

"You're the one who convinced us all to keep quiet in the first place!"

Pavel raised a hand between them. "Ladies, please. Stop bickering and just tell us what happened."

Jayn sighed. "This morning, after my lesson with Captain Lahmeer, Thalia joined me, and we were both waiting for Wave Mistress Bellos. She was running late, which has never happened before. Then we heard voices in the hall, so we poked our heads out. Mistress Bellos was speaking with a servant. A male servant whom I have never seen before. They were whispering, so we couldn't hear them, but then the man said, 'I will keep you informed.' Then he walked off. Mistress Bellos came in and taught our lesson, but she seemed... distracted the whole time."

"Was it him?" Shilo asked, her question coming out in a whisper.

"We can't be sure," Thalia said, just as Jayn responded, "I think it was."

Thalia sighed. "It might have been. He just didn't say enough. And the man from the Fish Docks had a normal voice. I mean, he didn't have a strong accent or anything distinctive." Jayn seemed about to add something, but Thalia cut her off. "And we can't be sure Mistress Bellos has anything to do with the conspiracy. I can think of a hundred legitimate reasons why she would need to speak with a servant."

Shilo gasped. "You think Mistress Bellos might be the servant's master?" she asked Jayn.

"We can't dismiss the possibility," Jayn said. "When that man spoke of a master, he might have meant a master Weaver."

A silence fell over the group. Clearly, they were out of their depth here and needed reinforcements. Pavel sighed. "I'm going to go have a chat with Captain Lahmeer. She is better equipped to deal with whatever is going on here."

Jayn bit her lip. "Are you certain we can trust her? Agia Bellos was her mentor."

Pavel shook his head. "If we can trust anyone here, we can trust Nyssa. The Kobolds cut down her entire Pentad right in front of her. I was there. Ryn and I traveled with her after that. She would wait until she thought we were asleep, and then she would cry herself to sleep each night. There's no way she would ever work for those creatures. And since she is close with Agia Bellos, she can tell us if Bellos has been acting strange lately."

Jayn nodded. "Fine. I'll go with you."

"No, I can handle it. What you and Thalia need to do is track down that servant. You saw his face, but we need his name or at least what job he does here in the compound. If he was working this morning, then his shift should be ending soon and he'll be headed back to the servants' quarters, or out into the city. Take the others with you and split up if you need to. Don't try to talk to him, or you might spook him. Just tail him, understood?"

They all nodded their agreement. He kind of liked being the leader for a change.

Chapter 21
Incursion

THALIA DID HER BEST to look casual as she and Ryn loitered near the front gates of the Watchkeepers' compound. She couldn't restrain herself from making furtive glances to either side several times a minute. She and Ryn faced one another, and looking past each other, they could see all approaches from within the compound. They had taken Pavel's advice and split up, with Jayn and Shilo covering the servants' dormitories.

Something seemed to have ignited a spark in Pavel today. When their Pentad first formed, Thalia had assumed that Pavel, with his age and personality, would have taken on a leadership role, yet he had spent the first two weeks of training apparently attempting to do as little work as possible. Perhaps, Captain Lahmeer had gotten to him too. Nyssa's Sunday morning conversation with Jayn certainly had affected a change in her. Thalia smiled at the idea.

"We should talk," Ryn said. He was too busy scanning over her shoulder to have noticed her smile.

"About?"

"I mean, it just looks weird that we're standing here and not talking."

"You're right, of course. Sorry, I'm still trying to figure out what exactly is happening here."

"Me too. I keep going over the details and trying to make sense of it."

"Any luck?"

He shook his head. "If we knew more about the missing Runeform, that would help."

"I'm sure that's one of the questions Pavel will be asking Nyssa."

"Probably." He paused. "You know he fancies her? I think so, anyway."

"Pavel Talvor and Captain Lahmeer?" She couldn't constrain her laugh at the thought. "Now that would be an odd couple."

Ryn smiled. They still weren't making eye contact as they scanned the yard for the servant. Thalia had done her best to describe the man to Ryn, though the servant's appearance was as unremarkable as his voice. As Pavel had predicted, a steady line of servants was filing out into the city. The two bored guards waved them all through without comment. Overhead, a layer of gray clouds obscured the sun and hinted at rain. She wondered how Pavel knew when the servants' shifts changed. Apparently, he paid more attention than his blasé attitude suggested.

When Ryn spoke again, Thalia realized how long the lull in their conversation had lasted. "Why a mirror? Out of all the Rune-forms in the compound, how will that one help them?"

"Well, on the surface, mirrors are pretty simple. Usually, it's a piece of glass over reflective metal, like polished bronze or silver. Of course, making one into a Runeform could give it any number of properties, but they would likely tie into the essential nature of a mirror. The attendant called it 'the mirror,' not a mirror. The reflective part must be the most salient feature of the device, if that's what they call it."

"The essential nature of a mirror? Hmm, well, that would be to show you your reflection, but maybe this one shows you something else. You look into this one and it shows you… well, something that helps you unlock the next door, I suppose. What if—" He cut himself short and changed whatever he was about to say, his voice dropping to a whisper. "Don't make it obvious, but tell me if that's him. He's about to pass us. On your right."

Thalia turned her head and covered her mouth, deciding to fake a yawn. Her jaw cracked as the charade became genuine; another day of Weaver training had worn her out, especially after Mistress Whitcomb had forced her and Shilo to spar with wooden practice staffs. The lightweight weapons were made of bundled reeds forced stiff by a thin layer of Stone. They could do no real harm, but a smart whack from one could still leave a bruise.

The green-liveried servant glanced at her but kept walking. Thanks to Jayn's invisibility Etching at the docks, the man had no reason to suspect that Thalia and Ryn were anything other than a couple of recruits chatting before dinner.

Ryn raised his eyebrows to silently ask the question. She nodded. He bit his lip. "Should we get the others?"

She shook her head. "Let's just follow him and see where he goes. Carefully though."

They joined the flow of traffic through the gates. One of the guards perked up when he saw their gray uniforms. "And where are you two headed?" he asked. Thalia and Ryn's lack of pins identified them as new recruits, whose movements in and out of the compound were generally restricted.

Thalia faltered, not having prepared an excuse, but one soon came to her. "We were told we could take our dinner in the city, if we so choose."

The guard shrugged. "Sure, if you got the coin, I suppose."

"The dining hall food is good enough; it just…"

"Gets old?" he supplied. "I understand that." He studied them a moment longer. Thalia grew impatient, worried the servant was getting away, but she fought to conceal her anxiety. Some of it must have shown through, or else her initial delay in answering the guard suggested she was lying. The man slowly shook his head. "It's not my place to say, but you two ought to be careful. Fraternizing beyond a certain level is discouraged among Training Pentads, and for good reason." With that, he waved them through.

Thalia felt heat rise in her cheeks as she followed Ryn through the gateway. What did that man think she and Ryn were sneaking off to do? The idea that they might be mistaken for a romantic couple surprised her. Sure, they were of an age, but she had several inches on the shy Root Weaver, and he looked especially pale and scrawny beside her broad and brown physique. As a couple they made as much sense as, well, as Pavel Talvor and Captain Lahmeer.

She had no time to dwell on such thoughts. She scanned the much denser crowd moving up and down the broad Falport avenue. If the man had worn the clothes of a regular laborer, instead of the gold-trimmed green uniform of a Watchkeeper servant, he would have vanished. He was of average build and height, with tan skin and short, curly hair. His face was remarkable in that it was wholly unremarkable. He was neither handsome nor ugly and had no distinctive features like a mole or scar. She felt that if someone were evil enough to work with Kobolds, it should show in their countenance somehow. They shouldn't be indistinguishable from the average man on the street. Even with the uniform, they almost lost him amongst the other servants dispersing in different directions. By chance most of the others who had left with him were all women and easy to rule out even when viewed from behind.

"There he is!" Thalia grabbed Ryn's arm and pointed.

They turned to follow the man, careful not to get too close. He traveled north, following along the outer wall of the compound. When that wall joined with the taller and thicker city wall, he turned and followed the road westward. Tailing the servant was not especially difficult at first. His uniform was easy to spot even in the crowded streets, as all the other servants quickly fell away, their destinations much closer or along side streets.

The man walked at a leisurely pace and never glanced back. He had no reason to suspect pursuit, Thalia told herself. He may not even know that the mirror's theft had been discovered yet. Belatedly, Thalia remembered the lax guards. Shouldn't the compound have been locked down? Their attendant had had plenty of time to report the missing mirror. The leadership's first assumption must have been the same as his—that the mirror had been borrowed or misplaced. They had no reason to suspect a theft yet.

Thalia gritted her teeth, questioning again her group's decision to keep quiet about what they had seen at the Fish Docks. Jayn had been so convincing five days ago, but now their silence only seemed foolish and reckless. If someone had been warned of the conspiracy to steal an artifact, the Watchkeepers would have recognized the significance of the missing Runeform immediately. Still, her regrets could not change the past. By now, Pavel should have finished informing Nyssa, and hopefully the compound would be locked down. There was still a chance the mirror had not been smuggled off the premises yet. The servant didn't seem to have it. True, it might have been a small handheld mirror that he could have secured under his uniform, but somehow Thalia doubted that. In her mind she envisioned a full-length mirror with an elaborate gilt frame and a heavy stand.

The crowds in the streets began to thin. Thalia slowed her pace to give the man more space, and Ryn followed her example. A glance at her companion's face told her Ryn's mind was just as racked by questions as hers. The man made a few turnings now, moving away from the outer wall, and when he disappeared around a corner, they hastened to catch up before dropping back to match his pace again. He still did not look back, and there were enough other people still about that their footsteps on the cobbled streets did not arouse suspicion.

She wondered if he was heading all the way back to the Fish Docks, as his path seemed to indicate. Already, they skirted along the edge of the seedy part of the city where they'd found Pavel on Sunday. Those streets were practically deserted. Business didn't truly pick up here until the sun went down. Thalia gave the servant as much space as she could without risking losing sight of him.

Eventually, most of the buildings gave way to large redbrick warehouses. They followed the servant onto a wide dirt lane. Thalia never understood why this section of Falport did not have paved streets; it was still within the city walls after all. The lane was completely empty, save for the servant and two men clearly standing guard before the entrance to one of the warehouses. The servant angled his steps toward the men. Thalia felt too exposed. On such an empty street, they would attract notice. If the servant saw their Watchkeeper gray uniforms, he would grow suspicious.

She grabbed Ryn's arm and yanked him into an alley between two buildings. She pressed her back to the brick wall, steadied her breathing, and listened for any sounds. She heard a murmur of voices as the servant exchanged some greetings with the guards, then the heavy metal door swung open on squeaky hinges, before slamming shut again. After several seconds, Thalia stole a glance around the corner. The two guards still stood at their post, and the servant was gone. She pulled her head back into the alley and studied the building opposite her. All the warehouses here were identical, with sloping tin roofs and narrow windows set high along the walls to let in light. If they could make their way around to the back of the building the servant had entered, she could perhaps give Ryn a boost high enough to peek in.

Ryn cleared his throat. "We should go back now," he said.

Thalia raised an eyebrow. She had not even considered turning back. "Why?" she asked.

"To tell the others. To tell someone, anyway. We know where he went."

"This may not be his final destination. He may only be stopping by for a minute."

"Fine, then we can wait here for a few minutes. We'll hear it if that door opens again."

"I think we should get closer. Some of these buildings have back doors. I don't think he saw us, but if he suspects he's being followed, he might try to slip out the back." She knew she was only making excuses to get closer. More than anything, she felt an overwhelming sense of curiosity to know what was in that warehouse.

Ryn sighed. He seemed to want to say more, but he just shook his head and said, "Fine, but let's go slow and careful."

Thalia nodded. She led the way down the alley, and he followed. This brought them into another sort of street, though not one meant for pedestrians. The backs of warehouses lined both sides of the space, forming a long, shared yard. The businesses that owned them used this area to store excess goods that could stand exposure to the elements, mostly piles of building materials, mixed in with plenty of empty crates and barrels waiting to be reused. A few warehouse owners had fenced off their yards for a small layer of security, so Thalia and Ryn had to weave their way back and forth through the piled junk and around the fences.

They came to the back of the servant's building, and Thalia was disheartened to see that this one also had a fence. They crouched down behind it. The wooden fence was crudely made, with plenty of gaps and knotholes, so they could peer inside with ease. The enclosed yard lay mostly empty, aside from a few crates stacked up against the back wall of the warehouse. If they could climb up those crates, they could easily peer in through the high windows. First, they needed to get over the fence. The posts rose well over her head. They could scramble over it, but not without making too much noise.

"No back door," Ryn whispered beside her.

"And no more guards, other than the two out front." She pointed to the stacked boxes. "If we can get into the yard, we can get a good look at what's going on inside. Then we'll have something to report."

Ryn chewed his lip. "Are you sure about this? We have to be absolutely quiet."

An idea came to her. "Trust me," she said.

Stone Weaving could be used to put things together and create firm bonds, but a lesser-known use for the force was taking things apart. She pressed her palms to one of the broad, flat pickets and infused it with Stone. She felt the grain of the wood, the strain and damage from weather and insects, and the rusty iron nails holding it in place. She spread her lacing into the top and bottom rails, focusing on the area around the nails. She constricted the wood to widen the holes, allowing the nails to ease their way out, smoothly and silently. She passed the wooden picket to Ryn, who laid it gently on the ground.

She'd need to remove three more pickets to fit through the gap. She strained her ears, listening for any sound of alarm or activity from the warehouse. She heard nothing. She removed the last two boards by rote, focusing most of her attention on looking and listening. The fence extended down either side of the warehouse, leaving two narrow alleys, which could conceivably conceal more sentries, but she doubted that. If someone desired to guard the building's rear, he would be here in the backyard.

She handed the last board to Ryn and made one final survey of the yard. She took a deep breath as if preparing to dive into an icy river and crept through the opening. Ryn followed behind her. They ghosted across the dirt lot to the back of the warehouse. The crates piled here seemed almost intentionally stacked for climbing, with three diminishing tiers. Ryn rested a hand atop one box.

"Wait," Thalia whispered. She set her hands to the same box and sent refracting strands of Stone throughout the entire jumble. Her senses told her the wood was weathered but sound. The crates could bear their weight without breaking. She nodded. "We're good," she said.

If Ryn wondered what she had done, he didn't ask. He hoisted himself atop a box and scrambled his way to the top. Apparently, his own curiosity had overcome his apprehension. She followed more slowly, picking her way carefully up. Ryn made room for her atop the highest crate. Sitting on their knees, they could raise themselves up just high enough to peer inside.

The window was dirty with soot, and the overcast sky muddied the daylight filtering through into the dim interior. Several moments passed before her eyes adjusted and Thalia could make sense of the busy scene below. Boxes and canvas-covered pallets stood in haphazard piles along all four walls of the single large room, as if a hasty attempt had been made to clear floor space in the middle. Over a dozen shadowed figures milled about inside. Most were clearly humans, but a few were short and squat, with gray skin and tight brown trousers and vests. Kobolds.

She barely even noticed the creatures, as the tableau at the center of the cleared floor drew the bulk of her attention. The mirror was not how she had envisioned it. It stood taller than her but was perfectly circular, set into a polished gold frame. The round frame was smooth and unadorned. Two points on opposite sides anchored it to the equally simple gold stand. The two uprights that supported the mirror tapered inward, following the curve of the mirror, before flaring outward toward the round pedestal base. The suspended mirror could be tilted up and down, and it also looked like it could be rotated in a complete circle on its base.

Five Weavers stood in a circle around the mirror. None wore the gray uniform of a Watchkeeper, but this group had to be a Pentad. The Five Forces were all represented, and each Weaver wove a complex lacing and funneled it into the mirror. Their control put Thalia's Training Pentad to shame. True, this group stood in complementary order. Each Weaver's lacings spilled into his neighbors and mixed together. Even that seemed part of the impossibly elaborate lacing they created. Thalia had never heard of a lacing that used all of the Five Forces. None involved more than two!

She noticed all this in a matter of moments. She saw too that none of the Weavers looked familiar, except the Stone Weaver, dressed in the green livery of a Watchkeeper servant. He constrained his lacings into a narrow beam by spiraling them around each other as they bent and split. That stunned her more than anything. She doubted even Master Caston knew such a technique. Thinking in three dimensions, Pavel had called it. The servant no doubt had concealed his ability to Weave when he sought employment with the Watchkeepers, or they would have dressed him in gray rather than green. Where then had he been trained? Clearly, his entire Pentad had worked together before, but Thalia thought only the Watchkeepers trained their Weavers in such a manner. She knew little of how other nations used their Weavers, but mainly they kept them separated. Stone Weavers only trained with other Stone Weavers, and so on. On top of that, the man had no foreign accent.

She braved a final glance at the other four Weavers before ducking back down. The two men and two women formed a disparate group. The Root Weaver, a woman in a fashionable blue dress, also wore what looked like a pair of Finston wooden clogs. The other woman, whose chubby face and simple blouse and skirt reminded Thalia of a baker, wove an impossibly tight channel of Flame that also extended in a spiral. Whether that was a way to keep it small or part of the lacing, Thalia couldn't say. The remaining men were equally mismatched. The slender Wave Weaver wore the tailored brown suit and bowler hat of a first-echelon gentleman, while the burly Aether Weaver curiously wore the leather apron of a smith.

Thalia ducked below the window and returned Ryn's wide-eyed stare with an equally bewildered look. "Now we go back," he whispered, no trace of a question in his voice. He turned and hopped carefully down the crates. Wordlessly, she followed him. A million questions swirled in her mind, but she knew they had to report what they'd seen. Whatever bizarre and elaborate lacing those Weavers were creating around the mirror Runeform, it could not be good, especially if the Kobolds were involved. No one knew what those creatures were truly after or why they had come to Aldria. Clearly, the threat was greater than anyone had yet realized. Ryn led the way now across the yard and back to their hole in the fence. He raised a foot to step over the bottom rail but then stumbled backwards.

"What is it?" Thalia whispered, but before she could even finish asking the question, she had her answer. A Kobold stepped into view on the other side of the fence. This one towered over her and wore a set of black leather armor in a style she had never seen before, secured by a lot of straps and buckles. A scar crossed diagonally across his hideous face, and he wore a curved sword at his waist. She couldn't be sure, but she guessed it was the same creature from a week ago, the one the servant had called Kalo.

Then there were dozens of Kobolds, crowding around behind their leader to peer through the fence and see what had caught his attention. They were all barefoot, with massive clawed feet. Some wore little more clothing than a pair of short breeches, but all carried some sort of weapon. Spying the two humans, the creatures broke into wide grins, showing far too many sharp teeth. Thalia and Ryn took several stumbling steps back away from the nightmarish fiends, but they had no means of escape. Yelling or running around to the front of the building would draw the attention of the human guards and the Weavers. A cold chill permeated Thalia's body, and she doubted she could muster the breath to scream if she had wanted to.

Kalo glanced over his shoulder at his followers. He raised a muscular arm and pointed to his left. "Gro," he grumbled. The shorter creatures looked up at their leader in apparent surprise. Without looking back at them, he grunted, a deep animal sound. The Kobolds flinched at the noise, then decided to heed his apparent order. The entire party turned and loped away in the same direction they had been headed, away from the Fish Docks and toward the heart of the city. More creatures than she had been able to see through the opening filed past. The invading force was at least fifty Kobolds strong, though she did not count them. Thalia's eyes were fixed on Kalo, who did not move. The message was clear. The Kobolds would continue on their mission, and only Kalo would stay behind to deal with these meddling humans.

He waited until the last Kobold had passed before stepping through the gap in the fence. He turned his shoulders sideways to fit. He'd been staring both of them down, but now he shifted his focus to Ryn, seeming to recognize him. "Gris ick scill allive?" Kalo asked.

When the creature's gaze left Thalia, it broke the spell that kept her frozen in fear, unable to act or think. She glanced about quickly for a weapon. She stood no chance against this hulking beast, but she had to try. She spied a wooden pole, likely the discarded broken handle of a broom. She darted toward it, stooped, and picked it up. She had still been in Kalo's field of vision, and he had to have seen her move, but the Kobold ignored her. He kept his gaze fixed on Ryn's face.

"Ghow?" Kalo asked. Ryn stood rooted with his mouth hanging open, his face gone a ghostly white.

Clearly, the Kobold had dismissed Thalia as any sort of threat. She would prove him wrong. She infused her improvised staff with a hasty lacing of Stone to strengthen and harden the wood. She stepped forward and swung, attempting to use the form Mistress Whitcomb had taught her. She'd aimed for his uncovered head, but he tilted away at the last moment, and she caught him on the shoulder pauldron. It felt like she'd swung on the brick wall behind her instead. Striking such a solid target sent shockwaves up her arms. She stumbled back and the staff fell from her grip and clattered to the floor.

With the reflexes of a cat, Kalo spun toward her and lashed out with his clawed hand. She raised her arms defensively, and he raked his talons across both her forearms, tearing into flesh and leaving searing gashes of pain. She reeled back and fell hard on her backside.

Now Ryn had been freed to act. He didn't think to find a weapon but merely threw himself at the towering creature. Ryn pummeled away uselessly with his fists, then tried an uppercut that caught Kalo right under the chin, forcing his mouth shut with a loud click. The Kobold had endured Ryn's assault with the same indifferent tolerance of a father withstanding the wailing tantrum of a toddler, until that last hit. Kalo turned and shoved Ryn backwards. Ryn stumbled under the blow but kept his feet.

In a single fluid motion, Kalo drew his curved sword and slashed toward Ryn in a horizontal arc. The scrawny Weaver danced back but not far enough. The Kobold's blade rent the front of Ryn's shirt and left a shallow gash across his stomach. He fell then, clutching his belly as blood stained his fingers. Kalo walked slowly forward to finish Ryn off. Thalia struggled to regain her feet, but bracing her hands against the ground sent shooting pain through her already throbbing arms.

In one final desperate attempt, Ryn lashed out again, not with his fists but with his Weaving. A green ethereal tree grew upward from his torn stomach, sending branches toward Kalo. Thalia had no idea what a Root lacing could do to stop an aggressive opponent, yet when the branches touched Kalo, he stopped and his whole body went rigid. His face contorted with something like disgust, and he lashed out with his free hand, not at Ryn, but at the lacing that stretched between them. Something like a puff of black smoke poured from Kalo's finger, and the tree suddenly vanished. He took a step away and glared at Ryn.

In the sudden lull, Thalia became aware of a distant noise. Screaming. Several streets away people were yelling. The invading Kobolds must have finally reached a populated street. Distantly, she knew the unprepared citizens of Falport were now fighting for their lives, but Kalo still held the bulk of her attention. He had turned his head, hearing the shouting as well. He glanced toward the opening in the fence, then back at Ryn. He shifted his grip and hefted his blade again. Ryn had shuffled back as far as he could, and his head rested against the stacked crates. Blood now seeped down the front of his trousers. Amazingly, he conjured his Root tree again. He kept the limbs constrained, but the threat was clear. Whatever he had done that so repulsed Kalo, he would do again.

Kalo grunted in clear frustration. He seemed torn between wanting to join the other Kobolds in their merciless slaughter and wanting to finish off these two Weavers first. Thalia spared a glance for her wounded arms. They weren't bleeding too much, but the skin around the scratches looked red and swollen. She clenched her fists, ignored the pain, and summoned her own lacings of Stone. She couldn't say what she would have done with them. She had some vague idea of targeting Kalo's sword and weakening it, though she doubted she would have accomplished much before he buried that blade in her chest.

Another noise helped Kalo decide his course. They all glanced toward the warehouse as the squealing doors on the far side slung open again. Kalo nodded to himself and gave Ryn one final look. He puckered his lips and spat, though the phlegm landed short of Ryn. Then he turned and sauntered off, twisting through the hole in the fence and disappearing around the side.

Thalia released her lacing with a sigh. Then her attention turned to the sounds coming from the other side of the warehouse. Several people or Kobolds had clearly exited the building, and she heard their indistinct remarks to one another. However, those voices diminished as they moved away. Apparently, the sounds of melee further down had drawn their attention, not the scuffle behind their own building. It seemed Thalia and Ryn would be left alone for now.

She finally managed to regain her feet and hobbled over to where Ryn still lay, clutching his belly. He had not released his Root tree. She dropped down to her knees beside him. "Move your hands," she said. "Let me see." She peeled back the blood-soaked front of his shirt, revealing an angry red gash just above his waist. She was afraid to probe the wound, but it did not look too deep. Gut wounds tended to bleed a lot, she had heard.

"Your arms," Ryn said through gritted teeth.

She looked at her wounds again. Blood dripped in rivulets down her forearms. "I'll live," she said. "I'm more worried about you. Can you use your Etching to heal yourself?"

He moved his arms back to clutch at his gut. "I think so, eventually. It takes a minute." Color had not returned to his face. He seemed on the verge of passing out. "But your arms…"

"They can keep. Save your energy."

"Maybe not. The claws, they're… poisoned."

Once again fear sent a cold chill rattling through her. Of course. Earlier in the week, Pavel and Ryn had filled them in on everything they knew pertaining to Kobolds. She had heard the general outline of the attack they'd endured on the road out of Aen's Hollow before, but this time they went into detail. Pavel shared his theory about poisoned claws that had killed the Root Weaver and likely would have killed him and Nyssa if Ryn had not healed them. How quickly did the poison take hold? Was she feeling it even now, coursing through her blood, or was that only panic? The last time Ryn had been seriously injured, according to him, he had passed out for hours while his Etching healed him. Could Thalia wait that long? Would he wake to find her dead? That was why he had not released his lacing. He'd known as soon as Kalo scratched her that he would have to heal her and quickly. *Trust the boy who saves your life*, the Rigel fountain had said.

She pressed her hands over Ryn's. "Please," she said. "If you are able…"

He wrapped her arms in green light. Once as a girl she had broken her leg, and she remembered well the strange tingling that healing produced. Alternating bands of cold and heat flowed through her. She watched as the wounds on her arms puckered and closed. As soon as the last red seam sealed itself and vanished, Ryn's tree flickered and disappeared. She looked down at the unconscious boy. The gentle rise and fall of his chest told her he still lived. His wound had not closed, but perhaps it bled less.

She could do nothing to speed up his healing. She could have easily carried him, but she didn't know which direction was safe, and she feared to move him while his Etching worked itself out. They were at the epicenter of the incursion, yet somehow they were safe for now. Kalo may eventually come back to finish them, but whatever they sought to do in Falport, the Kobolds would not have an easy time of it. The city guard and the Watchkeepers would recover quickly from the surprise attack and fight back. She wanted to join in that defense, but she couldn't leave Ryn unprotected. She sighed. She just had to wait until Ryn healed himself. However long that took.

She studied her arms. They felt normal. Had he managed to also purge the poison from her? Whether he had or not, there was nothing she could do about it now. She had to trust him. He had saved her life after all. She wondered why the Runeform had told her that. If Rigel had meant Ryn, it seemed unnecessary. She had no reason not to trust Ryn. She sighed again, looking down at the sleeping boy, or young man really. She could at least make him more comfortable. He'd get a crick in his neck lying like that against the crate.

She sat down beside him and carefully shifted him until his head rested in her lap. She leaned back against the crate and closed her eyes. The sounds of yelling and battle had moved further away. Either everyone nearby was dead, or they had fled from the attacking Kobolds. She couldn't help any of them yet. Absently, she ran her fingers through Ryn's hair. She remembered her mother stroking her head like that anytime she had taken ill as a little girl. She set her other hand lightly on Ryn's chest to know he still lived. He breathed, and the breaths were slow and deep, almost deliberate. Unconsciously at first, she matched her own breathing to his. As she did, her racing heart slowed and she felt calmer. He would heal, and they would make it away from here. Trust the boy.

The ground shook, pebbles danced across the yard, and the windows overhead rattled in their casements as a booming explosion sounded somewhere to the east. The people of Falport renewed their screaming. Still, Ryn did not wake. Thalia closed her eyes again and breathed.

Chapter 22
Captain Lahmeer

NYSSA SIGHED. "I DON'T EVEN know where to begin." Pavel kept his eyes on the ground and offered no further words. "You should have come to me right away, that should go without saying. Kobolds in the city? You know what kind of threat that poses."

He shrugged. "We did see them leave. And like I said, we had good reason to believe someone within the Watchkeepers was involved."

"Perhaps, but Agia Bellos? I've known her for years. There's no way she would work with the Kobolds."

He raised a defensive hand. "Jayn Eldragor made that suggestion. I'm merely passing it along."

Nyssa turned and walked away from him. She moved to the window and surveyed the green yard below without really looking at it. She'd been surprised to answer a knock at the door and find the handsome thief standing there. She'd seen little of Pavel in the last two weeks since delivering him over to the Watchkeepers. Their differing ranks and non-complementary forces gave them little reason to interact. She had been surprised he knew where to find her private room, and she was even more shocked by the tale he unfolded. Kobolds reaching into the Golden Lands, into the very heart of the Watchkeepers' stronghold? It sent a cold shiver up her spine.

Pavel cleared his throat. "What will you do?"

She spoke without turning back to him. "I'll have to make a report to the council. I'll tell them Kobolds were sighted along the Fish Docks. I'll keep your Pentad's names out of it, on the off chance there is some truth to this alleged conspiracy."

"A wise choice," he said, speaking barely above a whisper.

"I can tell you now that Agia Bellos had no part in this."

"I'm sure you are right." He hesitated before continuing, apparently taking pains not to agitate her. "The problem is, we don't know what the Kobolds want. What happened back in Aen's Hollow seemed like random, pointless slaughter. No rational human would be party to that, but there must be more to it. The kid thought they were searching for something or someone in particular. If we don't know their true goal, then we can't say whose purposes may or may not align with theirs—even someone within the Watchkeepers. Maybe someone is just using the Kobolds to accomplish an ulterior purpose."

She wondered why Pavel chose his words so carefully. Had his report agitated her? Certainly, the blackening of Agia's name had rankled her. She tried to soften her tone. "We can speculate all we want, but we just don't know enough." She sighed again. "I guess I'll go get this over with."

"Before you do, can I just ask, the missing mirror, what was it?"

"The Runeform? We can't know that it's connected, but... it probably is. Your attendant was right to be perplexed. Ordinarily, a Runeform would never be removed from the Gauntlet, especially when a Training Pentad is running it."

"What does it do? That might tell us why the Kobolds wanted it."

She hesitated. How much could she tell him? Now it was her turn to choose her words carefully. She turned to face him. "Ordinarily, no one is allowed to share details about the Gauntlet with recruits who are actively running it, but under the circumstances… Well, the short answer is, we don't really know what the mirror does."

He arched an eyebrow. "I think I'm going to need the long answer then."

"I'll do my best. You know better than most that quite a number of Runeforms survived the Burning. They're hardly commonplace, but not as rare as people think. Over the years, the Watchkeepers have amassed a substantial collection. You also know that Runeforms don't come with instructions. Some are easy to figure out and use, but not all. I won't tell you where, but we have a storage room filled with Runeforms that don't appear to do anything at all, or really we have no idea how to activate them. Even the ones we have found a way to use, well, we have no way to know if that was their original purpose. The mirror is definitely one of the stranger Runeforms we have, but when the Watchkeepers first built the Gauntlet a hundred years ago, they found a way to use it."

"How? You still haven't told me what it does."

"I know. I'm working my way to that." She decided to come at it a different way. "If the mirror hadn't disappeared, this is what would have happened. When your Pentad cleared the wheel, your attendant would have informed you that a switch to open the next door was concealed somewhere along one of the walls of the mirror chamber. The switch is impossible to see, but you can find it by feeling along the walls. Actually, there are several different switches, but only one is active at once and they're changed each time. Your attendant will tell you that the mirror will aid you in finding the switch, but he won't tell you how. You have to figure that out for yourself."

"And what would we figure out?"

"First you would study the mirror, but that would tell you nothing. It's on a stand that allows it to spin and tilt. You would spin it around, looking for some clue in what it reflected, like maybe the switches glow, but only in the mirror. This won't work. Eventually, in frustration, you will begin searching blindly for the switch, by feeling along the walls. Hopefully, you will leave one Pentad member to continue studying the mirror. Eventually, you will notice something... peculiar."

"What?" Pavel was trying to contain his impatience.

"The reflections in the mirror, they don't always match reality." Pavel's eyes widened at that, but he fought back another question. Nyssa pressed on quickly. She tried to keep it simple, but the mirror defied a straightforward explanation. She gestured as she spoke. "Imagine you are facing the mirror, and you step to the left. Your reflection might step to the right. It's not a distorted reflection, but a completely different movement. The mirror shows a different... version of you."

Pavel couldn't restrain himself. "What? How is that possible?"

"As I said, we don't know. Anyway, you would still find the switch by blind probing, but using the mirror speeds it up. Imagine Ryn is searching one section of the wall, while his reflection searches a different area, and you're watching the mirror. Either Ryn will find the switch first, or the mirror Ryn will. The Ryn in the mirror can't unlock your door, but he'll show you where your switch is."

"That's insane. The mirror does something that miraculous, and you use it to help solve a simple puzzle?"

"I didn't create the Gauntlet. That's been in place for decades. Sure, it's a peculiar novelty, but can you think of a practical use for it?"

He scoffed. "I don't know. Clearly it has some important use, if someone went to such great lengths to steal it. Can you tell me anything else about it?"

She hadn't given much thought to the mirror before, not since completing the Gauntlet with her own Training Pentad years ago. She thought back to those days. Tabbot had been part of that group; the others had all retired or switched units and been replaced over the years. "It is strange. I remember, the longer you looked into the mirror, the more obvious the differences became."

"How so?"

"Well, you might look away and then back and find your own appearance has changed. Your clothes might be different, or your hair." She pointed at him. "You might have a beard or walk with a limp. Once, I saw... Well, the me in the mirror was missing an arm. It was just a nub, severed right here." She grabbed her arm just below the elbow and shuddered at the suddenly recalled memory. She shook her head. "Still, I don't know how anyone could use the mirror for any nefarious or even practical purpose."

She could tell by the fevered look in his eyes that Pavel's mind raced as he considered all the possible uses for such a mirror, or maybe how much coin it could fetch on the underground market. Finally, he shook his head. "Clearly, we just don't have all the cards yet. I've held you long enough." He gestured toward the door. "You should make your report."

Outside an alarm bell began to sound. Nyssa rushed to the window. Her view showed her a grassy yard and the backs of three other barracks but no movement.

"What's that?" Pavel asked.

"I'm not sure." Nyssa quickly crossed her small room to the chest at the foot of her bed and retrieved her sword. She buckled the sword belt around her waist as she headed for the door. Pavel fell in step behind her.

It was early enough in the evening that few other officers were in their rooms. She joined the short line of women rushing down the stairs. She hoped none of them would suspect anything scandalous from Pavel's presence, but like her, they were all focused on getting outside and finding the source of the alarm. Some carried weapons, but not all. She'd never heard the alarm sound for anything other than a drill.

Outside they found a growing crowd of Watchkeepers, not all in uniform. She could tell by their confused looks and hurried conversations that none here knew what was going on. Then she spotted Rohan Caston striding purposely across the yard, his sword at his side. She angled her steps toward him and matched her pace to his. "Master Caston," she greeted him.

He nodded to them without slowing his pace. "Captain Lahmeer. Recruit Talvor." Pavel still shadowed her like a lanky hound dog.

"Do you know who sounded the alarm?"

"I did. There's trouble in the city." He gestured back toward the smithy. "Some city guards came running across the top of the wall, shouting down at us. Fighting in the streets, they said, between the Fish and the Appencourt gates."

"The city is being attacked? By whom?"

"I aim to find out."

Caston moved steadily toward the compound's entrance. Through a gap in the buildings, Nyssa could see a force already rallying there, awaiting direction. The Watchkeepers would aid the city in any way they could, though their numbers were few. At any given time, most Pentads were out on patrol or assignment, and their ranks were even more depleted at present. Several Watchkeepers were sequestered outside the city testing Thalia Moldo's luck charm, and even more Pentads had been sent west to scour the Sylphren Wood for Kobolds. Kobolds that had eluded them and found their way to Falport somehow. Kobolds that might even now be attacking the city. Her city.

She turned and placed a hand on Pavel's chest to stop him. He looked down at her in puzzlement. "Recruits are to remain in the compound in the event of an emergency in the city." He opened his mouth to protest, but she cut him off. "I know that won't mean anything to you, and I haven't the time to try to stop you." She looked away and lowered her voice. "Just don't be reckless and get yourself killed. Your Pentad needs you."

Before he could respond, she spun and hurried away to catch up with Master Caston. The Stone master was already barking directives by the time she joined the crowd near the entrance. "Commandant Lahey is away in the capital, so I'm taking charge. We have reports of fighting in the streets, and the city guard has requested our aid. If you're on the guard rotation, stay here and secure the gates. We've civilians and recruits inside. Everyone else, form up and move out. Improvise Pentads if needed."

Nyssa had no Pentad. She found herself hurrying out into the streets alongside Master Caston and three other Weavers she knew by sight but not by name. The broad avenue outside the Watchkeeper compound had been completely deserted. Likely everyone had bolted themselves indoors at the sound of the alarm. The Watchkeepers always warned their neighbors when they ran drills. A few faces peered out from upper windows. They turned and headed north. Caston directed some groups to go south, and others peeled off down side streets as they advanced. When they reached the wall, her group turned left and followed it. She saw no movement above. Any soldiers stationed on the wall must have descended to street level. She wondered again what had happened. Could there really be Kobolds in Falport? Should she tell Caston? This could be nothing. Either way, they would all know soon enough.

They stopped their advance, hearing a commotion down a side street. Several citizens milled about in front of a large stone building, one of the local Guild Halls. A red-faced man banged on the door. "Let us in, you blighted cowards!"

Several people waiting behind the man gasped and flinched as Caston's group approached. Something had clearly driven these people into an overwrought state. The man stopped his banging and glared at Caston. "Ah, the Grey Guard," he said. "Can you get these blasted Weavers to let us in?"

"What's going on?" Caston asked.

The frantic citizens spoke all at once.

"Monsters!"

"Creatures in the street are cutting people down with swords and axes!"

"We came to the Guild for help. They locked the door and won't even let us in."

Caston raised a quieting hand. He radiated authority, and the group quickly fell silent. "The streets behind us are empty and safe. Head to the Citadel, and the Watchkeepers will give you shelter."

The crowd readily obeyed. A few uttered parting curses for the Guild. Caston shook his head and led his improvised Pentad onward. Nyssa wondered what the citizens thought the Guild could do. They were Weavers but not trained for fighting. They could have at least offered shelter. She glanced back at the building. Several blue wards surrounded the structure, more than usual.

They hurried through empty streets and soon began to hear the distant sounds of metal on metal and screaming. Caston and the others broke into a trot. A moment later they faltered to a halt as the ground heaved beneath them. A large explosive blast sounded from somewhere behind them.

Caston looked back with wide eyes. "That sounded like it came from the Citadel!" He hesitated. Behind them they heard the tinkle of broken windowpanes clattering to the ground. Ahead they heard the sounds of fighting and slaughter. He was torn between two imperatives.

Nyssa grabbed his arm. "You should go back. An explosion means debris and collapsed buildings." She didn't need to explain further; a Stone Weaver was best suited to help anyone trapped by such a blast.

He nodded. "Rogin, with me," he said to the Root Weaver. "You two stay with Captain Lahmeer."

The Pentad split up, not an uncommon tactic in the field. Caston and the healer were best equipped for dealing with the aftermath of an explosion. The Aether and Flame Weavers, both men in fit condition, could put a stop to the fighting. Maybe. She led her two fellow Watchkeepers forward. She still could not recall their names, but with the danger waiting ahead, perhaps it was better that way. She recalled the fate that had befallen her Pentad when last she faced Kobolds. She would mourn these men less if she didn't know them.

She carried that bleak mood with her through the streets of Falport, but when she rounded a corner and stepped into a nightmare, she did not hesitate. She drew her blade and advanced. A dozen squat Kobolds surrounded a frenzied group of people. Five city guards fought to protect a knot of citizens, but they were losing. Each man wore red gashes and tears in his uniform where his light mail shirt had not protected him. Most of the citizens had been slashed or clawed, and a few clearly struggled to stay upright. Bodies lay everywhere outside the frenzied circle.

Nyssa struck down the closest Kobold before he had a chance to turn. They all wore a strange sort of brown leather clothing, but it lacked the protective thickness of armor. Her fellow Watch-keepers took up position beside her, the Flame Weaver landing powerful blows with the brass knuckles he wore on his fists, and the Aether Weaver making quick jabs with his shortsword. They quickly turned the tide against the Kobolds.

She stabbed the final monster through the throat, and as he fell sputtering to the ground, she stopped to catch her breath. One of the guards and several of the citizens had fallen before the melee ended. The Flame Weaver had a scratch across his cheek. She winced at the sight of that. Hopefully he could find a healer soon, if the Kobolds' claws really were poisoned.

One of the guards, wearing the stripes of an officer on his sleeve, saluted her and thanked her for her aid. She looked at the wounded citizenry. "We need to get these people inside somewhere."

The officer shook his head. "Everyone on this street has barred their doors, and I can't blame them." He gestured at the slain Kobolds. "This ain't the last of them. The streets are full of these star-cursed creatures."

Nyssa sighed. She knew she had to keep moving, to keep scouring the streets until not a Kobold remained. Most of the survivors had minor wounds, but half a dozen would not be walking out of here unless a healer found them. She almost told those who could to head east, but then she remembered the explosion. Was the compound still secure? "I can put up a shield that will stop almost anything. That should keep these people safe until it's all over, but someone will need to watch over them and go for a healer when the fighting dies down."

The officer nodded. "We can do that."

She raised her voice so everyone could hear. "Once we eliminate the threat, seek out the Watchkeepers for healing services. We won't charge like the Guild. Please, even if you've only been scratched, we think…" She didn't want to tell these people a fast-acting poison now coursed through their veins. "Their claws can cause a nasty infection if left untreated." She nodded significantly to the Flame Weaver. He touched his cheek and winced.

Precious minutes elapsed before it was over. A few of the unwounded civilians opted to keep moving in the hopes of finding less conspicuous shelter elsewhere. One of the guards went with them. She set a ward around the remaining group. It took a minute for her Etching to form, but she didn't want to risk using a lesser shield. They would be trapped inside the bubble until she or an Aether Weaver could free them, but they would be safe until the battle ended. If it ended. If the whole city didn't fall to the Kobolds. Then they were all as good as dead anyway.

She stumbled as she turned to walk away. The shield had taken too much energy. Her mouth was dry and her lips felt chapped. She longed for a drink of ice-cold water. She decided she could not keep making shields. Any other citizens she rescued would have to find shelter elsewhere. Her mission, she decided, was to kill Kobolds. She would not stop until they were all dead, or she was. Part of her had died weeks ago in the Sylphren Wood with the rest of her Pentad, she realized. She thought the loss had weakened her, and it had, but like a broken bottle, it left her with a jagged edge. She would use that edge to cut down the creatures that still haunted her dreams most nights. Before, she had dreaded the idea of facing the Kobolds again, but now that she was here facing it, a stony resolve settled over her heart. She could do this. For Tabbot. For Mercer, Brug, and Clayborne. For her friends.

Her fellow Watchkeepers followed her, and within a few street turnings, they plunged back into the chaos. Bodies filled the streets. The city guards fought with swords and spears. Citizens fought with improvised weapons. Weavers, not all of them Watchkeepers, lashed out with their lacings in any way they could. Kobolds were everywhere. There were seemingly hundreds of them. As she moved through the battle, she saw clumps of her gray-clad comrades fighting with weapons and lacings. The improvised Pentads had fallen apart, and most fought singly or in pairs, mere survival being their only goal now.

Survival was not a high priority for Nyssa. She cut down every Kobold she could and kept moving. As she learned last time, the beasts were strong and brutal but were barely competent in the use of their weapons. None stood a chance against her one-on-one. She knew a combined effort would end her, but she didn't think about that. She didn't think about anything as she gave her mind over to the battle. She flowed endlessly from slash, to parry, to stab. Time moved strangely in the flow of battle. Each moment stretched into an eternity, and yet it all rushed by in a blur of motion.

Dimly, she became aware of two things. First, she had lost the two Weavers with her somewhere along the way. Either they had fallen or been swept away from her in the tide of battle. Second, she was still alive. She seemed somehow charmed as she waded through the maelstrom. A blade had scratched her arm, and another had grazed her ribs, but they were superficial wounds. The Kobolds' dark blue blood coated her sword, her arms, her face, and her clothes, and every inch of skin the acidic fluid touched burned as if from a rash, but she could ignore that for now. She was a competent swordswoman, but she wasn't this good.

It came to her that the Kobolds seemed inclined to ignore her. Every time a creature came near her, it seemed intent on a different target. They barely even glanced at her. Pavel had been right. They somehow must have sensed the lingering traces of poison in her. To their minds, she was already dead, and they would go after other targets first. The Kobolds were not complete idiots. As soon as Nyssa showed any aggression toward them, they would turn and fight, but that initial disregard gave her an advantage. It kept her on her feet. She didn't think of it as a chance to survive this; it was just a chance to keep killing. And so, she did.

Sometime later—minutes? hours?—a shadow passed over her. She dispatched the creature before her and glanced up. She caught sight of something massive and covered in feathers swooping around the corner of a building. Was it some kind of eagle? She had no time to speculate. Her next opponent approached. She was the only human still alive on that particular street, so the Kobold headed straight toward her, willing to kill a poisoned woman for lack of a better target.

Time lurched forward again, and she was back in a crowd, fighting alongside six or so people, a mixture of city guards and Watchkeepers. She was merciless. She let the other humans draw the creatures' focus, while she moved in behind like a brazen assassin in broad daylight and cut the Kobolds down. Several times more the shadow of the great bird passed over her. She felt its gaze, but she could not stop to look up. If it would not attack her, she would ignore it.

The last of the Kobolds in that area fell. A few men cheered, but most turned like her with deadened eyes to seek the next fight. Some Watchkeeper she didn't know clapped her on the shoulder. "How were you doing that?" he asked, pride in her skill clear in his voice.

"GREAT FOOLS!"

They all looked up, hearing a booming voice from the rooftops. The voice was not human, but it certainly did not belong to a Kobold. A feathery creature crouched on the roof of a three-story building. Its shape and coloration reminded her of a barn owl, with tawny brown feathers on its wings and white ones on its breast, though it was larger than any bird she had ever seen. Its face was white and heart-shaped like a barn owl's, but there the similarities ended. No bird had those black almond-shaped eyes. They were human eyes, and indeed, though her mind recoiled at the idea, the creature had a human face. A slender nose with flaring nostrils, and soft lips, curved almost into a smile.

Some people screamed, others cursed, but Nyssa stood transfixed. Its eyes were solid black pools, yet it seemed to stare directly at her. Those human lips parted, revealing small human teeth. The creature leaned forward, extending its head along an unusually long neck. "She is Marked," the creature said in a softer voice, more akin to the purr of a cat than human speech, "but she lives."

The creature spread its massive wings and leapt from the edge of the building, extending its wicked curved talons. The others scattered, but Nyssa could not move. Faced with such impossible, grotesque creature, her mind buckled. She barely flinched as the human-faced owl dug its talons into her chest. Its weight forced her to the ground. Her head rebounded off the blood-soaked cobblestone streets and she knew no more.

Chapter 23
The Portal Opens

JAYN OPENED THE DOOR in response to Pavel's frantic knocking. "Here you are!" he said, stepping into their cramped room without waiting to be invited. "What are you two doing in here?"

Jayn glanced at Shilo, who sat on the edge of Thalia's bed. Shilo's was the top bunk, but she only clambered up there to sleep. Jayn's single bed lined the opposite wall. Light poured in through a narrow window, barely wider than an arrow slit on the far wall, nestled between built-in nooks and drawers, which held mostly clothes.

"Please come in," Jayn said, turning back to Pavel, who had already sidled past her to peer out the window. She noticed he wore a black harness over his gray uniform, which secured two bladed weapons to his back.

He glanced back at her. "Do you have any idea what's happening?"

"Not really. We were loitering outside the servants' dorms, like you suggested, when the alarm bell sounded. Everyone was heading for the front then. We started to follow, but Mistress Hinter found us. She told us there was trouble in the city and ordered us back to our dorms."

"Ah, and so you've just been sitting here? Where's Thalia?"

She cocked her head at his tone, but she forced herself to remain civil. "It was an order, Pavel. We couldn't disobey. All the servants sheltered in their dorms as well, so we weren't likely to see that man anyway."

"We haven't seen Thalia," Shilo added.

"Presumably, she is sheltering somewhere with Ryn," Jayn said.

Pavel scratched his chin. He'd been lax in his shaving, and black stubble covered the lower half of his face. "Hmm, they could be in trouble. If they saw the servant and followed him out into the city, well, they might have been caught in the attack."

"Do you think it's the Kobolds?" Shilo asked, rising from her seat, though there was little floor space for all three of them. "Did they come back?"

Pavel shrugged. "We should assume as much. They must have been waiting for the mirror to be moved, and now they're carrying out whatever it is they had planned."

Jayn recalled Pavel's task when they split up earlier that day. "What did Captain Lahmeer say? Did she tell you what the mirror did?"

"Well, she was planning on running our report up the chain of command, as you suspected, but the alarm bell sounded before she could do anything. She ran off with Caston. It would take too long to explain everything she said about the mirror, but the crux of it is that the Gray Guard found a way to use it that likely has nothing to do with its original purpose. But whoever took it must know what it really does."

Pavel seemed to be in a hurry. Already, he was scooting his way back toward the open door. "Where are you going?" Jayn asked.

"To find Thalia and Ryn, of course. We have to look out for our Pentad."

"What about the Kobolds?" Shilo asked.

"I've fought them before. You two should come with me. Jayn here has supposedly been trained for combat since birth, and those fists of yours could take down any Kobold."

Shilo chewed her lip in apprehension. Jayn narrowed her eyes. "Since when did you start caring about our Pentad?" she asked Pavel. "I think you just want to see what's going on out there."

He shrugged. "So, are you ladies coming or not?"

Jayn sighed. "I don't have any weapons here. I'll have to borrow a bow from the training yard."

Pavel gestured toward the door. Shilo didn't say anything, but she silently fell in step behind them as they left. The grassy yard of the compound seemed deserted. Everyone was either out facing whatever was going on in the streets, guarding the front gates, or holed up in their rooms.

Jayn didn't quite like the idea of disobeying an order. Normally, she wouldn't do anything that might reflect poorly on her service record, but these circumstances were far from normal. No enemy forces had penetrated into the Golden Lands in nearly a hundred years, if the Kobolds could be so classified. If she had not seen that hulking beast that night at the Fish Docks, she would still doubt such creatures actually existed, despite everything she had heard. She had years of training but had never seen a real fight, and certainly not one against actual monsters. She fought back that rising sense of dread. She would not turn coward now.

Probably, the fight would be over before they could join it anyway. The ship they saw on Sunday held perhaps a dozen

Kobolds, and while more could have hidden below deck, the attacking force could not be large. That made sense. No one could move an army of any size across half of Aldria without being spotted. This had to be a small, targeted strike force, if indeed the Kobolds had returned. For all they knew, this could just be a tavern brawl that had escalated into a minor riot.

Still, they had to be ready for the worst-case scenario. They did not know the target of this attack. Perhaps, the Kobolds were even now headed for the Citadel. If the compound were breached, as unlikely as that seemed, she had no desire to be caught hiding in her bunk unarmed. Finding a means to defend herself was the most logical course of action. She could then decide what to do next.

Halfway to the training yard, Pavel peeled off. "I need to grab something," he called over his shoulder as he continued at a trot. "I'll find you." Jayn and Shilo exchanged a glance and kept going. They found the training yard just as abandoned as the rest of the compound. Mistress Whitcomb had no doubt gone to join the fray. Jayn had heard a rumor that the weapons mistress, though a Stone Weaver, had such a weak gifting that the Watchkeepers would normally not have accepted her. She'd been recruited from the Standing Army, where she had reached the rank of Major, despite not being a Flame Weaver. The Watchkeepers had taken her in because of her expertise in combat training.

The training weapons were all housed under an open-sided metal pavilion, with shutters that could be lowered in inclement weather but had been left open today. Jayn found them all neatly stacked and untouched. All cadets—those who had earned their Weaver pins—and higher ranks kept and maintained their own weapons. Jayn found the bow she always used and a quiver that strapped diagonally across her back, which she filled with steel-tipped arrows, the good ones that Mistress Whitcomb did not let them use for regular target practice.

Jayn glanced at the swords and hesitated, remembering Mistress Whitcomb's comment on the first day of training that a sword was not a practical weapon for someone of her size. Still, it was her best weapon, and Jayn wanted to be prepared for any eventuality. The weapons master kept a few real swords, used not in sparring but for practicing forms. She pulled one free from its scabbard and ran her thumb along the edge. It would do. She hustled back out into the yard as she strapped the sword belt on. Shilo waited there, leaning on a wooden staff and glancing nervously about.

"Let's go," Jayn said.

They made it two steps, and then the ground lurched beneath their feet and a roaring blast nearly deafened them, accompanied by a sudden gust of air. Jayn fell to her knees, dropping her bow. Up ahead to the right, a massive cloud of gray dust hung over the wall where the Watchkeepers' smithy had stood. Bits of stone and debris rained down from the sky.

Shilo gasped. "Pavel!" He had turned in that direction when he left them.

Jayn pulled herself to her feet, picked up her bow, and sprinted toward the scene of the explosion. Every window within sight had shattered in the initial blast, but only the building directly opposite the smithy had taken substantial damage. The back wall of the three-story stone structure had collapsed, exposing the interior of each room. She glanced at it as she approached what remained of the smithy. She didn't know the building's purpose, but she knew it wasn't a barracks or used for training. A glimpse of shattered crates and chests spilling out their jumbled goods told her it was a storage building.

The smithy was gone. Jayn had not spent any time there, but she recalled a row of furnaces along the stone wall, work benches, anvils, lots of tools, and weapons and armor in various stages of assembly. The explosion seemed to have originated in one or more of the furnaces. A huge hole had been punched into the city wall, and large stone blocks lay yards away in the open plain that bordered the north side of Falport. Such was the strength of the Stone-laced masonry that the section of the thick wall above the hole had not collapsed into the gap. Glancing back at the fallen building, Jayn noticed twisted bits of metal and even whole anvils embedded in the shattered walls.

They nearly stepped on Pavel as they picked their way through the scattered debris. Floating gray dust still hung thick in the air, limiting visibility. Pavel lay face down beneath what had once been a wooden table, and his black hair now looked white under a caking of dust. Jayn and Shilo saw him at the same time, and wordlessly they moved to either side of the table and lifted it off him. The girls knelt down by his motionless body. Jayn set her bow aside and pressed two fingers to the side of Pavel's neck, as a tutor had once shown her, and felt a fluttering pulse. He bore no visible injuries beneath the coating of dirt.

"Help me turn him over," Jayn said. "Carefully."

Jayn and Shilo turned him over onto his back. As they did so, Pavel winced and seemed to wake up, though he kept his eyes screwed shut. Jayn surveyed his front. Blood dripped from one side of his temple, likely from where he'd hit his head as the explosion knocked him to the ground. It did not look severe, and in fact he seemed in remarkable condition for someone who had been so close to the epicenter of the blast.

"Pavel?" Jayn asked. "Can you hear us?"

Pavel groaned and then coughed feebly. "I hear you," he managed to say.

Jayn flinched as someone nearby shouted, "Get away from there!" She looked up to see Gwen Hinter, the Root mistress, picking her way through the rubble in her loose-fitting green robe. She wore a look of shock and consternation on her face.

"Mistress Hinter," Jayn said. "It's Pavel Talvor. He was caught in the blast."

"What?" Mistress Hinter seemed more annoyed than concerned. Her eyes narrowed as she finally spotted Pavel, lying between the two girls. "What were you even doing out here? I remember specifically telling you two young ladies to stay in your barracks." She wagged a rebuking finger.

Jayn dropped her eyes. She disliked the Root mistress, but any correction from a superior needled her. Her next thought was that Mistress Hinter was acting rather strange. She reacted as if the explosion represented little more than an inconvenience, rather than a serious attack on the Watchkeeper stronghold. Surely, the explosion had to have been deliberately set off. Experienced Stone Weavers would never put anything into a furnace that could react so catastrophically.

Mistress Hinter reached them, planted her fists on her hips, and stared down at Pavel. "Mr. Talvor," she said, "can you stand?"

"Maybe," he said and coughed again. Mistress Hinter sighed and actually rolled her eyes. After a moment, Pavel managed to add, "I used my Aether to cushion myself, like when I'm falling. I wasn't sure it would work in this case, but it was all I could do when I looked back and saw everything flying toward me."

"Hmm, well, thank your Aether reflexes you had time to do even that much." Mistress Hinter's voice held not a jot of sympathy for the injured man.

"Can you heal him?" Jayn asked, struggling not to sound incredulous. How could such a healer be so indifferent to pain?

Mistress Hinter didn't answer right away. She looked toward the tear in the wall and squinted her eyes to see through the still-lingering dust. Finally, she sighed. "Very well," she said and knelt carefully down, extending a hand toward Pavel without touching him. Her Root lacings, unlike Ryn's sprawling oak, resembled a slender date tree. Her lacing touched him for scant few seconds before dissolving, but it did the trick. Pavel gasped and finally opened his eyes and blinked up at them. The Root Mistress was already walking away. "Get him to the barracks," she called over her shoulder. "And stay there this time!"

Pavel watched her go, slowly shaking his head. Matted blood still stained his temple, but the wound had closed. "She is a strange one," he said softly, before climbing to his feet.

"Come on," Jayn said. "We should get out of here."

"One moment." Pavel stooped and picked up a small jeweler's bag.

Jayn had not noticed it amid all the debris. "What is that?" she asked. "Why did you come here?"

Pavel glanced again at Mistress Hinter's retreating backside. He drew open the bag and held it out to them. "Take a look," he said.

"Rings?" Shilo asked. Indeed, the bag held copper rings in varying sizes and styles.

"Thalia's luck charms," Pavel said. "I figured they would come in handy today."

Jayn sighed. "Pavel, you know those won't activate if Thalia doesn't personally hand them to us."

He shrugged. "Yeah, well, we'll have to find her first so she can give them to us."

Jayn shook her head. She stooped and retrieved her bow, and as she did so, she became aware of small sounds, like feet crunching through gravel. Mistress Hinter still picked her way steadily away from them, toward the collapsed building, but these noises were coming from behind them. She whirled around and saw a dark shape moving through the hanging gray dust. She had only glimpsed Kalo's face and hands once and in the dark. She had not realized how closely a Kobold's skin resembled a long-dead corpse. This was not Kalo; the creature was Jayn's height, though three times as broad, but it certainly was a Kobold. It carried a blade somewhere between a knife and a sword and had been attempting a stealthy approach toward them, crunching through the strewn rubble. It now stood within ten paces.

Jayn surprised herself with how quickly her hands shot up, one raising her bow, and the other reaching over her shoulder for an arrow. She nocked it and drew while Pavel and Shilo were still turning to see what had caught her attention. She aimed for its bare chest, but the shot sailed a little high, punching a hole into the Kobold's throat. Its blade clattered to the ground as the creature stumbled backward and clutched at its neck.

Pavel cursed and drew his blades. The sky had been gloomy and overcast all afternoon, and the sun had to be close to setting, but they could still clearly see a dozen broad figures clutching swords and clubs moving through the haze, spilling in through the opening the blast had created in the wall. Pavel raised his blades and seemed ready to make a stand. Jayn glanced around. The uneven terrain created by all the debris would make fighting difficult. She couldn't tell how many Kobolds were waiting to file in through the breach, but they were hopelessly outnumbered already.

"Fall back!" Jayn called to her companions, her voice a pale imitation of her mother's. "Head for the gate! There will be other Watchkeepers there."

She lowered her bow and turned on her heels. Shilo stooped to retrieve her staff and fell in behind Jayn. Pavel hesitated, but a glance back told her he was following. Mistress Hinter seemed to have vanished entirely. Jayn hoped the master Weaver could take care of herself. She would have to.

Halfway to the front gates, they ran into five gray-clad Watchkeepers, no doubt on their way to investigate the explosion. Jayn gestured with her free hand for them to go back. "Kobolds!" she said. "Kobolds have breached the wall."

Their looks of surprise and disbelief turned to horror as they stared past the sprinting recruits. Apparently, the Kobolds were still on their heels. Jayn did not spare a glance backward. The Watchkeepers halted. Two, a man and a woman, were archers. They drew and fired several arrows over Jayn's head before she reached their hastily assembled line. Then she stopped and turned to see her pursuers. A dozen Kobolds hurried toward them. She thought she had seen more than that coming through the breach but saw no signs of any other monsters. One had already fallen to the arrows. Another had been shot through the shoulder but kept coming.

Jayn drew an arrow of her own and fired on the advancing Kobolds. It sailed to the left and thunked uselessly into the ground. She was not used to aiming at moving targets with minimal time to line up the shot. The female archer glanced back at her. "Fall back, recruits!" she barked, repeating Jayn's own advice from moments ago. "Head for the front gate and warn them what's coming."

Jayn nodded and let the arrow she'd been reaching for slide back into her quiver. "Come on, Pavel," she said, for the Aether

Weaver seemed determined to fight with the Watchkeepers. He groaned and reluctantly lowered his blades again. Jayn noticed for the first time that they were not traditional swords. One was more like a tapered steel rod, and the other had notches all along its length. She half-remembered some conversation between Pavel and Thalia about how they were pre-Burning relics. No doubt he would have a chance to use them before the day was out.

The trio sprinted towards the gate, finding a flurry of confused activity there. Two dozen civilians stood huddled off to one side of the closed gate, apparently having fled to the Citadel after the initial attack in the city. A couple of the stretched-thin Watchkeeper guards attempted to corral them from wandering further into the compound. After the explosion, no one seemed to know where was a safe place to send the townsfolk. Just inside the gate Master Rohan Caston conversed with the guards. They seemed to be clamoring to know what was happening in the city, while he was trying to get a coherent report on the explosion. Pavel had said that Master Caston had gone out with Captain Lahmeer, but he must have returned upon hearing the blast. Amidst the disorder, no one seemed to notice the three recruits running up, though one was still covered in dust.

Jayn angled her steps toward Master Caston, clearly the highest ranking Watchkeeper here. The throng of guards around him prevented her from getting too close. "Master Caston!" she called, but her voice was drowned by the others. She tried again to get his attention.

"Caston!" Pavel shouted, using a volume Jayn had never heard before from the usually languid rogue. The one word cut through the din. Master Caston looked up, his attention caught either by the tone or the lack of a proper title. The guards fell silent, seeing Pavel's disheveled appearance. Pavel spoke before Jayn could.

"Someone blew your smithy halfway to Iscerna, there's a massive hole in the wall, and the compound is about to be overrun by Kobolds straight from the pit."

Master Caston's eyes widened in horror. "Curse me," he said into the silence that followed. "The attack on the city must have been a distraction to empty the Citadel." He looked around at the meager defense forces. "We're the true target."

Ryn lingered in a state midway between sleep and wakefulness. He had no memory of where he was or what had happened. He knew nothing and simply floated in a void for an interminable span of time. Gradually he became aware of a thrumming that was both a sound and a physical sensation. It enveloped him and filled him. Ryn's consciousness, such that it was, began to vibrate along the same frequency. It was the thrumming of the universe, of the Five Forces themselves. That thought was not his, but he accepted it and the warmth that followed and filled him. He allowed the thrumming and the warmth to permeate his mind with the same passivity of a suckling child, whose heart slows to match his mother's.

Eventually, he began to sense variations in the thrumming, a murmuring almost like voices. He became convinced that they were in fact voices. He decided this passively as well, like a drowsing man hearing rain outside his window. He accepts that it is raining but that will not wake him. Two voices separated themselves from the general susurration, one male and one female, though they were nothing like human voices. An eternity seemed to pass before Ryn could understand those voices.

The Portal opens, the female voice said.

We must cross over and head for the Reach, the male voice said.

Not right away.

We will be vulnerable on the other side.

Yes, but Kalo has been careless.

That name seemed vaguely familiar to Ryn. He reached for it, but it eluded him. No matter. The male was speaking again. *How many?* he thrummed.

Three have been Marked. No… It's four now.

Inconsequential.

Still, I will purge them if I can.

Do as you will.

Whether the voices said anything further, Ryn did not hear. He realized toward the end of the overheard conversation that he was sinking away from them. The male voice's last words came in a distorted whisper. Ryn floated downward, like a drowning man who no longer tries to fight it. Gradually, more sensations came to him, physical sensations belonging to the flesh and blood vessel that housed him. He felt a soft breeze against his skin. He felt fingers running through his hair.

Ryn opened his eyes. Thalia looked down at him and smiled when she saw he was awake. Two thick braids of black hair framed her face. His mind struggled for a moment to understand his perspective as she leaned over him. A sudden flash of memory came to him, of his own mother cradling his small body in her arms, tending to him in his sickness, even as ash fever ravaged her own body. The memory passed and he was jolted back into the present. He was lying on the ground outside somewhere, his head on Thalia's lap. Strange.

He sat up, and she let him. Blood stained his torn shirt and the front of his trousers as if he'd horrifically soiled himself. He touched his stomach. He didn't feel hurt. He felt great, like one of those rare mornings where you wake up of your own accord, bursting with energy and excitement for a long-anticipated day.

It all came back to him then. They had followed the servant through Falport. They had spied through a window at a Pentad doing... something to a large mirror. Then Kalo had found them. He'd slashed Thalia with his claws and sliced Ryn with his sword. Ryn's Etching had saved his life once again. Had he fully healed Thalia first? Ryn summoned his Root tree and Dowsed her without preamble. She shuddered at the sensation but said nothing. Ryn studied the knot of sensations that was Thalia. Everything was green, aside from some minor soreness from sitting still for so long, and the white light beneath it all that was perhaps her soul shone brightly. Her mind was as unique as any he had Dowsed before, and yet at the same time, they were all alike, except for...

Ryn dropped the lacing with a shiver as he remembered the last few details of the fight with Kalo. Ryn had no weapon, but after Kalo slashed Thalia's arms, Ryn had finally been able to stand up and fight. He'd been worse than useless. Kalo had pushed him back and slashed his stomach. Then in an act of desperation, Ryn had turned to Weaving. He had no idea what he was doing, but he found himself Dowsing Kalo. The cluster of sensations that made up Kalo was completely incomprehensible. Still, it seemed to have worked. Kalo reacted in shock and revulsion from the Dowsing.

He looked around, taking in their environment for the first time. They were still in the fenced yard behind the warehouse. "Are we safe here?" Ryn asked.

"Shh," Thalia said, gesturing for him to be quiet. "Not so loud. They're still in there doing something." She indicated the wall behind her with a tilt of her head.

He lowered his voice to a whisper. "Why have they left us alone?"

"I'm not sure. Kalo and his Kobolds went off to fight somewhere in the city. I could hear screaming but not for a long time now."

Every time it seemed like Ryn had fully come back to his senses, another revelation shook him. The first time he'd been wounded, hours had gone by while his Etching healed his body. Kalo's slash had not been as severe as those injuries, but how much time had passed? He asked Thalia.

She glanced up at the solid gray sky. "I'm not sure. The sun doesn't seem to have set yet, so it can't have been much more than an hour, maybe two."

"I guess I'm getting faster." Ryn looked around again. On their way through the warehouse district, Ryn had vaguely noticed as he always did the scattered signs of plant life that could be found even within city walls. Scraggly weeds, mostly beggar's knot and scabgrass, huddled in the shadows of buildings. Ryn spied the shriveled black husks of such weeds in the corners of the yard. Absently, he wondered whether his Etching could still work in a place without any vegetation. He shook his head, forcing his mind back to the present situation. "An hour or two," he said. "Still, I wonder why no one else found us?" He shrugged. "I guess we were just lucky."

He meant nothing by the comment, but still Thalia's eyes widened in realization. She looked to the hole they'd made in the fence and the neatly stacked boards. "The fence," she said. "When I removed those last two boards, I wasn't really paying attention. I think maybe I didn't hold back my Etching. I have to restrain it when I Weave or else whatever I'm working with gets the luck... And then I gave you the boards."

Ryn considered it. Other than the usual elation that followed his healing, he didn't feel anything, but he supposed luck did not involve a physical sensation. He shrugged it off and decided not to worry about it. "I'll take all the luck I can get right now."

"And you'll have it. For two days. Then you'll have to deal with the recoil."

"I'll worry about that then." *If I'm still alive in two days*, he added silently. He wondered how well the luck held in active mortal peril. Kalo had been able to wound him after all. Then again, Ryn had survived.

He became aware of a low humming sound. It seemed somehow familiar, like something half-recalled from a dream. "What is that?" he asked.

She shrugged. "I'm not sure. It seems to be coming from the warehouse. It's happened a few times before."

He looked up at the high windows. "You didn't look?"

She averted her eyes and stammered out a response. "I... didn't want to leave you."

Ryn only vaguely noticed her discomfort. He fixated on that humming sound. He needed to know what it was. It seemed suddenly terribly important. Without further comment, he clambered his way back up the stacked crates to peer in through the window.

"Careful," Thalia called after him in a whisper.

He reached the top crate and pressed his nose to the narrow glass pane. Inside only the five members of the Pentad remained, if indeed they were a Pentad. The mirror had turned and now faced away from Ryn's view, toward the open doors. The five Weavers still sent their carefully spiraled lacings into the mirror. Had they maintained the flow this whole time? They must all be strongly gifted.

The low droning sound was impossible to pinpoint, but it had to be coming from the mirror. The sky had darkened considerably since they'd set out after the servant, and no lanterns had been lit within the warehouse, yet bright light filled the center of the room. There could only be one source: the reflective surface of the mirror now emitted a beam of light, like sunshine spilling through a doorway.

Thalia climbed up next to Ryn and pressed her face to the glass. They said nothing, staring in growing anticipation at the back of the mirror. Ryn wished he could see the front of it. The humming noise grew louder, and the mirror brightened in response. Suddenly, a shape obstructed the light, casting a shadow across it. The Weavers stood five paces away from the mirror, and none stood directly in front of it. Nothing in the room could be creating shadows like that, unless it was something within the mirror.

Ryn suddenly knew it was not a mirror at all. "It's a portal," he breathed.

"What?" Thalia hissed beside him.

He didn't answer. He couldn't. The shadow grew and filled the mirror until no light shone forth. Seconds passed. Then a narrow shaft of light appeared from the top of the mirror, creating dappled shadows across some dark mass that had appeared in front of the mirror. It reminded Ryn of how the first rays of dawn could turn a grassy field into a maze of shadows. More light spilled out around the edges, and the dark shape elongated. No, it was moving forward, stepping through the Portal, which was a doorway to somewhere else. The creature that emerged was some sort of fur-covered animal, moving forward on four legs. Ryn could not see its head from this angle, or perhaps it was concealed by the harsh shadows thrown off by the mirror's brilliant flickering light.

Finally, the creature fully emerged, and the unimpeded light of the mirror shone on its broad backside. A round flat tail dangled between its wide haunches. Wiry black fur covered its entire body.

The creature was broad and barely had room to walk forward between the two Weavers on either side of it. It swayed as it walked, and it was nearly past when one of its back haunches brushed up against the green-clad Stone Weaver. The contact sent a convulsive shiver up the false servant. His stream of Stone faltered and vanished.

What happened next reminded Ryn of his Training Pentad's many failed attempts with the Gauntlet's wheel. The remaining four lacings began to unravel. One of the Weavers cried out as if in pain. Ryn expected the light to go out, but instead the mirror flared to a new brightness. Ryn raised a hand to shield his eyes, even though the light faced away from him. The thrumming noise, which had begun to fade after the creature's emergence, roared to a crescendo.

Only later did Ryn realize the full significance of what they saw. All Runeforms were over a thousand years old and indestructible. Even the flimsiest looking one could not be scratched or dented. The mirror was a Runeform. The mirror broke. It started at what would perhaps be the weakest points on a regular mirror. The two upright bits of metal that anchored the free-tilting mirror to the stand gave way. The round mirror fell free and clattered to the ground. They heard the sound of breaking glass, and the single beacon of light broke into a thousand jagged beams, which all quickly winked out. In the last shaft of light, Ryn saw the creature turn its head back to see what it had done. It had the face of a man.

Ryn reeled backward, the sight causing a physical reaction in him. He found himself falling from atop the stack of crates. A long time seemed to pass before he hit the ground. As he fell, he heard a voice rumble in his head, a voice he had never heard before, but one he still recognized.

"NO MATTER. WE ARE THROUGH."

Chapter 24
The Long Night

THALIA JOGGED THROUGH the empty darkening streets of Falport. She could not say whether she fled toward the Citadel or away from the beast they had glimpsed in the warehouse. Ryn ran beside her. He'd taken no injury from the fall—another stroke of luck—and been just as eager to sneak away. The sun finally seemed to have set behind the clouds. A dull rumble of thunder foretold rain. No lamplighters had risked carrying out their jobs that evening, so the streets were dark indeed. More than once the two Weavers nearly stumbled over bodies lying in the road. They had not the time or the light to see if the shadowed forms they passed were humans or Kobolds. The smell of death hung heavy in the air. They splashed through a puddle that likely was not water.

Hearing noises up ahead, Thalia staggered to a halt. Before them lay one of the city's many T-shaped intersections. A pair of shadowy figures emerged from the left, seemingly on a stroll down the broad street. Their size and the low, guttural voices in which they conversed made their identities clear. Thalia and Ryn stood rooted to the ground, hoping not to be seen. The nearest Kobold snuffed the air with its stubby nose. Its dark eyes glittered in the sudden moonlight as it regarded them. It gestured to its companion with the curved sword it held. "Grees uns?" it growled.

The other Kobold sniffed and seemed to shake its head. "Gread arready," it said.

The pair shared a gravelly laugh at that comment and kept right on walking, seeming to dismiss Thalia and Ryn entirely. It was a warm evening, but Thalia still shivered. She turned to Ryn, and his face looked pale in the moonlight filtering through a break in the clouds. "What just happened?" she asked.

Ryn ran a hand along the back of his head. "I think it's the poison," he said. "Back in the Sylphren Wood, after the first time I was attacked, the Kobolds seemed to ignore me. Pavel thought maybe they could tell somehow that I had been poisoned by the first Kobold to scratch me, even though I'd been healed, and so they figured I would drop dead soon. I'm starting to understand the way they talk. I think the second one just now said we were... dead already."

Thalia felt another shiver. "What about the big one earlier, Kalo? He still tried to kill you."

"I've met him before, back in the woods. The first time I saw Kalo, he walked right past me and went after Nyssa and Pavel. He seems somehow... more intelligent than the others. He must be their leader. When he saw me today, he must have recognized me from before. He asked how I was still alive."

Thalia recalled that now. She'd been too overwhelmed with horror at the time to really pay attention to what Kalo said. She shrugged. "Well, hopefully all the regular Kobolds will continue ignoring us. We need to get back to the Citadel." She wondered if the Watchkeeper stronghold still stood. She had not told Ryn about the explosion she'd heard while he was unconscious.

They resumed their run. Two weeks of Mistress Whitcomb's conditioning came in handy now. Several times they saw dark shapes moving along the streets. Whether they were human or Kobold, they ignored Ryn and Thalia. After the first few uneventful encounters, the two Weavers didn't even bother stopping or altering their stride.

They had nearly reached the entrance to the compound when something else found them. A small shape swooped low overhead. Thalia saw a circling pinprick of ghostly blue light and heard the cawing of a crow. They both stopped and stared up at Pavel's pet Runeform as it continued to circle and squawk at them.

"Corvus," Ryn greeted the bird, sounding more annoyed than anything. "Let me guess, everything's fine?"

The Runeform completed two more loops. "Everything's fine!" it repeated and flew off toward the Citadel.

Shilo crouched beside a broad-leafed plant inside the dark greenhouse. She struggled to control her breathing. A glass-sided building may not have been the best choice for a hiding spot, but she had given way to blind terror as she fled across the Watchkeeper campus and stumbled through the open doors of one of the greenhouses.

She'd done her best to stand and fight with the others, despite the terror that still gripped her. Things had gone well at first. With their backs to the barred front gates, the Watchkeepers had made a united stand. Jayn had been competent with her bow, and when she ran out of arrows, she drew her sword and fought alongside Master Caston. He seemed to trust her to have his back. Pavel had moved with blinding speed, catching and shattering the Kobolds' blades with his two ancient weapons. Shilo had not used her Etching. She feared getting in close enough to swing her fists. Instead, she used a common Flame lacing to strengthen her arms and lashed out with her staff. She was able to strike the Kobolds before they got close enough to use their blades or spike-studded clubs. She sent many of them sprawling back, but she didn't think she had actually killed any.

The attacks came in waves. In the lulls that followed, Master Caston and the remaining Watchkeeper officers discussed how to respond. They feared for the servants and anyone else who may have been left stranded inside the buildings. They didn't hear any screams or see any signs that the monsters were actively trying to break in anywhere, but the Watchkeeper compound was large and sprawling. They'd sent a few search parties out, but often they came running back minutes later, pursued by the next wave of Kobolds. One group of five never returned.

All order collapsed when the Kobolds rampaging in the city reached the gate. They heard the creatures banging on the wooden door and uttering their gravelly cries. Master Caston loudly assured everyone not to panic. Several Wave Weavers had reinforced the door with their strongest wards. Thinking back now as she sheltered within the greenhouse, Shilo decided that an Aether Weaver in the city had to be working with the Kobolds. She never saw such a person. The only sign that the wards had failed was when the splintered gate collapsed inward and a wave of Kobolds spilled through.

Assailed from both sides, the Watchkeeper line fractured and broke. A Kobold made a lucky grab and wrenched the staff from Shilo's hands. Suddenly disarmed, she had fled, leaving the others behind, thinking only of saving her own life. She felt a coward.

True, she'd seen most of the other Watchkeepers break away and flee for cover. Whoever hadn't retreated was probably dead now. How much time had passed since then? Hours? Minutes? She couldn't say.

The sun had set, plunging the campus into a starless night. Weaver lights mounted above doors illuminated much of the compound still. She'd avoided those areas, clinging to the shadows. Several times she had encountered roving bands of Kobolds, and each time she had fled. Her will to fight had vanished when she lost her weapon. She just wanted it to be over. If she could just hide somewhere until the dawn came, she felt she would survive this. The Kobolds had not come all the way here without reason. They wanted something. She prayed to the Maker that they would find it and leave. Unless they only wanted to exterminate the Watchkeepers.

Sweat beaded on her brow and the small of her back. Humidity from all the plants still lingered in the air, along with the sweet and heady smell of flowers and mulch. She shifted within her leafy shelter and peered through a gap in the foliage out into the night beyond the glass wall. Eventually, she spotted movement, a lone figure moving slowly across the lawn between greenhouses. A sudden parting of the clouds and a shaft of moonlight revealed the shape to be Mistress Gwen Hinter, the Root master. She carried no weapon that Shilo could see, and she plodded along steadily without any apparent fear or concern. Where had she been this whole time? Why wasn't she hiding or fighting?

Shilo longed to not be alone, to have even one fellow Weaver by her side, but something told her to keep still. Mistress Hinter's behavior now and even before at the smithy made little sense. Someone else spotted the Root mistress. Shilo gasped as a shape separated from the shadow of another greenhouse and jogged toward the lone woman.

"Mistress Hinter!" the man said in a loud whisper. Shilo couldn't tell in the dark, but he looked like the Root Weaver who had overseen their Gauntlet that afternoon, though it now felt like that had been days ago. He held a garden hoe in his hands as an improvised weapon.

Mistress Hinter offered a short greeting that Shilo could not hear. The thick glass wall of her shelter muffled their voices. The Root mistress stopped walking, planted her hands on her hips, and regarded the man.

"Thank the stars," he said. "I've been hiding for what feels like hours. I don't know who else is alive. Those creatures are everywhere."

"Yes, and you'd better keep your voice down."

As if reminded of the danger by her words, the man turned and scanned the surrounding greenhouses. His nerves were clearly frayed, and he rambled on. "This is madness. Are those really Kobolds? How can they be here? And in such numbers? They'll slaughter us all."

Mistress Hinter sighed, apparently annoyed by the man's presence. "I know," she said. "It wasn't supposed to happen this way."

He turned back toward her. "What?"

"I mean, this sort of thing isn't supposed to happen here. Not in Falport, not in the Golden Lands."

Her words drew the man's focus back to her. He stared and seemed to notice finally her peculiar demeanor and behavior. "How have you kept safe?" he asked her. "Have you no weapon?"

Mistress Hinter sighed. "Spare me your rambling and your questions. We should head for the main Citadel. If any Watchkeepers still stand, they will be holed up there."

Of course, the black stone cathedral of a building that stood in the middle of the compound was the heart of the Watchkeepers' organization. Shilo should have thought to flee there.

The man nodded. "Yes, ma'am." He seemed grateful to have someone else take charge. He turned to lead the way, and as he did, Mistress Hinter reached behind her back and drew something that had been tucked into the belt that cinched her robe. She surged forward with surprising speed and grabbed the man from behind. There was nothing romantic in her stiff embrace. She drew her hand back, and moonlight glinted off the knife she had stuck up under his ribs. He moaned in anguish and dropped his hoe. She raised a sandaled foot and kicked the back of his knee to drop the much taller man. As he fell, she pulled him back against her bosom and drew her knife across his throat. She held him close and made soft shushing noises as he sputtered and bled out. His body went still, she shoved him away, and he crumpled to the ground. She stooped and wiped her blade on the back of his shirt before returning it to her belt. Then she turned and walked away, resuming her casual pace.

Mistress Hinter's actions filled Shilo with more dread than anything she'd seen the Kobolds do that day. Why would she kill a fellow Watchkeeper? She had to be the traitor, the "master" that the false servant had mentioned at the Fish Docks. The others needed to know about this. Someone had to tell them. Shilo needed to get to the Citadel. She struggled to slow her breathing and then began to creep back toward the greenhouse door.

***

Pavel parried the Kobold's long knife with his bladecatcher, then shattered it with a swing from his bladebreaker. He'd lost track of how many times he'd done that maneuver. The Kobold, like most before it, lunged at Pavel with its jagged, broken blade. Pavel let the creature in close but sidestepped the thrust. The Kobold stumbled forward and struggled to turn back toward him. Pavel anticipated this too, and he jammed his bladebreaker toward its face as it came back around. The tip of his weapon found the creature's eye and then the back of its skull. Pavel's blades were primarily defensive weapons, and he had to resort to such messy tactics for a quick kill.

He wrenched his blade from the fallen creature's face and flicked it to remove most of the blood and viscera. He used the edge of his sleeve to wipe blood splatter from his face. Left on the skin too long, the blue fluid began to burn. He turned to find that Jayn had dispatched her foe. Pavel glanced around. He'd gotten so turned about that he did not know where in the compound they were anymore. After the initial melee when the gate fell, even the ranks of Kobolds broke apart. For the last several skirmishes, Pavel and Jayn had faced only two or three creatures at a time, and those came at increasingly longer intervals. Most of the Kobolds seemed to have fled or else been slain. He stopped to ponder once again what they had been after. He and Jayn hadn't seen any other Watchkeepers for some time now. He hoped Nyssa was safe, out in the city somewhere.

He nodded to Jayn and they moved off at a slow walk. Though just a girl, the Fourth Pentarch's daughter had done admirably in the fighting. She and Pavel had put aside their petty differences and fought back-to-back at times. Twice they had stopped to rest, and she had sheltered them with her invisibility ward. She carried her sword in one hand and her bow in the other, though she had long since run out of arrows. She'd managed to salvage a few from fallen Kobold corpses, before firing them off again. Jayn had not hesitated to do so, though it clearly disgusted her. Pavel had come to admire the girl, in the same way he imagined he would respect a precocious younger sister, if he'd had one.

Jayn sheathed her sword and unslung the water skin she carried over her shoulder. She had found it somewhere along the way. He averted his eyes as she took a long swig. Seeing a Wave Weaver slake her thirst reminded him of the hunger that hollowed his stomach and filled it with a dull ache. He'd missed dinner, and after a long day of Weaver training, he'd used even more Aether in the fighting. He would reach his limit soon if he didn't get anything to eat. He had to admire the Watchkeepers for their intensive training program; never before had he been able to wield Aether for so long. His stomach growled loud enough to alert any Kobolds in the area. Jayn wiped her mouth and gave him a sympathetic wince.

"Do you know where we are right now?" he asked. "If we can get to the main Citadel, maybe I can raid the kitchens."

She looked around. "I think it might be that way." She pointed with her head.

He nodded. She looped the waterskin over her shoulder and drew her blade before setting off again. In the growing darkness, they had not always had much warning of approaching Kobolds. Just as they rounded the side of a building that might have been a barracks, a small shape flitted over their heads. Pavel knew right away it was Corvus. His Runeform circled once around their heads, regarding him with a single cerulean eye, before darting off again. Pavel turned upon hearing footsteps. Two shadowed figures approached at a trot, neither with the girth of a Kobold.

"Pavel?" the shorter one called, and he recognized Ryn's voice. Thalia ran alongside the kid. She'd picked up someone's dropped staff.

"Thalia! Ryn!" Jayn greeted them in a loud whisper.

"What's happening?" Thalia asked when they reached Pavel. "The gate was down and unguarded. We followed Corvus to you, though it looks like he's flown off again."

The four Weavers huddled together and kept their voices low, making frequent glances over their shoulders. Pavel and Jayn put away their blades and took turns relating what little they knew, starting with the explosion that had blasted a hole through the city wall. Thalia expressed horror over the loss of the smithy.

"We think maybe the attack on the city was a distraction," Pavel said. "They drew most of the Watchkeepers out before attacking here. Maybe they're trying to steal more Runeforms? No one has a clue, really."

"What about you two?" Jayn asked. "Why'd you go out into the city?"

Thalia and Ryn seemed reluctant to tell the full story. They sketched a vague narrative about following the false servant out to the warehouse district and being attacked by the big armor-wearing Kobold named Kalo. They saw something involving the stolen mirror and a full Pentad, but they couldn't comprehend it themselves and their brief attempt to explain it made little sense.

"Anyway," Thalia said, "after we saw whatever it was that happened with the mirror, we came straight back here. We passed several Kobolds in the streets, but they just ignored us."

"You were right, Pavel," Ryn said. "They must be able to sense traces of the poison in us. Kalo scratched Thalia, but I managed to heal her." He paused. "What about you?"

Pavel thought it over. "I can't say they've been avoiding me, but it could be this one is drawing them in." He hooked a thumb at Jayn.

She scoffed. "Wow, sorry I haven't been poisoned like the rest of you."

Thalia laughed at that but then cut herself short. "Where's everyone else? Where's Shilo?"

Pavel shook his head. "We don't know. Everyone split up when the gate came down. It's been just us two for a while now. The number of Kobolds seems to be dwindling, but it's not over yet." He remembered the jeweler's pouch crammed into his pocket and dug it out. He handed it to Thalia. "Here, I managed to salvage some of your luck charms before the smithy blew."

She took the bag and opened it to peer inside. "Are you saying you want one of these?" she asked. "No doubt it would have been handy earlier, but if things are dying down…"

"I'll leave it up to you," Pavel said. "I just think it's better to be safe."

She mulled it over but then finally nodded. "All right, but just remember this also sets a two-day timer and then something bad *will* happen to you."

He nodded. "I am well aware."

Thalia fished a ring out of the bag and handed it to Pavel. It was a tad small, but he managed to slip it over his little finger. Jayn held out an expectant hand. Thalia sighed and gave her a ring. Thalia glanced at Ryn. "I… accidently gave him a luck charm earlier," she said. She closed the bag and tucked it into her pocket.

"Excellent," Pavel said. "But what about you?"

She shrugged. "I'm not exactly sure if it will work for me. Master Caston never allowed me to try, and since it activates by me giving someone the charm, I don't know if I can give it to myself."

"Just try," Jayn said. She smiled. "If you believe it will work, then it will."

Thalia thought it over. "All right," she said. "I suppose it can't hurt." She pulled the bag back out and selected a ring. She held the band of copper up in front of her face, and the glinting metal caught the glow of a nearby Weaver light. Very deliberately she placed the ring on her left hand. "I give this to myself," she said, and then smiled at her own apparent foolishness.

A single caw was his only warning, and then Corvus plopped down on Pavel's shoulder.

"I've found you," someone said, and they all turned to see Shilo running up. She stopped short of their knot and lowered her eyes. "I was headed for the Citadel, when Corvus found me. He wouldn't stop squawking until I followed him. I… I'm sorry I ran away earlier."

Jayn surprised them all when she stepped forward and embraced Shilo, a little awkwardly with a bow still in one hand. "Forgot all that," Jayn said. "I'm just glad you're still alive."

Thalia put a hand on Shilo's shoulder and dug out another ring. "Put this on," she told Shilo, who did so without question, apparently too overwhelmed by their sentiment to speak. Ryn grinned like an idiot. Thalia turned back toward them. "I suppose we should all head for the Citadel."

"Wait," Shilo said, stepping away from the other two girls. "I have to tell you all something. When I was hiding, I saw… Mistress Hinter is the traitor."

"What?" Jayn asked, just as Ryn said, "How do you know?"

"I saw her stab another Watchkeeper. She had no reason to do it. She just attacked him and slit his throat."

Jayn slowly shook her head. "I never would have suspected that woman. Well, we have to find Caston or one of the other masters and report it."

Thalia nodded. "Are we all ready to move out?"

"Oh, just a moment," Shilo said. She unslung a canvas bag from her arm that Pavel had not noticed in the dark. "Someone must have dropped this. Corvus seemed to want me to pick it up. You probably need it the most." She stepped forward and handed the bag to Pavel.

Curious, he opened the bag, and the unmistakable scent of fresh bread filled his nostrils. Shilo had found someone's packed lunch, a large yeasty roll and a wedge of the sharp yellow cheese the kitchen staff made on the premises. It was simple fare, but it seemed like the food of the stars to a starving Aether Weaver. "My luck is improving already," he said and stuffed as much as he could of the roll into his mouth. He didn't even think to share it. The others laughed and shook their heads, but they knew he needed it to refuel. They waited for him to down the bread and then the cheese. It took less than a minute. He longed for a drink of water to wash it all down, but he would not trouble Jayn. He knew how jealously a Wave Weaver would guard her water. The food did little to assuage his hunger, but it would keep him on his feet for at least a little longer. He let the bag fall to the ground, as he wiped his hands on his shirt.

"One last thing," he said and stuck out his right hand, pinky out.

"Seriously?" Jayn said.

"Don't leave me hanging, team."

The others scoffed and rolled their eyes, but they all gathered in a circle and locked their hands together just like that first time in the dining hall, which now seemed like ages ago. He locked eyes with each of them in turn before saying, "One, two, three…"

"Pentad," they all said in unison. It wasn't a shout but a statement, and he heard the steel in each of their voices.

"Let's go," Thalia said.

They advanced only a few paces before Corvus lifted from Pavel's shoulder. The Runeform squawked and flew two loops over their heads. He dropped back onto Pavel's shoulder for a moment and shouted, "Your mother is here!" before darting off into the night.

Jayn looked back at him and cocked her head. "Pavel, did your bird just insult you?"

Pavel glanced around. He didn't really know what Corvus had meant by that, but he knew that in his roundabout way, the Runeform had been trying to tell him something. He felt a presence behind him, and he drew his blades as he turned.

A tall Kobold growled as it emerged from the shadows not ten paces away. Even in the dark, Pavel recognized Kalo by his height and the long curved sword he held. Pavel took up a fighting stance. "You four head to the Citadel," he called over his shoulder.

"No," Ryn said. "I'm not running away." When had the kid developed a spine?

Jayn stepped up beside him. She'd dropped her bow and held her sword with both hands. "I thought I'd proven myself by now," she said.

He knew without looking the others would not flee either. "Our luck will hold," Thalia said.

Pavel regarded Kalo again. The beast had not moved. He was bigger than the other Kobolds and seemingly more intelligent. Plus, he could Weave. Maybe. Still, Pavel had a full Pentad at his back now. When last they fought, Kalo had easily disarmed and defeated Pavel, but Pavel had underestimated him then. Pavel was prepared this time, and he had his lucky charm.

Pavel puffed his chest out and addressed the creature. "Kalo, is it?"

Kalo did not respond. He only glared at them.

"Listen, Kalo," Pavel continued, "you're clearly outmatched here. It's five against one. You're better off running while you can."

Kalo slowly shook his head. "Gree no tink so," he growled. Kalo raised his sword, squared his own stance, and began moving sideways, as if to circle around the Pentad. Pavel turned, keeping himself between the Kobold and the others. Kalo moved with the grace of a big cat, until suddenly he stumbled. He fell flat on the ground, apparently having tripped over a rock.

Pavel laughed, more from shock than anything else. "Ooh," he said. "That was unlucky." That's precisely what it was. Five Weavers had brought their enhanced luck to bear against Kalo, and the Kobold didn't stand a chance. He was likely to fall and break his own neck before he did any of them real harm. Pavel took a step forward. He would end this quickly.

Kalo turned where he lay on the ground and raised an empty hand toward Pavel. Pavel frowned. Kalo made his clawed fingers into a fist and then splayed them wide. As he did so, something shot from his hand. It reached Pavel before he could even comprehend it. Tendrils of black smoke, somehow darker even than the night, raced toward the Pentad. The twisted lacing washed over Pavel, though he couldn't feel it. Pavel glanced down at his hands. Some subtle shift had drawn his attention. He saw nothing. He shifted his grip on his blades, and suddenly the copper ring on his little finger fell away, having split into two equal pieces.

Pavel took a step back and nearly toppled over himself. A collective gasp from the three girls told him their rings had also shattered. Impossible. Kalo's dark Weaving had broken their rings. Had he broken their luck as well? Would they still feel the recoil and would it happen now? Pavel felt as if the ground had shifted beneath his feet. A glance at the others' stricken faces told him they feared the same thing. Kalo was climbing slowly to his feet.

"On second thought," Pavel said, "we should all run."

He bolted to the right and the others followed. They were well into the night now, and they stumbled on through the dark voids between the dimly lit buildings. They rounded a corner, and Pavel knew where they were. They'd missed the central Citadel and wound their way back to the blown-out smithy. Thalia gasped in recognition. Pavel stared at the gaping hole in the wall and the pitch-black night beyond. Should they flee the city entirely? To reach the gap though, they would have to pick their way through strewn debris in the dark. Even if no one turned an ankle, they would not make it out before Kalo caught up. Pavel's gaze swung to the partially collapsed building to the right. The wall had given way, revealing a cross-section of exposed rooms.

Pavel pointed to the nearest open chamber. "In there," he whispered. Maybe they could hide. Barring that, they could fight with their backs against a wall. He hurdled the pile of debris and clambered into the dark room. The others followed without question. A stack of now broken crates filled half the space. Dozens of spare gray Watchkeeper uniforms spilled across the floor. A door set into the far wall no doubt led to an interior hallway. Pavel tried the knob and found it locked from the other side. Ryn and the girls crouched behind the mass of boxes.

"Hide us," Thalia whispered.

"I'm trying," Jayn shot back.

Pavel could barely make out the blue lines emerging from Jayn's boots. If he hadn't known to look, he wouldn't have seen it. He crouched down beside the others. From the inside, the wavering bubble of Wave and Pavel's companions were clearly visible, but Kalo would only see an empty room. He still might hear them. Pavel did his best to slow and quiet his breathing. The others struggled to do likewise.

Moments passed. They heard large feet crunching through the rubble, and then Kalo appeared, silhouetted in the moonlight. The clouds seemed to be breaking up; perhaps it would not rain after all. Kalo took a few steps toward the hole in the city wall. Pavel held his breath and silently willed the Kobold to leave.

Slowly, Kalo turned back toward them. His eyes did not fall on their hiding spot, but he clearly regarded the damaged building. He took a few steps forward. He still held his sword, but he carried it loosely at his side. He did not snuff the air, but nevertheless, he seemed to be following some trail. When Kalo set his large bare foot on the broken pieces of wall, Pavel knew they could not hide. Kalo would find them. He climbed into their room. The luck charms had not held, and the invisibility ward would not either. That trick had only worked the first time.

Pavel shifted his grip on his blades and waited for Kalo to draw closer. The last time they had clashed, Kalo's sword had not broken. It too had to be a pre-Burning relic. Pavel took advantage of the element of surprise while he still had it. He shrouded himself in the last of his Aether, sprang to his feet, and charged. To Kalo's eyes, he must have materialized from the air. Pavel thrusted with his bladebreaker. The pointed tip pierced but could not fully penetrate the black leather armor on Kalo's chest. The Kobold staggered backward. Kalo recovered quickly and swung his scimitar. Pavel parried with his bladecatcher. Blue sparks flew from the clash of metal, and Kalo's sword slid into one of the slots. Pavel twisted his wrist and tried to pry the blade loose from Kalo's grip. Kalo held on tight and yanked back. Pavel allowed himself to be pulled forward and pressed all his weight into the bladebreaker, driving the tip in deeper. A grunt from Kalo told Pavel he had pushed through the armor and found flesh, but he must have struck a rib, as the blade sank no further. Pavel pressed his advantage and delivered a swift kick to what would have been a sensitive area on a human man. Kalo groaned and fell bodily against the wall behind him. Pavel felt the brute's grip loosen on the scimitar. He flicked his wrist and sent the sinister blade flying off to the left, through the opening where the back wall had once been.

Pavel raised the bladecatcher to slash at Kalo with the unnotched edge. The Kobold had long arms, and he shoved his hands against Pavel's chest. Kalo's action was a defensive flailing; he did not even try to use his claws. The creature was strong, and Pavel staggered backward, his narrow blade pulling free. The others had finally reacted. Jayn appeared on his left, having dropped her ward and drawn her sword. Ryn stood on his right, enveloped in a Root tree.

Pavel kept his eyes on Kalo but addressed Ryn. "What are you doing, kid?"

Ryn gestured toward Kalo, who still leaned against the wall. "He doesn't like it when I Dowse him."

"Well, then by all means, Dowse away."

Ryn shot his branches toward Kalo, who simply swiped his hands and dissolved the lacings in a puff of black smoke.

Pavel shook his head. "This guy learns fast."

"How is he doing that?" Jayn asked. "Is he… a Weaver?"

Pavel didn't respond. He couldn't. He kept his eyes fixed on Kalo. They may have disarmed the Kobold, but he was still a deadly threat. Kalo pressed his hands to the wall and pushed himself off it. The stone groaned under the strain. A large crack had formed, running the length of the wall. Kalo looked up at the ceiling as a shower of dust came down. Then his eyes met Pavel's. He smiled and did something completely unexpected. He turned and threw himself against the wall again with all his weight. The structure had clearly been weakened in the blast. The entire wall fell into the next room, and Kalo rode it down.

Pavel looked up as the ceiling and the whole upper floor fell toward him. Aether enhanced his reflexes, but he only had a fraction of a moment to react. He'd always been a leftie, which was perhaps why he leaned toward Jayn and away from Ryn. He shoved her as hard as he could, and then the building hit him.

Chapter 25
A Blending

JAYN COUGHED AND STRUGGLED to raise herself from the ground. Her ears were ringing, and she'd scraped her knees on the jagged stone rubble. A crate from the second floor had fallen on her back, but apparently it was empty. She wriggled her way out from under it. She got up on her hands and knees and scrambled further away, before turning over to sit with her legs sprawled out in front of her. Her trousers had definitely torn at the knees.

She surveyed the exposed cross-section of the three-story building. Kalo had knocked down a wall, and the ceiling above had swung downward like a trapdoor, taking the contents of the second-floor room down with it. The bulk of the collapse had fallen right where Jayn had been standing. Where Pavel and Ryn had been.

She staggered to her feet and stepped cautiously forward. Scraping sounds to her right caught her attention. That side of the room had stayed mostly intact, sheltered in a lean-to created by the intact outer wall and the fallen ceiling. Broken boxes of uniforms filled the gap. Someone was attempting to push them out through the triangular opening. Thalia and Shilo had been back there.

Jayn hobbled over and began yanking out clothes and scraps of wood, flinging them behind herself. She soon excavated an opening wide enough to see Thalia and Shilo's black silhouettes. She offered her hand and helped the two girls climb out.

Thalia wiped her dust-coated hands on her trousers. "The others?" she managed to ask.

Jayn couldn't tell in the dark if the girls had been injured, but they were both on their feet and steady. She pointed to the rubble on the other side of the room. "They must be buried under there," she said. "Pavel shoved me out of the way." She shook her head. The man's bravery that night had done much to change her opinion of him. She hoped he was still alive under all that stonework. And Ryn too. The boy wasn't good for much, but he hadn't run. He was part of her Pentad.

Thalia picked her way toward the fresh debris. "We should dig them out quick," she said.

"What about…" Shilo started to ask but trailed off as all three girls heard a low growl.

From the shadows of the next room over, Kalo's hulking form appeared, as he staggered to his feet. Jayn glanced around. What had happened to her sword? She must have dropped it when Pavel shoved her. A glint of metal in the moonlight caught her eye. She rushed toward it, knelt, and drew out a sword from beneath a piece of flung wood. It was not hers. This wicked curved blade belonged to Kalo. She hefted it and turned back toward the Kobold.

He stood not ten paces from her, his dark eyes glimmering in the moonlight. He held out a large hand. "Griv tat to me," he said in a voice like grinding rocks.

"Come and take it, you brute," she said, surprising herself with the venom in her own voice.

Hearing rustling behind her, Jayn spared a glance back to the girls. Thalia had reached back into the collapsed room and pulled out her staff. Shilo simply stood and stared in slack-jawed horror at Kalo. The girl was not much of a fighter, despite her gifting. Jayn had no time to dwell on that. She turned her full attention to Kalo. The creature circled to his right. Jayn brandished her blade, threatening him not to come any closer. He towered over her, but he was unarmed. He might be able to overpower her, but he would bleed for it.

Kalo made a strange rumbling noise in his throat. It took Jayn a moment to realize he was laughing. "Grave little girrl," he said.

Jayn stepped forward and made a threatening slash with the sword. Kalo reacted with the speed of a striking snake. His hand shot up. Black tendrils enveloped his body, and a blast of what could not possibly be—yet had to be—Weaving flowed toward Jayn. Foolishly, she slashed at it with the sword. The dark mass surrounded her. A dizzying wave of pain shot through her, and her whole body stiffened, as if from a convulsion. It did not pass. Her back arched, and she rose to the balls of her feet, yet she did not fall. Some unseen force kept her fixed in place, like a butterfly pinned to a board. Her arms hung rigid and useless at her sides.

Her mind revolted against it. This could not be happening. Kalo advanced slowly toward her. Her whole body wanted to squirm, but she could only stare in frozen terror. Her eyelids refused to even blink. This wasn't real. No lacings existed that could do this to her. It was a dream, a nightmare. Pavel hadn't pushed her. She'd been knocked out by the collapsing floor.

Kalo loomed over her now, his face twisted into the mockery of a smile. Distantly, Jayn heard shouting. Then Thalia was there, striking Kalo on the back with her staff. He barely flinched. His eyes never left Jayn as he swung his arm and backhanded Thalia across the face. She reeled back and crumpled to the ground, falling from Jayn's narrowing field of vision.

Kalo reached down. He had to bend his knees to grab the sword that Jayn still clutched in her paralyzed hand. He pulled it free as easily as one might take a toy from the arms of a sleeping child. Deliberately, he returned the blade to his scabbard. Then Shilo was there, jabbing a staff into Kalo's ribs. She must have picked it up from where Thalia had dropped it. Kalo groaned and staggered away from the blow. Shilo tried for another jab, but Kalo gripped the wooden pole. He tried twisting it from her hands, but Shilo didn't let go. Her hands began to glow with lacings of Flame. Kalo gripped the pole and shoved. Shilo staggered backward and fell out of view. Jayn heard the staff clatter across the shattered stones.

Kalo turned his attention back to Jayn. He seemed annoyed by the distractions. His dark lacings had never faltered. Jayn still could not move any part of her body. Her heart beat frantically, as if trying to escape when the rest of her could not. She could barely breathe. Kalo gripped her chin in one massive hand. There was nothing of tenderness in the gesture. He dragged a single clawed finger down her cheek. She felt the skin tear and a trickle of warm blood run down her neck. He lashed out with his other hand and struck her in the stomach.

She thought she'd been run through on his sword, but as the black lacings finally released her and she fell slowly backward, she saw he had punched her in the gut with an open palm, driving his claws into her flesh and knocking the wind out of her. Her head hit the ground and she nearly blacked out. She clutched her stomach and struggled to breathe. She wormed her way backward through the debris and ran up against a large stone slab. She managed to sit up against it just enough to see, as Kalo now turned his attention to the other two girls.

Thalia lay motionless on the ground, but Shilo was already pulling herself back to her feet, leaning on her recovered staff. Her Flame had gone out, but now it returned. Her hands again began to glow from within. Kalo drew his sword. Shilo just managed to bring the staff up for a block as Kalo made a downward slash with his blade. The sword snagged for a moment and then sliced cleanly through the wooden pole. Shilo staggered backward under the blow, dropping the two halves.

Jayn tried unsuccessfully to stand. She couldn't take a full breath, and each attempt came out in a ragged wheeze. Her entire chest ached. Had he cracked her ribs? Punctured a lung? She struggled to put her own fears aside and focus on the others.

Kalo's free hand shot out. He grabbed Shilo by the throat and lifted her bodily from the ground. Only muffled choking noises escaped her mouth as she tried to scream. Kalo's claws dug into her face. Poisoned claws, Jayn suddenly remembered. Was that why she couldn't breathe? Was the poison already killing her? She nearly blacked out then. She stayed conscious through sheer force of will. She had to know what would happen to the others. Kalo had his blade up now. He set the tip against Shilo's stomach and then drove it slowly into her. Jayn watched in helpless horror. The monster clearly liked to inflict painful wounds that would not grant a quick death.

Faced with the slow crushing of her throat and the blade slicing into her guts, Shilo lashed out. Her body had gone limp when Kalo grabbed her, but it was fear and not Weaving that held her. Shilo brought up her right hand and swung a glowing fist into the side of Kalo's jaw. The Kobold staggered back. As he did, his blade pulled free and he dropped Shilo. Miraculously, she did not collapse when her feet hit the ground. Her knees buckled, but she caught herself and then launched forward. The light in her hand suddenly flared to an astonishing brightness, like the sun itself. She delivered a powerful uppercut to Kalo's chest.

Jayn blinked rapidly to try clearing the glowing afterimage from her eyes. When she could see again, Kalo simply was not there. The desolate remnants of the smithy stretched before Shilo, all the way to the rend in the city wall. Had the force of Shilo's Etching sent Kalo flying all the way out of the compound? Shilo wavered and then collapsed. The silence was punctuated by the sounds of all the broken supply crates crumbling to pieces, the wood completely drained to fuel Shilo's final attack.

"Shilo!" Thalia called. She had awoken at some point during the struggle. She pulled herself up and crawled over to Shilo. Her roving eyes then found Jayn. "Are you all right?"

"For now," Jayn managed to wheeze.

Thalia turned her attention back to Shilo. She lifted her shirt and winced. "She's bleeding bad." Thalia looked about. She picked up a piece of cloth. It was a shirt from the scattered uniforms that had spilled from the ruined crates. She shook the dust and splinters from it and then pressed it to the wound in Shilo's stomach. She gathered up more bits of uniform and began improvising a bandage around Shilo's midsection. The Flame Weaver had apparently blacked out.

Jayn struggled to move again. She managed to sit up more fully against the bit of masonry behind her. Her breathing was almost normal now. She grabbed a nearby pair of trousers and pressed it to her own stomach wound. She felt she would live. Except for the poison. She glanced toward the collapsed building. There'd been no signs or sounds from Ryn or Pavel. Despite her desire to find a healer, she could only sit there and breathe. Her energy was completely spent. Fighting was exhausting, and she'd been doing it for hours.

Thalia finished what she could do for Shilo and then moved to Jayn. Kalo's fist had blackened Thalia's eye, but she was the least injured of the three. Thalia tied several pairs of trousers together and wrapped them around Jayn's midsection. Jayn winced as the bandages tightened.

Thalia glanced toward the broken building. "Just wait here." Jayn could only nod.

Thalia moved over to the pile of rubble that covered Pavel and Ryn. She began systematically pulling out and shifting broken crates and slabs of stone. Jayn had once thought that Thalia's bulging arms spoiled what was otherwise a lovely figure, but they came in handy now. Jayn longed to help, but she doubted she could even stand. She closed her eyes and focused on her breathing. Her ribs were definitely bruised, if not broken. She listened to the sounds of shifting rubble. Between the steady thuds, she heard another noise, a tinkling of pebbles coming from the wrong direction.

Her eyes shot open. She found the source of that soft noise. A dark shape emerged from the gap in the city wall. Kalo. He had one hand clutched to his chest, and he staggered with each step, but still he came. He'd even held onto his long scimitar, though he let the tip drag along the ground behind him. Thalia had not noticed. She kept shifting debris, searching desperately for Ryn and Pavel, or at least their bodies.

Jayn coughed. She needed to warn her. She forced the word out. "Thalia..." Her wheezing voice had been too soft. Thalia didn't hear. Kalo drew ever closer, plodding doggedly along. Jayn's tongue felt bloated in her dry mouth, but she dragged it across her cracked lips in an attempt to wet them. She had to get Thalia's attention.

"THERE YOU ARE!"

The booming voice sounded directly behind Jayn. She had never heard such a sound but knew it was neither Kobold nor human. Thalia whipped around and staggered back, clearly stricken with horror by whatever it was she saw beyond Jayn. Unbelievably, Kalo ignored the voice. He did not halt his march toward the girls.

"ENOUGH!" the voice said. It sounded feminine, though Jayn could not explain precisely why. She could not bring herself to turn her neck.

Kalo finally stopped at that. He turned and glowered at the presence.

"Leave them be," the voice said, dropping its volume to an almost musical tinkling. "The Five have emerged. We are bound for the Reach."

Kalo's only response was to sheath his blade. A sudden breeze battered against Jayn as a white shape overshadowed her. Something like an enormous bird swooped toward Kalo. He offered no resistance as it grabbed him by the shoulders with its massive talons, though they must have sunk deep into his flesh. The great brown and white bird began to batter its wings against the air. Impossibly, it lifted Kalo from the ground. Kalo shut his eyes and seemed to accept what was happening. The bird struggled to ascend, but it managed somehow, despite the burden it carried. As it rose up and over the city wall, it twisted its head around backwards to regard Jayn with a horrifically human face.

"WE WILL REMEMBER THOSE WHO BEAR THE MARK," it said, and the voice seemed to come from inside Jayn's skull. Her eyes rolled back into her head, and she blacked out.

***

"Wake up!"

Someone slapped Ryn's face.

"You have to wake up," Thalia said, desperation in her voice. She slapped him again. Hard.

Ryn groaned. He tried to open his eyes fully but could only squint up at her in the dim moonlight. Then he tried to sit up but couldn't. He had no feeling in his legs, a hauntingly familiar sensation. Thalia tried to pour water into his mouth from Jayn's mostly empty waterskin. He sputtered and coughed it up. He managed to prop himself up on his elbows and look down. A large slab of stone pinned him to the ground, just above his knees. His legs didn't hurt; he just couldn't feel them. All at once, he remembered the fight with Kalo and the collapsing ceiling. He glanced to his left. Nothing but rubble. He looked right. Pavel lay beside him, facedown and pinned under the same slab of stone, though it had caught him on the back. He seemed to be awake.

"Pavel?" Ryn asked.

"Hey, kid," Pavel said. His voice sounded strained, but he managed a smile.

"Are you all right?"

"I've been better."

Ryn looked back up at Thalia who sat crouched behind him. "Where are the others?" he asked.

Thalia glanced toward the massive opening where the back wall had once been. "They're out in the yard. They're alive, but... They need healing, Ryn. Kalo scratched both of them."

"Where is Kalo?"

"He... he's gone now. It took some time to dig you out. I don't know how much longer they'll hold on. They need you, Ryn."

Ryn squeezed his eyes shut and tried to pull himself free, but his legs wouldn't budge. "Can you get this off me?"

Thalia studied the large slab. "Maybe," she said. "Hang on."

She stood and left him. She seemed to be gone for a long time. Ryn steadied his breathing and summoned his tree. Maybe he could reach Jayn and Shilo from here. He spread his roots wide. He became aware of the ubiquitous grass that grew all across the Watchkeeper compound. It wasn't normal grass, though he had never quite figured out that mystery. Perhaps some Runeform helped it grow so robustly. He sent out his roots and drained the grass mercilessly. It would regrow. He allowed the energy to fill and strengthen him. He extended his branches as far as they would go, but the girls were clearly well out of range. Pavel was not. Ryn Dowsed him. Pavel had been banged up and bruised, and he was desperately hungry. Without asking permission, Ryn infused him with Root, healing him and removing his fatigue, though Ryn knew now that was only a masking.

Pavel gasped. "Thanks, kid," he managed to say.

Ryn let the lacings fade. He had to get free to reach the others. Finally, Thalia returned, carrying the broken half of a staff. "I checked on the others first," she said. "Their breathing is steady, for now." She hefted the piece of wood. "I think I can wedge this in and use it as a lever."

He nodded. "Go for it."

She hesitated and glanced back toward where she left the girls. "They both bled a lot. I'm afraid to move them, but maybe I could carry them in here?"

He shook his head. "I don't think I'm hurt too bad. Try to get me loose first. You can carry me to the others if you have to."

Thalia assented. She set to work, wedging the wooden haft under the slab. The piece of ceiling had split in between Ryn and

Pavel, and a large crack ran down it. She used a stone block as a fulcrum and leaned her entire body on the lever. The slab budged an inch. She wedged her lever in deeper and shoved bits of stone into the gap to support it. She worked tirelessly. As the weight lessened, Ryn began to feel a tingling in his lower legs.

Thalia released her lever, which remained wedged in tight. "I'm going to try just lifting it now. Try to wriggle your way out if you can."

She squatted down beside him and dug her hands under the stone. She grunted as she began to lift. As the pressure on his legs lessened, a wave of pain surged to his brain. The jagged edge of the stone ceiling had sliced into him. Nevertheless, he did as he'd been told, scrambling back on his hands and butt and dragging his crushed legs with him. Thalia let the slab drop. "Oh, Ryn!" she cried, staring at his legs. She dropped to her knees and pressed her hands to his thigh. "I shouldn't have moved it. You're bleeding bad."

Pavel swore. He still remained pinned beneath his section of floor, but he had a clear view of Ryn's legs. "That's too much blood," he said. "The weight must have been keeping it in. He's gonna bleed out!"

"I'm trying!" Thalia said, pressing hard against the ragged wound. "His other leg is bleeding too, I think."

Ryn gritted his teeth. He felt dizzy.

"Use your Etching, kid," Pavel said.

"I can't," Ryn said. "I never learned."

"Now's the time to figure it out, kid. You'll be dead in another minute."

Ryn screwed his eyes shut and tried to focus his frantic mind. Was this the end? Was he going to die? He couldn't even feel the flow of blood as it sapped his life away. He willed his Etching to work. Always it had been a subconscious thing, working subtle changes and healing him without him even realizing it. He had no time to wait. He summoned his Root tree. He sent his roots out as far as they would go, draining life from every blade of grass he could reach. He turned his branches inward and tried to Dowse himself. It didn't work. It couldn't work. No Root Weaver could heal himself. The lacings could only be directed outward. How did his Etching work then?

It was impossible. A handful of weeks ago he had just been a mushroom hunter, living in the woods with his aunt and his pig, and knowing next to nothing about Weavers. He didn't know enough. He cast his mind back over the previous month, trying to recall every conversation he'd had about Weaving and Etchings. He thought about Nyssa's shield Etching, how hers was the strongest and used only Wave, and yet any Wave Weaver could make a similar, if weaker, shield through Blending in Stone. There had to be something he could do, maybe with the others' help. He tried to focus. He felt light-headed. Every time he opened his eyes, the room spun. Thalia and Pavel were speaking to him, but he did not listen.

He was dying.

He would never be able to explain exactly how the idea came to him. Perhaps it was a stroke of Thalia's luck. Kalo had broken the others' charms, but Ryn's charm had been a piece of wood on the other side of town. He recalled one of the first things Pavel had ever told him, as if the rogue whispered it in his ear: "That's the whole rub of Root Weaving. You can't use it to heal yourself. Maybe if you could lace it with Aether... but no, that's impossible too."

The words had meant nothing to Ryn at the time, but he understood now. And yet he didn't. Aether and Root couldn't mix.

Aether always flowed inward, and Root always flowed outward. They were opposing forces. Root consumed Aether, just as trees break the wind, someone had told him. Trees break the wind? It was the weakest metaphor he had ever heard. The Watchkeepers had plenty of them. Stone consumes Root, as a blade hews the wood. Flame subsumes Root, as branches fuel the fire. "Subsumes" meant they were complementary, but did even that make sense? One could easily say the fire consumes the wood. Why then do Root and Flame Blend and not destroy each other? The Watchkeepers viewed the relationship of the Five Forces as an unassailable and logical reality, but was it?

Why could Root and Aether not Blend? If it all existed in the mind anyway, and so much of Weaving depended on believing it would work, could he make it happen? Could he Blend them through sheer force of will? He needed a new metaphor. No real antagonism existed between trees and the wind. Sure, a strong storm could knock a tree down, but many plants relied on the wind to carry their pollen or scatter their seeds. Aunt Marla, who perhaps had been a Root Weaver, had taught Ryn much about trees and plants. Like humans and animals, they too could breathe, in their own way. They did it through their leaves. Aether meant breath. Aether meant life. Plants need the wind to survive. Wind invigorates trees through their leaves. Wind stirs the leaves. He latched onto that thought and repeated it like a mantra. Wind stirs the leaves. Root does not consume Aether, it subsumes it, just as wind stirs the leaves.

"Wind stirs the leaves," Ryn mumbled.

"What?" Thalia asked from somewhere high above him.

Ryn opened his eyes but saw only darkness. He closed them again. He reached out an arm and fumbled for Pavel. The man's rough hand seized his. "I'm here, kid," Pavel said. His voice sounded strange.

"Aether," Ryn said. "Feed me... Aether..."

"What do you mean, kid?"

"That won't work, Ryn," Thalia said.

"No..." Ryn forced the words out. "Trust me."

A long silence followed.

"Do it," Thalia said, her voice suddenly calm. "Just do it, Pavel."

Pavel squeezed his hand. Physical touch helped. Ryn sent all of his branches curving toward Pavel. He stopped short of Dowsing him. Something brushed against his lacings.

"This isn't doing anything," Pavel said.

"Just keep it up," Thalia said. "Don't stop. Give him everything you've got left."

Again, something brushed against Ryn's lacings, like ghostly fingertips. Pavel sent him a continuous stream of Aether, which frayed apart upon contact with Ryn's Root. He could feel something though. That faint brush of contact. Like a light breeze. Like wind through the leaves. Wind stirs the leaves. He invited it in. Stir the leaves. Fill the branches with life. Breathe it in.

Something caught. A single tendril of white Aether. Someone gasped. It might have been Ryn. The strand tried to pull away or fray apart to nothing. Ryn didn't let it. He breathed it in through his leaves, sucked it down into the very heart of the tree. More tendrils came with it. Pavel kept feeding him. No, Ryn reached into Pavel and pulled it out. Pavel couldn't stop now if he wanted to.

The Aether poured into Ryn and infused every inch of his body. It wasn't anything like Dowsing. That was an image conjured in the mind. This was the deep physical awareness of one's own body that only an Aether Weaver could feel. Ryn found the wounds in his legs, the broken bones, the torn vessels. He channeled the Aether into those areas of his body. No, it was Root. It was a Blending of two opposing forces, mending his body and replenishing his blood.

Ryn opened his eyes, and he could see as if it were day. Aether enhanced the senses. Thalia drew her hands back in shock or perhaps horror over what he had done. He extended his awareness outward, drawing fuel from the surrounding vegetation, as well as his own revitalized lifeforce, as an Aether Weaver could. His roving branches found Shilo and Jayn. He would not need to move closer. He Dowsed them simultaneously. It was easy. Almost as an afterthought, he wrapped a branch around Thalia. He healed her black eye. He healed Jayn's scratches and punctures. He healed Shilo's bruised neck and the slice in her gut that had punctured… some organ. He knew plant anatomy better than human. It didn't matter. He healed them all the same, flooding every disordered part of their bodies with green light, tinted to a lighter shade by Aether. Shilo and Jayn gasped simultaneously as they awoke.

Ryn dissolved his lacings and lay back on the ground, feeling reborn.

"What did you do?" Thalia asked.

He followed her line of sight. Pavel had lost consciousness during the ordeal.

"Don't worry," Ryn said. "Pavel will be fine. He's just drained."

Thalia turned her wide eyes on him. "No, Ryn, *what* did you *do?*"

Everything changed that night.

***

Nyssa opened her eyes to the gray light of morning, as the familiar tingle of Root healing washed over her. She saw Agia Bellos kneeling beside her. Agia was one of the few Wave Weavers to achieve any competence with Root, so that did not surprise her. What surprised Nyssa was that she was still alive. She remembered the endless fighting and then the monstrous bird and its talons. She touched her chest, feeling the holes in her shirt where the claws had gone in.

Agia rested a hand on her shoulder. "Easy now," she said.

"What happened?"

Agia frowned. "We were hoping you could tell us."

Nyssa turned her head and saw two other Watchkeepers—Master Trevor Flint and a Stone Weaver whose name she could not recall—smiling down at her. Nyssa rubbed her eyes and sat up. "The claws…" she said, mainly to herself. "I thought she was going to kill me." She only then realized that she had perceived the owl as female.

"Who?"

"I… I'll tell you later."

Agia nodded. "You did have punctures in your chest, but they were relatively shallow. No major damage, thank the Maker. We've been combing the streets for hours, looking for survivors. We thought you were dead when we first came upon you lying here."

Nyssa sat up and looked around then, seeing corpses all around her, both human and Kobold. The stench of decay suddenly hit her nostrils. Agia grimaced in sympathy, extended a hand, and helped Nyssa to her feet. The healing had done its job, and Nyssa had no trouble standing, but she gripped Agia's arm all the same. "What's happened?" she asked. "Is it over?"

"For now, it seems. The Kobolds have fled. I don't know how much you know, but they didn't just attack Falport. A separate force breached a city wall and attacked the Citadel."

"The Citadel? I heard an explosion, but I didn't know…"

Agia nodded gravely. "We're still tallying up the dead, but the losses were substantial."

"Why did the Kobolds retreat?"

"It seems they found what they were looking for."

"What did they take?"

"Runeforms. It's peculiar, though. As far as we can tell, only a single storage room was looted. They took only… uncategorized Runeforms."

Uncategorized. That meant the Runeforms that no one had figured out how to use in the past thousand years—the Runeforms that didn't seem to do anything at all. Somehow the Kobolds must know what they do. Or whomever the Kobolds worked for. That owl… Though it was far less humanlike than the Kobolds, that creature had seemed far more intelligent. That giant bird was the true master of the Kobolds, though Nyssa could not say how she knew that. She touched her chest again. How had the wounds been shallow? The owl's massive talons should have pierced through her heart. If it wasn't trying to kill her, then why did it grab her? Why had she been spared? She shook her head. "I wonder why they wanted those."

"I fear we will find that out someday. But come, let's get you back to the Citadel." Agia took her by the arm and steered her through the maze of corpses. Nyssa wondered how many Watchkeepers had fallen, how many more friends she had lost to the monsters. This was only the beginning. The owl and its minions would not stop here. They would use those stolen Runeforms to accomplish some darker purpose in Aldria. That owl had seemed so foreign, so otherworldly. Perhaps, it was. Perhaps the mirror Runeform had been used to summon it from another world, another reality, like the one in which she was missing an arm. If the mirror gave glimpses of other worlds, maybe it also could serve as a bridge, a portal. Maybe the owl wasn't the only thing to cross over.

Agia seemed to sense her dark thoughts. She squeezed Nyssa's hand and spoke in a soft voice as she led her through the streets. "Most of the masters seem to have made it through the night. No confirmed casualties there, but we're still looking for Mistress Hinter. No one remembers seeing her since before the fighting began. A tragedy if the Kobolds did get her. In better news, you will be pleased to know our newest Training Pentad members have all survived, apparently unscathed. I saw them briefly as I headed out this morning. I'm sure they had quite the night, but I think I'll leave it you to debrief them."

Nyssa couldn't help but smile at that. Her Training Pentad, as she had come to view the group, all had a great deal of potential. Even Pavel.

Epilogue
An Answered Question

TERRON LAITH GHOSTED across the rooftops of Rigel. He was in his element here. Aether masked his footsteps, and another Blending masked even his presence, so if anyone happened to glance upward, their eyes would want to slide past him. That was a clever bit of lacing that not even the Watchkeepers across the river in Falport knew. The Academy of the Ways carefully guarded its secrets. Even Terron did not know them all, but someday he would. He had talent and drive and was determined to work his way into the Sanctum. Doing so meant sometimes taking on the more unsavory jobs, like spying on a fellow Scholar.

He caught sight of his quarry, walking down a broad avenue. This late at night the streets were empty, and he had no trouble keeping up with her. He'd shadowed her all the way from Lon's Watch, undetected. Terron had been surprised when Rense Gilhart had found him in the Aether Library and assigned him the task, but he had known not to ask questions. Respective ranks among the Sanctum were not known to common Scholars, but Terron was fairly certain Rense stood near the top. Rense was Terron's key to joining the Sanctum and learning all those delicious secrets, so he could not say no.

Down below, Mina Bellain turned a corner and entered another one of Rigel's many squares. Terron leapt to the next rooftop with an Aether-enhanced jump and crept forward to peer over the edge of the building. Mina had reached Falport after nightfall, and Terron had expected her to stop there for the night. The city had seen quite a bit of excitement a week ago, which he thought might have attracted her interest. She had stabled her horse at an inn near the river, but less than an hour later, she'd slipped out the back and crossed the bridge into the far less interesting town of Rigel. Her pressing onward meant she had to be nearing her final destination.

They didn't discuss it openly, not with him, but Terron got the sense that Mina was not well liked by her fellow Sanctum members. She was known for being peculiar, even among a group that tended to attract the eccentrics. She guarded her own secrets jealously. For starters, no one seemed to know where her main gifting lay. Terron had it on good authority that she had once healed a fellow Scholar who'd been bitten by a dust adder while on one of the more remote Maer Isles, which meant she surely had to be a Root Weaver or at least wield a complementary gift, yet she was also known to Blend Aether and Stone to make her own enchantments. The woman was an enigma and embodied one of the juicier secrets in the Academy.

He caught sight of her standing before a fountain at the center of the square. He recognized it by reputation alone. He leaned in closer over the edge of the building, eager to hear whatever question she would ask the Rigel fountain. Suddenly, she turned and looked directly up at his perch. "You can come closer, Terron," she said.

How had she seen him? His lacings had been flawless. There was no way she could have sensed him. Maybe he had slipped up somewhere along the road. Yet she had continued to behave as if she were unaware of his pursuit. Why? Had she wanted him to follow her? He sighed and shook his head. It would be foolish to try hiding now. He jumped from the rooftop. A pillow of Aether cushioned his landing. He decided to play it cool. "Good evening, Mina," he said.

She laughed at him. He frowned. She was a member of the Sanctum, so he could not be rude to her. She arched an eyebrow. "Was it Rense Gilhart who sent you after me?"

He shrugged. There was no use denying it; she clearly knew, but he still wouldn't give Rense up. "I don't know what you mean."

She turned back toward the fountain, seemingly dismissing him as any threat. He had to admire her confidence, though it also rankled him. He would play along. He strolled up and stood beside her, leaving a respectful distance. Water tinkled softly as it spilled from one tier of the fountain down into the next.

"What do you know of the attack on Falport?" Mina asked without looking at him.

He considered what he should say, but only for a moment. "Not much beyond the rumors I've heard along the road. A week back Kobolds attacked the city and the Watchkeepers' so-called Citadel. Many people were killed. A number of artifacts were stolen, presumably Runeforms, which the Gray Guard had no right to have in the first place. A Drake was supposedly seen flying over the city."

"It wasn't a Drake."

"How do you know?"

"Trust that I do." She glanced sideways at him. "And what about you, Terron Laith? What do you know?"

He chose his words carefully. He walked a fine line here between respectful and probing. "I know that you have been absent from the Academy for some months. I know that you returned unexpectedly and then left again after less than a day. I know you have traveled directly here to this fountain. Are you going to ask it a question?"

"In a moment, perhaps. First, tell me what you know about this." She stuck a hand in the front pocket of her blue dress and retrieved something. She held it out so he could see it by the lanternlight.

He tried to contain his reaction when he recognized it. The thick ivory bracelet, covered in intricately carved runes, could only be one thing. "That's what you took from the Academy?"

"Borrowed, as is my right."

"Of course, but what could you possibly want with the Keeper's Bracelet?"

"Just a little experiment, though I'm glad you are here to witness this. Please report everything that happens tonight back to Rense Gilhart."

He could make no reply to that.

She shook her head. "You're a clever one, Terron. Tell me what you know of the bracelet."

"Only what everyone knows. Any oaths made while wearing that Runeform become permanently binding. No force of will can break it. I've never known anyone to actually use it though."

"Hmm, well, pay attention." She slipped the bracelet over her hand. It was large, and she had to slide it halfway up her forearm to get it to stay. She hesitated. "I'll need to be careful how I phrase this," she said with a smirk, but clearly she had already composed her oath. In a confident, carrying voice, she intoned, "I swear that after I ask this Runeform fountain one final question, I will never again attempt to ask it any other questions, for any reason, under any circumstances."

She slid the bracelet from her arm, and instead of putting it away, she offered it to Terron. He quirked an eyebrow, but he took it from her, carefully, as if being given a venomous snake. He quickly stuffed it in his own pocket. With no further explanation, she looked up at the fountain.

"Rigel," she said. The stone face sprang to life, and she asked her question. "Who or what can stop the greatest threat currently facing Aldria?"

The Runeform immediately boomed out its response. "BRAISED CHICKEN AND FENNEL."

Mina nodded, as if that non sequitur actually meant something to her. Terron struggled not to gawk. "What?" he asked, and the word contained many questions.

She offered Terron a smile. "My second question and my first answer," she said, then turned and strolled away. She called over her shoulder, "Write it down if you need to. I'm off to dinner."

~

Michael Hardcastle

ABOUT THE AUTHOR

Michael Hardcastle teaches high school English and writing in Tampa, Florida, and has an MFA in Creative Writing from the University of Tampa. His fiction has been published in The William & Mary Review and West Trade Review, and his poetry has been published in Common Ground Review and Torrid Literature Journal. *Root Weaver* is his debut fantasy novel.

If you enjoyed reading, please rate and review *Root Weaver* on Amazon and Goodreads.

The Five Forces series will continue with *Wave Weaver*.

Visit www.hardcastlewrites.com for more information and to sign up for the newsletter.